PRAISE FOR RACHEL HOWZELL HALL

"A fresh voice in crime fiction."

—Lee Child

"Devilishly clever . . . Hall's writing sizzles and pops."

—Meg Gardiner

"Hall slips from funny to darkly frightening with elegant ease."

—*Publishers Weekly*

PRAISE FOR *FOG AND FURY*

"This captivating blend of angst, mystery, and page-turning suspense delivers a top-notch reading experience."

—*Kirkus Reviews* (starred review)

"Enough nuance and complexity to make things feel fresh. Readers will be eager to return to this series soon."

—*Publishers Weekly*

"A gripping series debut."

—*Booklist*

"Of immense appeal for readers with an interest in mysteries and thrillers featuring a female sleuth, a myriad of unexpected plot twists, and a memorably 'big reveal' finale. Unreservedly recommended."

—*Midwest Book Review*

"A new Rachel Howzell Hall thriller is always call for celebration, and this one may be her very best. *Fog and Fury* is a PI page-turner, full of investigative twists, deeply rendered characters, and lush, evocative writing that could come from no one else. Pick this book up now."

—Jess Lourey, Edgar Award–nominated author of *The Taken Ones*

"Rachel Howzell Hall once again proves why she's one of the best crime fiction authors writing today. *Fog and Fury* combines whip-smart observations about race and class with a twisty mystery and cliff-hanger ending that'll have you already wanting to put the next book on your TBR list. It's a must read for noir fans, especially if you loved her Lou Norton series."

—Kellye Garrett, award-winning author of *Missing White Woman*

"Rachel Howzell Hall has done it again with *Fog and Fury*. This is a story with depth, heart, and terror, and it cements her as one of the strongest voices in crime fiction today. Newly minted PI Alyson 'Sonny' Rush is a character to root for. Add in her extended family, the dark secrets in the town of Haven, the messy relationships and social growing pains, all at once familiar and frightening, and you have the recipe for a stellar thriller. Don't miss it!"

—J.T. Ellison, *New York Times* bestselling author of *A Very Bad Thing*

PRAISE FOR *WHAT FIRE BRINGS*

"Rachel Howzell Hall is a master of the psychological-suspense thriller. *What Fire Brings* delivers shocking secrets, surprises on every page, and a killer twist that will leave you breathless. A must-read!"

—Melinda Leigh, #1 *Wall Street Journal* bestselling author

"This one will keep you guessing! Hall's considerable talent is on full display as she expertly deploys misdirection and subterfuge in a riveting tale of intrigue and suspense where nothing is as it seems. The past collides with the present to forever alter the future while the twists keep coming until the final shocking reveal. If you love an intricate plot with well-crafted prose, incisive insight, and complex characters, do not miss this propulsive mystery by a superb storyteller!"

—Isabella Maldonado, *Wall Street Journal* bestselling author

"Crackling wildfires, dark secrets, and a serial killer on the loose. Rachel Howzell Hall's *What Fire Brings* is a captivating and creepy thrill ride through the California canyons, right up to the final and fiery twisty end."

—Wanda M. Morris, award-winning author of *All Her Little Secrets* and *Anywhere You Run*

"Rachel Howzell Hall is simply one of the finest crime writers of her generation, and *What Fire Brings* is her most assured novel yet . . . and one that hits a little close to home for everyone who puts pen to paper or finger to keyboard. Tense, illuminating, and filled with surprises on every page. A masterwork that will leave you flipping pages to see what you might have missed."

—Tod Goldberg, *New York Times* bestselling author

PRAISE FOR *WHAT NEVER HAPPENED*

"Rachel Howzell Hall does it again. *What Never Happened* blends blade-sharp writing and indelible characters with a suspenseful story that pulls you in and won't let go, as a seeming paradise grows dark with storms, suspicion, and murder. I couldn't put it down."

—Meg Gardiner, #1 *New York Times* bestselling author

"*What Never Happened* opens with a gut punch and doesn't let up from there. Rachel Howzell Hall's twist on the you-can't-go-home-again story is smart, dizzying, and thrilling. She not only handles the mystery elements expertly, but she honors the grief and rage of our past and present."

—Paul Tremblay, bestselling author of *The Cabin at the End of the World* and *The Pallbearers Club*

"Rachel Howzell Hall has crafted her own genre of slow-boiling, powerfully emotional thrillers. Her realistic characters are ordinary people, haunted by past horrors that won't stay buried, forcing them to face pure evil to find their own redemption."

—Lee Goldberg, #1 *New York Times* bestselling author

"In *What Never Happened*, Rachel Howzell Hall seamlessly weaves together the past and the present, decorating her breakneck plot with dark secrets and unexpected reveals that glitter like jewels. I couldn't turn the pages fast enough."

—Jess Lourey, Amazon Charts bestselling author of *The Quarry Girls*

"*What Never Happened* is superb. Beautifully and smartly written, it is an engrossing thriller with an ending that will leave your head spinning. It is deliciously creepy and perfectly crafted. In a word, stunning! Don't miss this one!"

—Lisa Regan, *USA Today* and *Wall Street Journal* bestselling author

"Rachel Howzell Hall's *What Never Happened* is a spine-tingling twist of a roller coaster that keeps you on the edge of your seat to the very last page and will have you saying 'Thanks a lot, Rachel, for my lack of sleep.'"

—Yasmin Angoe, award-winning author of the critically acclaimed Nena Knight series, *Her Name Is Knight* and *They Come at Knight*

PRAISE FOR *WE LIE HERE*

"*We Lie Here* is another fast and surprisingly funny thriller from Rachel Howzell Hall. I was on the edge of my seat through all the revelations, twists, and turns in a fast-paced third act. Get this book and relax with the knowledge that you are in the hands of a fantastic crime novelist."

—Adrian McKinty, Edgar Award–winning author of the Sean Duffy series

"In *We Lie Here*, Rachel Howzell Hall gives us a tight, lean, eye-level look at the Gibson family—flawed, normal, abnormal, and each affected by a deadly secret left buried for years—while weaving a page-turning tapestry of dread, cold-blooded murder, and nail-biting tension. What a ride. What a wonderful writer. More, please."

—Tracy Clark, award-winning author of the Det. Harriet Foster series

"*We Lie Here* is definitive proof that it's impossible to be disappointed by Rachel Howzell Hall, who just gets better and better with each book. She has tools and tricks to spare as she pulls you to the edge of your seat with her razor-sharp plotting and keen eye for the darker side of human behavior that's too easily obscured by the California sunshine."

—Ivy Pochoda, author of *These Women*, a *New York Times* Best Thriller of 2020

"Loaded with surprises and shocking secrets, and propelled by Rachel Howzell Hall's magnificent prose, *We Lie Here* is a captivating thriller that I couldn't put down. It's very clear to me that Hall is one of the best crime writers working today, and she keeps getting better. *We Lie Here* is a can't-miss book."

—Alex Segura, acclaimed author of *Secret Identity*, *Star Wars Poe Dameron: Free Fall*, and *Blackout*

"Rachel Howzell Hall continues to prove why she's one of crime fiction's leading writers. *We Lie Here* is a psychological-suspense fan's dream with both a heroine you'll want to root for and a story you'll want to keep reading late into the night. A must-read!"

—Kellye Garrett, Agatha, Anthony, and Lefty Award–winning author of *Like a Sister*

PRAISE FOR *THESE TOXIC THINGS*

An Amazon Best Book of the Month: Mystery, Thriller & Suspense

"This cleverly plotted, surprise-filled novel offers well-drawn and original characters, lively dialogue, and a refreshing take on the serial killer theme. Hall continues to impress."

—*Publishers Weekly* (starred review)

"A mystery/thriller/coming-of-age story you won't be able to put down till the final revelation."

—Kirkus Reviews

"Tense and pacey, with an appealing central character, this is a coming-of-age story as well as a gripping mystery."

—*The Guardian*

"The mystery plots are twisty and grabby, but also worth noting is the realistic rendering of a Black LA neighborhood locked in a battle over gentrification."

—*Los Angeles Times*

"Rachel Howzell Hall . . . just gets better and better with each book."

—CrimeReads

"Rachel Howzell Hall continues to shatter the boundaries of crime fiction through the sheer force of her indomitable talent. *These Toxic Things* is a master class in tension and suspense. You think you are ready for it. But. You. Are. Not."

—S. A. Cosby, author of *Blacktop Wasteland*

"*These Toxic Things* is taut and terrifying, packed with page-turning suspense and breathtaking reveals. But what I loved most is the mother-daughter relationship at the heart of this gripping thriller. Plan on reading it twice: once because you won't be able to stop, and the second time to savor the razor's edge balance of plot and poetry that only Rachel Howzell Hall can pull off."

—Jess Lourey, Amazon Charts bestselling author of *Unspeakable Things*

"The brilliant Rachel Howzell Hall becomes the queen of mind games with this twisty and thought-provoking cat-and-mouse thriller. Where memories are weaponized, keepsakes are deadly, and the past gets ugly when you disturb it. As original, compelling, and sinister as a story can be, with a message that will haunt you long after you race through the pages."

—Hank Phillippi Ryan, *USA Today* bestselling author of *Her Perfect Life*

PRAISE FOR *AND NOW SHE'S GONE*

"It's a feat to keep high humor and crushing sorrow in plausible equilibrium in a mystery novel, and few writers are as adept at it as Rachel Howzell Hall."

—*Washington Post*

"One of the best books of the year . . . whip-smart and emotionally deep, *And Now She's Gone* is a deceptively straightforward mystery, blending a fledgling PI's first 'woman is missing' case with underlying stories about racial identity, domestic abuse, and rank evil."

—*Los Angeles Times*

"Smart, razor-sharp . . . Full of wry, dark humor, this nuanced tale of two extraordinary women is un-put-downable."

—*Publishers Weekly* (starred review)

"Smart, packed with dialogue that sings on the page, Hall's novel turns the tables on our expectations at every turn, bringing us closer to truth than if it were forced on us in school."

—Walter Mosley

"A fierce PI running from her own dark past chases a missing woman around buzzy LA. Breathlessly suspenseful, as glamorous as the city itself, *And Now She's Gone* should be at the top of your must-read list."

—Michele Campbell, bestselling author of *A Stranger on the Beach*

"One of crime fiction's leading writers at her very best. The final twist will make you want to immediately turn back to page one and read it all over again. *And Now She's Gone* is a perfect blend of PI novel and psychological suspense that will have readers wanting more."

—Kellye Garrett, Anthony, Agatha, and Lefty Award–winning author of *Hollywood Homicide* and *Hollywood Ending*

"Sharp, witty, and perfectly paced, *And Now She's Gone* is one hell of a read!"

—Wendy Walker, bestselling author of *The Night Before*

"Hall once again proves to be an accomplished maestro who has composed a symphony of increasing tension and near-unbearable suspense. Rachel brilliantly reveals the bone and soul of our shared humanity and the struggle to contain the nightmares of human faults and failings. I am a fan, pure and simple."

—Stephen Mack Jones, award-winning author of the August Snow thrillers

"Heartfelt and gripping . . . I'm a perennial member of the Rachel Howzell Hall fan club, and her latest is a winning display of her wit and compassion and mastery of suspense."

—Steph Cha, award-winning author of *Your House Will Pay*

"An entertainingly twisty plot, a rich and layered sense of place, and most of all, a main character who pops off the page. Gray Sykes is hugely engaging and deeply complex, a descendant of Philip Marlowe and Easy Rawlins who is also definitely, absolutely her own woman."

—Lou Berney, award-winning author of *November Road*

"A deeply human protagonist, an intricate and twisty plot, and sentences that make me swoon with jealousy . . . Rachel Howzell Hall will flip every expectation you have—this is a magic trick of a book."

—Rob Hart, author of *The Warehouse*

"*And Now She's Gone* has all the mystery of a classic whodunit, with an undeniably fresh and clever voice. Hall exemplifies the best of the modern PI novel."

—Alafair Burke, *New York Times* bestselling author

PRAISE FOR *THEY ALL FALL DOWN*

"A riotous and wild ride."

—Attica Locke

"Dramatic, thrilling, and even compulsive."

—James Patterson

"An intense, feverish novel with riveting plot twists."

—Sara Paretsky

"Hall is beyond able and ready to take her place among the ranks of contemporary crime fiction's best and brightest."

—Strand

MIST AND MALICE

OTHER TITLES BY RACHEL HOWZELL HALL

Fog and Fury
The Cruel Dawn
The Last One
What Fire Brings
What Never Happened
We Lie Here
These Toxic Things
And Now She's Gone
They All Fall Down
City of Saviors
Trail of Echoes
Skies of Ash
Land of Shadows

MIST AND MALICE

A HAVEN THRILLER

RACHEL HOWZELL HALL

This is a work of fiction. Names, characters, organizations, places, events, and incidents are either products of the author's imagination or are used fictitiously. Otherwise, any resemblance to actual persons, living or dead, is purely coincidental.

Published by Thomas & Mercer, Seattle

www.apub.com

EU product safety contact:
Amazon Media EU S. à r.l.
38, avenue John F. Kennedy, L-1855 Luxembourg
amazonpublishing-gpsr@amazon.com

ISBN-13: 9781662522871 (hardcover)
ISBN-13: 9781662522888 (paperback)
ISBN-13: 9781662522864 (digital)

Cover design by Lisa Amoroso
Cover image: © Florian Kainz / Getty; © Hlib Shabashnyi / Shutterstock

Printed in the United States of America

First edition

For DevCom, for letting me be me . . .

There is only one day left, always starting over:
it is given to us at dawn and taken away
from us at dusk.

—Jean-Paul Sartre

PART I

The Girl Who Came Back

May 13, 2023

This is so freakin' stupid.

He paces across the bare basement that he'd helped to build.

Those stupid wood ceiling beams. And the stupid wet bar nook? Him.

Took six weeks to scrub the mold and dirt off the cinder block walls, hang the drywall, put in recessed lighting, new outlets, the carpet . . .

The lock on the door at the top of the staircase with steps that he sanded?

He installed it. Even hung the freakin' door.

And now, that locked door kept him from leaving. If he had a screwdriver, he could undo those hinges, unscrew that lock. He checks the pockets of his cargo shorts—he only has a deck of Uno cards and a cheap lighter.

He glances at his watch—he's been gone for three hours. Celi's worried by now. If he had his phone, it would be blowin' up with texts.

Where you at????

Did u get lost?

WTF??!

The spicy nacho Takis flaming hots

Hello??

They can't keep him down here forever. What would be the point? He ain't got no money. Neither does Celi. So this can't be for ransom. He'd heard that folks up here fuck around with weird sex stuff. Is that what this is? They want him to be some kinda sex slave?

He rubs his arms. Getting cold. If it got too cold, he could burn his socks. He needs to take a piss. Ain't no bathroom down here. Plumbing costs too much. The closest thing to a toilet is the empty plant holder in the corner . . .

"Hey!" he yells to the ceiling. "What the fuck, man?"

He takes the stairs two at a time. Kicks the door three times. Leaves black scuff marks on top of the ones he made ten minutes ago.

Nobody answers. The only noise he can hear is his own heart pounding in his ears. And his growling stomach. He hasn't eaten all day cuz he'd been saving his appetite for all the meat he was supposed to be grilling today.

Carne asada. Al pastor. Bacon-wrapped hot dogs. Street corn.

Right now, he was supposed to be fucked up, his third Corona in one hand, his BBQ tool in the other, dancing to some bullshit Pitbull song.

Not this. Whatever the hell "this" was.

If the news cared about people like him, they'd write LOCAL MAN KIDNAPPED IN PROPANE TANK REFILL RUN. He chuckles. First, who the hell gets kidnapped during propane tank runs? And second, "local man" cuz they wouldn't know what to call him. Sometimes, he doesn't know what to call himself.

Mi cielo. That's what Moms called him.

Corazón. That's what Celi calls him.

Illegal. Alien. Day laborer. Rapist. Murderer.

He is everything to everybody.

And now: victim.

"Fuck that," he grumbles, scanning the basement for something, *anything*, to escape with.

Fire.

Yeah. And then, when they come down to feed him—cuz they won't let him starve—he'll pull out the cards and the lighter and start burning them up. *Draw Two, bitches!* If he gotta burn every card in the deck, he will. *Skip*, you fuckin' weirdos! Then, he'll run up the stairs, grab the keys to the car, and drive. Not home—they'd come looking for him at home. No—he'd drive all the way to LA or San Diego. He got homies down there, and they'd protect him. Maybe he'd convince Celi to leave this fuckin' town and start a new life, for real this time. If she loves him, she'll join him down in El Pueblo de Nuestra Señora la Reina de los Ángeles del Río Porciúncula.

Outside, tires crunch against the driveway.

Ah.

Nobody opened the basement door cuz ain't nobody home. Any minute now, that door is gonna open, and then . . . ?

Should he bum-rush them? Or play nice and sneaky? Act sick and crouch in the corner like his stomach hurts, and when they bend over to check on him, *BAM*!

What would John Wick do?

That punch wrist throw. Or a two-shoulder grab—

The car door slams. The car alarm toots twice. Then . . . silence.

His stomach growls. The beep-beep-beeping of the security system near the foyer.

6-7-3-8. They'd given him the code during construction. *Cuz you're like family,* they said. Fuckin' gringos.

The ceiling above him creaks. Closer . . . closer . . .

They're both big. He is not. But he is young and angry and wants to get out of here more than they want to keep him locked in a basement that he fucking built.

Home is seven miles away. If he needed to run it, he could. He's walked fifty times that. If he needed to dumpster-dive to eat, he will—cuz he's done that too.

The thought of some asada fries makes his mouth water.

Focus.

He will pretend to be sick, yeah, clutch his stomach, make his face twist. Maybe he should piss his pants, make it look authentic, cuz what grown-ass man would do that on purpose?

The corner beneath the slot window—the perfect place to pretend. He drops to the ground, pees his pants, pulls out his lighter and a bunch of cards before clenching into a ball, and starts to writhe and whimper. He prays hard to be delivered, to be forgiven, to wake up from this nightmare.

No one will believe him. Shit like this doesn't happen in towns like this. But this local man knows: ain't no place like Haven.

This town is the pretty bitch at the party. If you take her home, don't be shocked if she puts Visine in your rum and Coke and steals your cash and the P.F. Chang's gift card your godmother gave you for Christmas.

The floorboards at the top of the landing creak, and someone walks down the stairs. The wood groans.

"Open the door," he whispers as he clenches.

Open the door.

Open—

1.

Or maybe this is how I end.

Not in a hail of gunfire but by party bike.

I was one of twelve people powering this wine-bike trolley through downtown Sableport as House of Pain blasted from its speakers. My best friend, India, was flirting with Anthony, a law school professor visiting from Berkeley. Shekinah, the second wife of our college friend, Dustin, was performing a drunken striptease on the pole at the pedal crusher's rear. The other passengers on the bike laughed, "Woo-hoo"-ed, and "Yas, kween"-ed as Shekinah performed and as we swerved around a stalled three-wheeled motorcycle.

"And I'm, like, why is she texting me like she hasn't been MIA for the past three years," Dustin was saying to me. "Like . . . *bitch*. You left me. You left our marriage. What is there to talk about?" He scowled and rolled his eyes.

I said, "Wow."

But I accepted this invitation to leave Haven, if only for an afternoon.

I needed distraction from all the . . . *everything*.

He took a swig from his bottled water and rubbed his right knee. "I didn't tell Shekinah. She'd flip the fuck out. She don't play that."

The woman twerking on the back of a party bike wasn't into ex-wife shenanigans? You don't say.

"And what have you been doing since, what?" He squinted as he tried to remember the last time we'd all hung out. "Cherise's wedding?"

I pedaled harder. "I'm now a PI down in Haven."

He raised his eyebrows. "So, Cherise is still in the FBI, but you *left* left the LAPD?"

"Yep."

He glanced down at my hands. "I don't see any rings on those fingers."

"Came close, though."

"Cuz you were always the goddess atop Mount Olympus," Dustin said, nodding. "If we weren't scared of crossing your dad, we sure as hell didn't wanna cross Miss Val. We know she'd cut a fool."

I laughed. "My parents weren't overprotective."

"No—they were *retributive*. The original flavor of 'fuck around and find out.'"

House of Pain morphed into Eminem, and I guess we were in the Down-Ass White Boy section of the driver's mix. Good music, but none of it—this bullshit conversation with Dustin, the twerking second wife, and India giggling—made sense to me. How was I supposed to act natural when, hours ago, a seventeen-year-old girl had landed on my front porch, no longer lost? When another young woman now wore a toe tag in one of India's steel drawers?

Murder, mayhem, and merlot.

Okay, then, life.

Months ago, my therapist down in Los Angeles had advised me to leave my apartment once a week and do something life affirming. "The dead aren't coming back to life, Sonny," Dr. Molina had said, "even if you hid out for the rest of yours. Do you really want to die of vitamin D deficiency because you haven't seen the sun since Christmas?"

No, I didn't want to die from rickets or scurvy. Death by bar-crawl party bike would do.

Even though it was only four o'clock, the temperature had dropped, and fog now butted against the rolling green hills of Sableport. Misty halos formed around the streetlights and made neon bar signs sexier than what they were. Fog did that—to things, to people. I also looked more alluring than what I truly was—a thirty-five-year-old disgraced LAPD detective who moved to a town six hundred miles north of Los Angeles to find stolen dogs and lost people.

The party bike parked in front of Lulubelle, our fifth and final winery. This tasting room, tucked near a hillside, had ivy-covered brick walls and twinkling lights strung around its courtyard and walkways.

India slipped her arm through mine. She wore blue jeans and a tube top with incredible boob support. I wore the same miraculous tube top, but denim shorts and OG red, black, and white high-top Jordans. With bronzed cheeks and lip gloss, India and I looked like we owned 51 percent of this damned town.

The tasting room reminded me of the living rooms seen in *The Bachelor* episodes. Kinda Spanish. Kinda California. Kinda posh but a little trashy with dark wood finishes and chairs that don't look sturdy enough for American asses.

"Still having fun?" India shouted over the Billie Eilish song playing on the winery's stereo.

I placed my cheek against hers. "I'm good."

"I don't know much about this place," India said, "but . . . *wine*."

At my request, we'd made one change in our itinerary: no Bengtsson Vineyards. London Sutton's family owned that winery.

My phone rang.

Before I pulled the device from my cross-body bag, India took my hand. "No working."

"I'm not."

"Why are you checking your phone, then?"

"Making sure Mom's—"

"El and Gio are looking after her," India said. "And you're not drinking enough."

"True."

"You *love* wine."

"But at this point, I need something that will make me forget." I scanned the variety of bottles on the bar shelves and shook my head. "Not one bottle of Hpnotiq."

India snorted. "Sorry. This place doesn't serve vodka-cognac-infused melted blue Jolly Ranchers."

"Sometimes, all we need in this world is a big red cup of vodka-cognac-infused melted blue Jolly Ranchers."

India thrust a short port glass at my lips. "Taste this."

"What is it?" I asked, sniffing the plum-colored liquid.

"Dunno."

I blinked at her. *Really?* But I sipped it anyway and frowned. "Anise."

"Yeah. It's nasty." Then, she took the glass and downed the rest. "On this day, I'm not paying hundreds to be analytical or to drink what I know. I can be Brooke and Sam's momma tomorrow. Today? Tonight? Right now? I drink what the good Lord pours into my glass."

Now it was my time to snort. "Living on the edge, huh?"

"Maybe if I had before, Tyler wouldn't have cheated on me—"

"Not true," I said. "You could've been the Black Angelina Jolie, and he *still* would've fucked y'all's praise and worship leader."

She rolled her eyes. "You're my best friend—you're supposed to tell me that I'm sexy and exciting."

I wrapped my arm around her waist. "You're sexy and exciting and worthy of nonjudgmental love. Don't forget that."

India lifted her empty port glass. "Drink more. Talk less."

I nodded. "Heard."

And so I sipped a liqueur that tasted like boozy coffee, and I flirted with Noah, the winetender who had tousled brown hair and a square jaw, and looked young enough to be the starting quarterback for the Oregon Ducks.

My phone vibrated, and this time, I let it rescue me from the quicksand. I'd missed a bunch of calls, and now there were a few voicemails. I read the transcripts of each.

"This is Stanley Cain, and I'll be representing London Sutton. Over the next few days, I'll be scheduling time to talk with—"

I pressed Stop and mumbled, "Kiss my ass, Stanley Cain." His client had killed a seventeen-year-old boy, had probably killed her daughter, and had definitely tried to kill me.

Next.

"Hi, Sonny. It's Lori Monroe. Devon and I have a favor to ask. Could you call me when you get a chance?"

Xander's mother, Lori, and I had developed a friendship that lived past the typical expiration date for a cop befriending her victim's family. We were sorority sisters who'd pledged Alpha Kappa Alpha around the same time, but she'd crossed at UC Berkeley and I'd crossed at UC Santa Barbara with India.

I'd call her tomorrow.

Next voicemail: Mom.

"All good here. You'll never guess who called me today. Quincy Johns. We went to Jordan High together. He lives in Ojai now—"

She sounded healthy. She sounded occupied. Good.

Next: Ivan.

"Hey! Just got a few cases for you to pick from. Missing person, cheating husband, or insurance scam. Talk tomorrow or later tonight if you're sober."

Ivan was pretending that it was all good between us. Maybe it was—I didn't know.

A few text messages also clogged my inbox. Sales on hair bundles. Fundraising for the election . . . Nothing from Cooper.

It had been a wicked two weeks for him—I'd go silent too. His wife was in jail for killing her seventeen-year-old patient-victim-lover and possibly their daughter and had been caught by his girlfriend, who quickly became an ex because she hadn't known he'd still been married. Yeah, Cooper Sutton was an asshole, but I still worried about him.

"Get off the phone," India slurred, swiping for my phone and missing.

"Go tongue down Anthony," I said.

"Done!" She swiveled on her stool and promptly stuck her tongue into Anthony's mouth. Then she laughed—and that made me smile. She cut up dead bodies all day to determine how they got dead. And her ex-husband had married the leader of the praise and worship team at their church. She deserved to tongue down every man in this town if that's what she wanted.

As for me . . .

I leaned more toward sad drunk, and guilt now rolled through me, surfing on the waves of coffee-flavored sherry. How dare I have fun while so many horrible things were disrupting the peace and destroying the lives of innocent people?

To be or not to be or *Slings and arrows of outrageous fortune* or *Take arms against a sea of troubles*?

Hamlet heavy, I stumbled out of the tasting room and settled on a bench in the courtyard.

Honking car horns. Bells ringing on another party bike. Music blaring. "Woo-hoos" and "No ways" and "Holla!" Laughter, lots of laughter.

Fun abounded, but all was not right in the world.

Ivan answered on the first ring. "Aren't you supposed to be cavorting right now?"

"Taking a break before my next romp," I said. "What's this missing person case?"

Ivan chuckled. "I shouldn't have texted you."

"Why not? It's no longer a thing?"

"It's still a 'thing,'" he said, "but it's distracted you from having fun."

"I had fun," I said. "I experienced normal life. I even almost kissed a bartender ten years younger than me. Fun was had. So what's this case?"

"You know," he said, "you're not the only god on earth."

"Yeah, but there's only one Batman."

"And how many guys played *him*?"

"I'm not talking about the depiction. I'm talking about the real-life Batman. She exists, and she's irreplaceable."

My phone buzzed.

A text message from Brady Kwon, the lead investigator at the Mendocino County Sheriff's Department.

She's good

KB was thrilled to see her

Talk tomorrow

Brady's text message made my shoulders soften some. Because Honor Butler was now home with her mother, Keely.

"So," I said to Ivan, "the missing person case?"

"Fine. Let me get the . . ." Paper rustled in his part of the world. "She didn't write much on the intake form, but she lives on the other side of Haven—"

"There's another side of Haven?" I asked.

"Yeah. East. Anyway, her husband's been gone since May. The sheriff's department hasn't made any progress, and she wants us to find him."

"Do you know her?" I asked.

"Nope."

"Sound legit?"

"For the moment? Yeah. But that will be up to you."

"When is she coming in?"

"I told her tomorrow afternoon. So go back to romping and cavorting."

I lost India to old-school Jodeci songs and Anthony, the Boalt School of Law professor. She reminded me that I had the key to her house and an Uber account. So, I returned to her lovely seaside Victorian with its large sunken tub and custom cabinetry, wide-planked oak floors, and guest bedroom with its own view of Point Something-or-Other lighthouse.

I'd passed out the moment my head hit the pillow only to startle awake an hour later. I sat up in bed and realized that I hadn't called to check in on Mom. Yes, I'd left her alone in Haven for the first time—but it was also two-thirty in the morning. Too late to call. Instead, I confirmed that she hadn't left the cottage from the AirTags I'd placed in her favorite pairs of shoes.

At four in the morning, a text from India woke me up.

I hooked up with Anthony!

No shit.

We're at the Radisson near the harbor

I closed my eyes and fell back asleep.

At seven in the morning, I reached for my phone again and tapped into the cottage's security system app. Activity: No one had crept around this morning in search of Honor or me.

Twenty minutes later, I pulled on soft joggers and a softer T-shirt. I shuffled to the kitchen and stared at India's cold stove and the fresh veggies we'd purchased to make Sunday-morning frittatas. Even the empty coffee maker rolled its eyes at me—neither India nor I had set the timer to brew a fresh pot. Beyond the kitchen windows, fog had disappeared the world, leaving behind a few crape myrtle trees to serve as proof the world still existed. Anyone could be out there, hiding in the mist, watching me . . .

Like the pissed-off family of Autumn Suarez, the young woman murdered by another young woman who I hadn't arrested for stealing bologna and baby food from a liquor store.

The worry I now felt standing in India's kitchen was rice-grain sized. Ricin was dangerous rice sized, though.

Time to go.

Since my vandalized Bronco was still in the shop and London Sutton had wrecked the Nissan Sentra loaned to me by my landlord Giovanni, I used a rideshare—and that's what I hailed to take me back to Haven.

My phone pulsed three separate times. Pulse one: "Axel" would be picking me up in a silver Toyota Camry. The second pulse came from Mom's text message:

Good morning daughter

Driving with Elliott to the farm to deliver cupcakes!

Love you more!

The third pulse came from Elliott's text.

GM!

Enroute to wedding site w/Val

TTYL

I pushed out a breath—all was well at eight forty in the morning. *For now.* There was plenty of Sunday left.

No one jumped out of the fog to accost me as I hurried from India's house to Axel's silver Toyota Camry. Inside, the sedan smelled of allspice, and the stereo played mostly commercials.

Axel said "How are you?" and I said "Great," and we rolled through India's Sableport neighborhood and back to Highway 1 South.

Axel turned off the radio and cracked the window. He obeyed all traffic rules and let a squirrel cross the road.

My phone rang.

"You on your way back?" Mom sounded . . . *easy*.

"Yep," I said, "but I'm stopping at the office first."

"Was someone in our house last night?" she asked. "I found white-girl hair in the sink and bathtub."

My pulse quickened by a beat, and I said, "Someone stopped by who needed help." I cleared my throat, then asked, "Excited for the wedding today?"

Mom grunted.

"What's wrong?" I asked, closing my eyes, wondering what could've possibly set her off this early in the day.

"If you talk to your father," she said, "tell him we're out of cardamom. I can't make that bread pudding he likes without cardamom. I tried calling him, but he's not answering."

He wasn't answering because he'd been dead for five years now.

Mom sighed. "I guess I can go out—"

"No," I said, "I'll pick some up before I go home. And I'll try calling Dad. There's a lot going on out there, and you need to focus on the wedding."

How could she notice a random white-girl hair in the bathroom sink but not remember that Dad was dead? She'd been doing good these last few days. Had all the wedding cupcaking taken too much from her?

"Yeah, I know you're a cop," she was saying now, "but don't ever marry one."

I was no longer an *active-duty* cop. As for marrying one? I said, "Sure, Mom."

My parents had been together for forty-six years before his liver rebuked another short glass of Jack Daniels on the rocks and gave up the spirit. Mom had blamed the LAPD and, specifically, Ivan for Dad's death. Since then, she'd iced Ivan out of her life. I thought it would've been impossible to live in a town of only a thousand people and Mom and Ivan not talk, but with Val Rush, all things were possible.

Axel drove past the WELCOME TO HAVEN highway sign.

I snorted. "Whatever."

That placard needed an asterisk and small type. *Watch your back and protect your neck.*

"You say something?" Axel's eyes met mine in the rearview mirror's reflection.

The nerve around my left temple twitched as I chuckled. "Just this town. It puts on as charming and safe, and it's . . ." *Bullshit.* "More complicated."

He nodded and grinned. "Everything has been figured out except how to live."

I cocked an eyebrow. "Jean-Paul Sartre."

"Yes. You like him?"

"I do," I said, squinting out at Haven's bright-colored shops and restaurants. "He depresses the hell out of me, though."

The fog had cleared, and now I could see almost all of Haven. Three square miles had been crammed with those qualities that made California a spectacular state. North of San Francisco and filled with redwoods and rolling hills speckled with California grapes on one side and an ocean filled with tall kelp forests on the other. Tourism drove the economy here, and there'd been a push to revitalize the old and expand the town's boundaries to make it new—from forcing aging businesses to finance facelifts for their storefronts to courting and landing new companies to make a home here. Some residents were all in for the development—my landlords, Elliott and Giovanni, had moved their bakery from San Jose and served as Haven's poster boys of economic growth. Some residents were against the expansion, and they didn't want more diversity—not in food, not in politics, not in people. Pride flags had been burned, and only four full-time Black residents—Mom, Lori and Devon Monroe, and me—called Haven home.

Change was coming to this town, no matter how many flags were burned, no matter how much blood was spilled.

Axel slowed for the red traffic signal. "Just like we all must figure out why we're here," he said, "as well as our purpose in life, so must this town. How to live—that's what Haven's parents must decide. A fancy place like Pebble Beach or a town without locals and no new development? A ghost town? A town of long-term renters? The little town that could or the little town that won't?"

I said "Hmm," not really caring about Haven's identity problem. "I'm worried more about how they treat each other, not necessarily how they slap on new paint and host golf tournaments."

Axel made the right turn that would take us to downtown Haven. "But isn't it all related?" he asked. "How to live—with each other, with ourselves, in a place bustling with its own anxiety and identity crisis?"

I squinted at him and smiled. "Your accent."

"Cameroon," he said with a toothy grin.

"Former philosophy professor?" I asked.

"And part-time professional mourner." He paused, then added, "A lot of research and study doing both. It comes in handy for this job too."

I tossed him a smile and turned back to look out at Haven.

My eyes burned from too much wine and not enough sleep, and I thanked the heavens that Axel didn't need to take Highway 128, the most beautiful, twistiest, and deadliest road I'd ever driven. Since moving to Haven, I had yet to wrap myself around a redwood or run headlong into a logging truck. However, London Sutton had tried to run me over in a parking lot off that deadly highway, and I thanked the fates again that she failed.

The charming storefronts of downtown Haven stood out from the fog. Roll-Roll-Roll-Your-Dough already had a line of old folks wanting to eat German pancakes and bacon. Shoppers at Good Pickings pushed carts heavy with bottled waters and boxes of long-neck Coronas. Sweetlife still pushed out cinnamon rolls and lattes, even though the bakery's three principal bakers were miles away, setting up for a wedding. Yes, Mayberry-by-the-Sea smelled of fried sweet dough and fresh-brewed coffee, spilled wine and sea salt, and anyone could taste it all from the air, if they tried. So many secrets hid all around this coastal paradise—and I now mined those secrets and stored them in the file cabinets of Poole Investigations.

Since my arrival to Haven just weeks ago, two young people had been killed . . .

And life had moved on.

That was the fucked-up thing about living—even as the worst things that could happen to you *did* happen, you still had to brush your teeth, pee, blink, and see the world move on even as you moved on, too, even as grief pressed down on your shoulders like all the gravity in the universe. Even though your own heart kept beating as your lungs threatened to quit and your mind threatened to drown you with so many thoughts.

As a teenager, I'd never dreamed of working on a Sunday morning. In my high school fantasies of Sunday mornings, I was slipping on my Macy's-bought dress, shoving my feet into a pair of Jimmy Choo heels and grabbing a matching handbag, then heading to church with my two children, Anya and Lucas, in my BMW 745, being driven by my fine-ass male-model husband, Tyson, the Ralph Lauren Polo Guy, to our church in Santa Barbara. There, we'd pray and put lots of money into the offering plate and, afterward, drive down to Disneyland.

There was a chill in the air as I stepped across the threshold of Poole Investigations. The bell above the doorway tinkled.

"That you, Sonny?" Ivan shouted from somewhere beyond the lobby. A rhetorical question since he had a security camera posted at the entryway.

"Yeah," I still shouted back.

The television in the waiting area to my left played an episode of *Cheers*, but no one sat in the chairs to watch. The candy dispenser had been refilled with Skittles, proof that we'd had visitors. A pot of mediocre-tasting coffee sat near the empty reception desk along with mail from yesterday. No blinking light on the answering machine—Ivan must've picked up the messages. The overhead fluorescent lights didn't flicker. The wallpaper and paint weren't faded, and the gray carpet wasn't stained or frayed. No newspapers piled or yellowed in dusty corners. This could've been any space in Anyplace, USA—from molars to murder, this office could do it all.

And somehow, I fit in, a failed cop turned PI, who'd solved Ivan's case—*London Sutton did it*—but not mine—Figgy the goldendoodle still hadn't been brought home to the Suttons.

I passed the receptionist's desk without scooping up the mail. It *was* Sunday, my day of More Rest than a Wednesday. I launched down the hall and stood in the doorway of Ivan's office.

My godfather wore gray Dickies and a blue golf shirt and *those cop shoes*. He was flipping through a manila folder with one hand and holding a coffee mug in the other. He smelled like moss and fire.

"Look what the cat dragged in," I said.

If Robert De Niro turned into a polar bear, he'd look just like Ivan. That twice-broken Roman nose. Thick white hair. A smirk that believed that 98 percent of the world population were lying and murdering assholes.

"How was drinking and driving?" he asked.

"I'm sore and have a headache in my ankles," I said, plopping into his guest chair. "Never doing *that* again."

Ivan smiled. "But I bet you laughed and fluttered your eyelashes and made a bunch of men miserable."

I snorted and rolled my eyes. "I do *that* every Thursday."

"You're a hoot and a holler, Alyson. You deserve more downtime. Working too hard gets you dead, and Al didn't bust his ass for you to have a heart attack at thirty-five."

"So what is this case that required me to come in on a Sunday?" I asked.

Ivan tilted his head. "Who said you were required to come in today? I didn't."

I squinted at him. "Well, you said the client was coming in—"

"But I didn't tell you that *you* had to. Your hours are your hours," he said, watching that realization flare in my eyes. "This ain't the LAPD." Ivan slid that manila folder across the desk.

I opened the folder to find the intake form.

NAME: Araceli Rivas
RELATIONSHIP WITH THE MISSING PERSON: Wife
MISSING PERSON'S NAME: Emiliano Rivas
DATE OF MISSING: Saturday, May 13, 2023
AGE AT DATE OF MISSING: 23 years old
LOCATION LAST SEEN: 7-Eleven on 32250 78th Street, Haven, CA

"Missing for almost three months?" I asked. "How does she know that he's missing and didn't just leave?"

No laws forbade an adult to lawfully leave their home or their families.

The bell above the front door jangled.

"That's probably her," Ivan said, pushing up from the chair. "You get to ask her that yourself."

2.

I grabbed my leather binder and the intake form and followed my godfather to the reception area. On my phone, I launched Scriptor—a transcription app I'd read about—and was now ready for my first interview of the day.

The woman standing in the lobby had a slicked-back hair bun the color of cherry Kool-Aid. She wore a mustard-yellow cardigan over a tank top that said Good Vibes Only. Rings twinkled on almost every finger, and her neck was adorned with a bunch of necklaces weighed down by charms—seashells, dolphins, and MAMA. She was very Wine O'Clock, even with a missing husband.

"Araceli?" Ivan asked.

The woman nodded and all the earrings on her earlobes and bracelets on her wrists jangled their "hello." She gave Ivan and me a grateful smile—those sharp cheekbones were the real deal, not a contour-Sephora conjure. "Thank you for talking to me," she said. "I know it's a Sunday, but . . . I need your help."

Her voice made me think of soy candles that smelled of pumpkins and chardonnay.

Ivan led the three of us up to the loft. His shoes creaked the entire way—the man who'd assaulted me across from Deegan's had worn silent shoes. And he'd smelled of cigarettes and cheeseburgers, not moss and fire.

We reached the loft, and Araceli let out a small gasp of surprise, seeing a ribbon of the Pacific from the windows. Ivan made us K-Cup coffees as our potential client settled on the graying brown leather couch with its mismatched pillows. Even though Araceli Rivas was the embodiment of fairy lights and wine time, she wore sadness and exhaustion too. She was the opposite of London and Mackenzie Sutton with their lululemon, Stanley mugs, and Louis Vuitton.

Araceli's hazel eyes brightened as she accepted the cup of Café Mocha from Ivan. She rummaged in her bag and pulled out a purse-size leather organizer. From there, she pulled out a small framed picture and sat it on the coffee table, giving it a slight pat.

"Is this Emiliano?" I asked.

She nodded. "My heart."

I plucked the picture from the table and settled in the armchair.

Emiliano Rivas had hard brown eyes and a soft smile. You crushed on him because back in elementary school, he'd always pick you first for kickball. But then, in middle school, he'd forget that he knew you as you passed each other in the hall . . . which made you crush on him harder. Adult Emiliano still had dark hair—long on the top, short on the sides. He still wore a crucifix, tiny and gold, around his tatted neck. He must've decided to finally remember a woman like Araceli, because here she was, seated on this couch, carrying a picture of him in her purse.

"How long were you married?" I asked, opening my binder.

"It would've been a year tomorrow," she whispered, eyes on the picture.

"How has year one been?" I asked.

"Rough," she said, "but all newlyweds face some obstacles at first, right?"

Beats me, Araceli.

I offered her a sad grin instead of a solid answer and handed Ivan the picture.

"Missing since May?" Ivan asked, giving the photo the briefest look before plopping into the other armchair.

"Feels longer than that," Araceli said, tears burning in her eyes. "On the last day I saw him, we'd been getting ready for a Mother's Day barbecue over at my parents' house. We ran out of propane, and he went to get more from the store. And that was it. He—" She dropped her head and her shoulders shook. She whispered, "Sorry."

"No need to apologize." Ivan pushed the box of tissues on the table closer to her. We watched silently as Araceli cried. When enough time had passed, Ivan said, "When did you report him missing to the police?"

Araceli snatched more tissues from the box and dried her tears. "A week after Mother's Day." She bit her lip and looked at me, her cheeks flushed. "I only waited that long because of his status."

"Status?" Ivan said. "Meaning?"

"He was undocumented?" I whispered, eyes on Araceli.

Araceli winced and nodded. "He'd been in the States for almost two years, and we got married because I thought that would help. I thought by now that we'd be living our happily ever after, but we're not, and I don't know if he left because he didn't love me anymore or because something bad happened. I'm stuck between grieving and being pissed off because, if he left, why, and if he didn't leave, why would he put himself in danger? Why didn't I go get the stupid propane tank refilled and—"

She pushed out a long breath and pushed her hand through her bright hair. "I don't . . ." She shook her head and shrugged. Her chin quivered, and her eyes turned glassy. "I don't know what to do, what to think."

"Did he come to the US with a work permit?" I asked.

She gave the smallest headshake.

"Did he have a criminal history?" I asked.

She hesitated before saying, "No."

Ivan and I exchanged looks.

"We love each other," Araceli said, "and I wasn't about to go live in fucking . . . *Jalisco*, where he's from, especially since I have a home and my family and a nice life here. He found a good job in construction over at Lumière, the spa they're building."

Cooper had shown me the plans and renderings for Lumière, named after his mother's Louisiana-Creole family. Natural mineral-water springs, every body treatment possible, seasonal California cuisine, adults only. He'd designed a private villa with our own hot spring just for us. Sonny's Serenity and Lumière were scheduled to open Winter 2025.

The villa was supposed to be my wedding gift.

"Emiliano was actually a licensed contractor back in Jalisco," Araceli said. "Everybody over at Lumière liked him."

"Is it possible that he got detained by ICE?" Ivan asked.

"Me and my family thought that too," Araceli said, "and I called the detention centers way down in Adelanto and Calexico, but they don't have a record of him. He wasn't in jail at the sheriff's, neither."

"Could he have gone back to Jalisco?" I asked.

Araceli shook her head. "They're saying that he's not there."

"*They* meaning . . . ?" I asked.

"His mother, his brothers." She paused, then added, "Emiliano used to always go drinking after his shift with this guy. Umm . . ." She closed her eyes as she thought. "Hector Montez, I think. I tried calling him, but he won't answer my calls or text messages. And I can't even see his phone on Find My anymore."

I jotted Hector Montez's contact information onto my legal pad.

Araceli plucked new tissues from the box as tears welled in her eyes again. "We were talking about starting a family. I was putting money away for an immigration lawyer. We were happy."

Patrick McDermott and Olivia Newton-John had dated "happily" for nine years until he faked his death. Another guy intentionally overturned his kayak near the deepest part of Green Lake in Wisconsin, all so that he could fake his death and start a life with some chick over in Uzbekistan. Folks were always happy . . .

until they weren't. "Happy couples" were always involved in shit that people "never saw coming." Except . . . yeah, you saw that shit coming. He disappeared on "work trips" a lot. She's drinking way too much. Then, he's dead from eating poisoned banana pudding, she's almost dead after drinking her morning smoothie tainted with antifreeze, and you learn about the adultery, the beatings, and the money. Sometimes, for cops, "we were happy" reeked more than a corpse pulled from Lake Mead.

"And the sheriff's case?" I asked Araceli now.

Araceli sucked her teeth and scowled. "To them, Lee is just another 'illegal.' I mean, they had me fill out papers and they went to his job, but other than that? They haven't done nothing cuz they don't care. And that's why I came to talk to you guys. I've had enough of nothing happening, you know?"

Ivan sighed and ran his hand over his whiskered cheek. "Well . . . missing persons cases aren't cheap. We do analysis and gather information—that's phase one. We analyze all areas of interest. Where he could be, for instance. We talk to family, create flyers, do traces, locate witnesses. We charge two hundred an hour or a flat rate of four thousand dollars for forty hours. We may find him in three days or three months. Depends."

Araceli's eyes bugged. "Four k? That's a lot of money."

Ivan nodded. "Sure."

She turned to me, tension ratcheting off her body. She had lots of questions—but I couldn't afford to answer them without being paid. I, too, was broke—that $4,000 would keep the lights on and phones working. I took a sip of K-Cup coffee and frowned. Cold. Not that it would've tasted any better if it had been the temperature of Pompeii lava.

Getting no support from the other BIPOC woman in the room, Araceli's face quivered with a flash of anger. "You don't have a special rate or a Groupon?" Her cherry Kool-Aid hair was coming undone from its tight bun. She closed her eyes and slowly exhaled. "How is this my life?" she whispered to herself.

There were cameras and phones everywhere. Location devices and satellites. Data collection nowadays was nonstop. How people still managed to disappear, I would never understand. We knew so much and still knew nothing at all.

Ivan said, "I know. The price sounds like a lot, but—"

"What if I could pay for some of those hours?" she asked, squeezing the handle of her canvas bag.

"That would be up to you and your budget," Ivan said. "We take these matters seriously. I ran missing persons for the LAPD for four decades. Miss Rush here worked homicide, also with the LAPD. We've solved countless cases—"

"I know, it's just . . ." Araceli gazed out that long window to the Pacific Ocean, chewing on her bottom lip as she thought. Once she'd thought enough, she stood from the sofa. "Maybe I can start a GoFundMe or . . . something?"

She chuckled even as tears slipped down her cheeks. "Loving him has cost me a lot, and I feel like a bitch for even saying that . . ." She took another long breath in with her eyes squeezed shut. "Because what if I get the money, and you find him, and I learn that he just didn't want to be married to me now that he's *here*?"

Ivan placed a large bear paw on her shoulder. "That *is* a risk, I hate to say."

"Can I think about it?" Araceli asked. "Can I call you later today?"

I said, "Of course."

Ivan said, "We'll be here, ready to help."

We escorted Araceli Rivas back down the stairs and to the entrance. No one spoke until that last "Thank you" from her and "Anytime" from Ivan. We watched her walk to an ancient green Honda Civic.

"We don't have the resources for pro bono work, coupons, and specials," Ivan said. "You wanna get paid, right?"

"Yep. Sounds messy, though."

"Yeah."

"You think he's *gone* gone," I asked, "or do you think there could be foul play?"

"No clue," Ivan said. "He wouldn't be the first asshole to leave his wife. She seems like a nice kid, though." He waited a beat, then added, "Speaking of assholes: Another case. Cheating husband. Wife wants hard proof. Won't take long, but she doesn't need to know that. We need the money, so you'd pad it out to about twenty hours."

I took the intake form completed by scorned wife Lyric Sydney to my office next to Ivan's, a nice space with a window that offered a view of downtown Haven. I'd pinned only one flyer on the corkboard behind my desk.

MISSING DOG
HELP US FIND OUR LOVED ONE

Finding Figgy had been my first case, and I'd . . . *not failed*, but neither had I succeeded. The dog was now living with a family who I'd named Jen, Jack, and Hazel-Wrenley Minivan. The mom, Jen, had backed into my borrowed Nissan Sentra on the afternoon I'd confronted them about the dog. But before I could do anything about that, I'd found Mackenzie Sutton dead in a Beemer. Cooper had more fucked-up things to deal with other than his family's missing goldendoodle.

But I *would* bring Figgy home, cross my heart, swear.

Before completely shifting gears, though, I typed, "Araceli Rivas at 677 Eighteenth Street, Haven, CA" into PeopleFinder. She worked as a receptionist at Liberty Tires & Brakes and had graduated from Haven High School in 2013. No children. No property. She drove that Honda and owned Celi's Secrets on Etsy. Her Instagram and TikTok profiles shared that same name. She made cutesy things: jewelry and bathroom art, friendship bracelets and candles. Highly rated by more than a thousand customers.

Next, I typed in “Emiliano Rivas.” No social media profiles—and no record of a man with that name living on Eighteenth Street. And now, he was gone.

I clicked into my emails.

> FROM: Sam_Schmidt@oaklandtribune.com
> SUBJECT: Happening in Haven — Have a minute?

No, I didn’t.

> FROM: GiannaPilper@sfgate.com
> SUBJECT: Murders in Haven — Introduction

No, thanks.

Seven more emails from reporters up and down the coast of California—but nothing from Haven’s own Tanner Orr, editor in chief of the *Haven Voice*. No news articles yet on London Sutton. No pictures of the pretty, middle-aged blonde who, if you squinted, could pass for that actress, the one who played the crazy wife in *Gone Girl*. But then, Orr hadn’t received permission to report on *real* crime in this town. No David Lynch–ification of Haven on Orr’s editorial watch. Just stories about skinny-dipping and loud music calls. That’s what the paper’s owner, Boomer Levy, a.k.a. the Suttons, demanded.

How long would it take for a producer to adapt this story with Nicole Kidman as lead actress? They’d cast a white woman in my role, even though Gabrielle Union was *right there*.

In the office next to mine, Ivan’s fingers tapped at his computer keyboard.

My throat tightened as I pulled out my phone and pulled up that grainy video from Deegan’s security camera. There I was, just a few nights ago, standing by Giovanni’s Sentra, my arms filled with manila folders I’d taken from our file room. My attacker came behind me, his face hidden by a mask and cap, his hands hidden by gloves. He’d stood at least six feet tall, and he weighed about two hundred twenty pounds. He wore a tactical watch—white digital numbers against a black face—and cop shoes—not quite Oxfords but not really sneakers either. Ivan wore a similar watch *and* similar shoes.

But I'd hesitated pointing the finger at my godfather. Just yesterday in Sableport, I'd spotted on the wine-bike trolley at least seven burly white men of a certain age wearing tactical watches and old-man ex-first-responder comfort shoes. Each man could've easily slipped his arm around my neck and dragged me down Seaview Way. Because a woman didn't have to "do" anything to be attacked.

Two hundred dollars an hour was a lot of money, especially for a twenty-something-year-old receptionist at a tire shop with a missing husband who'd been in the States without permission. I'd be shocked if Araceli Rivas ever sipped a second cup of K-Cup Café Mocha in Poole Investigations' loft again.

Cheating husband. I'd hop on this case, but not today. The two unlikeable characters already had existing files in Poole's file room. Lyric Sydney had married Kameron Trevino just six years ago. Except Kameron hadn't divorced his *other* wife, Itzel, and Lyric hadn't signed off on her divorce from *her* wife, Elena. So Lyric's accusation that Kameron was cheating . . . Well . . . *Yeah.* With *her*. And *she* was cheating on Elena with *him*. Or maybe there were agreements or . . .

Ugh. Too much thinking for a Sunday.

This time, "Ronin" picked me up in a red Kia Sorrento. He drove with his hand at three and nine and listened to the soundtrack of *Kinky Boots*. I'd added a stop between Lori and Devon Monroe's house and my cottage: 1 Pearl Way.

"Wanna get out?" Ronin parked in front of the modern estate that looked Japanese inspired there and American inspired over there with its terraces, trees, clean lines, bluff, and view of the ocean and redwood forest.

His Porsche sat in the driveway, dirty and cold. Newspapers piled around the sports car's wheels and restaurant circulars remained rubber-banded to the front doorknob.

"No," I said, peering at the house's darkened windows. "I just wanted to see . . ." I held my breath, hoping to glimpse Cooper in the yard or garage, some proof that he was still alive.

I never thought I'd be sitting in the back seat of a Kia, slowly pulling past Cooper's magnificent house without entering it. I never thought that we'd be broken up and that he'd be broken down, the second father in Haven that London had destroyed.

Cooper had dealt with Xander's murder, and then the death of his daughter, because Mackenzie had been a sociopath like her mother and had threatened them both with ruin if they divorced. Mackenzie knew about Cooper and me and hadn't wanted us together. She'd extorted him, not about our relationship, which hadn't been secret—but she'd threatened to send development secrets to his competitors if he divorced London just as he'd planned. He hadn't stayed married to London because he loved her, like I'd believed. But he'd still chosen life with her instead of life with me.

Haven was heaven for some, and hell for the rest. I wanted to make life better—for Lori and Devon, for Mom, for Cooper. Even if I could, though, better was only temporary. Evil always returned—that was certain. But I had some capability, though limited, to beat evil back.

Guess that's why Uncle Ivan ran a private investigation firm in this town of a thousand. Bad shit happened here, and sometimes, you didn't know why or who'd caused it. All you knew was that you needed to stop it.

Everything has been figured out, except how to live.

And that was my job—figuring out some of the "how" to make bad things stop so that we could all enjoy peace . . . if only for a day.

3.

Just like I'd requested, Ronin and his Kia Sorrento dropped me off in front of Devon and Lori Monroe's ranch-style home on Oyster Road without providing me with a lesson in existentialism.

In just a few days, the Monroes' house's brown paint had faded, and the landscape had become shaggy with brown patches in the lawn and ignored newspapers left on the driveway. The ocean roared on the other side of this property with a back deck overlooking a white-sand beach. They'd moved from Oakland up to Haven because they'd feared that their son, Xander, had been in danger—gangs, drugs, and the Oakland Police Department. But it had been a middle-aged blond child psychiatrist wearing yoga pants and TOM FORD Vanilla Sex Parfum that had ripped Xander away from them in a seaside town that sold "H(e)aven" T-shirts and baseball caps.

Fucked up.

And this place . . .

Waves crashing against the shore.

Seabirds squawking from the air.

My heart pounding in my ears.

Never-ending.

Maybe I should've come here yesterday instead of drinking and flirting and "moving on."

My soul ached as I left Ronin's Sorrento and headed to the front porch. I passed the Monroes' Honda Accord in the driveway, the back seats crammed with suitcases and boxes.

Were they leaving Haven?

The front door opened before I knocked. Lori Monroe, PhD, stood at the threshold, her brown skin ashen, her hair pulled back into a ponytail. Her red-rimmed eyes looked hollow, and her smile drooped just like the lavender growing around the front yard.

"Thanks for stopping by," she said, pulling me into a hug. She took my hand and guided me into the foyer. "I look a mess." She wore track pants like mine and a pink hoodie.

Unlike India's house, the air here smelled of bacon, toast, and potatoes. My stomach growled.

The living room still burst with pictures of handsome Xander wearing his football uniform, white lab coat, and swim trunks during a family vacation to Mykonos. The couches and armchair held no dents from people sitting in them. No crooked pillows from clutching. No ashes in the fireplace. No dishes stacked in the see-through kitchen cabinets. No rumbling clothes dryer or whooshing dishwasher.

"Devon drove down to Oakland." Lori dumped ground coffee into the maker.

"Preaching today?" I settled on a stool at the breakfast bar.

"No. He's . . ." Lori hit BREW. "He resigned from his position as pastor over at Haven Methodist. He no longer believes in Haven's goodness and light."

"And you?"

She stared out at the backyard. "I think we're gonna sell the house. We'd get over three million for it." She shrugged and said, "That bitch's bail arraignment is Tuesday. Devon's driving back up for it. We hired an attorney from San Francisco. Nikolai Farrell. Really smart. No bullshit."

Xander's funeral would not take place in Haven.

"Fuck Haven," Lori spat. "The people in Haven who cared enough for us can drive down to Oakland. As for the rest . . ." She stared at her closed fists. "It wasn't supposed to be this way."

Lori groaned and her head fell back. "Wish I had some Patrón to slut up this coffee." She pushed out a breath, and said, "I'm not ready to completely sever my connection to this place. To this house. But I don't want to live here right now either. Anyway. The favor."

But she didn't speak for a long moment. Instead, she watched coffee drip into the empty pot. She wrung her hands as she waited.

"What do you need?" I asked.

"This may be totally inappropriate to ask, and if so, I'd totally understand . . ." Lori plucked two mugs from the cabinet and placed both on the counter. She grabbed the sugar tin from the counter and creamer from the near-empty fridge. We both fixed our coffee. She lifted her mug, thought for a moment, then sipped. Her eyes filled with tears.

Lori Monroe, PhD, was not a woman prone to tears. She was a geochemist and studied the interaction between water and rock. She donned waders and mucked around in contaminated mud. As a Black woman in science, tears would expose her to rock hounds who thought she was there because of DEI quotas. She was strong, but Haven had broken her heart, and now, teardrops slid down her cheeks.

She took a deep breath, and said, "Will you be a pallbearer at Xander's funeral?" She clamped her hand over her mouth to catch a sob. But too many came, and a tsunami of grief washed over her.

I rose from my stool and pulled the broken woman into my arms. We stood there, just steps away from the beautiful Pacific Ocean, mourning the loss of a kid gone too soon.

"If we'd just stayed in Oakland . . ." she whispered. "If I'd just found another solution . . . If I'd just had faith . . ."

I held her close as she muttered her regrets into my shoulder. Yes, I'd help carry her son to his final earthly resting place. That's what friends were for. And I'd also make sure that the woman who took him away from his parents, his family, friends, and community, who stole him from California and science and comics and a world that needed his light, laughter, and love . . . I'd make sure London Sutton never walked the streets as a free person again.

4.

Last Saturday Morning
2:15 a.m.

A sharp rapping sound pulled me from sleep. The television now played an infomercial for wrinkle cream starring that lady who used to be in *Dynasty* . . . or *Falcon Crest*. My eyes burned with exhaustion. I sat there, alone on the couch, heart racing from the jarring noise, wearing filthy, ripped white jeans with a crocheted blanket spread across my shoulders.

Another sharp rap—someone was knocking on the door.

I glanced at the clock on my phone: fifteen minutes past two in the morning.

Nowadays, nothing good ever happened after two in the morning.

I tapped my waist. Gun. I slid my Glock from its holster, crept to the door, and peeked through the peephole.

A young woman with matted brown hair stood on the porch, her dirty, rumpled Abercrombie & Fitch T-shirt and jeans clinging to her thin frame. She knocked again and looked back over her shoulder. A canvas shopping bag was slung over her shoulder, and it looked like it weighed more than she did.

Who the fuck . . . ?

My hand hovered over the doorknob. "Yes?" I asked, my tone even.

"Can I talk to Alyson Rush, please?" She sounded scratchy. A teardrop tumbled down her gaunt cheek.

Something about this girl seemed familiar.

I opened the door wide enough for the girl to see the gun.

The stranger's brown eyes bugged—yeah, she saw it—and quickly popped back up to meet mine. "You don't know me," she said, her voice trembling, "but—" She looked back to the forest.

"Who are you?" I demanded, lifting the gun just a bit so that the young woman could see the Glock was not a toy. Now was not the time to try me.

The stranger closed her eyes, took a deep, shuddering breath, and then met my gaze again. "I'm . . . I'm Honor Butler."

My grip on the gun loosened. "Honor?" I whispered. "Shit. Come in."

The young woman stumbled over the threshold. Immediately, her body sagged as though she carried the weight of the world in that canvas shopping bag on her shoulder. She smelled like dirt and sweat, bruises darkened her already-filthy arms, and a nasty cut on her lip had pebbled over with dried blood. She trembled as she clutched her elbows, and her eyes darted around the living room like she expected someone to ooze out of the shadows.

My eyes did the same, except that Honor had been the one to ooze out of the shadows.

I guided Honor to the living room couch, grabbed the crocheted blanket, and draped it over her shoulders.

The girl sat but kept that bag tight against her chest. Her Puma sneakers had been white once upon a time. Now, they looked like she'd walked the soil of seven continents.

"Want something to eat?" I asked.

"Yes, please."

Good. Time to stall. Time to force my mind back to work. Especially after being nearly run over by a family of dog thieves and almost killed by a lululemon-wearing psychopath in one of the prettiest locations in California.

And now, a teenager who'd been missing since April sat on my couch, looking like she'd been thrown out of a car and kicked in the head.

Yeah, my brain needed time. More time than required to make that turkey sandwich. I needed the time it took to fully roast a frozen turkey. But that wasn't possible.

Since Honor looked like she hadn't eaten in days, I made two sandwiches, opened the new bag of Cheetos, and grabbed a big bottled water from the fridge. I placed the food on the coffee table before my guest and smiled.

Honor whispered, "Thank you," and ate in silence as tears slipped down her cheeks.

I thought about calling the girl's mother, Keely Butler. When Honor had first gone missing, Keely hadn't immediately reported the girl as missing—Honor had run away before. After deciding that her missing daughter was an emergency, Keely had pleaded with Ivan to make finding Honor a priority. He hadn't.

Probably because Keely had never looked to see if Honor's phone still worked.

Probably because Keely had accused Ivan and me of racism—Honor was half Mexican. Keely planned to run for mayor and, as retribution, had threatened to come after us when she won.

I didn't like that woman, but Keely was still a worried mother who deserved to know that her daughter was alive.

At the same time . . . it was two something in the morning. Why was Honor sitting in *my* living room eating and not her mother's? Honor didn't know me, and yet, here she was, chowing down on a stranger's turkey sandwiches. Why? And who told her to come here?

I knew Honor would spill her secrets—I just had to wait. And Honor would also show me the contents of that shopping bag. *Time, time, time.* A full belly made a clear mind . . . but turkey sometimes did the opposite . . . which was why we all fell asleep after Thanksgiving dinner.

Well, shit, Sonny.

I sat beside Honor, praying that the girl would stay awake long enough to give at least three answers to six million questions.

Honor finished her meal and drained the bottled water. Then, she let out a long sigh and a chuckle. "This is random, huh?"

I offered a quick smile. "Totally."

The young woman's face clouded some before she forced a smile to her lips. "I don't even know how . . ." She shook her head.

"Just . . . say whatever comes into your head," I said, "and then we'll fill in the holes."

She whispered, "I . . . I thought I could trust them. They were friends. Or at least I thought they were."

"Who?" I asked.

"Liam. Caitlin. Mackenzie." She paused, then said, "Especially Mackenzie. She's, like, my play big sister. I'm pissed at her most of all."

"Do you mean . . . Mackenzie Sutton?" I asked, eyebrows high.

Honor nodded and swiped at the teardrops tumbling down her cheeks.

She was speaking of Mackenzie in present tense. Which meant she didn't know that, hours ago, I'd found Mackenzie Sutton dead in her BMW, foam drying on her lips. But I wouldn't tell Honor any of this right now—too much, too soon for the both of us.

Honor tugged at her earlobe. "Guess I should tell you where I've been and everything, but it's just too . . ." Her face tensed, moments away from cracking.

I placed my hand on Honor's wrist. "Just . . . give me, like, the Snapchat version."

Honor nodded, relieved that she could speak in her native tongue.

Back in April, on the morning of her track meet, Honor and Mackenzie had met Liam and Caitlin at this café up in Sableport ten miles north of Haven. She knew Caitlin and had only known Liam on Instagram.

"Cuz he, like, used to run cross-country when he was in high school," Honor explained. "He's, like, totally hot. And rich."

That April morning, she and Liam had flirted over chilaquiles and spicy Bloody Marias. Everyone had been twenty-one years old except

Honor. She got drunk that afternoon, and she and Liam hooked up at his parents' beach house not far from the café. He asked her to stay with him, and she said, "Yes." Her dreams had come true—she'd landed the perfect boyfriend. They partied that weekend, and Liam bought her gifts, everything that she'd ever wanted: a Michael Kors purse, new Adidas Sambas, good weed, good food. She didn't want to go back home.

"I hated Haven, like, you can't imagine how much," she told me.

But Mackenzie told Honor that she needed to finish one last year and graduate from high school. "She begged me to come back," Honor said, "but I didn't want to leave Liam."

Mackenzie returned to Haven, but Honor stayed with Liam and Caitlin. Life had been perfect until, one day, a week later, Liam just shut down.

"Like, he wouldn't touch me or talk to me," Honor said, staring at the empty plate. "I was, like, what did I do to make him hate me?"

Then, Liam told Honor that he wanted her to come with him to a party. He drove her to the mall and bought her sexy clothes. "Like, from a real store," Honor said. "Nordstrom."

They went to the party in this house with decks and infinity pools and half-naked waitresses, and everyone there was male and over thirty. "Total geezers," she said, scowling. "But they had, like, E and some good weed, and these strong drinks. I totally got fucked up." And then she woke up naked in the bathroom of this swanky house.

"I couldn't remember what happened," Honor said, shaking her head, "but I knew that I'd had sex. Liam was happy. He had all this cash in his hands, and he told me that he loved me, and we were happy again until he got mad again, and like, I told him that I didn't want to do it anymore, but he kept promising one last time and that I could go, but he never let me go, and he'd drive me up and down California to these parties, and one time? He handcuffed me, and . . . I escaped and just ran, and I didn't want to get in a car cuz I didn't know . . . And I came here because . . ."

Eyes wet and wild, she gaped at me. "Don't tell anybody I'm here. At least not yet. Especially Mackenzie or my mother. I can't—"

A sob burst from her chest, and she wept into her hands.

So this just got a whole lot worse. "Worse" the size of Mount Everest.

"I'm gonna get them back," Honor said between tears. "For what they did to me. Mackenzie knew, but did she ever come looking for me?"

"Honor," I said.

The girl's phone vibrated from the bag. She fished it out.

My pulse jumped. "Have you kept your phone on all this time?"

She nodded. "Does it matter?"

I jumped up from the couch and peeked out the living room window.

Nothing but fog, trees, and darkness.

"Someone may have followed you here," I said. "They could be using Find My."

Honor gasped and held the button on the phone's side to turn it off.

I snatched the phone from Honor's hands. "Not good."

Honor whispered, "I'm so sorry. I wasn't thinking."

I nodded. Couldn't even say "It's okay" because it was so not okay. If this was indeed sex trafficking involving rich kids and old geezers, they'd bristle at the idea of a victim knowing their secrets.

"It's not like it matters," Honor grumbled. "My life is over anyway. I'm trash. No one will feel sorry for me. I did this willingly. I deserve—"

"Stop," I said, looking away from the dark tree line. "Lick your wounds later. We got shit to figure out." Including whoever had just texted her.

Another teenage girl had swerved into my orbit. Penance for failing Autumn Sanchez back in Los Angeles.

Honor glanced up at me, her eyes filled with desperation and hope. "You're a private investigator, right? You help people?"

"Yes."

"Can you help me?"

Do I have a choice?

Yes, I did have a choice. I was no longer a sworn officer or a mandatory reporter. I was now a private citizen. Alyson Rush, private eye, trying to make a dollar out of straight nonsense.

But this . . . I didn't know how . . . who . . . what . . .

Call Ivan.

Back in the day, Ivan Poole had worked hundreds of sex trafficking cases. He'd know what to do.

I called his number, but Ivan didn't answer.

"I can't go back home until you help me," Honor said, tears in her eyes, "cuz Liam probably knows I'm here."

My stomach twisted, and I wanted to vomit. I said, "Yeah," pissed that my life had become one trash fire after the other with no possibility of blue sky in the forecast. I had more chances of getting hit by a meteor than finding—and holding on to—a happily ever after.

Brady Kwon. He was the only other option.

Days had passed since we'd seen each other. Would he come if I called?

Honor couldn't stay at my house. I didn't even *know* this girl. I didn't *trust* this girl.

"Honor," I said, "I need to keep your phone for now."

"Okay."

"If I'm helping you, I'll need access—"

"Six-nine-zero-six-one-four."

"Wanna take a shower?"

Honor's eyes filled with longing, and she nodded. Clean towels, a fresh new pair of scrubbing gloves, boxers, and a T-shirt. The first steps toward normalcy.

As she disappeared into the bathroom still clutching that shopping bag, I dialed Brady Kwon's number. My hands shook—this was only the beginning. Whatever had brought Honor to my doorstep had now involved me, and I had no idea what kind of danger I'd just invited in for two turkey sandwiches and a shower.

5.

I still hadn't eaten breakfast and was now experiencing bubble gut from drinking too much wine and Lori Monroe's coffee. The crankies were coming, and I bade adieu to Lori and stepped outside. Oh yeah—my Bronco was still in the shop for repairs.

My phone rang: India.

"Hey," I said, my eyes on the long road ahead.

"Ohmigod," India said, breathless. "Was that the best time you've had in, like, forever?"

"It was fun," I said, heading to the sidewalk.

"What's wrong?"

"Trying to figure out how to get home from Lori's house. An Uber or . . . ?"

"Girl, walk your ass home," India said, cackling. "Two miles ain't gonna kill you."

I sighed—it was actually only a mile and a half—and I set off, heading east toward the trees. Okay, so feeling fresh air against my face just two minutes in made me smile. Taking my time to get somewhere would also give me the space to think.

My phone vibrated again, this time with a text message from Dallas the mechanic.

Your truck will be ready tomorrow AM

I'll drop it at your place

My smile broadened—insurance would cover 90 percent of the costs.

I reached the one traffic light at Highway 1, which separated downtown Haven from the forest that hosted my cottage. The light turned green, and I crossed the road, gaining on the evergreens and those spectacular homes purchased by rich people or the old folks who'd bought these million-dollar homes seventy years ago for fifty dollars and a basket of persimmons.

By the time I reached Summer Way, my knees were burning, my calves were burning, and the linings of my throat and lungs were burning. *I should really walk more.* Dallas was dropping off my Bronco tomorrow, and driving Fabulous Ass Bronco (a.k.a. FaB) gave me joy. Didn't I deserve joy? I also liked living, and by the way my body signaled that she wouldn't do that for long if I didn't walk more . . . *Fine, I'll walk to work twice a week.*

Before taking the road that led down to my cottage, I stopped at our lighthouse-shaped, roadside mailbox. As I walked down our gravel pathway, I sorted through today's mail. Restaurant menus, AARP magazine, an envelope for Mom and Dad from Lenderful Financial Services. I cocked an eyebrow at seeing my dead father still receiving mail. And here I thought that only my mother believed he was still alive. I knew Lenderful—I'd passed their billboards down in Los Angeles every day. "The Right Solution for the Wrong in Your Life."

Why were my parents receiving mail from them? Was this simple junk mail or legitimate Al and Val Rush–branded bullshit?

Mom now lived with me in Haven because Dad had borrowed on his pension without telling her and also because they'd taken out a reverse mortgage on the house now owned by the bank. She hadn't wanted to relocate to Haven, but she didn't have a lot of money, and living alone in Los Angeles, especially, required more than Social Security checks.

And now . . . mail from Lenderful Financial Services.

If I asked Mom about it, she'd say "Probably junk, it's nothing" with a bright smile.

Why were they getting mail from a fast-cash place, though?

My father had retired from the LAPD five years before his death, and Ivan had retired not long after. Both men had bled blue but left the force before they were required to.

Dad had squeezed his pension dry, leaving Mom with a dribbling of cash. Ivan had retired but had opened Poole Investigations to make ends meet. He needed money, which was why he needed Araceli Rivas to pay our fee. And I needed Araceli to pay our fee because I had to pay off the settlement to Autumn Suarez's family. Even though Cooper had lopped off 75 percent of the $97,210, I still had about $25,000 left—and I didn't have $25,000 just waiting to be spent.

No one in my family had great financial outlooks.

Recognizing my own financial shenanigans, however, didn't loosen the worry knot in my stomach about my parents' money mistakes.

My landlord, Elliott Frye, wasn't rich, but he'd sold his house in San Jose to relocate to Haven. Together with his husband, Giovanni Espinoza, he'd purchased this house of cedar shingles and a wraparound deck along with the miniature version of the main house that Mom and I rented. And now, the couple tossed me a wave as they washed their Ford Explorer, their one surviving car.

"*Walking?*" Elliott asked, eyebrows high.

"I *know*," I said, then pointed at him. "Did my insurance company call about the Sentra?"

Giovanni nodded. "And they totaled it."

"Sorry again."

Elliott flapped his hand. "Gio wanted a new car, and now he's getting a new car, and we may end up suing the Suttons if you don't sue them first."

"Line is pretty long," I said.

"How was the wine-booze-bike-cruise trolley?" Elliott asked, pulling on his Tiffany-blue Sweetlife sweatshirt.

"I drank, I toasted, I sang 'Sweet Caroline.' I'm done for the rest of the year. Thanks for watching over Mom. And the wedding? I thought you all were gonna stay over?"

Both men grimaced, and Giovanni aimed the hose at the Explorer's tires.

"We were," Elliott said, "until we saw the groomsmen taking pictures wearing those red baseball caps."

"Oh dear," I said.

"We got the fuck outta there with a quickness," Giovanni said.

"Oh, Haven," I said, shaking my head, "you never disappoint."

Elliott wagged his finger. "Don't paint Haven with one broad brush."

I rolled my eyes. "You know this town is a lie—"

"One bad apple," he said.

"More like one bad strawberry," Giovanni said. "One rots and the whole basket's fucked up. Haven is like a basket of strawberries—"

"You live here now," Elliott pointed out.

I cocked my head. "Yep."

Giovanni returned to washing the hood of the Ford.

"No place is perfect," Elliott said. "This place is the closest."

Both Giovanni and I said, "Okay."

Elliott needed Haven to behave. He needed to trust this place. Like me, like Giovanni, he didn't trust it, but he couldn't admit to Giovanni that he'd been wrong to leave San Jose. Haven *had* to work out. What's a Pride flag burned and red-hatted clients when you had these beautiful trees and that ocean?

I thumbed at the cottage. "And how is she?"

"Good," Elliott continued. "She's texting a lot. Like *a lot* a lot." He moved closer to me. "She almost burned a batch of cupcakes yesterday cuz she was texting like a sixteen-year-old."

I scrunched my eyebrows.

He gave me a sly smile. "Does she, like, have a boyfriend or . . . ?"

I snorted. "Uhh, *no*."

"Wrong answer," Elliott said. "Her face gets all bright, and her eyes get all misty."

I said "Uhh, *no*" again.

Giovanni splashed me with the hose. "Let that woman carpe diem, especially if it's gonna keep her off the highway and out of the forest."

On our second day in Haven, Mom had left the cottage and gotten lost among the redwoods and pine trees. A few days later, she'd wandered away from the community center—I had found her at the pier, talking to a strange man I later saw leaving a house owned by Ivan and rented by Keely Butler.

Maybe Elliott was right—whoever was holding Mom's attention could keep her ass planted in one spot. I could have all the AirTags in the world pasted all over her, but if I didn't chain her down . . .

Yeah, maybe I *should* put mSpy on her phone.

Mom was sitting at the kitchen table with the phone to her ear. She tossed me a wave, her face bright with a smile. Instead of her favorite purple sweatsuit, she wore yellow leggings, a white flowing shirt, and lip gloss. She looked like that lady in the type 2 diabetes medication commercial.

"I remember that!" she was saying to the person on the phone. She laughed, then said, "You talk to her recently? . . . Umm . . . Hmm . . ." She threw her head back and cackled.

That smile. Those eyes. *Yellow leggings?*

Who was he? What did he do? Was he divorced? Who were his kids, what was his economic status, did he have a record?

I smelled lunch, and my growling stomach tore my attention away from my mother. I peeked into the pots: smothered pork chops, buttered potatoes, and green peas. She'd baked peach cobbler for dessert. We called it "P4," and it was my favorite dinner. Usually, she'd bake hella-complicated pastries like pavlovas and lemon soufflés to prove that she remembered things, but now, she was baking cobbler, which could mean *anything*.

Shit.

My bedroom was just as I'd left it, with Honor Butler's canvas shopping bag in the corner and the boxers and T-shirt she wore crumpled in the hamper. When would I go through that shopping bag and her cell phone?

After taking a shower, yes. After eating my first meal of the day, definitely.

Before doing either, I checked the security app again on my phone and saw the live feed from the front doorbell camera and the pantry door camera.

Birds, trees, and bees right now.

I tapped ACTIVITY.

10:00 a.m.: Me leaving yesterday morning and climbing into a hired car for Sableport for bike-trolley shenanigans.

10:30 a.m.: Elliott and Giovanni loaded up the Explorer with supplies and my mother.

1:00 p.m.: A buck led two does and three fawns past the cottage.

2:20 p.m.: A gaze of raccoons sniffed around the spot where one of their own had eaten a poisoned cupcake that had been left by a phantom for me to eat.

5:15 p.m.: Giovanni and Mom tromping into the house after baking a hundred cupcakes.

As for today, nothing interesting had happened so far. *Good.*

The cupcake poisoner . . . There'd been video of a man purchasing them at Sweetlife, and he resembled the man who'd stood with Mom on the pier that night. Brady Kwon and the Mendocino County Sheriff's Department now had the security camera footage from the bakery—but like the camera footage from Deegan's of my assaulter, they couldn't make out much detail.

Was it possible that my assaulter and the cupcake phantom were the same men?

Yes.

Did I feel any better knowing that I was looking for one asshole instead of two?

Not really—but at least he hadn't shown his face in the forest again. I wasn't actively carrying my gun, but if shit kept happening to me, I'd wear her like I wore a bra.

I pulled on another pair of sweats and a slouchy T-shirt. My belly growled again, and I tapped it. *Soon, baby, soon.*

Mom was humming Chaka Khan's "Sweet Thing" as she set the table. Snapping her fingers, she looked back at me and smiled.

"Who have *you* been talking to that's making you groove and grin like this?" I asked.

She blushed, and said, "Quincy Johns. You met him a long time ago. We went to Jordan High together. Tall. Looks like Billy Dee Williams's cousin?"

"Oh. Yeah."

He'd come to cookouts and holiday parties, and all the women would flutter around him like butterflies and honeybees. He had wavy hair and a trim mustache, drove a silver-gray Cadillac, and showed everyone around him the picture of his boat. Quincy Johns had attended my father's funeral, too, and now here he was, five years later, making my mother hum and cackle while wearing yellow leggings.

"So what's he calling you for now?" I playfully crossed my arms.

"He lives down in Ojai now. Retired from the air force—he'd been stationed at Vandenberg near Santa Barbara. He visited LA a few days ago and heard that I'd closed the bakeries and moved—"

She remembered all that today!

Hooray!

"—and he got my number from Charlene—"

Mom's friend.

"—and he called me back on Thursday, and we've been talking and texting and . . ." She set down the glasses with a nod and shrugged. "It's . . . *nice*."

I dared to offer an encouraging grin.

By just letting her talk, I learned that Quincy's first wife, Gloria, died sixteen years ago. He divorced his second wife, Phyllis, three years ago. His grown children—Yolanda, Quincy Jr., and Sharla—lived in Phoenix, Baltimore, and Lisbon.

"Sounds good so far." I placed my elbows on the kitchen counter and watched her turn off the burners on the stove.

My mother had a long-distance boyfriend. Weird. And . . . *normal.*

"Hungry?" she asked.

"Starving—I haven't eaten since yesterday. And supper smells incredible."

She curtsied and waved to the pots. "Go for it." She kissed my forehead and hummed "Sweet Thing" as I scooped meat, potatoes, and veggies onto my plate. She grabbed a bottle of Cab from the wine rack and the corkscrew from a drawer.

With the late-afternoon sunlight shifting around the living room, and the house smelling of garlic, onions, and meat like that, and the television playing on mute, it felt like old times again.

"Quincy was just telling me," Mom said, cutting into her chop, "about the Taos Mountain Balloon Rally in October. This year's the fortieth annual."

"I'm sure that's absolutely beautiful," I said, my mouth full. "All those bright colors and the sunrise . . ."

"Yeah, one of his buddies from the air force has a balloon business, and he was saying how this festival is better because it's smaller." She spooned peas into her potatoes. "Must be incredible to see all that in person."

"Yeah." My phone buzzed: an alert from the security system. I tapped to see . . .

Giovanni pulling the Explorer out of the driveway.

"And I thought," Mom was saying, "I *should* see it in person. What's stopping me?"

I snorted. "Money."

She gathered the peas and potatoes onto her fork. "Q said that he'd pay my way." She ate her forkful of food and nodded. "This *is* good."

I slowed my chewing as my stomach twisted around peas and pork. And we'd been doing so good today. "I don't think . . . You probably . . . No."

Her eyebrows scrunched—a flash of anger—but then she gave me the fakest of fake smiles. "May I ask why not, since I'm not your child and don't need to ask for your permission to be a grown-ass woman who does grown-ass-woman things like going on hot air balloons?"

She fixed me with a steely gaze, her empty fork tapping at the potatoes. She was still the strong-willed woman she'd been all my life and was now waiting for me to fuck up further.

What could I say that would keep that fork in the potatoes and not in my eye?

Because your mind doesn't work well in places you know.

Because just this morning, you mentioned Dad forgetting to buy cardamom.

Because I wouldn't be able to find you if you wandered off into the fucking scrublands of New Mexico.

My lips clamped shut, tighter than before. No response was better than *any* response. Like with a T. rex, if I kept still . . .

"I know what you're thinking," Mom said, frowning and sawing with too much vigor at her pork chop. "But I'm too young to be old, and so what, my hip hurts a little, but your shoulder hurts sometimes. The doctor said that I'm years away from replacement surgery—"

Huh? What? Her hip? No. I could give zero fucks about her *hip*.

I opened my mouth to say that but knew that my true concerns would bring rain I'd been avoiding successfully since sunrise. But I had to say *something*. "You knew Quincy forty years ago—"

"Do a background check on him, then."

"What would I find?"

"Retired lieutenant colonel. Father of three. Licensed pilot. Lives in Ojai."

"Anything else?"

She cocked an eyebrow. "His ex-wife isn't in jail for murder, and his daughters are living productive lives without having to blackmail their father—"

"Whoa." My head snapped back. "Unnecessary roughness, Mother."

"Just proving a point," she said, pointing her fork at me. "I don't plan to work in a bakery and come home and cook for you for the rest of my life—"

"I didn't—"

"Can I want something more?" she asked. "And have that *more* with someone else?"

My phone buzzed—security system again. Giovanni at the Explorer, but this time, he was unloading supplies to the garage.

"I don't need your permission to go," Mom said. "I'm not a child. I want to see fucking balloons floating every-fucking-where—"

I could no longer taste this delicious pork chop because this meal had been a setup.

"And I'm going to see balloons." She nodded, then scowled at her plate. But the anger passed, and her frown turned upside down as she thought about those balloons and kissing Quincy at five hundred feet in the air, sipping New Mexico wine, and yeah, I totally understood, but . . . shit.

If I let her go, then *I'd* have to go—and I wasn't trying to watch my mom canoodling with a man not my—

My phone buzzed: India texting.

U there already?

I texted back.

??

Did you find it?

Did I find what?

India's response made me hop up from the table and rush to my bedroom.

Mom shouted, "What's wrong?"

I grabbed my gun box from the top shelf in the closet and plucked my Glock from the foam cushion. I checked the magazine and slammed it up and into the gun's ass. My arms filled with steel and my spine straightened, galvanized by adrenaline. I returned to the living room and raced past my mother.

She asked, "Everything okay?"

"No. There's a dead man in our forest."

6.

India sent me a pin of a location that was entirely too close to my front door.

I shoved my phone into my sweatpants' zippered pocket. "Lock the door behind me." Just in case whoever made that body in the forest dead was trying to hide.

"Yep." Mom sprang from her seat and grabbed from the knife block a high-carbon stainless steel butcher's knife that cut rib roast like butter. Bad guys needed to avoid this kitchen cuz Val Rush, former hood girl, would definitely stab their asses up.

Cold air slammed into me as I stepped onto the porch. The golden hour had passed, and the sun was closer to the sea than the sky. Darkness stretched across the forest before me. The aromas of Mom's chops and Giovanni's grilled onions mixed with the scent of evergreens.

Pop! Crack!

The sounds of snapping branches—people in the woods—pulled my attention north to the copse of pine trees. Gun ready, I took a trip around the cottage—all clear—before taking a deep breath and running north and into the forest. My eyes adjusted to darkened spaces around me. Fallen logs now looked like the legs of sleeping giants, and shrubs resembled big furry dogs. I heard the murmurs of people talking now, and I quickly followed that sound.

The funky smell of skunk made me slow but only for a moment. The buzz and bite of insects against my bared arms annoyed me, and I hoped that I had itch cream in the medicine cabinet. I looked up to see a slice of sky between the trees and—*shit!* My ankle twisted, but I didn't stop. The trees grew tighter, their tops rustling in the evening breeze. Sweat beaded under my arms, and my legs cramped—I'd only taken a few bites of pork chop, definitely not enough to sustain my body. Strong beams from flashlights danced across the forest—

What's that? I slowed down and sniffed.

This was no longer the scents of dinner food, evergreens, or skunk.

My stomach churned, familiar with this sickening sweet odor.

Heart pounding, I inched closer to those lights and that chatter, dreading the discovery hidden beneath this forest debris. Once the smell couldn't get any stronger, I fished my cell phone from my pocket.

"You can't be here," a man said.

"This part of the forest is off limits," another man said.

I said "Okay" but tapped the flashlight icon anyway and shone its light on the forest floor before me. I knew the ending to this story. Still, I prayed, *Let this be another dead raccoon. Or a fallen deer. Just don't let it be . . .*

That.

A forest at night was the worst possible scenario for a crime scene.

And then, I was a problem that investigators would need to solve: a big-mouthed contaminant with past experience working crime scenes who no longer carried a badge.

Fortunately, I had reception in this forest, and made two calls:

Elliott, to let him know that scary shit was happening in our neck of the woods and who'd keep Mom calm. And then I called Ivan, who didn't answer. He, too, should know that a body had been found in the forests of Haven.

I didn't have a lot of time—the first deputy was stringing slick yellow tape around the trees as a second deputy tried to block my view.

But I had three inches on him and could see over his head. And since he wasn't doing what he *should've* been doing, I did his job for him.

First, I noted the time and temperature in my Notes app.

7:15 pm
58 degrees

From my spot—about twelve feet away from the body—I took pictures and video of the trees, of the decedent, and made more notes.

White or Hispanic male
Dark hair
No beard/mustache

John Doe wore no shirt, and his pale skin stood out like a sheet against the deep-red bark of the redwood he sat against. He wore black boxer briefs. A few large tattoos were on his chest: a crucifix, praying hands, and a rose. So ubiquitous, those tats. Everybody's mother wore those tats. Still, I hoped they'd be useful in identification.

I aimed my phone's camera and snapped close-up and midrange shots. Despite the deputy's belief that I wanted to get closer, I'd never move from my spot now—investigators would have a hard enough time searching a forest for evidence. They didn't need me making new footprints or smashing a bullet case deeper into the dirt. I didn't have a pencil or pad to sketch the scene, so the pictures would have to do. Not that I'd be allowed to investigate.

I shone the light across his body.

"Can you not?" the deputy whined.

"I'm helping you out, bro," I told him. "You can't blame me for doing your job."

No obvious gunshot wounds from my vantage point. Dried blood crusted in his nose, on his lips. Nothing had been chewed away yet by forest creatures—raccoons, stray cats, and other scavengers living in these woods. But the blowflies had come, and though I couldn't see them yet, eggs were being left on this John Doe. Flies were awful at picnics but helpful at crime scenes—they helped determine time of death and the environment around the body. A person found with an American lady caterpillar in their mouth would tell an entomologist that this body may have come from Texas or Mexico first since those butterflies didn't flutter all the way up to frigid Northern California.

Though I'd worked over a hundred crime scenes during my career—and had solved 85 percent of my cases—forest scenes like this . . . Narnia to me, and I felt bad for the lead investigator. At least it wasn't raining. At least the ground was basically level. At least this wasn't hunting season. At least there were no campers.

No police helicopters lit up the night sky.

No side streets or alleys to tape off to keep civilians—yikes, I was now a civilian—from tromping across the crime scene. But this civilian had handled more homicide investigations than any of these uniformed men—and they were all men—had ever faced in Haven.

The fog rolled in from the Pacific Ocean, and the floodlights set up by sheriff's deputies weren't strong enough to push through the haze.

Detective Brady Kwon smiled as he saw me standing twenty steps away from John Doe. The deputy had tired of my intrusion and directed me to this spot, and I stayed. Brady wore a windbreaker tonight instead of a blazer. Work boots instead of oxfords. He'd shaven tonight—I smelled fresh melon-scented aftershave and, in this light, saw just how smooth his camel-colored cheeks were. Edged-up and good-smelling, Brady Kwon was Mendocino County Sheriff's Office's finest.

"Fancy meeting you here," he said. *"Again."*

I shrugged. "An unexpected detour from my quiet and boring Sunday."

He scowled at the rolling banks of fog. There were . . . *ten . . . eleven* . . . fifteen deputies at this crime scene standing around, doing nothing.

"You'll have to hold the scene tonight, and start at first light," I said, watching the fog race among the trees.

A muscle in his jaw ticked—annoyed with me just that quick. His gaze skipped from the black tent now erected over the dead man up to the treetops, over to the do-nothing deputies, and back to me again. He sighed, whipped out his pen, and opened his leather binder. "How did you find out?"

"Around six o'clock, India texted and asked if I'd been the one who called it in."

"Ah. It was an anonymous caller."

Hmm.

"Anyway," I said, "I ran over, aware that a bad guy could still be around. And then I smelled him—"

He gaped at me. "He's barely dead and you *smelled* him?"

"Barely dead?" I blinked at him. "His arm is raised over his head, defying gravity, my dude. That means he's been in that position for several hours before whoever the fuck left him against that tree—"

He held up his hands. "Thank you, *Miss* Rush."

Not *Detective* Rush.

"Don't patronize me or diminish me with 'miss,'" I spat. "'Sonny' is fine. 'Alyson' if you want to completely be an asshole."

He touched his heart and gave me a little nod. "Apologies. Didn't mean any disrespect. I just wanted you to know that we're not idiots—"

I heard a splash and turned around. The deputy who'd set up the tent gagged, retched again, and vomited all over the crime scene.

"Get him outta there," Brady shouted.

I covered my smile with my hand.

Brady pointed at me, wanting to remain serious but knowing that this night was all kinds of fucked up, and if he at least didn't smile, he'd return to his car and cry. So, he tossed me a grin and made a note of Deputy Nevin upchucking six feet from the decedent.

"You think the person who dumped him here is watching us right now?" I stared out to the trees and the fog.

"You keep saying 'dumped,'" Brady said, still writing. "Who's to say that John Doe didn't walk out here and get lost and rested against the tree to wait it out?"

"His feet say that didn't happen," I said, not blinking.

Brady started to rebut, but instead, he tromped over to the tent, peeked inside.

I knew what he'd see and had taken pictures of John Doe's clean soles. Not one leaf or twig had been caught between his toes, no dirt or gravel pressed into his heel.

Brady returned to me and started writing again in his binder.

I leaned in closer. "You saw that, right? *Everything?*"

He looked at me, looked back at the tent, tromped over again.

Heaven help us. Help this dead guy. Help his family.

Brady returned to me again, his eyebrows high. "Thanks for that."

"Yep."

The man's foot appeared mottled purple . . . except for the side of his foot and the white letters that spelled ADIDAS. Seemed like he'd died wearing Adidas socks and had worn them long enough that his dying blood had settled around that imprint, leaving the skin there pale.

"So someone undressed him and dumped him here?" Kwon asked.

I grunted.

Brady clicked his teeth. "Yeah, we're gonna have to hold the scene until the morning. Can't see shit out here."

I folded my arms and kept my mouth shut.

"Why this spot?" he wondered.

"Isolated but not unreachable," I said. "He'd be found, but not immediately."

"To give the murderer time?"

"Yeah, but time for what?"

And who had carried John Doe out here? That anonymous caller? And from which direction? There were no direct trails to this spot, so the dropper had to have parked somewhere nearby—unless the bad guy lived in one of these nearby houses. Three houses south of this spot:

Elliott and Giovanni, Mom and me, and the Zimmermans, an elderly couple who used walkers and canes. Two houses north of this spot: Soren Bourne, also old, and a big cottage now an Airbnb.

And I mentioned that rental now to Brady Kwon.

He said, "You know that you're not—"

"Yes."

"Are we gonna have a problem?"

I cocked an eyebrow. "Are we?"

If he didn't put on his thinking cap, and if he kept missing shit like clean feet and gravity-defying, reaching limbs, then . . . yes, we were.

From a trolley-bike wine crawl to a body being dumped in the forest. California was giving me her all this weekend. Yesterday this time, I'd been sipping reds and ports and flirting with a hot winetender. Now I stood on the perimeter of a crime scene, watching sworn officers tromp through the clump of trees with flashlights.

"Where's your partner, Will?" I asked Brady now. "Altar-boy duties at church? Science fair project? California Missions report?"

Brady chuckled. "McCann's on his way." He squinted at me. "Why aren't you asking to help out with . . . ?" He nodded toward the officers looking for clues in this foggy dark.

"Because it's a dark and foggy forest, and I know that you won't let me because it would compromise the case once you're in court trying to lock up whoever killed your John Doe."

He held his squint longer, then pushed out air. "And yet, even on the sidelines, you're still the main character."

I gave him a big grin. "Sorry about that, then."

He cocked his head. "Why?"

"That means you're either destined to fall in love with me or die a tragic death."

Someone called out, "Hey! I found some footprints!"

"Footprints or shoeprints?" I asked.

A deputy overheard my question, and snorted, "What difference does it make?"

Brady frowned. "If you're asking that question, go back to the road and keep people from contaminating the scene any more than your dumbass question."

The deputy huffed away from us. Another deputy reported, "Shoe."

"Drop a tent," Kwon said.

The CSI team would make a cast of it. Could be something. Could be nothing.

Soon, yellow tents peppered the forest.

And the fog kept rolling in. And the musky scent of normal forest mixed with the damp air. Eventually, I heard the crunch of tires against leaves, branches, and gravel. I looked at my phone: It was almost nine o'clock. Fifty degrees.

Deputies allowing someone to drive this close meant that it could only be one vehicle.

"Med examiner's here," Brady said, reading my mind.

I made another note on my phone.

The van parked at the yellow tape and carried India and her assistant, Troy. Tonight, she wasn't charming-flirt Indy, my best friend. Wearing her official fleece and badge, she was now India Laster, MD, medical examiner of Mendocino County, the only one in this forest authorized to actually handle the body.

She tossed me a nod as Brady marched to join her on the other side of the yellow tape. Before he dipped into the tent, he looked back at me. "We got it from here," he said, "and McCann will meet you at your house."

I cocked an eyebrow. "I can't even be a lookie-loo?"

"You're doing more than looking." He paused, then added, "Don't worry. I'm not an idiot—I can keep up with the famous Sonny Rush."

"May I join the autopsy?"

"This isn't like the Monroe case," he said. "You aren't connected to this guy at all."

"Other than him being dumped less than half a mile from my house?" I held out my arms. "Forgive me for wanting to help solve your case."

He mirrored my gesture. "Forgive me, but this is *my* case, and if circumstances were different—"

"Fine. You got it, Big Shot."

"I got it. Stop worrying."

The famous Sonny Rush.

Unnecessary roughness.

And I *was* a great cop.

So why aren't you a cop tonight?

My neck warmed, and I sighed, pulling up the pictures on my phone.

Trees, logs, leaves, John Doe's feet, John Doe's neck, and . . .

I squinted, then zoomed in on the picture of the dead man's left calf: the Grim Reaper but as a woman dressed in a wedding gown, candles at her feet, a scythe in her left hand, a globe in her right. *Santa Muerte.*

"Can we start a week in this fucking town without a body turning up?" Ivan's voicemail, delivered in his "old man from SoCal" voice, made me smile. *"If you don't mind, I'm gonna skip tonight's festivities of watching MCSO fuck up a crime scene."*

Before coming to my home, Investigator Will McCann had stopped by a Boy Scouts jamboree to pick up his merit badges in sustainability and personal management. He wore the suit his grandpa bought for law school and had slicked-back brown hair like David Niven in *Please Don't Eat the Daisies*. Even in that suit and with that hair, he still lacked style and savoir faire. A sixty-year-old cocker spaniel had more bite than Will McCann, and the more he smirked at me, the tighter my fists closed.

Good on Ivan for saying "Yeah, no, I'm staying home."

Because now McCann sat at my small dining table with his little iPad and Apple Pencil like that was a good idea. But then, he had a badge, and I didn't, so maybe he was onto something.

He frowned at his note-taking setup. "So what you're saying is . . . ?"

Or maybe he wasn't onto anything, just as I'd suspected.

"Cookies ampersand shots at-symbol three four exclamation point," I said.

He tapped his iPad again, and his scowl deepened.

"Maybe you should just use a pad and pen," I suggested.

He kept tapping, though. "I didn't bring a pad and pen."

I stepped over to the everything drawer and grabbed both a pen and pad. I slid them to the detective without comment.

McCann eyed the old-fashioned tools, looked at his iWatch—time was a-wasting, and he'd spent five minutes just trying to log on to my Wi-Fi. "Fine, but you should . . ."

I cocked an eyebrow. "Should what?"

He flicked his hand, now irritated by my patience. And he didn't know if he could say what I should do. *Respect me because I have authority here* sounded like it would come from a man dressed up as his granddad.

"Why are you here?" I asked, irritated now. "I didn't call it in."

"I'm talking to everyone who lives in the area," Will McCann said. "And you—"

"I know, I know." I rubbed the bridge of my nose.

"Let's keep going," he decided, scribbling on the pad. "You left here and took a gun."

"Certainly."

No, I didn't know the victim. No, I'd never seen him before today. "You've asked these questions three times now," I said, "and my answers won't change. Are you all gonna—"

Will McCann held up his hand and cocked his chin. "Someone was found dead, ma'am, and it may seem pointless to you, but my questions—"

"I didn't say they were pointless—"

"But you're on the other side of the tape now," he said, daring to flick his direct gaze at me before sending his eyes back to the borrowed pad. "And you'll swear in court, under oath, that you didn't touch the body."

"I did not touch the body. The deputy at the scene can also testify to that."

"And . . ." He scribbled some more. "You're in possession of your gun? The gun found beneath John Doe won't come back registered to you?"

My brain chimed like a tuning fork, but I kept my expression muted. "I am in possession of my gun."

I didn't know that a gun had been found beneath John Doe—and McCann wasn't supposed to share that, the big dummy. Before he could accidentally leak any other details about the crime scene, Brady knocked on the front screen door like a dad picking up his kid from a Boy Scouts merit-badge check-in.

"We're just finishing up," McCann said, flipping past the two pages of his notes.

I placed my chin on my fist, waiting for any more inane questions.

McCann nodded and nodded, then tapped the table. "Yep. Got everything."

My mother shuffled from her bedroom to the kitchen.

I sat up, yanked out of my arrogance—I'd forgotten that she was here.

She poured herself a glass of orange juice, not acknowledging the two visitors.

McCann gathered his nonfunctioning iPad and digital pencil and stood from the table. He started to rip the pages he'd used from the notepad, but I placed my hand on the pad, and said, "Keep it."

Brady gave the smallest head shake. "Thanks for your help, Alyson."

McCann sauntered to the door and to his partner-dad. He said "We'll be in touch" before stepping onto the porch.

"Sure," I said, rolling my eyes.

Brady looked back at me and mouthed "Thanks" before winking.

My knees wobbled just as they had while pedaling that damned booze bike.

The taps of texting pulled me out of my lust cloud and back into the cottage.

Mom, with the volume of her phone set on a hundred, sat on the couch, phone to her face, one finger slowly doing the work of a thousand. *Tap . . . tap-tap . . . tap . . .*

"You sending a message using Morse code?" I asked, wanting to finish my pork chops, potatoes, and peas—but not on my sour stomach and being this exhausted. Instead of warming up food, I grabbed a mug and the box of Sleepytime tea from the kitchen cabinet.

Mom grinned, but not because of my question. Her face shone, and her eyes looked bright and clear.

I poured hot water over the tea bag, and as it steeped, I watched my mother being some man's girlfriend. Eventually, she sensed me watching and tore her focus from the phone. "I was telling Quincy about all the excitement around here tonight," she said.

I said "Hmm," then reached for the honey bear in the cabinet.

"He said we should be sure to lock up tonight."

I smirked as I squeezed honey into my cup. "Good idea."

"I told him that you have a gun."

I held up two fingers. "Plural."

She flicked her hand, dismissing my comment. "He doesn't need to know all that."

I cocked an eyebrow. "You sure? You've shared everything else."

"I told him that they found a gun—"

"Can you not?" I snapped, nearly dropping my mug.

She frowned. "What? It's not like that was a secret."

"McCann wasn't supposed to even tell me that, Mom." I sat down the mug, fearful that I'd throw it at a wall in frustration. "This is an active investigation, and MCSO will probably need my help, and I can't have you telling Mr. Quincy everything that's happening here—"

"He lives down in Ojai—"

"I don't care," I said.

"Then you shouldn't talk about this shit with me around, then."

"Or maybe you shouldn't rush to tell everything you hear because you're trying to be interesting," I shot back.

"You don't think I'm interesting?" Her eyes glinted with hurt and anger.

"I'm saying that this ain't an episode of *Law & Order*. There's real danger here. For you. For me. Even for Mr. Quincy." I exhaled and closed my eyes. "Please, Mom. Use discretion. You're worthy of love even if all you tell him about are the deer family that lives around here and the cupcakes you baked for the Red Hats."

Mom curled her lip and returned to texting. *Tap-tap . . . tap-tap-tap . . . tap.* She muttered "Like I'm some child" before stomping to her bedroom and slamming the door.

I was living with sixteen-year-old me all over again.

7.

Last Saturday Morning
3:30 a.m.

The air in the cottage felt heavy—trying to breathe in Haven hadn't been easy, and my already-ragged breathing due to the shenanigans earlier in the day now turned into sips of breath. My head swam, even though plenty of oxygen swirled around the living room.

Alabama, Alaska, Arkansas, California . . .

As much as I wanted to rebuke this grounding technique recommended by my former therapist, I had to admit: Dr. Tess Molina knew her shit.

Colorado, Connecticut, Delaware . . .

Because little by little, that death grip around my throat eased, and my thinking cleared, and I achieved thinking an ordered thought . . .

Don't wake Mom.

Too much was already happening at three thirty in the morning. I didn't need Val Rush trying to run the show and asking Honor why she would ever follow nonsense over the cliff. "Ain't you got sense? If they told you to drink Pine-Sol, would you do that too?"

Honor's phone vibrated again in my hand. A text from "BOO-FRIEND."

Ur not smarter then me

I accepted *Ur* for *your*, but *then*? No, Boo.

Above that taunt, I spotted an earlier text from "BIG SIS."

OMG WHERE R U??

I'LL COME GET U!!

My own phone buzzed with a message from BKWON.

Got your VM

About an hour away

See you soon

I exhaled—Brady would know what to do about Honor. This was his world up here. Didn't matter all that had shaken out between us over Xander's case. Honor Butler needed help.

And now the seventeen-year-old girl crept out of the bathroom, wearing a pair of my boxer shorts and a Beyoncé concert T-shirt. Her dirty clothes were balled up and clutched to her chest. Honor had scrubbed the grime off her skin, but bruises and cuts still spilled across the exposed spaces like melted licorice whips.

I winced. "Need something for pain?"

She nodded.

I grabbed a tub of Advil from the kitchen counter and gave the girl two caplets and another bottled water. "Who hurt you?"

Honor glugged water to chase the pills. "Liam. He's into . . ." Her cheeks reddened. "That violent stuff." She sat back on the living room couch and gripped the crocheted blanket like it kept her tethered to this space. "Are we alone here?"

I shook my head. "My mother's in the other bedroom."

Honor grunted, tried to smile. "My friends and me used to break into this cottage all the time. I thought that was gonna be the stupidest thing I'd ever do." She chuckled as tears shone in her eyes. "I shoulda got in trouble back then. Maybe that's why this is happening to me now."

"No, no, no," I said, moving to the couch. "You've done nothing to deserve this."

"I'm never gonna be 'Honor' again," she said, her eyes glued to the coffee table. "It's not like Liam would say my name anyway—he'd call me his pretty prossie."

"Prossie?"

"Prostitute. He went to England with his dad a bunch of times and heard them say it over there. I was his pretty prossie. After that perfect first week together, he didn't call me 'Honor' or 'sweetie' or anything cutesy. I don't deserve 'Honor.'" She pressed her bruised cheekbones. "He would text me 'Ho,' and at first, I was, like, cool, like n-o-r was too much to add, but he meant it. 'Ho.'"

"You'll be 'Honor' again," I said, taking the girl's hand. "I promise you that."

I'd met trafficked people who'd been caught standing over the corpses of their abusers or "dates." Working with the district attorney, I'd help return agency to that exploited victim, reclaim their name, take their breath back. Helping them to love themselves again—or for the first time—had been the most difficult task, and a few never achieved the strength to swim against the tide.

"How did you get here?" I asked now.

Honor said, "Walked."

"From?"

"Sableport."

My eyes bugged. "To here?"

She nodded.

Ten miles.

A fifteen-minute drive without traffic. How long did it take to walk?

"Ten hours," Honor said, reading my mind. "Sometimes I'd walk beside Highway 1, but then I'd feel like Liam could see me, and so I'd walk through the forest." She sniffled and rubbed her nose. "I escaped yesterday morning. He had to go to his baby cousin's baptism." She pushed out a breath and whispered, "It's been a long day."

Gurl. This had also been the longest day of my *life*. After leaving the jail, I thought I'd be able to sleep in, watch an episode of *The Golden Girls*, and take a shower.

"You should sleep," I said, standing from the couch. "My friend will be here in a few hours. You can take my bed."

Honor's gaze flitted toward the hallway that led to the bedrooms. "What about you?"

I flicked my hand. "Don't worry about me. The couch and I are old friends." That way, I could also watch the door and the forest.

Honor followed me like a shadow and disappeared into the bedroom and slipped beneath the comforter. The young woman whispered "Good night" and started snoring before I even reached the door.

Pretty prossie. Liam deserved an ass kicking for that alone.

I held my breath as I eased open Mom's bedroom door.

Her form rising and falling with each breath. She was asleep.

Back in the pantry, I opened the dryer and grabbed clean track pants, a hoodie, and washcloth. I took a quick sink bath in the kitchen—didn't want to wake Mom or Honor with noise from creaky pipes. Then I made a turkey sandwich with extra mayo and returned to sit on the couch with that and the bag of Cheetos. I ate and stared at the dark television until the first light of dawn pierced the redwood forest.

At ten minutes after five in the morning, car wheels crunched against the gravel.

I peeked past the living room curtains to see a blacked-out Yukon pulling into my empty parking space.

Brady Kwon.

My pulse thrummed. *Let this go right. Please. One thing.*

Private citizen Alyson thought Brady Kwon was a hero. Former homicide detective Alyson thought he was a pain in the ass. Right now, I needed both to help Honor Butler.

Brady Kwon knocked on the door, cop-style, all knuckles.

As soon as I opened the door, he grimaced. "Sutton really fucked you up."

I shushed him. "People are still asleep, believe it or not." I tapped my bruised cheek—I'd forgotten about my own injuries. The tussle on the coast with London Sutton had done some harm. But that was then, this was now, and now, I said to Brady, "I'm not the one you're helping."

I opened the door wider, inviting him in.

He glided past me, leaving a wake of woody aftershave. He had his Black mother's full lips and his Korean father's sharp, freckled cheekbones. He was six feet tall and casket sharp in his black hoodie, black jeans, and black boots.

"Coffee?" I asked, already pouring him a mug.

He grunted his thanks and took the cup. He drank his coffee like he was drinking water.

I refilled his mug without comment.

This time, he sipped and sighed. "So. Celebrated LAPD homicide detective Sonny Rush calls a bumpkin investigator for help in the wee hours of the morning."

"I know, right? What the fuck?" I took a deep breath and said, "Her name is Honor, and she's in trouble. Don't know how much, but sex and rich men and underage girls? Never good."

I told him all that Honor had told me, adding information about Honor's mother, Keely, as well as the connection between Honor and Mackenzie Sutton, who had introduced the teen to Liam.

That made Brady lift his eyebrows. "Does she know that Mackenzie's dead?"

I shook my head and pointed to the canvas shopping bag on the floor. "I have a feeling that some answers live in there and—" I plucked Honor's phone from my front hoodie pocket. "—and in here."

He pointed to the phone. "I can't do anything about that. Honestly, I can't do anything about any of this. You haven't proven anything to me yet. Is it worrisome? Of course, but—"

"I know," I said. "Let me poke around and learn more. But Ivan doesn't have a lot of resources."

"I'll do as much as I can."

"Off book?"

"At this point, yes." He nodded at Honor's bag. "You look in there yet?"

"No."

Brady grabbed the bag and dumped its contents onto the coffee table.

Phone cord, lip gloss, tampons, a dead phone, a dead digital camera, instant camera photos, pieces of mail, a gas station map of Mendocino County, wrapping papers, matchbooks, speeding ticket, FasTrak sensor, unopened pack of Bubble Yum, and a paring knife.

"The hell?" he said, chuckling.

"There's order here," I said.

"Yeah, but . . ." He scratched his neck. "If this is sex trafficking . . . These are bad men—you know this. Where's the kid?"

I gestured toward the bedrooms. "Asleep. She's a mess, blaming herself for everything, of course."

"She for real?"

"I detected no lies."

"I'll drive her home and keep up after her. Make sure people know that she's not alone, that she's being protected. Then, when you find out enough evidence . . ."

I said "Yeah" and rubbed my tired eyes.

Longest day ever.

I hated to do it, but I finally nudged Honor out of a peaceful slumber—the girl's first, probably, in months. After the young woman pulled on a pair of my leggings and a hoodie, she tiptoed out to the living room. Honor looked a little less haunted than she had four hours ago, but her eyes were still wary. She saw Brady Kwon standing at the window. She tilted her head and squinted at him.

Before speaking, I launched the Scriptor app on my phone for a test run. Then: "Honor, this is my friend, Brady. He's a police officer, but still a good guy."

Brady rolled his eyes and said, "Ha ha."

I smirked, and said to Honor, "He's gonna help us out."

Brady's chin dipped to his chest to meet Honor's gaze. "If this is gonna work out, you gotta do what I ask, okay?"

Honor nodded.

"First thing," I said, "your phone. You gave me permission. Can you grant Brady the same privilege?"

She whispered, "Yes."

I gave Brady the phone, and he immediately turned it on. He swiped, tapped, and sighed. "Yep, you're being tracked."

Honor's eyes bugged. "Find My?"

"That and . . ." He held up the girl's phone and pointed to an app: mSpy.

"It's marketed as a tool for parents," he explained, "and it captures who you've messaged, who you've called, your last locations—including Sonny's."

Honor covered her mouth and peered at me. "I'm so sorry."

"I'm uninstalling it," Brady said. "Whoever put this on your phone will know that it's been taken off."

As Brady Kwon searched her phone, I made Honor buttered toast and coffee. We sat at the small kitchen table as morning light spilled across the wood.

"Nicknames," Brady said, a notepad alongside his cup of coffee. "Who is 'BIG SIS'?"

"Mackenzie," Honor said.

He paused as he wrote. "'BOO-FRIEND'?"

"Liam."

"HAG" was Keely. "CAP" was Caitlin.

"And 'BIG BABY'?" he asked.

Honor swallowed, and her nostrils flared. "My driver." She said nothing else, but in that space, it was obvious that BIG BABY scared her.

That didn't worry me as much as someone texting from Mackenzie's number. *Dead* Mackenzie's number.

Honor's hands curled around the coffee mug. "Please don't tell my mom that I came here first. She'll flip out." She looked down, her hair falling into her face. "It's her fault that I'm fucked up like this."

No argument from me. But did Honor mean "She fucked me up from childhood" or "She ignored the signs of my distress"?

Honor's shoulders sagged with relief. "And you can keep my bag. I took a bunch of evidence."

"We should get going," Brady said.

Honor crammed the rest of her toast into her mouth and hurried to the bathroom.

I wanted to be relieved that Honor had come here, that she was now safe. But as I stared at that canvas shopping bag . . .

What the hell am I supposed to do with a pack of Bubble Yum?

"So," I said to Brady. "Thoughts?"

He held up Honor's phone before tossing it to me. "It's possible that her mother put that tracker on her phone."

Which meant that Keely knew Honor had come here—and that I hadn't called her with the good news that Honor had returned to Haven.

"But that also implicates Keely," I pointed out. "Your kid isn't truly missing if you know exactly where they are."

Brady Kwon shrugged.

I pushed out a breath. "If I'd looked for her sooner, Honor wouldn't have been—"

"You've lived in Haven for all of, what, three weeks?" Brady Kwon asked, wandering over to the front door. "This isn't about you not doing your job, Sonny. There's enough shit in your backyard to shovel. Leave this 'I shoulda' bullshit to Ivan."

I folded my arms and joined him at the door.

"You're in danger," Brady said.

"Every Saturday."

"I guess."

"You got her?" I asked.

"You trust me now?"

I shrugged. "Maybe, but ask me if I like you."

"Rather have your trust than your love," he said and winked. Then he looked past me. "Ready?"

Honor said, "Yes."

I opened the front door. The forest's cold air chased out the cottage's warm air. Fog hugged the trees, and somewhere in those woods, birds chirped and squawked their morning songs.

8.

I was too amped up to sleep, even though I wanted to, even though chamomile and ashwagandha dribbled through my bloodstream. I retreated to my dimly lit bedroom and lifted my mattress. I pulled out the thin folder that now held Honor's crumpled papers, an amuse-bouche to the documents I had yet to acquire. First, though, I kicked off my Jordans, stripped out of my changed clothes—I smelled like the outside and fried food—and showered. Clean again, I grabbed my laptop and Honor's canvas shopping bag from the corner. I powered up the girl's phone, using my own charger.

The walls creaked around me as fog continued to roll over the cottage.

First things first: sorting and printing text messages. Photos. Notes in the Notes app. Emails. Snapchats and DMs and digital cash transactions. I didn't read any of it, not yet, and simply swiped, screenshotted, and hit print. My bedroom filled with the *zzt-zzt-shfff* of the printer on my desk, the most noise I'd made so far between these four walls.

Honor Butler had been missing since April, and the first texts to Mackenzie Sutton predicted just how bad the following months would be.

Honor: KB won't be at the meet

Mackenzie: U don't even run anymore lol

She doesn't care what I do

She's busy chasing dick 2

Hmmm sounds familiar

I want ALLLLLLL THE D!!

I will get you ALLLL THE D!!

That's what Big Sisters R4!!

"KB." Must stand for "Keely Butler."

Why, at seventeen years old, was Honor talking about *any* of this? She should've been fretting about College Decision Day and if Keely had correctly filled out the FAFSA. She should've been worried about final grades and stubborn zits instead of smoking out and popping E with losers and predators.

Mackenzie: Do u need money or not??!

Fine but I'll tell Liam

THIS IS ALL ON YOU!!!

Honor: Whatever

I can't control his reaction

Fine

Don't want 2 do this anymore

I CANNOT BELIEVE U!!!

U CAN'T LEAVE!!

But Honor *did* leave—and she came *here* because someone told her to find me. Who? She wouldn't say because snitches get stitches, and as the saying goes, "A closed mouth catches no flies." Or fists. Or bullets.

Pictures, there were so many pictures, and each made my stomach churn with rage.

Topless Honor sailing on a boat and sitting on the lap of a man old enough to be her grandfather.

Honor with a Blue Sky meth tablet on her tongue.

Honor passed out as three men held her like a prized yellowfin tuna.

I searched through the April pictures and stopped once I found a shot with Honor, Mackenzie, and a brassy-auburn-haired Lindsay Lohan lookalike. Was the redhead Caitlin? Each girl wore a bikini. The redhead appeared ten more times until June, and then she disappeared from the selfies and party shots.

A note taken on July 2 listed Honor meeting Orville K at the Deluxe Inn in Oakland, then at Mustang Motor Inn outside of Solvang, and finally at Starlite Motel in Richmond. Nothing good ever happened at hotels named Mustang or Starlite or Deluxe.

Digital cash transactions included $400 from Orville Klein for "party supplies," $175 from Big Poppa D for "mini," and $600 from the Mayor for "Grand Slam."

Yet Honor's mother, Keely, wanted to be Haven's next mayor? Keely wasn't a safe harbor for her daughter, and that's why Honor must've come to *me*, a stranger, for help.

Anyway, it was obvious that Honor hadn't just been missing—she'd been trafficked. Would one former LAPD homicide detective turned private investigator and her hyperlinked Excel spreadsheet be enough to launch a proper investigation? Especially with guys named the Mayor and Big Poppa D hiding in the shadows?

Let the sheriff's department deal with it. That's what my cop voice told me. The Mendocino County Sheriff's Department had the people power, the jurisdiction, the databases, and the budget. Would Honor find justice, though? Would her case fall into the cracks? Would all these names and locations and transactions simply become statistics? What would make the cops and courts pay attention, especially knowing that snitches got stitches, knowing that people weren't bulletproof?

I needed a big name. A powerful man whose name would make news organizations pay attention. Like the true identities of the Mayor and Big Poppa D, Orville Klein, the grandpa on the boat—I found his picture again. Gray-haired, tanned white guy with veneers . . . I saved the shot for an image search.

I shoved all my documents back into the folder and slid it back beneath the mattress. Honor and Araceli both wanted me to help them—and I wanted to help so that they could both live happier lives.

And to be honest: Even if I solved a case, problems sometimes persisted. No such thing as happily ever after. A bullet had been successfully removed from my shoulder, but that shoulder still ached on damp days. Successfully finding Emiliano Rivas—I knew he was that John Doe in the forest—would expose any secrets Araceli feared being exposed. Punishing those who hurt her meant Honor would learn that some of her closest friends and family would prefer to see her die if that meant that they could live.

9.

My mind was broken—I'd gone more than twenty-four hours without meaningful rest. Digging into the contents of either Honor's phone or that shopping bag would have to wait until I restarted, reset, and returned from a few hours of sleep.

After setting the alarm on my phone for six o'clock, I fell into bed with scratchy eyes, scratchy skin, sore back. Just like the good ol' days of bulletproof vests, murder books, and . . .

. . .

. . .

My eyes popped open to a light-filled room.

Somehow, time passed—that's what the chiming on my phone was telling me.

I groaned and tapped Stop instead of Snooze. I'd sweat through my T-shirt—that had been some deep sleep.

Mom, wearing her matching purple and green kimono and headscarf, stood in the middle of the kitchen, her eyes narrowed.

"You good?" I asked, grabbing a clean bath towel from the washing machine.

"Um-hmm. It's just . . ." Her eyes skipped from the clean mugs in the drying tray. *Something's off*—that's what her expression said. Someone new had been in her kitchen, but she wasn't completely confident in saying that. But she didn't want to look as though she was having memory problems. Her eyes landed on me. "You look like shit."

I said "Ha" and shuffled to the bathroom.

"How was the wine thing?" she asked, following behind me. "I never asked."

"Fine. I'll probably pass the next time."

"You need to have some fun for a change," Mom said, leaning against the bathroom door. "What's the point of you helping people live if you don't live yourself?"

"You're so wise," I said, turning the shower knob to HOT.

"Be young and beautiful, and drink and flirt and enjoy the light and the laughter—"

"With all your sayings, I should hang you on the wall."

Mom harrumphed and said, "No one gives a shit or a fuck or a rat's ass if you work your tail off, Alyson."

I pointed at her. "There she is!"

"The world keeps turning," Mom said, "so move your ass and drink some wine."

I smiled at her and crossed my arms. "And what are you and your delightful candor doing today?"

Her brown face shone with rest and glee. Straight eyeliner and lip liner. A hint of blush and rust-colored eyeshadow. Hair slicked back into a neat ponytail. Yes, Valerie Rush had a clear mind this morning.

"Retirement cupcakes," she said, heading back to the living room. "Six hundred hand-frosted cupcakes."

In all the Monday mornings I'd lived through in Haven so far, this Monday morning was one of the best. Simply because Dallas dropped off my Bronco as the sun blinked through the trees. Fog? What fog? And for a moment, I even forgot that Brady and India were working a crime scene a half mile away from my front porch. Sure, my arms were itchy from all of last night's mosquito bites, and yeah, my heart hurt as I handed the mechanic my debit card to pay what the insurance company hadn't, but the bite cream was working, and the 1970 Bronco's new windshield sparkled, and her slate-blue paint sparkled, and the repaired driver's side taillight and two new tires made me grin so hard that I almost cried.

Dallas had saved her, and he'd washed her, and as I climbed behind the shiny wood steering wheel, funky fresh in denim cargo pants and clean Air Jordans, I took in a deep breath. She smelled of baby powder and dreams.

Guilt tugged at my conscience, though—as Mom showered this morning, I'd placed mSpy on her phone. Just as an experiment. Too much was happening in Haven, and I needed to pay attention to my job instead of worrying if she chose to wore sneakers that didn't have the AirTags. Just when I'd changed my mind and wanted to take off the location app, Mom had left the bathroom and grabbed her phone from the dining room table.

And now she rode shotgun, misty eyed in her Sweetlife sweatshirt. She patted the dashboard—she'd been with Dad when they'd visited Downy Ford to buy this truck so many years ago. She took a picture of the truck's interior and texted it to Mr. Quincy.

"Don't make me take that phone away," I said, backing out of the driveway. "You can't be burning pastries today."

"You worry about all the dead bodies piling up around you," she said, "and let me worry about my business." But she slipped the phone into her purse and resisted pulling it out, even though her phone went *bing-bong*, the ringtone now connected to her special friend.

This morning, I couldn't even see the coastline as I drove us into town. The fog had muted the bright colors of the storefronts. If the mist hadn't been hiding a murderer, I would've appreciated the quiet after a night lousy with police radios and tires crunching against twigs.

I pulled in front of Sweetlife and accepted Mom's peck on the cheek. "Love you."

She said "Love you" and was off, ready to charm this town with sweet treats.

Me? I was off, ready to expose the rot of Haven, starting with the bigamist who'd hired us to follow the bigamist she loved. But before I did that . . . more lidocaine cream for my arms.

The cleaning lady had come overnight, and my office smelled like lemons and lavender. Ivan hadn't made it in yet, and after settling down with a K-Cup of crappy coffee, I slathered more Gold Bond itch cream on my arms, then opened my laptop and logged on to PeopleFinder. I tapped "QUINCY JOHNS" into the search bar.

Five names popped up. I selected the sixty-five-year-old resident of Ojai, California, the one with the 850 credit score and Social Security number ending in 6-8-9-3.

So far, so good.

Quincy Johns was still an attractive man with his silver mustache-goatee combo and wavy silver hair. He could've been a dashing spokesperson for Newport menthols or male testosterone. He wore glasses to drive and was an organ donor. He'd attended Jordan High School in Watts, California, and graduated the same year as my mother. Instead of drilling further into education, I skipped to the part I cared about most:

CRIMINAL HISTORY.
No cases listed.

My phone buzzed with a text message from Ivan.

Araceli Rivas came up with the money

Case is yours

Proceed

Wow, I texted back.

I'm impressed

Will start this morning

It may be for nothing though

I think last night's John Doe was him

Ivan texted back:

Oh well

Let's see if she'll want anything else then

Oh, Monday morning, I could kiss you. And good for Araceli Rivas!

I didn't like *not* helping her, but I liked having money too. Now, though, she'd receive a partial refund if John Doe was her husband. Until then . . .

I grabbed from the corner of my desk the thin folder that held the original intake form. I stared at that picture of the missing man.

This guy in my file didn't look like the diminished John Doe sitting against the redwood. Emiliano had nearly fifty pounds on John Doe, first of all, and Araceli didn't list a crucifix tattoo on the dead man's chest. I scanned the information she'd shared and that I'd jotted down.

LOCATION LAST SEEN: 7-Eleven on 32250 78th Street

Time for a field trip to this *other* side of Haven.

Rows of lush green vines stretched across the hills that separated oceanside Haven from East Haven—and also the home of Lumière, Cooper's next big project.

Since the fog couldn't push its way over the hills, the sun shone down on this part of the world. That heat penetrated the Bronco's windshield and warmed my skin, and I wanted to bathe in this light.

This was the side of Haven that I hadn't visited. How many people lived among these swells of land, these vine-covered hillsides? That would change, alas, with the opening of the spa. More traffic, more people, more crime . . .

I'd dreamed with Cooper about this spa—and not just a day spa but an oasis with mineral baths and natural light and farm-to-table menus, and I'd dreamed of being the chief of security, and in the evenings, Cooper would rub my feet and pour me the first glass of red from our SunCoop label, and shit, I'd actually believed all of it.

Lumière's wood-framed edifice already gave off luxury and relaxation among California's best grapes. Even though the air smelled of rich, turned soil, sawdust, and hot metal, I wanted to grab a soft blanket and take a nap. I could already taste the Cabs and Sauvignon Blancs as I stood at the hurricane fence. The persistent beeping of trucks backing up and the vicious whirs of power saws interrupted my fantasies, though. The boards posted around the property showed architect renderings of the forty-six-acre resort and hotel that would offer spa treatments, yoga, Michelin-starred cuisine, and wine.

Would that change as a result of Cooper's recent personal tragedies? Or would the world keep moving, stepping over its dead and depressed because it had to?

Did any of the workers wearing hard hats care what was going on with Lumière's developer? I hated to think it, but I'm sure that as long as their checks cleared, no one gave a fuck that Cooper had lost so much in the last week. They now pounded hammers and lifted beams and pointed this way and that.

But I hadn't come to talk to these workers with the clipboards and California-issued contractor licenses. At least, not today. No, I wanted to talk to the men on the fringes, the ones who didn't have licenses or even valid Social Security numbers. Right now, the day laborers crouched in the shadows, waiting for a cue from the foreman to grab a saw or a toolbelt to do just enough to keep them coming back for more work.

I pulled out my picture of Emiliano Rivas from the file, tapped Scriptor on my phone, and headed toward the group waiting in the shadows.

The men leered at me as men do—until someone whispered, "La migra."

Shit. Was it my upright posture? My clean Air Jordans? How many Black women have they met in California who fucked with ICE? If we'd been in Florida, closer to the Caribbean, *maybe*, but here in California, why the hell would I hook up with la migra?

An older man with scarred hands and a weathered face was peeling an orange. He flicked his eyes at me. He froze as I smiled at him, realizing his mistake.

I stood before him, and said, "Hola, buenos días. Me llamo Sonny Rush and I'm . . . estoy buscando Emiliano Rivas."

The old man's gaze flicked back at my Bronco. "No hablo con ICE."

I looked back at my *so not a government car.* "I'm not ICE. I'm looking for a missing—"

Too late. The group was dispersing, melting like foam into the edges of the parking lot.

Frustration burned like acid in my throat as the mosquito bites beneath my shirtsleeves reactivated. If I wanted to know more about Emiliano Rivas, I needed to talk to these folks, and I needed them to trust me. Then again, was I the right person for this job? I stood out already in the land of private investigators—a Black woman was like a lemon in a bank of snow. And since I didn't have a badge, these guys sure as *shit* didn't have to say *jack* to me.

Yeah, no matter how much I cared, how much I wanted to make a difference, my gut told me that I was the wrong person for this job. But who else was there? I climbed back into my not-government-issued Ford, scratched my arms, and let out a few breaths through clenched teeth.

Genesis, Exodus, Leviticus, Numbers . . .

Araceli Rivas had scraped the funds together for me to find her husband. But one hour in, I'd already thrown up my hands.

I blame the mosquitoes.

The foreman's trailer smelled like sawdust and sweat. The plastic nameplate on the desk said Dave Kruger, and his office was a cramped space, the kind of room that shrank the longer you sat there. Outside, the sunlight of inland Haven was warm and bright, a stark contrast to the fog I'd driven through along the coast.

In Dave Kruger's office, a different kind of fog hung around—people fog, made of avoidance and half-truths. He hadn't said a word to me yet, but the barrel-chested man with the perpetual scowl carved into his face looked like he obfuscated a *lot*. His calloused hands gripped a coffee cup, and his gray hair hid beneath a battered Giants cap. His work boots could kick a dragon and win, they were so strong looking and fire born.

I turned on the transcription app, then told him who I was and smiled as I spoke. *Be nice, Dave. Let's be friends, Dave.*

"I've already told the cops everything I know." His voice sounded rough, like he gargled gravel every morning before slipping on his daily scowl. "Emiliano was just another guy on the crew. He was a hard worker. Kept to himself, mostly."

"I know we don't like talking about these things," I said, my tone light but pointed, "but you knew he was undocumented. Did it not matter? And to be honest? I'm a PI, not a cop. I'm not here to arrest anybody. I'm just working for this guy's wife."

Dave rubbed his hand along his scalp. "Look. I'm on schedule. I don't care if the papers these guys show me are real or less real. If he can read a schematic and not be an asshole, I'll throw him a parade and a couple of months of work. Like an internship."

I held up my hand and nodded. "Understood—but if they don't show up one day . . . ?"

He shrugged. "What am I gonna do? Send out a search party? You know this, Miss Rush. These guys come and go." He leaned back, his chair creaking under his weight. "We don't ask questions. Emiliano showed up, did his job, and got paid cash. That's it."

"Who could've seen him last?" I asked. "Like . . . the day before he went missing?"

Dave scratched his chin, his eyes narrowing as he thought. "Probably one of the guys he carpooled with. Hector . . . or Francisco. Something like that. Those two were always speaking in Spanish and laughing. He'd know better than me."

"Hector" didn't sound anything *like* "Francisco."

"Do you have Francisco-Hector's number?" I asked.

"Nope. Sorry."

Snitches got stitches.

"But the guys usually grab a bite to eat at the roach coach on the other side of the site."

"Good to know," I said. "Anyone ever have a problem with Emiliano? Any arguments, grudges, bad blood?"

Dave shrugged, his jaw tight. Then: "I know he had a beef with one guy. Maybe he's Hector." Dave's face brightened. "Now, *that* guy is problematic. A hothead but good with a jackhammer. Now, *that* info I can give you. Yeah, Hector Something . . ." He rambled off an address on Twenty-Third Avenue, then said, "I've come close to kicking his ass off my site. If Emiliano ran into any static, that guy . . ."

He glanced at the door—he'd rather be anywhere else. "To be honest, Emiliano was an asshole in the way guys who build shit are assholes. He might've rubbed some people the wrong way but nothing that would've . . ." His gaze dropped to his coffee cup.

"Would've gotten him killed?" I finished for him.

"I didn't say that," he snapped. Then, softer: "Look, Miss Rush, I've got a crew to run. I didn't *disappear* Emiliano, and I don't know who did. He may be back in Mexico or Guatemala or wherever else the fuck these guys come from. If you want to waste your time digging, be my guest. But you won't find anything here."

Ten minutes later, I found that food truck, Angie's Tacos, but not Francisco or Hotheaded Hector, Jackhammer Enthusiast. I ordered a cup of coffee and sipped slowly, hoping that someone—*anyone*—would show up. No luck. The word had spread that la migra was hanging at Angie's Tacos. Alone, I sipped my hot beverage to the musical stylings of Celia Cruz, who sang about life being a carnival.

Then I returned to Dave Kruger's trailer.

He was gone too.

This was not the Haven advertised in the Chamber of Commerce brochure. According to Google Maps, though, this Subway sandwich store, the donut and nails shop, and the Metro by T-Mobile store had Haven addresses. More Forty-First Street and Browning Avenue than Seaview Way and Oyster Road. There were a few storefront immigration attorneys, a laundromat, and an Iglesia Remanente Fiel Central. Billboards—I hadn't seen any on the other side of the hill—advertised STD testing, an online traffic school, and . . . The corners were peeling on this last billboard, the red letters fading. No one had the funds to replace or repair it. The ad's simple line drawing stood out more than its dilapidation, the side profile of a god with a long wavy beard.

I knew this graphic.

Ivan and my father wore a tattoo with a similar drawing on their biceps. On this billboard, though, Plutus spoke a word bubble:

CALL NOW!
OBSIDIAN FINANCIAL SOLUTIONS

A quick search on my phone told me that Obsidian was one of those fast-cash, payday loan businesses, the kind that thrived in working-class communities. Back in the day, folks called establishments like these "loan sharks." The name may have changed, but the 30 percent interest rate had not.

Just like the bullshit served up by Lenderful.

Liberty Tires & Brakes, located at 8923 Main Street, had dirty plate glass windows, barely there carpet in the waiting room, and three hard-backed chairs for waiting customers. The newish television over the receptionist desk played a soccer match on mute. Today's soundtrack came from the hydraulic tools being used in the tire bay.

A young woman with a cheek stud and stiff, wet-looking hair sat behind that desk. She smelled like laundry sheets, and that scent rode on the breeze produced by her giant fake lashes.

"How are you today?" she asked me.

"Good," I said, smiling. "Is Araceli in?"

"She's on break. May I help you with something?"

I leaned against the counter. "Just wanted to say hi. I'm new in town, and Araceli and I met yesterday. I've already had to have two tires replaced since I moved to Haven, and she mentioned that she worked here."

The woman frowned. "Let me guess—you went to Dallas first?"

I nodded.

She wiggled her nose. "He's for them people over there. But if you want good prices and the same tires? We'll hook you up. Our little spot ain't pretty—"

I chuckled and gave a joking nod.

"But we're not making our customers pay for Wi-Fi and fancy coffee," she said.

A hood spot. In Haven. Wow. And yay.

"I didn't get your name?" I said.

"Jessica, hi. But if you're waiting for Celi, you're gonna be waiting awhile."

"Yeah?" I looked at the clock on my phone: a little past ten thirty.

"Family stuff—she's dealing with a lot right now."

A missing husband disrupted any fucks one would give about selling tires.

I nodded. "I'm gonna get some breakfast, then. I may pop over before driving back to . . ."

"The oceanside?" Jessica said, eyebrow high, sensing that I was about to call it "Haven." Because, unfortunately, I was.

"Yep," I said. "The oceanside."

"I'll let her know that . . ." She squinted at me.

"Alyson."

"That you were looking for her."

My phone vibrated: a text from Brady.

We need to talk

Where are you?

I texted back:

Liberty Tires

Let's meet in the lot of Polly's

Be there in an hour

Jessica was scribbling a note on a sticky that included my name. "Don't schedule your day around her, though. Eat, do your errands and all that, but we don't plan on her showing up to stuff."

I shrugged. "Hopefully, Emiliano turns up and she can get back to living."

The young woman blinked at me—*you know, then*. She sucked her teeth. "He can stay gone—but you ain't heard that from me."

Just as I was moseying to the door. "You don't like . . . ?"

She wiggled her nose again, then tapped at the old computer keyboard. "He's . . ." She shrugged. "My 'lita used to always say, 'No todos los que chiflan son arrieros.'" When she saw my eyebrows scrunch, she added, "Not all who whistle are mule drivers."

I nodded. "Don't trust appearances. So you think—"

She held up one hand and grabbed a bunch of invoices with the other. "And my grandpa would say, 'La lengua guarda el pescuezo.'"

I nodded. "Right. The tongue guards the throat, which means you're about to shut up now to stay out of trouble."

Jessia laughed. "You got that right."

A wind pushed through the room, and the glass door leading from the garage opened. A short man wearing grimy overalls stood there. The name patch on his chest said MATAIS, and he had the prettiest hazel eyes I'd ever seen on a mechanic.

"Car's ready," he told Jessica. To me: "Sorry, I forgot what you dropped off—"

"She's here to talk to Celi," Jessica said.

"Oh." His interest in me waned, and he backed out of the door and returned to the bay.

Jessica pointed to her invoices. "I gotta handle these, but I'll tell her that you dropped by."

I left Liberty Tires and walked back to the Bronco. Before I climbed behind the steering wheel, I peeked over my shoulder.

Matais was staring—but was he staring at me or the Bronco?

FaB always stole any light I shone. She got men to talk who were only interested in her braking system and engine build. Next time I visited, Matais would talk to me—men like Matais always did.

10.

More than custom-built, classic Broncos, everyone liked breakfast, even a woman who'd been wrongly accused of being la migra. American cops especially liked bacon and eggs and strong, hot coffee. When I wore a badge, I'd been no different. Greasy-spoon diners got me all that, cheap, along with a bucket of helpful information about the people I'd been investigating.

Back in LA, I'd grab meals at Romie's Diner—sometimes chicken maple sausage instead of bacon, breakfast fried rice, or a breakfast burrito if I felt adventurous. I'd go to the Serving Spoon in Inglewood on Tuesdays for their turkey wings or to Tal's on Florence Avenue for fried pork chops and grits, which had been my partner's favorite spot.

Polly's sat around the corner from Liberty Tires. It was the kind of place with paper menus covered in plastic but only after someone had left a jelly thumbprint and a splotch of ketchup on it. There were springy pleather booths with rips here and there and tabletops that smelled of Pine-Sol. All of this run-me-down, though, convinced me that I was moments away from an orgasmic moment with hash browns.

Men of every shade filled booths and counter stools as a Norteña song oompahed from the stereo and battled against the chatter of English and Spanish and sizzling breakfast food.

A waitress with a freckled Victorian bosom beneath a Polly's T-shirt and wearing knee sleeves pointed me to a corner half-booth.

Perfect.

All eyes followed me—some eyes that had already pecked at me back over at the construction site found me here again, the outsider in the group of outsiders. I knew what it meant to not be heard, to not have a voice, and to be treated like a second-class citizen. But at least I had a passport and spoke the language and didn't have to pray their prayer of protection. No, my prayer of protection had different words but were ultimately the same. *Let me and my loved ones move about this city, state, country, without being assaulted or killed by someone who thinks I shouldn't be here.*

The chatting died down some, and that tuba and accordion got louder.

I wanted to stand in the middle of Polly's and shout "I'm not a fucking ICE agent," but the waitress with the bad knees now stood at my table with a mug, a menu, and a pot of coffee. Her red plastic name tag said DIANE, but she looked more like a Carla with that rat's-nest black hair and mother's bosom. She looked to be about sixty-five, which meant that she was probably fifty—breathing diner fumes every day had aged her.

"Welcome, Officer," she said, her voice cautious as she poured hot brew into my cup.

I snorted. "I'm not a cop." *Not anymore.*

She made a slight perplexed frown. "Then why the hell are you here?"

"Sure as hell not to arrest anybody." I took a sip from my mug.

Hot, rich, strong. If coffee could marry me, I'd demand that ring *today*. And anyway, what was it about the coffee in these diners? Was it like the way the water in New York made bagels and pizza delicious? Was it the scorched filters? Or had we been bamboozled into thinking that Folgers wasn't good enough? Didn't know, but I was digging this rich brown brew steaming from this chipped mug discolored from years of use. If I smoked cigarettes, I'd want to be alive with pleasure sipping this cup of coffee as I read the *Los Angeles Times* as *Young and Restless* played on the RCA.

"Cop or not," Diane said, "you just made a whole bunch of people nervous."

"Not my intention." I tried to smile at her, but the coffee wanted all my attention. "I tried to talk with a few of those guys earlier. But they weren't having it."

"Because you're a stranger and possibly a troublemaker from the other side of the hill."

My smile died some. "I'm actually trying to make it right for someone who lives here."

She squinted at me—she saw it—but shrugged. "Good intentions—the road to hell and all that, right?" She chinned at the menu. "Need a moment?"

I said "Yes, please" because I needed more time: more time for her to spread the word that I wasn't la migra, a marshal, nor a sheriff's deputy.

The menu offered the same as greasy-spoon diners offered all across America. No avocado toast or chia seeds, ancient grains or acai bowls on this side of the hill.

Diane returned with the coffee pot, prepared to jot my order down on a mental pad filled with other orders. "So?"

Bacon, fried egg over hard, hash browns, wheat toast, God bless America. Then, I said, "I'm actually a private investigator, and I'm looking for a missing man."

"Oh yeah?" Diane's expression didn't change. "Men go missing around here all the time. Some of 'em disappear cuz they want to. Others disappear when they don't want to. Either way, it ain't my business. I've helped people like you before, those good-intentions people, and they were liars, and families were busted up, and people I cared about were taken away. So now I see nothing, and I know even less. Just safer that way."

She refilled my cup and tossed out "Food will be up in a minute" before turning on her heel and fading back into the dingy paint, the ripped-seat booths, and the Mexican polka music.

Instead of brooding, I swiped over to Instagram and found Araceli Rivas's carefully curated profile and posts.

Look at me looking at this perfect California sunset!

Look at Emiliano and me holding hands at the beach!

Look at Emiliano napping with his Dodgers cap over his eyes as we relax together in this hammock!

Family barbecues. Family weddings. Fourth of July manicure. New black Dodge Charger. Araceli's and Emiliano's happiness burst from my iPhone like sunshine.

I didn't have an active social media presence. People didn't need to know that a cop drove that Bronco. People didn't need to know that fabulous baker was my mother. Thieves, murderers, and bad cops didn't need to meet my friends or know what coffee or boutique or steakhouse or cocktail or beachside resort I enjoyed. Angry men were the worst—I didn't need them to know that long drives on straight roads alone helped me reset.

Back when she ran the bakeries, Mom's staff ran those social media accounts filled with bright lemony things and bright powdery white things—but they never posted pictures of me. Nor did they ever post pictures of Mom, disheveled, standing in the middle of her kitchen, lost in that cloud of confusion. Always shiny pics, aspirational shots, outright lies of life sometimes.

Yes, outright lies of life, I said it, standing on all ten toes too.

I'd investigated cases with dead women who wore their murderers' DNA beneath their new Easter Sunday manicures. Evildoers had driven or had pushed people off cliffs just like the ones in Araceli's feed. Posing in this light and with my hair behaving like it should, along with a caption that read "Haven is Heaven," would have folks back in Los Angeles thinking that my life here was absurdly perfect. Because behold the hair, behold that light. They'd have no clue that I'd broken up with Cooper, that his wife had tried to kill me, that a dead man had been dumped in the forest not far from my house, and that I now sat in a greasy-spoon diner in the working-class part of Haven. This pretty house had holes in the attic, and no one wanted to talk to the alleged *migra* with great hair . . . and good intentions.

Thank Plutus, Diane returned to me with my American breakfast. She set the plate down a little harder than she needed to, but then she cocked her head to look at the picture on my phone. "Oh, I've seen her."

"Yeah?" With great intent, I placed my napkin across my lap to not scare the waitress.

"Nice girl. Works at the tire place around the block. Comes in with friends. Tips."

"Araceli Rivas," I said. "I'm working for her." I tapped on a picture of Emiliano posed before the Charger. "This is her husband—he's the missing one."

Diane grunted. "Hmm. Never seen him before."

"He works over at the spa construction site."

She snorted. "So do ninety-eight percent of the people around you right now, but I've seen *them*." She tapped my phone. "This guy? I don't know this guy. They're not gonna help you find this guy."

"But you can," I said.

"Don't know you, sweetie," she said. "You're living the high life over on the other side—"

"I'm only trying to help Mrs. Rivas."

"Enjoy your breakfast." She ripped the check from the notepad and set it on the table.

So Diane had served Araceli and her friends but had never met Emiliano. How was that possible?

Did he not like diner food? Were his hours weird, and by the time he clocked out, Polly's was closed? Did he hide during those times he wasn't working?

Not one to surrender, I wrote my work number on the check—Diane would see it hidden beneath the twenty-dollar bill. Maybe she'd change her mind and call me.

Maybe.

This was nothing new.

How many cases had I worked with girlfriends and wives and baby-mommas who hadn't recognized the man who'd beat them or tried to kill them—even though the bad guy climbed in bed beside her every night? How many cases had I worked with folks who didn't recognize the shooter—but the shooter had been their homeboy? How many cases had I closed with honest people who'd experienced trauma after a bad thing had happened to them, and they just had an honest-to-goodness bad case of the blanks?

The Hillside Strangler case: Multiple witnesses had identified different people as the bad guy—they'd experienced trauma and some of those witnesses had been pressured by the cops to change their testimony. Perception—how our brain focused on what we considered important—was subjective. Memory didn't record perfectly. Memory decayed and wrapped itself in bias. Then there was physical distance and lighting, or someone focusing on the weapon instead of the person carrying it . . .

So was it possible—and truthful—that Diane didn't recognize Emiliano?

Certainly.

And it was also possible that the law of the land—*snitches get stitches*—kept her mouth shut. The threat of retaliation was real. And this law was one of the many I chose to believe in as I left Polly's to meet Brady in the parking lot.

Keep your head down and mind your own business.

Don't get involved, especially in a community of secret lives.

But if Diane thought I'd move on from her, though, she thought wrong—I'd been paid to mind everybody's business now, and that included a waitress at a diner serving delicious hash browns.

Judging by Liberty Tire Jessica's reaction—*he can stay gone, but you didn't hear that from me*—Emiliano may have been problematic. She, too, didn't want to say much. More secrets.

I climbed behind the steering wheel of my Bronco just as my phone buzzed.

Hi Miss Rush

Jessica said you were looking for me

Why did you go to my job??

Araceli's energy . . . I sensed fear and a little anger.
In the neighborhood, I texted back.

I didn't tell her that I was an investigator.

OK good

I took a sick day

Why are you talking to people?

I laughed, and said, "Child, nuh-uh."
You're not paying me thousands of dollars just to surf the web.

I do use searches on the computer

but talking to potential witnesses is best

And I want to make sure you get your money's worth

The houses across the street from the diner were far from posh and lacked curbside appeal. No lawns or gardens evoked specific architecture styles or movement—but the windows were large enough to let in light, the walls sturdy enough to block the chill. One house with brown roof tiles had kids' toys scattered around the front yard. An ancient Chevy Blazer had been parked in this driveway since Clinton's first presidential inauguration—the cobwebs across the truck's tires and back windows were more permanent than the grungy front door. Mail had been tossed on the stoop. Then: *tchek-tchek-tchek*. The sprinklers sprayed everything in its path—from the abandoned toys to the rear right tires of that dilapidated Blazer.

Through the windows, I saw an old woman seated in a living room armchair. Floral housecoat, hair bun, and leathery skin. She was aiming the remote control at a TV mounted to the wall until she settled on a Mexican soap opera. This world was hard enough for her, for my mother, for all of us who just needed to sometimes lose ourselves in the land of soap.

11.

As I waited for Brady, I listened to '90s on 9 on the truck's stereo. My phone buzzed, lighting up with the investigator's number.

I said, "Hey. Where are you?"

"Almost there," Brady said. "Construction trucks causing traffic jams. You find out anything yet?"

I turned down the SWV song. "Dedicating the rest of the day to finding stuff out. And what's up with you?"

"Honor's worried that you're gonna do something that hurts Big Sister."

Mackenzie Sutton.

I frowned. "She still doesn't know that Big Sister is dead?"

"Guess not. And I'm telling you this just so you know. Honor Butler is still a kid and still wants people to like her."

I clicked my teeth. "You're telling me this because . . . ?"

"Future knowledge." He paused, then said, "See you in five minutes."

So, he told me this—but what *wasn't* he telling me?

I pushed out a cleansing breath as En Vogue told me to hold on. I tried to relax, but their tight harmonies were making me feel tighter, like I was already driving back over that curvy road to the other side of Haven.

Brady parked his Yukon beside my Bronco, and a minute later, he slid into my passenger seat. He looked delicious this morning, all business in his blue MCSO polo and khakis. Since we'd already talked, he skipped the formalities and said, "We're still waiting to confirm one last thing, but the John Doe on Dr. Laster's table is Emiliano Rivas."

"Why haven't you or India confirmed?" I asked.

"He isn't in AFIS."

Automated Fingerprint Identification System, a database able to search a billion fingerprint records in the blink of an eye. But not a billion and one.

"But I'll send them out for a national search," Brady said. "If he's a Mexican national, though, they won't be in the fed's database either." He ran his hand over the Bronco's wood steering wheel. "Nice."

"Mm-hmm."

He needed to tell me something—and it wouldn't be good for me, not with him stalling like this.

I found Araceli's Instagram profile and tapped on the picture of Emiliano relaxing in a hammock. The way his eyes were hooded matched those hooded—and dead—eyes on the man on steel instead of mesh.

Brady barely looked at the photo before blurting, "Honor won't talk. If she won't share details or names, then how do we know what she's saying is true?"

My stomach tightened as I thought about the photos I'd found in her phone and remembered the payments from Orville Klein and the Mayor.

"She's problematic," he said, "and while I believe her . . ." He gazed in the distance.

"I'm working on proving it," I said, my mouth dry.

He jiggled his knees, nervous. "I hate that I'm relying on you for this."

"I can tell. I'm thinking about the future too."

Like Honor, I was also problematic.

"Back to Emiliano," I said, now. "Whose gun was that?"

"Did McCann mention the gun?" Brady asked, eyes closed.

"Yeah, he's an idiot."

"Someone left Rivas there," Brady admitted.

"He's been gone since May," I said, "but found dead in August. Where did they keep him?"

"Wherever that weird pattern is."

"Which weird pattern?"

"The weird pattern India found on his back."

"Oh, yeah." Playing it off since I didn't *know* about the weird pattern on John Doe's back.

"He'd been lying against whatever that was as long as he'd been the Adidas logo."

I said, "Yeah. You got a picture of it?"

Brady opened his file and selected a photo of Emiliano's back.

There were crisscrossed lines against the skin of his lower back.

I swiped back over to Araceli's Instagram page and found that hammock picture of Emiliano. Hmm. Could he have been wrapped in this hammock?

"When are you telling Araceli?" I asked.

Brady was staring at that picture, silent.

"If you don't, I will. That's her husband."

Not that I enjoyed death notifications. I'd been both hugged and attacked during visits to the next of kin. Sorrow to anger, tragedy to violence. From *How could this happen* to *What did y'all do to him?* Under the care of a doctor, my own father had passed, and I still wept, and I still growled at his care team. They'd done so much for him. They hadn't done enough for him.

Araceli, with all her aspirational signs and sweetness, there was no clue how she'd swing.

Brady let out a long breath. "I'll tell her."

"I'm going with you," I said, my tone leaving no room for argument. "She hired me to find him—I'll have questions. She will too. You? Probably not. I'll follow you over."

He remained seated, his thumb rubbing his lip.

"What, Brady?"

"Just . . ." He exhaled again and shook his head.

I held up my hands. "I won't fuck this up for you."

But it was too late for that—I already had.

Araceli and Emiliano Rivas lived in a modest bungalow on Eighteenth Street. The battered green Civic was parked in the driveway—she was still home.

I parked two houses down and killed the Bronco's engine.

Brady parked behind me.

Neither of us spoke as we walked up the pathway and stood on the front porch. A flowered wreath hung on the front door. Two rocking chairs with potted plants lit by fairy lights. Pumpkins—orange and white ones. A welcome mat that said:

Did You Bring Snacks?

There were aspirational signs here, too, including a fake weathered one:

Welcome To Our Porch
Sit Long, Talk Much, Laugh Often!

The door opened. Araceli stood there, bright eyed. Then she noticed Brady Kwon standing behind me. She said, "Oh no . . ." She wore a fuzzy blue housedress that looked as soft as ducklings. She'd been eating a grilled cheese sandwich and a bowl of tomato soup. *Real Housewives of Beverly Hills* was playing on the living room television. Her cell phone sat near her lunch plate.

This was an all-too-familiar scene for me. Swap out grilled cheese for a Big Mac or a plate of leftover spaghetti. *Real Housewives* for *Matlock, Love & Hip Hop*, or CNN.

Araceli Rivas wouldn't finish her lunch today nor would she find the antics of the Real Housewives to be funny for months. Nothing on television hit the same after foul, real-life shit.

My gaze stopped at a picture of Araceli and Emiliano on their wedding day. Her smile had been as radiant as that white dress she wore. Emiliano, stylish in his gray tux, had stood behind her. A happy man. A happy wife. A new life.

Brady sat on the couch beside Araceli. He handed her the picture of the man now in the morgue. "Is this Emiliano?"

Araceli's face crumpled as the image sank in. She let out a broken sob and buried her face in her hands. Her shoulders shook as she wept.

"I'm so sorry," I whispered, sliding the box of tissue across the coffee table.

Araceli leaned over to clutch her stomach like we'd punched her. We had.

I muted the television and let this woman's sobs be our soundtrack—she deserved that much. I glanced over to her project table and all the crafts stuff in bins and carts—she was making snowmen from book pages with hats made of acorns.

After she'd temporarily run out of tears, Araceli grabbed a tissue from the box and tried to chuckle. "I thought I was ready to hear the news." She looked at me with sad eyes. "Especially after I heard they'd found someone in the forest . . ." She tore at the damp tissue and whispered, "Was that him?"

I nodded and took her hand.

She dropped her head. "How?"

"We're still figuring that out," I said, my gaze flicking to Brady.

"Can you tell me . . . ?" Araceli swallowed. "Was it natural? Like . . . heart attack or . . . ? His only brother died last year. He had some undiagnosed . . ." Her hand fluttered around her chest. "Emiliano was scared that the same would happen to him."

"We don't believe it was a natural death," Brady said.

She said "Okay," but the way her chin quivered, she was moments from losing it again.

"Could you provide us with something of his?" Brady asked. "A toothbrush, for instance. For confirmation."

Araceli nodded and left the living room.

Brady stood and wandered to the craft table. Flipped through the book that would live again as ornamentation.

Araceli returned with a toothbrush. "He was supposed to be helping me make those snowmen."

Brady pulled a small evidence bag from his jacket pocket and placed the toothbrush inside the bag.

"That's how we met," Araceli said, gazing at the table. "At a crafting con. He was working at the convention center down in Fresno, and we saw each other . . . I didn't ask for his papers, if he was American or . . ." She shook her head. "Love knows no bounds. Love has no nationality. Love is heart, not . . ."

She wiped her face on the backs of her wrists. "Who would do this to him?" she asked, her voice trembling.

"That's what we're trying to figure out," Brady said. "Did Emiliano have any enemies? Anyone who might have wanted to hurt him? Or even . . . hurt *you*?"

Araceli shook her head slowly, then hesitated. "He had secrets. Things he wouldn't tell me. But I grew up knowing not to ask too many questions. It's just how things are, you know? Sometimes it's better if you don't ask. And what do you mean, someone wanting to hurt *me*?" She chuckled. "Maybe the lady who didn't like the pink felt baby chick I made for her. She said that I was 'pushing an agenda' by making a pink baby chick." She rolled her eyes. "So, no enemies. We were just regular people."

"What about ex-girlfriends?" I asked. "Or the parents and family of ex-girlfriends? Any disagreements with neighbors? Someone pissed that you didn't give them back the lawn mower they let you borrow? Someone angry that you cut back their tree without asking?"

Araceli said, "Nope. And ex-girlfriends: He didn't date anyone in the States."

"Did Emiliano own a gun?" I asked.

Her eyes widened. "No, never. We don't have guns in this house."

"Just ruling out road rage or . . ." I shrugged.

"Mind if we look around?" Brady asked. "Just to get a better understanding of things. We may see something that may seem irrelevant but could break open the case."

Araceli said, "Of course. Whatever you need."

I followed Brady for a moment but lingered in the kitchen. No missing knives. The bathroom—one less toothbrush in the holder. Lemon-printed hand towels. Moss wall art along the hallway. Butterfly suncatchers and driftwood candleholders. Dried-flower glass terrariums. Crystal-beaded this. Stained glass that.

In their bedroom, cute embroidered pillows. A big black-and-white portrait hung above the bed's headboard. In the closet, one side was hers, the other side . . . Shelves filled with rows of men's sneakers, some still in boxes. I took pictures of it all, from the hummingbird glass art to the seventeen pairs of sneakers.

We left the house for the backyard. I'd seen this space on Araceli's Instagram profile. There was the hammock. Large black butterflies with yellow diagonal and horizontal stripes fluttered near a tall, wood-framed butterfly habitat near the lemon trees. The garage door opened easily—but it was crammed with boxes and bikes and a Ping-Pong table. Four tall white poles were leaned against the side of the house.

"Soccer goal," Brady said.

No net, though.

"Emiliano was a coach," Araceli said from the back door. "He taught little ones who are barely taller than the ball."

Both Brady and I chuckled at that.

"You said he'd gone to get propane on the last day you saw him," I said as a butterfly glided around my head. "You know from which store?"

"No idea," she said.

We returned to the living room.

Araceli sat back on the couch with her hands clasped tightly in her lap. "What happens now?" Her eyes darted over to a candle burning on a small table. A picture of Emiliano sat behind it. Her face collapsed, and she tottered over to the candle and blew it out. She bowed her head, whispered a prayer, and made the sign of the cross.

That made me think about his calf tattoo. The Saint of Death.

Araceli looked at us over her shoulder. "I've kept a lit candle here since he left, and now that he's been found . . ." She bit her lower lip and stared down at the smoking candle. "If we hadn't met, if we hadn't fallen in love, maybe . . . maybe he'd still be alive."

"Another question," I said. "The tat on his calf."

She nodded. "Santa Muerte."

"Was he still an active believer?"

She squinted at me. "Are you asking me if he was a member of a death cult or if he was in a cartel?"

"Both possibilities are insults," I admitted, "but both possibilities could help explain his death."

She tilted her head. "You see any shrines to skeletons wearing wedding dresses around here? Any red, black, or white candles? Any cigarettes or little bottles of fucking tequila?"

"Why the tat, then?" Brady asked.

"Cuz it's a fucking cool image." She closed her eyes, took a deep breath to tamp down further bursts of anger. She exhaled through pursed lips and opened her eyes. "Sorry about that."

"The investigation is officially a homicide case now," Brady said, "and I'll be leading it, and we'll do everything we can to find out who did this."

"Maybe it's the same person," she said.

I frowned. "Same . . . person?"

"Who killed the other two guys," Araceli said. When neither Brady nor I spoke, she tilted her head and zeroed in on Brady. "Emiliano is the third man from the spa site who went missing. Since those other men were probably undocumented, too, y'all didn't look into it."

"On construction jobs like this," he said, "men are nomads. Going where the work is."

"And if ICE is involved . . ." I said, shaking my head.

"Less workers, no money," Brady said.

She turned back to me. "Emiliano's the only one who was found—and that's because of you."

I blushed. "But I didn't find him. And really, you hired me to look—"

"And my tax dollars hired *him*," she said, nodding at Brady. "And *he* didn't find him either. So what am I paying for?"

Neither Brady nor I answered.

"I just know that something janky is going on over there," Araceli said, picking up the memorial candle from the table and sniffing it. "Miss Rush, maybe you should look into it since nobody else will."

Brady said, "No one told us that people have gone missing from the construction site, but now that I'm aware . . . Now that your husband's been found . . ." He cleared his throat, then made a note in his pad.

"What do I do now?" Araceli said. "What about his . . . his body?"

"The medical examiner will contact you soon about making arrangements," I said.

"Here's the number for the coroner." Brady handed Araceli a business card.

Haven's newest widow stared at the card, then twisted the wedding band on her left ring finger. "Thank you, Miss Rush, for believing me."

"I'm very sorry for your loss," I said. "We'll do our best to get you answers."

Back in the Bronco, I sat for a moment, looking out my windshield but seeing nothing. I glanced in my rearview mirror at Brady's reflection. He also sat, but he was talking to someone on his phone. The neighborhood was coming alive with the scent of frying meat and the sounds of skateboards and lawn sprinklers.

I needed to call—

I tapped my pocket. *No phone.* I searched my bag. No phone. *Must've left it.* I exited my car, which made Brady look up and roll down his window. "Be right back," I told him. "Left my phone." I hurried up the walkway. Before I could knock, I glimpsed Araceli through the window.

She was standing at the altar again, that memorial candle for Emiliano back on the table and relit. Phone held out, she recorded herself blowing out the candle.

Fucking social media.

Araceli paused long enough to return my phone, throwing in a hug as a bonus. "If you see something in my Etsy shop, let me know and it's yours."

I returned to Brady Kwon in his Yukon and shook my phone at him.

"Intentional," he asked, eyebrow cocked, "or did you truly forget?"

I winked at him. "I'll never tell."

He smiled.

I asked, "Did you know about the missing men over at the spa construction site or were you as surprised as you looked?"

His turn to wink. "I'll never tell."

PART II

The Girl Who Interrupted

12.

Keely Butler burst into the lobby of Poole Investigations like a tornado hurtling across a Texarkana highway. The door slammed against the wall so hard that it rattled the Skittles in the candy machine. Even though it was a little past noon, it was still too early in the day for this shit. But here she was, barging into my life, ready to celebrate her daughter's return.

Or not.

Keely stood there, pink faced, her chest heaving beneath her blue Rise & Grind T-shirt. Her hair was slicked back into a bun that wasn't nearly as tight as the nerves in her face. Did this woman know any expressions other than "glower"?

"You two just can't help driving the stake through my heart, can you?" she asked.

We weren't driving it deep enough, though, because here she was, alive, heart beating.

"Good afternoon, Miss Butler," I said, nonplussed. "How can I help you?"

"You're *not* helping me," she spat. "You're helping everybody in Haven *except* me."

I refrained from snorting and extended my hand toward the waiting area. "It's great news about Honor. I'm glad she's alive. Glad that somehow she found me—"

"Somehow." She stomped over to the chairs and dropped into one.

So, Keely wasn't a vampire who could be killed by a stake in the heart. How *would* one kill a werewolf, a swamp creature, or a balrog like Keely Butler?

"Your kid's home," I said, sitting in the chair across from her. "Isn't that what you wanted?"

She leaned forward and sneered at me. "But what *happened* to her?"

I wiped my damp hands on the thighs of my jeans. My gold silk shirt now felt damp and heavy with sweat. "She didn't tell you?"

"No, she didn't tell me. Aren't you gonna find that out?" she asked.

"Solving crime is not our job at Poole Investigations—"

"How am I supposed to help her if I don't know what happened?" she shrieked.

"Investigator Brady Kwon—"

"But you'll go out of your way, helping illegal aliens instead of helping American citizens, right? Fuck helping me save my kid."

"*Your* kid, not ours," I said. "And who we help isn't your business."

Here she was, in Bad Mom form, who hadn't paid attention and ignored the signs of her child's slide into danger. Now, she was demanding that everyone else help her pick up the pieces without taking a moment to admit her own lapses, her own need to divest from the facade of Perfect Family.

I'd seen parents do this a million times in my previous life—and I understood . . . until the "faking it" hindered investigators like me from uncovering the truth. And Keely Butler was doing just that.

Now I cocked my head and squinted at her, steadily gazing but saying nothing, unafraid of her brand of fucking crazy.

"I saw Araceli Rivas leaving here yesterday," Keely continued. "The same woman who can't find her husband, a man who snuck into this community without permission. The same man who goes around Haven, preying on young girls like Honor. Leering at them. Just disgusting. Leeching off our system and stealing catalytic converters from people's cars and copper from the streetlights—"

"Miss Butler," I interrupted, "my clients and their needs are none of your—"

"Did Araceli Rivas tell you that her husband is a *creeper*?" she asked.

I didn't respond—because the Rivas case wasn't anyone's business and because I'd been paid to work the Rivas case, and to Araceli, to *me*, Emiliano mattered. They'd both deserved resolution—he'd been lost, and he should've been found.

"So now you've looked for a dog," Keely Butler said, holding up one finger, and then a second finger. "You helped out the Monroes, who only moved here in June, and yet, Honor had been missing since April. When do I get priority?"

I crossed my legs and let my chin rest in my hands. "First of all, your case was never assigned to me. If Investigator Kwon and the sheriff's office need my help, they will ask me."

"Until then?"

"It remains their case." Simple—and I shrugged to underscore that. But my stomach tightened because in truth: Honor's situation was far from simple. The girl had returned, leaving a bag of evidence documenting bad men hurting her—and I didn't know what to do about that in my new capacity.

"Can you at least *pretend* to care?" Keely asked, then clapped her hand over her mouth. *"Please?"*

I pushed out a breath, tapped the Scriptor app, then grabbed a pen and notepad from the reception desk. "Did you put a tracker on Honor's phone?" I wrote that question on the first sheet of paper and looked up at her. "If you used a software, say . . . mSpy, you could help Investigator Kwon figure out where she's been all this time."

Keely Butler shook her head. "If I'd done that, I would've found her a long time ago."

Okay, so that cleared up the question about who could've been tracking Honor.

"Who were her best friends?" I asked.

Keely nibbled at a thumbnail and stared at the coffee table. "Umm . . . Caitlin? I don't remember her last name. Umm . . . Mackenzie Sutton was her big sister at high school, but that was a long time ago. Once Mack graduated, they never talked again."

Wrong.

"Umm . . ." Keely Butler tapped her foot, searched for answers in the fluorescent lights that ran along the ceiling.

"Any boyfriend or guys she liked?" I asked.

She shook her head. "She wasn't into boys. She was scared of getting pregnant or catching STDs."

Wrong again. So very, *very* wrong.

"Anyone you think Investigator Kwon should talk to? Obviously not Mackenzie since . . ."

"Yeah, I told Honor all about that," Keely Butler said, nodding. "She's not talking even more now. She just said, 'Karma's a bitch.' Guess she's still angry." She gazed at her hands for a long time, then shrugged. "Maybe one of the kids on the cross-country team. They all had their little secrets."

Honor had a big secret—she wasn't on the cross-country team anymore and hadn't been for months before that April meet.

"Speaking of cross-country," I said, "are you sure she ran that morning?"

"Positive," Keely Butler said, nodding. "She loved running. And someone knew that and stole her off the course."

I wrote *Clueless STILL* on the pad. To the woman sitting across from me: "I'll share all of this with Investigator Kwon. Like I said, he's the lead—"

Keely kicked the edge of the coffee table. "It doesn't bother you that you're wasting resources on someone who isn't even supposed to *be* here? If I'm mayor next year this time, you can bet your ass that I'm gonna clean this town up. Get rid of all the illegal trash predators hunting down our kids, once and for all."

From my preliminary peeks through Honor's phone, I, too, had found predator trash—Orville Klein, Big Poppa D, Liam the boyfriend—and they all looked very American to me. Still, her words were a punch to my gut, not because I'd expected better from this woman—I didn't—but because her sentiments were becoming all too familiar and easy to say.

Keely hadn't been the first person to blame immigrants for Haven's woes nor would she be the last. For me, though? I was tired of hearing this shit, especially since Mackenzie Sutton had died by a white woman's hands. Xander Monroe had too. Honor had been hanging around dangerous white boys with dangerous ways of living. A white man had burned my landlords' Pride flags. Haven was 98 percent white, with most of the remaining 2 percent living on the other side of the hill, minding their business and paying less for tires. I didn't believe that all immigrants were noble, law-abiding folks, but I knew that Keely Butler preferred her piping-hot cup of racism more than the heavy syrup of reality—her people were fucked up and always stayed in trouble. If she wanted to truly take out the trash, she'd end up lining Highway 1 with orange trash bags of folks who looked like her.

"I'm not sure how being a racist will help you find out what happened to Honor," I said to her now, my voice steady even as I bubbled with anger. I gripped both armrests of my chair like I was riding a roller coaster with its next drop hidden from view. All the snapbacks and retorts were gathering in me like a hurricane, and my muscles bundled with tension.

"First of all," Keely Butler said, raising her Karen finger at me. "Honor's Mexican American. I *can't* be racist. And second: Mexicans are the ones who took her. You just got to Haven, so you don't know what's been going on around here. These people come to this town, and they're bringing drugs, and they're bringing crime, and they're taking our kids. One of them is even going around stealing people's dogs out of their yards. None of you cops care about missing girls of color."

None? Was she fucking *kidding* me?

Bile burned in my throat—I wanted to gag.

Too early in the day, though.

Lift ev'ry voice and sing . . .

Till earth and heaven ring . . .

Ring with the harmony of liberty . . .

And after thinking about the Black National Anthem, I thought of Polly's Diner and that delicious, perfect breakfast, and I thought about the people who lived in East Haven, who were now building New Haven, including Lumière Spa and Resort. They were doing the best they could to make a life in a town that considered them to be trash.

I pushed out a sigh and stood from the armchair. I'd shown enough patience to Keely Butler—in the past, she'd called me uppity and disrespectful. "I'll share what you've told me with Investigator Kwon. If you'll excuse me, I need to get back to my work."

She glared at me with flared nostrils, her hands clenched into fists.

I parted my feet and waited. *Please hit me. Please, please, PLEASE.*

Keely Butler bit her bottom lip, probably wondering why I wouldn't do as she'd commanded, probably wondering if smacking me would do the trick. But some unseen force told her to unclench her fists and tug her purse onto her shoulder. "This isn't over," she snarled. "I'll make sure that everyone in Haven knows that you don't care if Haven's girls are victimized and terrorized."

Was this what she wanted to leave me with? *A threat?* I swear: This woman was a crab walking backward to find the ocean. She still hadn't learned—and I wasn't a difficult lesson. Threaten me and you'd get less than what you started with. Fortunately, for Honor's sake, I had already been trying to figure out who'd hurt that girl.

Keely Butler stormed out of the front door as loudly as she came, and that bell banged again.

Till earth and heaven ring . . . And I slowly lifted my left fist. Better that it hung in the air than slammed into that bitch's face, right? Right.

Keely Butler wore two kinds of perfume: freesia and rage. The latter's acrid stink lingered in the waiting room long after she'd left, permeating the chairs and carpet.

I needed to do some quick work to counteract that odor. I grabbed the TV's remote control and found *Sanford and Son* on Tubi—the first step toward a cure. I didn't have any of Mom's sweet potato cupcakes to place around the office as offering to the ancestors, but I *did* have music, and I found the best of Aretha Franklin on my playlist and connected it to the intercom system's Bluetooth. Black folks' sage to ensure Keely Butler's energy wouldn't blossom like that corpse flower down in Indonesia. I needed to guard against loud and nonsensical racism—bigotry moved through the world like a cancer discovered too late. No one survived *and* thrived on a steady stream of fear and division. Ask Ms. Butler, though, and she'd deny it all cuz she fucked a Mexican dude once.

Alone again, I released a long, slow breath, rolling my head and shoulders to release the tension settling there. My skin, though, still prickled with tiny wounds.

As mayor, Keely would kill anything good in this town. But was she *really* planning to run, or was this just another act? Her opponent would play hardball during the march toward election day, exposing the truth: Bad Person, Bad Mother. Did Keely really want that?

I stomped back to my office with Aretha singing "Think," my own personal soundtrack. I sank into my chair as the room spun around me.

Why did I let that woman shake my compass like that?

I squeezed the bridge of my nose and squeezed my eyes closed even tighter, waiting for the world to reset. Reset to what, though? What was *normal* Haven?

Past my windows, tourists and townspeople wandered from shop to diner to car. City workers were stringing up a Fall Harvest Festival banner across Seaview Way. Back when Cooper and I had been together, I'd been looking forward to attending that festival. I'd been looking forward to picking out pumpkins with him. Making spiked apple cider and getting deliciously tanked as we watched the sun sink over the ocean. Now, I was watching two dogs sniff each other's butts and the sun pushing past the haze to make Haven twinkle with light.

13.

The drive up to Sableport was quiet except for the hum of my Bronco's new tires against Highway 1. The closer I got to the next town, the brighter the sunlight, and soon, rolling hills, scrub oaks, and dry grass took the place of mist and ocean. Sableport had its own mysteries, but I brought along a few of my own to solve, including the most important one:

What happened to Emiliano Rivas, the man who'd been found in my forest and now lived on India's steel table?

My best friend's office smelled like Pine-Sol and lemons—but the room where I now stood across from her reeked of Pine-Sol and dead body: round, sour smells. A sheet covered the body on the table, the outline of broad shoulders and a stocky build telling me that a dead man lay before us. India, gloved up, had stuffed her locs beneath a surgeon's cap as the rest of her hid under blue scrubs.

"So," she said, "he was wearing black boxer briefs. Temperature was fifty degrees. Nothing unusual with his organs—everything was where they were supposed to be. Enlarged right heart, organs dark and congested, fluid in his lungs. No mummification or substantial decomposition. No animal scavenging. No skin or scalp slippage."

"Fresh dead," I said.

"Mm-hmm. No alcohol. No drugs. But the story is in his eyes." India pulled the sheet from Emiliano's head and shone her penlight into his brown eyes.

Red specks in the white part—petechial hemorrhaging. Broken blood vessels that came from strangulation and suffocation. India aimed her light at thin purple lines around his neck.

"A bag over his head, maybe?" I asked. "The seam making it tighter?"

"Possibly. Abrasion across his tongue."

"He bit it while trying to breathe?"

India shrugged.

Deduction was my job, not hers.

"Foamy material in his nose and mouth, which meant a fluid build-up in his lungs. You see the bluish discoloration of his face?"

I nodded. Lack of oxygen. That, along with the bulging eyes and tongue . . .

"But how do we know it wasn't a sexual kink or suicide?" I asked.

"The ligature—a bag or tie or whatever—it would've been around his neck or on his head."

I tossed her a gun finger. "Let me guess: There wasn't a bag nearby. And I'm guessing there were no ligatures found in the forest."

Homicidal asphyxia—not as popular as death by gun, knife, or car / baseball bat / fist, all known as instances of blunt-force trauma.

"No bite marks," India continued.

Sometimes, bite marks indicated sexual activity.

"I took fingernail clippings," India said, "in case there was someone else around."

I'd had cases thought to be homicidal asphyxia but the family of the decedent had discovered the body, then been embarrassed by what they'd found and cleaned up the scene before dialing 9-1-1.

"The imprint left by the ADIDAS on his foot," she said.

"Fixed blood at that point, right?"

She bobbed her head, a yes and no. "But that arm, the one held up despite gravity, still told me that he was in rigor mortis. Rigor generally leaves thirty-six hours after death, so . . . with all that we know so far . . . time of death would be Saturday morning. He'd been dead for about twenty-four hours by the time you found him. But we'll confirm everything once we get back results from his lung samples."

"And the gun?" I asked.

India's eyebrows furrowed. "Who told you about the gun?"

"Bargain-basement Encyclopedia Brown mentioned it."

"Ugh. McCann."

"You have a picture of it?"

Using the room's computer, she pulled up the picture of a compact 9mm with a black glitter slide and a pink rose printed on its grip.

"Not the cutest gun," I said. "Effective, though."

She sighed. "Well, he didn't die by gunshot."

No—he died by manual arts.

"I'm glad you know who he is now," India said. "One more family receiving some closure." She dropped her head and muttered, "Damn."

"You do the best you can," I told her.

"I need to do better."

"*Science* needs to do better," I pointed out. "Your little brain is smoking right now. Smells like bacon."

She laughed.

Back in her office, India gave me printouts of the rose and glitter Glock, the dead man's face, the crisscross marks on his back, and the intricate Santa Muerte leg tattoo.

"I hear you and Kwon notified Mrs. Rivas together," India asked.

I smirked. "Is that a problem?"

A smile played across her lips. "The man has it bad for you. Like they always do." India clicked around her computer as pages of reports turned from digital pixels to printed things spitting from her printer.

"You hear anything about London's arraignment?" I asked.

"Not yet." She plucked the pages from the tray.

"Lori told me she was going," I said. "Wonder if Coop went."

India said, "Another ME is handling Mackenzie's autopsy. I couldn't—not as a friend, well, *former* friend of her father."

I gazed at India, then sank in my chair. "I wish I had a badge."

"If you had a badge, you wouldn't be here."

"Untrue—I was gonna move to Haven to be with him."

She twisted in her chair and squinted at me. "That's right—you were eventually gonna handle the spa's security."

"Yep." I drummed my fingers against India's desk. "My Uber driver back on Sunday shared an interesting Sartre quote—"

"Not Sartre," India said, rolling her eyes.

"Everything has been figured out except how to live."

She stared at me, then nodded. "We got the dying thing down to a science."

Yeah.

My phone vibrated.

You around?

"Speaking of Investigator Brady Kwon," I said, tapping back:

Yep

Wanna talk?

Yeah we need to

14.

For the second time that day, I met Brady Kwon, this time at Lucy's, a dive bar with a great view. Calamari and Coronas, peanuts and darts. The Eagles on the jukebox, and the Eagles on ESPN. There was no theme except for that ocean, that sunset, and the dead neon *K* between the *C* and the *Y*. I liked Lucy's better than Lucky's.

As Brady finished a phone call, I pulled up Araceli's Instagram page. She'd recorded herself saying that Emiliano had been found, that he was with the ancestors now, that he no longer needed the candle to guide him home. And then she blew out that candle. Over five thousand people had "liked" it, many of them posting comments:

Your love will never die.

You're so brave.

Emiliano loved you so much.

Hugs and kisses

ILY!

Inspiration!

Kween!!!

I knew this wasn't fair, but I thought of my Uber driver and his job as a professional mourner. While this wasn't the same—Araceli Rivas *did* lose her husband—there was something . . . *performative* about grieving like this on social media. Thinking the worst about Haven's newest widow made my stomach cramp with guilt.

Brady and I ordered and handed our menus back to a server named Sienna. Button nosed, she was pretty and perky, and for a millisecond, I felt eel-slick jealousy writhing in my chest each time she touched Brady's shoulder.

"Come here often?" I asked him, sipping from my water glass, attempting nonchalance.

Brady nodded, shelled a few peanuts. "Pretty. Quiet. I pop in to think things through. I'm the only regular from the station, and I keep my mouth shut about how good the burgers and key lime pie are. I'm keeping Lucky's a secret."

I lifted my eyebrows. "But you brought *me*."

He gave me a small smile. "You don't count—and don't ask me why."

Sienna brought him a bottle of Dos Equis and my glass of Napa Cab.

Brady lifted his bottle. "To solving shit in time to go home and watch *Game of Thrones*."

Cheers to that.

I sipped my wine. "Tell me: Can I now eat porch cupcakes without the fear of dying?"

"Not yet." He sipped his beer and winced. "Working on it. Swear."

"It's been days—"

"But not months." He pushed aside the tin bucket of salted peanuts and leaned forward. "So there's something non-case-related I want to ask you—"

"No."

He blinked at me. "I haven't even—"

"I'm not joining the sheriff's department." I cracked open the peanut shell in my hand.

"Why not?" he asked. "It's good pay. Investigating cases, arresting bad guys . . ."

"He says as he presses his calf against mine beneath the table." I met his eyes and waited for him to move his leg away.

He didn't.

"Do you understand what it would mean if I got hired to your department?" I asked.

He blushed. "We couldn't . . . be together."

I rolled my eyes. "No, idiot. I'd be senior to you. I'd be your boss. I have ten years, you have five. No way I'd let you tell me what to do. And then you'd resent me, and then you'd try to kill me like the scorned cops on those true crime TV shows. *Fatal Love* or some shit, and then Ivan would have to kill *you*, and . . ." I waved my hand. "So, no. For both our sakes."

He tapped the tabletop. "Guess we're done with non-case-related items, then."

We laughed. Drank. Sighed.

"Now that you've brought Emiliano home," he said, "what's your next case?"

"Cheating spouses *or* insurance fraud," I said.

He scratched his temple. "Give it a minute—either case may have a body at the end."

"Solving homicides. How fucking weird of me."

He held up his hands. "I don't yuck someone's yum."

"You like it too."

"I do." He shrugged. "But I like a lot of things that I probably shouldn't." He stared at me. "Like the woman seated across from me."

I rolled my eyes. "Allow me to yuck your yum before you even go there."

"You're a more-normal desire than solving murders."

I pointed at him. "You just asked me to join your team. We can't be sleeping together and solving murders at the same time on the people's dime."

"I thought I was quitting this murder-police thing after kicking the cupcake assassin's ass?"

I wagged my finger at him. "I forgot. And then, afterward, we'd rule the seven cities of Mendo County."

"We'll be like that couple on *Remington Steele*."

I hooted to the sky. "I'm Pierce Brosnan." I circled my finger. "Back to business for a moment. Have you heard anything about Emiliano Rivas being a lurker?"

He frowned and growled, "No." He paused, then asked, "Why? Did you hear something?"

"Keely Butler," I said. "She hurled that accusation, and now, if she Karens her way back to the office, I can tell her that I looked into it."

Brady blinked at me, then said, "But you're taking *my* word for it."

"Maybe." I held up both hands. "I'm just bringing it up for *you* to investigate. I'm done. The man's been found."

He rolled his eyes. "Done? Sure, you are."

"I am."

"At this very moment, you don't have a file in your bag with autopsy reports and pictures?"

I sipped my wine. "Curiosity."

Brady placed his chin in his hand and grinned at me.

"What?" I asked. "You got this. You'll find out whodunit any minute now."

"If that were true—that you're content with leaving me to solve the whodunit part—you wouldn't be seated across from me, eating mediocre calamari."

"More than mediocre, but less than superb." I chomped one and chewed. "Fine. Something's bothering me about this case, and I'm not letting go . . . *for now*." Then I stuck my tongue out at him.

Brady needed to take another call, and he stepped away to the end of the pier.

I texted India.

Drinks w/Brady K right now

Flirting

Working

Confused

HELP!!

Ellipses immediately bubbled on the screen.

He asked you out?!

Yay yay yay!!

I squinted at the screen, then looked up at Brady, still talking.

You encouraged him??!

YES

So you approve??

YES!!

And our jobs??

Yall work for different people

You're an adult and you're smart

Figure the shit out

And Cooper?

New phone who dis?

"Sorry about that." Brady slid back onto his stool.

"You know what made me the saddest talking to Araceli today?" I asked, picking at the crust left in the basket. "When she regretted her and Emiliano meeting at the crafts con in Fresno. *That* felt . . . authentic. Truth without any of the cutesy affirmation shit."

Brady said "Yeah" and stared into his beer bottle. "Of all the shit to regret, falling in love . . ." He took a swig of beer and shook his head. "And in this business of ours . . ."

"Right? Where everyone wants to put on with the 'light up a room' and 'never had an enemy' bullshit." I took his beer and took a quick pull. "So I don't even know your origin story," I said, pushing back the beer bottle. "*Your* true authentic self."

"What do you want to know?" he asked, wiping his mouth with a napkin.

I stared at him. "Tell me about your family."

He nodded. "My dad came from this little town outside of Seoul. Met my mother at the San Francisco International Airport—she pushed people around in the wheelchairs, and he'd broken his foot. One morning, she saw him limping along and offered to push him to baggage claim, and that was that. He worked his ass off—from dry cleaners to dishwasher to karaoke DJ. He finally listened to my mother, and they started this car service for people needing special accommodations while getting around the Bay. At one point, they had seven cars.

"Worked almost every day of his life, even now, and he's eighty. Mom drives with him sometimes. They're not perfect but . . ." He shrugged. "I wouldn't mind what they have."

I said, "Yeah."

"They're why I'm a little extra sensitive about this Rivas case. It's not that I don't want to solve this. It's just that . . . that . . ."

"Investigating means exposing," I said, wineglass to my lips.

"And exposing sometimes results in deporting. My own father stayed well past his visa expiration date. He couldn't bear going back and leaving behind his 'Yeob Gongjunim.'"

"Sounds sweet, whatever that means," I said, smiling.

"Darling Princess."

I mouthed the words, then said, "But if we don't investigate, the bad guys win."

"The bad guys won when they killed Emiliano. He's not coming back even if the bad guys get the needle."

I snorted. "Way to ruin your dad calling your mom 'Yeob Gongjunim.'"

After splitting a slice of that incredible key lime pie, Brady and I paid our bill—split evenly—and walked back to the parking lot. Standing at my truck, he gazed down at me, brushed my bangs from my forehead.

I looked up at him and studied his eyes. I smoothed his eyebrow.

He leaned in.

I shook my head. "Before I can kiss you, I need you to protect me."

"Cupcake assassin," he said.

"Um-hmm."

He squinted into space. "I'll work ten days a week instead of eight to find out who tried to kill you."

"And then?" I wrapped my arms around his neck and pressed against him.

"And then . . ." He wrapped his arms around my waist and pulled me closer. "I'll kick their ass, arrest them for attempted murder, and turn in my badge. I'll come work for Ivan, and we'll rule Haven and the seven cities of Mendo County forever more."

I chuckled, then I kissed him quick, and squinted at his surprised expression. Then, I kissed him again, longer this time. He tasted like citrus and graham crackers. "That's on credit," I told him, my nose nuzzling his. Then I pushed him away. He held my hand until I was too far away and he had to let go. "Good night, Investigator Kwon."

"Good night, Alyson," he whispered, breathless.

Lucy's had been a nice liminal space where a girl could be whoever she needed to be as long as she had a basket of fried food and the beverage of her choice at hand. Now, though, it was time to no longer smile and flirt with pretty detectives and return to the fucked-up mad world—and the people who made life hard, even though calamari, key lime pie, and wine existed.

Sitting back at my office desk, I sank into my chair and powered up my laptop. I'd barely exhaled when a breaking news notification rolled down on the screen's upper right corner.

> Family of Five Found Murdered in NorCal—Victims Include Mother and Child

I clicked the link and scanned the small article.

> . . . Witnesses saw the shooter stand over a young woman holding a baby and shot and killed them in Creekwood, a Northern California rural community, leaving five dead. The other three victims ranged from twenty to thirty-six, including a woman who was shot as she slept. Their autopsies are expected to be completed later this week. GO HOME had been

> spray-painted on their front door.
> Authorities said they were searching for two suspects . . .

I squeezed the computer mouse with one hand to steady my pulse and waved my now-warm face with the other, taking deep breaths to keep from crying. Humans killing humans wasn't new but taking the lives of the woman and the baby . . . Some of us had finally evolved to a new state of cored-out, fucked-up, mega evil, and I hoped that reading stories like this would forever take my breath away. I shifted in my seat and reread the article again, the sting diminished, but the shock still zapping around my heart.

This read like a typical murder story until GO HOME. That addition made my mind race. *Anti-immigration.* Could this case be connected to Emiliano Rivas's? To the other missing men from the spa site?

I shared the link to the article with Brady with a text.

Saw this

Any chance it's tied to Emiliano?

I reread the article a third time in case I'd missed a word or a meaning. Finding nothing, I leaned back in my chair and watched the laptop screen.

GO HOME.

My final task before leaving the office . . .

I found his number and dialed. Held my breath as the line rang . . . rang . . .

"This is Sergeant Tank Goffman with the Department of Immigration and Customs Enforcement . . ." Voicemail instead of the live person.

At the beep, I said, "Hey, Tank. This is Sonny Rush. Long time, yeah? I'm working up in Haven now in the private sector, and I have a question that I hope you can help with." I left him my new work phone number—even back in our days together with the LAPD, I'd never wanted ICE Tank to have my real number—and today, in this world, in *this* climate, I sure as hell didn't want him to have it now.

Honor Butler lived with her mother, Keely, in a gray Victorian with dingy pink eaves. I hadn't heard from the girl since she'd left my house yesterday morning, and I was starting to worry. My anxiety upticked as I parked across the street from that dingy Victorian and made my way up the walkway. With my stomach in knots, I rang the doorbell and waited.

Alabama, Arizona, Alaska, Arkansas . . .

The porch light popped on and the front door opened. Keely Butler stood there wearing a sweaty yoga set, her skin bright pink. "What do *you* want?" she asked.

Still no "Thank you for bringing my girl home."

"Just wanted to check on . . ." I tried to peek past the woman in front of me. As far as I could tell, Honor wasn't sitting in the living or dining rooms.

Just days ago, I'd hid under that tableclothed dining table as I'd searched for Mackenzie's dog. I'd crept along hallway walls that led to Honor's bedroom, crammed with exercise equipment and piles of clean laundry. That room gave off a weird vibe, like Keely had never intended for her daughter to return.

Keely crossed her arms. "She's sleeping, and I'm not waking her up."

I tried to smile. "I wouldn't ask you to."

Really, what had I done to this woman for her to be so . . . *offended*?

"And you don't have to check up on her anymore," Keely said, stepping back, preparing to close the door. "She's back to being Honor."

I squinted at her. "Being Honor is what led her to leaving."

Oops. Shit, Sonny.

"Excuse me?" Keely asked, eyes narrowed.

In for a penny, in for a pound.

"She needs help, Miss Butler," I said. "Counseling. Therapy. She's going through—"

"How many children do you have?" Keely asked.

I smiled. "I'm not a mother."

"We have nothing to talk about, then." She tried to slam the door.

But I held out my palm and stopped the door from closing. "Since you know so much, you should know that she hated cross-country and never intended to run that day she disappeared. In fact, she'd quit cross-country weeks before then but let you think otherwise."

Keely blinked at me, looking for something to say, but her brain knew that Honor needed help. Her heart, though, didn't want to admit defeat.

"I'm not a mother," I said, my own heart now softer, "but I *do* know distress and danger—and your daughter is experiencing both. You never hired me nor did Ivan ever assign your case to me—no matter how much you keep saying that he did—but I'm looking into a few things on your daughter's behalf."

"Like?"

"Like where she's been all this time. All I ask is that you keep monitoring her movements. Who she hangs out with. If something or someone strikes you as strange or trouble, listen to your gut and keep them away from her, and then let either me or Investigator Kwon know as soon as you can. He's aware of the situation—he'll actually lead Honor's investigation once we have solid information."

Keely looked back over her shoulder—was Honor sitting in a place I couldn't see? Then Keely looked back at me with red-rimmed eyes. She nodded and pushed the door to close it.

This time, I let her.

15.

I tugged at the neck of my sweater and wished that I'd chosen to wear a T-shirt this morning instead. Mom, riding shotgun, had her window rolled down. Even though the ride to Sweetlife was only five minutes long, she jabbed the radio button, found the yacht rock channel, and snapped her fingers as Champaign sang "How 'Bout Us."

I made a face—at the cold air, at her singing. "What's gotten into you today?"

She cackled. "Love. You should try it."

"Uhh. Read the room. Why do you think I moved to this . . . ?" I whipped my hand at the town waiting for me across Highway 1.

"So is he the only man in Haven?" Mom asked, eyebrow cocked.

I didn't answer.

"You know what your problem is?"

"It's sweet that you think I only have one."

"You want happily ever after," Mom said, "but you only want one version of it. You keep staring at the sun too long, you're gonna go blind."

"Thanks, Mom."

"What are you expecting to get out of going over there?"

The light turned green. I looked both ways before crossing, then said, "I just need to be sure he's okay."

Mom scowled. "He ain't okay. His daughter is dead. His wife is in jail. And his girlfriend—*you*—broke up with him. That man ain't ever gon' be okay. But here you are, hoping to save his life."

I gripped the steering wheel tighter. "Up until three weeks ago, he was the love of my life. I still care about all that's going on with him. Is that wrong?"

"I was talking to Quincy about you—"

"Please, don't." The cold breeze from the open window made my eyes fill with tears. So I bit the inside of my cheek to keep those tears in check.

"And he said something to think about. You have to uncross your arms to hug someone."

I scrunched my face. "Okay."

"It sounded relevant at the moment."

"Maybe you left out a part."

"Yeah." She paused, then said, "Don't let your past keep you from your future, Alyson. Love exists here—and you are lovable. Remember that."

I pulled in front of the bakery.

Customers were already snaked out of the front door.

Mom kissed my cheek, then climbed out as Champaign continued to sing.

Other than the hum of fluorescent lights and the faint creak of floorboards beneath my shoes, the office was quiet. I headed for the file room and opened the A–D drawer and pulled out BUTLER, KEELY. There were many reasons to keep Keely's file on my desk. Maybe she knew Liam or Orville Klein. Maybe Honor's father was a bad guy—the Clyde to Keely's Bonnie. Maybe Ivan had discovered a secret that didn't seem so terrible back in the day but had come back to ensnare a seventeen-year-old girl.

Back at my desk, I typed Dave Kruger Lumiere into Google.

Sixty-one results.

The foreman of Cooper's spa had been the captain of his high school football team in Sausalito, California. Last year, he'd attended homecoming and . . . that was the last "normal" thing about the man helping to build Lumière.

He got kicked out of SeaWorld for assaulting a mime right before an orca show.

During the nineties, he'd been a member of a Philippines-based cult charged by the feds with immigration fraud and human trafficking.

Five years ago, a transient had died of a drug overdose in a house he owned.

He sang lead in a Bruce Springsteen cover band.

And most recently, he was an associate of a Cal/OSHA official involved in the death of a day laborer on another construction site who'd fallen from scaffolding. The undocumented man hadn't been harnessed correctly and had plunged fifty feet to his death. Dave Kruger, the foreman of that site, should've been criminally charged, but lucky for him, the OSHA investigator had been recently convicted of soliciting bribes in three other cases.

Dave Kruger was not just an asshole—he was also a negligent and not-adjudicated murderer.

My phone rang and I answered.

"Miss Rush," the woman said, "this is Diane, the waitress from Polly's."

I grabbed a pad and pen from the corner of my desk. "Hey, how—"

"Good, good." She sounded rushed and hushed. "Listen, I'm on break. But something just happened you should know about. Emiliano Rivas just came into the diner."

I paused, then wrote down what she'd just said. "A dead man came into . . . Huh?"

"Emiliano Rivas," she said. "And he's not dead."

Diane was either smoking that good shit or she'd worked too hard today.

My eyebrows knitted together. "But Emiliano Rivas—"

"Is dead. Yeah, you told me that. But I served him a sausage breakfast burrito, coffee, and three slices of toast just an hour ago. He was with a girl—"

"Araceli?"

"No. She looked Chinese or something."

I dropped my pen and rubbed the temple of my nose. "Okay."

"I gotta go—"

"Wait, Diane," I said. "Can you give me a description? And what was he driving?"

"A turquoise Subaru, and he wore a green Oakland A's baseball cap and black hoodie. And he had a Gucci wallet. That's when I saw his license and his debit card," she said. "Both said Emiliano Rivas, and he lives in Sableport. 7-3-7-7 Heron Avenue."

I wrote all this down, then said, "Real quick: Dave Kruger. He's the—"

"Foreman at Lumière," Diane said.

"Do you hear much about how he treats his workers?" I asked.

Silence on the other end.

"Hello?"

Diane cleared her throat, and said, "I really gotta go."

"Yes or no—should I be concerned if I was the sweetheart of someone who worked at the spa site?"

Silence, and then: "Yes."

As soon as I ended my call with Diane, Tank Goffman's name showed up on my phone.

I was thrilled but not happy.

"How's the girl with the best-looking ass in the Pacific Division doing?" His voice was deeper than Khazad-dûm—and his dysfunction ran even deeper.

"You're the same as you were the last time we talked," I said, my eyes squeezed shut. "How's the biggest asshole in the universe doing?"

He laughed. "Can't complain. Busy."

Armed to the teeth while breaking windows and tearing families apart.

"You working for Ivan now?" Tank asked.

"Yep. Up in Haven. This town ain't all that it's cracked up to be. People are awful even in beautiful places."

"Yeah," he said, "but I'd rather be cracking skulls by the beach instead of fucking Norco where it's a hundred-seventy degrees right now. Where'd Ivan get the money to move up there and open a firm?"

"'Firm' is a generous word. It's just him and me. And he got that sweet, sweet LAPD pension, that's how. He's no different than any other old cop who becomes a PI or goes into private security."

He laughed. "Of course you'd defend him. Anyway—"

"Anyway," I said, "I'm working a case. Undocumented worker. His prints don't show up in AFIS. Could you run 'em on your system?"

"If I remember correctly, you turned me down three times—"

"I don't date cops—"

"And now you want me to help—"

"Will you do me a solid or no?" I asked, closing my eyes again.

"Sure, Rush. You owe me."

That made me open my eyes. Were Emiliano's fingerprints and any information that came with them worth dealing with ICE Tank Goffman?

Fucking justice.

I took down Tank's email address and sent him Emiliano's fingerprints as soon as I ended the call. My desk looked like puppies had scrambled across its surface. Too many file folders and printouts, Keely Butler's among them.

I held my breath as I opened her file—and I didn't take a deep breath as I flipped through page after page of her dossier. Aliases: Teri Fields, Rochelle Acevedo, Rochelle Fields. "Teri Fields" had been charged with disorderly conduct. "Rochelle Fields" had been arrested for burglary. The real Keely Butler had served a few months in jail for larceny. Guess her parents had given her Rise & Grind because she'd never be hired to do anything else.

How sad for them. Then again, what part had they played in young Keely's life that led her to squat in a nice lady's ADU for two years until being evicted by the sheriff's department?

Mad world.

I kept reading and came to KNOWN ASSOCIATES.

Carlos Vega. This guy had a record as long as my legs. Trespassing, drug dealing, obstructing wife's burial, assault and battery, criminal mischief . . .

I typed his name into image search and—

Shit.

That's him. The man who'd stood beside my mother at the pier during one of her memory lapses. He'd also been seen on camera purchasing—

"Murder cupcakes," I said, my face losing all feeling, my tongue heavy as cold lard.

This was the man who'd tried to kill me. *Allegedly.* And he was a "known associate" of a woman who hated me—the same woman whose daughter ran away from home. Vega had stood with Keely at the curb moments before I snuck into her house to search for Figgy. Now I had his name—and his laundry list of crimes he'd committed.

With fingers I couldn't feel, I texted Brady.

I have the name of the cupcake assassin!

Fighting a swell of dizziness, I emailed him copies of Carlos Vega's rap sheet as well as the video clips from Sweetlife's security camera.

I'll look into it

Do more than that!

Figure of speech

Relax

Get a cup of coffee

Take a breath

Don't worry about my next steps

Worry about yours and this asshole's

My thoughts sounded like locusts had found a secret entrance through my pores.

Carlos Vega.

I'd talked to that asshole. Even thanked him for keeping my mother from wandering into the ocean. Hands no longer numb but now shaking, I clicked back into his record. Six feet two inches. Two hundred thirty pounds. A bear, like Ivan. He could've easily jumped me.

"Shit," I whispered. "Shit, shit, shit."

"Why are you cussing this early in the morning?" Ivan stood at the threshold of my office door. He wore a blue suit and a blue-and-red-striped tie.

"Carlos Vega," I said, slumping in my chair.

"I know that name," he said, running a cigar beneath his nose.

"I didn't, but I know his face."

"Who is he?"

"The man who left the poisoned cupcakes. The man who jumped me on the street."

Ivan's spine straightened, and his ears flushed. "You really think this asshole's good for it?"

"We have him holding that box of cupcakes and the CCTV footage from Deegan's—"

"Circumstantial."

"Whatever," I said, waving a hand. "Not enough for an arrest warrant, but at least we have a viable suspect now."

"Kwon's good. He'll make the connections if connections exist." Ivan paused, then added, "Especially now that he has extra incentive."

My face warmed. "Huh?"

"Promotion," Ivan said. "He wants that top position, and I can help make that possible, especially if he's put away the fucker who tried to kill my goddaughter. A good word from me and even *you*? The job's his."

"I wanna show you something." I brought up Araceli's Instagram page on my monitor.

Ivan lumbered over to my desk and peered at the screen. "That's our client, yeah?"

"Yeah. She posted this after Kwon and I gave her the death notification."

Ivan watched the video twice, then looked at me and shrugged. "Okay."

I tilted my head. "That's normal to you?"

He chuckled. "Sonny, I'm closer to a hundred years old than I am to thirty. What you all do with all this social media? I'll understand underwater backward Byzantine temple rites before I understand what the fuck TikTok is. But this—" He waved at the social media profile on the screen. "—this bothers you for some reason. Why?"

I sighed. "Don't know."

He beckoned me to follow him. His office smelled of old coffee and good cigars. I plopped down into one of his guest chairs as he sat in the chair on the other side of the desk. He handed me one of two carryout cups of coffee. "Two creams, three sugars, right?"

I smiled. "Yep."

"What's the grin for?" he asked.

"Remembering that you bought me my first cup of coffee."

My parents would always say that coffee stunted your growth. Once I passed five-five, Ivan had shrugged and said "I think she's fine, Al" and then pulled into the parking lot of Winchell's Donuts.

"A glaze and a coffee," he said, now smiling. "Good times."

"Yeah." I squinted, then said, "I just realized. I haven't even been to your house here."

"Sure you have . . ." But then his eyes softened. "No, you haven't."

"Weird, especially with you being my godfather."

He loosened his tie and laced his hands behind his head. He almost—*almost*—looked approachable. "Come over on Wednesday," he said and rattled off an address on Sea Cove Lane.

"How many houses do you own in this town?" I asked, tapping his address into my phone.

He shrugged. "Just investment properties. Why? You looking to buy?"

I snorted, and said, "You tell me. It's payday, right?"

He laughed. "We'll get to that."

"I ask because, when I was looking for Figgy, the house that came up in one of my searches was listed under your name. I just assumed you lived there."

He shook his head. "Keely Butler's renting that house right now. I don't keep tabs on every little thing that happens in them, either, so don't ask. Is that a problem?"

I raised my hands in a gesture of surrender. "Not a problem. I'm just trying to show up at the right place, that's all."

He squinted at me. "Back to Araceli: Why do you care what that lady does? You found her husband."

I ran my coffee cup along my lips. "Guess because his fingerprints didn't show up in AFIS."

"If he's an illegal—*undocumented*—alien, person, who didn't commit any crimes, he wouldn't be."

I said, "I know, but . . . What's our budget for hiring outside help?"

"We don't need outside help."

"For like . . . consultants with access to the fingerprint databases in Mexico, for instance."

Ivan stared at me, then said, "I'm not paying for that. We're not a big agency, if you haven't noticed."

"I know."

"You wanna be Superman. Give everybody their happily ever after."

"I guess."

"Haven needs Batman—"

"But we ain't got Batman's budget," I said, eyebrow cocked.

Ivan chuckled and lit his cigar. "Baby Gotham. One day, we'll have all the toys. To do that, though . . ." He puffs his cigar. "You gotta catch husbands fucking cheerleaders, wives trying to kill said cheerleaders, and the VP of HR stealing from the birthday cake fund. One case at a time, Sonny. You gotta move on. Let Araceli Rivas mourn her husband. This place is a breeding ground of deception, and we got some collecting to do."

He took a gulp of coffee. "At least there's good coffee in this fucked-up world."

Yeah. At least.

"Payday, right?" He swung away to bend down and open the safe beneath his credenza. He reached into the darkness and pulled out a sealed envelope. Then he smiled at me and slid that envelope across the desk. "Including a bonus for closing the Monroe case."

I took the envelope—I could smell the money even with the flap glued shut like that. "Speaking of . . . London's arraignment?"

"Took all of fifteen minutes," Ivan said, leaning back in his chair. "They brought her in wearing that orange jumpsuit. Charged her with one felony count of murder, one attempted murder—of *you*—with premeditation and special circumstances. She pleaded not guilty. What's his face, Superstar Lawyer, is representing her. No bail."

"No bail?" My eyebrows lifted. *"Really?"*

"She's a flight risk. A danger to others."

"And Cooper?"

"Sat with the Monroes."

I blinked at Ivan and said again, *"Really?"*

He nodded. "London's attorney, Stan Cain, may ask for change of venue, but . . ." He shrugged. "Not many people know what happened between her and Xander."

I frowned, my sense of wonder diminished. "Because no one was allowed to report on it."

"Well, now, that's a good thing. She'll get a fair trial and justice will be served. Amen."

After finishing our coffees, Ivan walked me to my truck. The thick mist smelled of bacon and the ocean. His eyes jumped around Seaview Way and narrowed as drunken college boys stumbled down the foggy street.

"Mom has a boyfriend," I told him with a smile.

That made his gaze snap back to me. *"What?"*

I nodded. "I know." I told him that Quincy Johns had snagged Mom's attention. "You remember him?"

"Yeah, I remember that Schlitz malt-liquor-looking asshole. That stupid air force uniform got on my fucking nerves." He ran his hand over his thick white hair. "Don't know how to feel about that."

"Same. But I'm doing background on him. I haven't found anything about him being an ax murderer yet."

Ivan said, "I'm going home to catch a few winks." Then: "Be productive."

My stomach churned as I climbed into the Bronco and watched as Ivan climbed into his Toyota Tundra. I gripped the wheel tightly, my palms slick with sudden sweat.

Washington, Adams, Jefferson . . .

I sat in my spot and watched the taillights on Ivan's truck disappear into the fog.

16.

The bell over the door *bing-bong*ed as I stepped into Pacific Guns & Ammo. The shop reeked of gun oil and cheap tobacco, its walls lined with rifles, shotguns, handguns, and gun bags and cleaning supplies. Since my last visit, Harvey Parrish had hung more American flags than before, just in case we forgot. And now this patriotic United States American looked up from the counter with his raisin eyes. He clenched his American ham-hock hands and pushed back his broad American shoulders strong enough to fire both the UZI and AR-15 pegged to his wall.

"What do you want, Rush?" he growled, rolling up the sleeves of his green-and-black flannel shirt. His wrist tattoos—WLM and 13/90—were a reminder that he wasn't a good dude.

"Happy Tuesday, Harvey," I said, my tone even. "I have a few questions for you."

He snorted. "And why would I answer them?"

"Because it's your civic duty." I paused, then said, "A guy named Emiliano Rivas was found dead in the forest." I placed the printout on the countertop of Emiliano in the hammock. "You see him before?"

He shrugged. "Maybe. Those guys all look alike."

"Yikes, Harvey."

"This one," he said. "Didn't he work over at the spa?"

"Yep."

He muttered, "Fucking ridiculous. Taking our jobs—"

"What job did Emiliano Rivas take from you? Or are you using the royal 'our' to mean racist dickheads always excited to blame their shortcomings on more skilled men with bigger, better . . . *tools*?"

"Fuck you."

"No, thanks, and I don't think Fuchsia Little would appreciate you sharing your busy penis with yet another Black woman."

Harvey froze. Like . . . he did not move. Like . . . this time, I was a T. rex . . . or a PI who knew his darkest secrets.

"Tell me the truth, Harvey," I said, leaning against the counter. "You don't hate Black women at all, do you? It just sounds good. You just have to make your Aryan Nation friends think you're as hateful as them."

He still hadn't moved.

Too bad—my eyesight was perfect, and I could see him *good*. I placed the photo from the "Parrish, Harvey" file before him.

His eyes flicked down to see 2018 Harvey Parrish holding his then-four-year-old son, Nasir, at Disneyland with one hand and his other hand lost in Fuchsia Little's hair. A happy interracial family visiting the happiest place on Earth.

I studied the picture. "I always cry during Fantasmic! Do you cry, Harvey?"

He swallowed, his eyes still stuck on the picture. "What do you want?"

I pulled out my phone and opened the photos of the gun. "Tell me about this Glock."

He squinted closely at one of the shots. "Serial number's been scratched off."

"No shit. That's not my question. How do I see what it used to say?"

He laughed. "You can't—that's the point of scratching it off."

I blinked at him.

He stared at me.

I waited, then smiled. "How do I get to know what it used to say?"

He crossed his arms. When I didn't speak, he rolled his eyes. "They're using this magnetic liquid to wipe down the area." Then he described how magnetic particles migrated to the scratches to create the number's outline. He frowned at me. "Thought you used to be a hotshot cop—they came up with that tech in 2015."

I nodded. "I know all about magneto-optical sensors. My question actually is this: Did this gun come from your shop? I mean . . . you'd remember selling a Glock with a black glitter slide and a pink rose on the grip, wouldn't you?"

He nodded. "Yeah. I don't sell pink guns."

My eyes skirted the shelves—didn't see any. "Do you know anyone in Mendo County who does?"

"Nope."

My gaze dropped to the pictures of the gun before shifting to pictures of Harvey with his secret Black family. "You sure?"

"Yep."

I cocked an eyebrow.

"I'm not lying."

"Okay." I took a step back. "Thanks for your help."

He nodded at the Disneyland picture. "You forgot this."

"I got plenty of copies. You keep that one. It will help you remember." I opened the door.

The doorbell *bing-bong*ed.

"Hey, Rush," Harvey shouted.

I didn't turn to look back at him.

"Chippy's up in Sableport," he said. "Big inventory. Check there."

Now I looked back at him and smiled. "Thanks, Harvey."

Cooper's house sat on the bluffs of Haven, overlooking the Pacific Ocean. The view was breathtaking—rolling waves crashing against jagged rocks below, the horizon stretching endlessly in shades of blue and gray with an ocean breeze carrying the scent of salt and seaweed. Despite this beauty, the house looked like a fortress, and the two-story with large windows now loomed dark and cold against the coastline.

I'd visited only once, days ago, and he hadn't been my host.

This morning, Cooper opened the door, the sole occupant of an architectural masterpiece.

"Sonny. Hey." Dark circles hung beneath his eyes. Hair unbrushed, cowlicks untamed, stubble on his jaw. His gray hoodie was stained with some kind of red sauce. He stank of sweat and sorrow. Even though he looked like hell, he was still a beautiful man. That jawline. Those eyes, even bloodshot. The way he filled the doorway.

Breathless, I said, "Hey."

His eyes shone with tears. "You're here."

I said, "Yeah."

He sniffled, blushed, swiped at his eyes. "It's just that . . . ten seconds ago, I picked up the phone and thought about calling you, but I changed my mind, but then I said your name aloud, and the doorbell rang, and . . . you're here."

"It's not the Resurrection," I cracked.

"But it *is* a miracle, maybe not to millions of Catholics, but to this lapsed one . . ."

"If that's what you want to think."

"That's what I want to think." He gestured for me to come in.

I forced myself to step inside.

The foyer was dark and cold. The sleek furniture and tasteful art still remained, but the air felt stale, and despite its tidiness, the house felt . . . *empty*. Like no one lived here at all.

On my last visit, I'd shared a glass of wine with London. That's when she told me that she knew about Cooper and me.

Awkward.

During that trip, I had also spotted a pair of women's orange Nikes in the laundry room. The woman who had jogged with Xander Monroe on the last morning he was alive had also worn orange Nikes. Now, those fancy sneakers lived in an evidence locker in Sableport, and the owner waited behind bars, her bail denied.

Sneakers weren't the only things missing here. All the pictures of London . . . gone from the mantels, the walls . . . Their bedroom, maybe? There was no "allegedly" and "due process" in the Sutton home. Cooper had deleted his wife.

Photographs of Mackenzie still remained. There she was, wearing her high school graduation cap and gown. There she was, partying in Ibiza, DJ headphones to her ear. There she was, cuddling with Figgy who I still needed to retrieve from those awful Minivan people.

Vases of fresh yellow tulips sat on the living room coffee table, the mantel, and the breakfast bar. Three coffee cups sat in the drying rack near the kitchen sink.

Cooper noticed me noticing. "The LaPlanches are here. She insisted on coming up."

Emilie LaPlanche and her husband Frank. Auntie Lee was Cooper's mother's sister.

"She cook?" I asked.

He tried to smile. "Of course." He paused, then added, "She asked about you. She put étouffée in the freezer for you."

My eyes widened, and I smiled. "Ooh! Tell her thank you. Where are they?"

He shuffled over to the fridge and pulled out the frozen dish of crayfish and shrimp étouffée. "Driving down the coast. They've never been to Northern California."

During Mardi Gras, Cooper and I had taken a trip down to the LaPlanche home outside of New Orleans. There, Auntie Lee had expressed her excitement for Cooper's new future with me.

"You know . . ." I said, "you gotta take care of yourself. You're about to go through even more shit."

"What's the point?" he muttered, staring at the coffee table.

"No, you're not doing this today." I grabbed his arm and pulled him toward the staircase. "Shower. *Now.* You're not sitting here like this while I'm in this house. Go. And run a brush over your head."

He groaned and shuffled up the stairs.

"I'm shocked Auntie Lee didn't shove you in there herself," I shouted after him.

He groaned again but didn't argue—which worried me more than him shouting back. Cooper wasn't the kind of man to take orders without comment.

I waited at the bottom of the staircase until I heard the shower water running. Then, I headed to the kitchen.

The fridge was filled with food—the LaPlanches believed in butter, salt, and the holy trinity. But Cooper needed simple. I grabbed the carton of eggs and the big tub of precooked rice meant for gumbo and étouffée. Then I dumped coffee into the maker and hit Brew.

He eventually shuffled back into the living room, his hair damp and his face shaven.

"That's better." I offered him a smile as he sat at the breakfast bar smelling of soap and orange blossoms. I set a plate of rice and scrambled eggs before him, then made myself a plate.

He sprinkled seasoned salt and splashed Tabasco over his meal—Cooper may have passed for white, but his taste in food showed his truth. But he barely picked at his breakfast.

I ate in silence for a few minutes, giving him space. Then: "You've been through hell—I get it. But you're still here—"

He flinched and said, "Can we not . . . ?" He shook his head and scratched his jaw. "Sorry. It's just . . . This isn't the life I thought I'd have. Even last year this time, I thought we . . ."

Our happily ever after was supposed to start the day I moved to Haven.

"So, if you don't mind," he said, "let's talk about something else."

I nodded, pushed around rice and eggs with my fork, then said, "One of the day laborers at Lumière was found murdered."

He looked up sharply, his eyes narrowing. "*What?* Who?"

"His name was Emiliano Rivas," I said. "Someone dumped him in the forest not too far from my place." Then I told him all that had happened since Sunday. "Emiliano's widow, Araceli, mentioned that two other men from the site had also disappeared."

Cooper shoved a forkful of rice and eggs into his mouth. After chewing for a moment, he said, "I'm not in the trenches, but I should've heard about this. Ain't nobody said nothing, except for you."

I nodded, then refreshed our cups of coffee. "Dave Kruger."

"What about him?"

I dumped sugar and cream into my mug. "Problematic."

Cooper dumped a teaspoon of sugar into his cup. "The OSHA investigation."

I froze with the cup's rim against my lips. "You knew and yet he still works for you?"

"I didn't find out until two months ago. Ivan did all the background, so if anybody fucked up, it was your uncle. But then the case was dismissed. I had no grounds to fire him."

I stared at him. "He killed a man."

Cooper grunted and ate more of his rice and eggs.

"And then a dead man showed up a stone's throw from my house."

Cooper sighed and set his fork down. "What do you want me to do?"

I opened my mouth and closed it. Then I stared at the ceiling—no answer there. "Don't know yet. Stop exploiting poor people?"

His face darkened. "Is that what you think I'm doing? Exploiting poor people?"

"I . . . don't think you are, personally, but . . . I don't know. I'm handling it, okay?"

"I don't exploit anyone," he growled. "I don't hire the workers directly, Sonny—that's on the contractors. And I make it clear that everyone gets paid fairly, no exceptions. *And* I contract mobile health clinics and baby lawyers to come to the site twice a week. Not just for the workers but for their families and any member of the community who needs that kind of help."

"Fine," I said. "You don't exploit, but if you hear anything, let me know. Okay?"

He nodded and kept his jaw tight.

"I heard you sat with the Monroes at the arraignment this morning."

He dropped his fork and snorted. "Fuck, babe, you want me to eat or not?"

I grinned as I sipped coffee.

"I'm not supporting London. She's a fucking psycho . . ." He gathered rice and eggs on his fork. He chewed, and it took great effort for him to swallow. "I told Lori and Devon that whatever they needed . . ." His eyebrows crumpled, and this time, he let a teardrop tumble down his cheek.

I stared into my cup of coffee, biting my cheek again to keep from crying.

"They're doing Mack's autopsy today," he said. "Then I guess I'll plan her . . . her . . ." He stared at his hands. "If I'd just divorced her, and not cared about what Mackenzie wanted . . ."

"But Mackenzie was blackmailing you," I pointed out.

Cooper scowled. "*Money.* I gave in to her cuz I thought losing money was more important than losing you. If I'd just followed my heart—"

"You'd be broke."

He shook his head, then pushed back his hair. "But then you'd be here, and Mack would be alive. Maybe even Xander would be alive."

My chin was quivering, my tears standing on the brink of my heart. I left my stool at the breakfast bar and wandered over to the patio window. I gazed out to the shore, to the waves rolling in and rolling out. Once I'd gained enough control: "When I first met Auntie Lee, during all that was happening with Autumn and Royalty, she told me, 'Tracasse-toi pas.'"

"'Don't worry,'" Cooper said, coming to stand beside me.

"But it meant more than that," I said, squinting out at the sea. "It meant, 'It's gonna work out in the end, no matter what that end is. Enjoy life as much as you can. Be calm.' So . . . tracasse-toi pas, Cooper." I squeezed his shoulder.

He fought back tears as he watched those waves roll in and out.

This was not the moment to ask to see Mackenzie's room like I'd planned to. This was not the time to mention that his daughter could've been involved in a sex trafficking ring. That revelation was as far from "tracasse-toi pas" as one could get.

Cooper cleared his throat and swiped at his eyes and nose. He leveled his shoulders and said, "How are you on money? I know you were supposed to be . . . We were supposed to be . . . I was supposed to be actively helping you with everything. Including your mom."

There was a memory care facility in Sableport—but Cooper had offered to pay only if I'd left Haven. Now, with everything like it was . . .

"She's better this week. But . . ." I shrugged.

"The offer still stands. And that offer includes home care." Cooper's mother, Sophia, had suffered with dementia. He'd provided her with in-home care and an occupational therapist, and she'd done well until the afternoon she climbed into her nurse's Prius. Days later, California Highway Patrol had found Sophia behind the wheel of the car, dead, a hundred miles east of Palm Desert. He remembered that pain.

"And when the time comes," I said, "I'll take your offer to help. I *did* get paid today. And he threw in a bonus for my work on Xander's—"

But Cooper didn't wince. His wife was in jail for that murder. Her pictures had been removed for good reason.

Together, we washed dishes just as we'd done in our life as a couple. Then he poured more coffee into his cup.

"I should head out," I said, grabbing my bag from the couch.

"Okay."

I hesitated, unsure how to feel. Part of me was relieved—staying would only complicate things. But another part of me—the part that still remembered the man he used to be—felt like I was leaving him behind when he needed me the most.

"In other news," I said, making my way toward the foyer, "not sure if you've heard, but Honor Butler's back home."

He grunted. "I know I'm supposed to care about that, but . . ."

"She and Mackenzie were close," I said.

A veil draped over his face, and his shoulders tensed.

"They weren't close?" I asked.

"Girls," he said, shrugging. "They loved each other on Thursday morning and hated each other by lunchtime. I stopped getting involved." He paused, then added, "I let London deal with all that. Maybe that's why my kid is dead."

I wanted to take Cooper in my arms, hug him, and say "There, there," but my anger had heated up to "simmer." If he'd been better at a lot of things, our lives wouldn't be shit right now. This master of the universe in real estate development should've worked that hard at being a parent and husband. He should've noted what wasn't working and done something about it. He'd never let one of his projects languish the way his family had. He needed to acknowledge all the shit he'd done that brought all of us—including the poor Monroe family—to ruin. The masquerade had failed, and the truth had resulted in a bloody mess.

"I'm still gonna get Figgy back," I said. "The family that has her rammed their minivan into Giovanni's Sentra. This ain't over, okay?"

He smiled and light found his eyes. "I'd like her back, now more than ever."

He touched the small of my back and that brief three seconds of physical touch sent fire up my spine. I thought about kissing him that first time on the Ferris wheel. Then I thought about kissing Brady Kwon at Lucy's.

There was no comparison.

I loved Cooper Sutton.

And I didn't know what to do about that.

17.

Cooper bristled at my saying "exploiting poor people." But then, using cheap labor to build nice things without offering that labor force benefits, security, or safety measures was the very definition of exploitation. Desperate people did desperate things—from leaving behind their homeland in search of a better life in a strange country to a development titan hiring as many workers as he could to finish a project as quick and cheap as possible.

No, Cooper didn't hire Emiliano and the other men directly—he was right about that. Contractors hired those workers, including Emiliano—he was right about that too. But Cooper didn't kick anyone off the site for doing wrong—contractors knew that if they came in or under budget, they'd land another job with Sutton Partners. Unskilled laborers would help that happen.

The file room still scared me—on my first trip without Ivan, I hadn't used the door stop to prop the door open, and I'd locked myself in. But I'd learned two valuable lessons that day. *Always take your cell phone* and *Always use a doorstop.*

Right now, I did both—I'd put back Keely Butler's thick file after going through her encyclopedia of aliases, arrests, and murky connections only to pull it back out now. For the second time in less than twenty-four hours, I was searching her past for another connection: Honor's father.

Honor was a vulnerable girl—those who found themselves being trafficked tended to be. Some victims had experienced physical, emotional, or sexual abuse in their Before Life. Unstable homes, substance abuse, domestic violence, poverty, poor mental health . . . Honor had run away from home several times before finally disappearing back in April.

Why?

Keely was a fucked-up human being, but what about Honor's father? If he'd been around, maybe he would've been able to counter some of his babymomma's dysfunction, providing Honor with the attention she often sought. If he'd been around, maybe Honor wouldn't have developed the emotional vacuum she'd eventually fill with older men.

There he was, on the last page of Keely's dossier: Javier Taufua. When we'd first met, Keely had told me that he'd been deported to Mexico, but according to PeopleFinder, Taufua lived in San Diego. He was born in July, fixed motorcycles, and had an honorable discharge from the navy.

The picture on PeopleFinder showed a broad-shouldered man with dark skin and thick black hair tied back into a ponytail. His features—that nose, that brow, the chin—screamed Samoan. Even his last name, Taufua, was *not* Mexican, which was what Keely had always claimed he was.

I called the listed phone number.

The line rang twice before a deep voice answered. "Jav here."

I cleared my throat and said, "Mr. Taufua, hi. My name is Alyson Rush, and I'm a private investigator up in Haven. I'm calling about Keely Butler."

There was a pause followed by a weary sigh. "What's this about?"

"It's about Honor," I said carefully. "Keely's daughter . . . *Your* daughter."

He laughed but not with joy. "Allegedly."

I paused before saying, "Sounds like you and Keely aren't on good terms. I'm looking through my background on Miss Butler and there's enough that I'm concerned about Honor's present and future. Any insight from you would—"

"What's this about?" he asked again. "Keely trying to set me up like she did before?"

"This is more about your daughter and not necessarily—"

"Keely swore she couldn't get pregnant, but then she did, like immediately. Did she tell you that? Did she tell you that she wouldn't even let me see the baby—just demanded that I send child support? She tell you that?"

"No," I said. "Did you send child support?"

"Yup," he said, "hoping that one day she'd let me in. Nope. I even thought about suing for custody but . . . lawyers cost money, and I already didn't make enough as is. All she does is lie. She could tell me the sun was shining, and I still wouldn't believe her."

"So, how do you know that Honor is your daughter?" I asked. "I mean . . . Keely's told all of Haven that Honor's father is Mexican—"

"What?"

"Yeah."

"Cuz she sees a vowel at the end of my name?"

"Probably."

"Cuz my skin's brown?"

"Probably."

"I'm Samoan American."

"Yeah. I guessed that."

"But Keely won't let me do a damn DNA test," he growled. "Said it was insulting, like I was calling her a whore. Look, Miss Rush, I knew Keely for maybe a month before she told me she was pregnant. She claimed the baby was mine, and I . . . I tried to do the right thing. But I'm not Mexican, and I'm pretty sure that I'm not Honor's father.

"I'm ashamed to even admit this, but . . ." He took in a breath and exhaled. "I've never even met my daughter in person."

I frowned. "Really?"

"Nope. I have absolutely no connection to her—except for the money I send every month. But no calls from Honor, no nothing. I stopped sending Christmas gifts—I've never received a thank-you or a candy cane. It's like I don't even exist." He chuckled. "But my wish has obviously come true."

"How?"

"I prayed that Keely would have a miserable life, and from what I can tell, she has."

"Your daughter—and that's why I called. She's in danger, and I'm trying to understand what led her to run away from home several times."

He grunted. "Do you know Keely?"

"Yes."

"There's your answer right there."

After ending my call with Javier Taufua, I stared at the phone in my hand, then looked outside my window. The wind was picking up, and the air now looked gritty. I thought about Keely's story as my fingers tapped the edge of the desk. Why would she lie? If she wanted Honor to check a box, she still could—just not as Hispanic.

My phone buzzed again. The name on the screen made my stomach twist.

ICE Tank Goffman.

He and I never got along. I believed in due process. He believed in Guantanamo Bay. I believed everyone should have health care. He believed that only the strongest should survive—and if you couldn't hack it, he shouldn't have to pay your way. He thought women were too weak and emotional to be law enforcement officers. That our brains were too small, our hands were too tiny, our vision of the world too small.

I absolutely hated the man and didn't feel a thing when he was ambushed by his second ex-wife's brothers for hitting her. A woman—me—had saved his life that day, using my tiny girl hands to press his chest long enough to stop the bleeding, using tampons to stanch the manic flow of blood. Yeah, my small hands carried out the plan that my small brain came up with.

"I owe you my life," Tank had said from his hospital bed, "and whatever you need, I'll come through for you. No expiration date."

I never thought I'd use the ICE Tank chit—he left the LAPD for ICE, and I moved to Haven and was now investigating the murder of an undocumented man whose prints weren't in the system. Here we were.

"What's up, Tank?" I asked now.

"Same shit, different day," he said in his gravelly voice. "Just found a bunch of migrants hiding in an old boxcar, six minutes from death. How's the ocean?"

"Cold."

"You should join me down here. You speak Español, don't you?"

"I do, but no thanks."

"You still got that bleeding heart," he said, chuckling. "That'll get you dead down here."

"A hot gun and a stripper in Mar Vista almost got *you* dead, though."

"Yeah," Tank said, "but we would've been able to find her. These people I deal with? They're fucking ghosts."

Almost 10 million pedestrians crossed from Mexico into California last year, and more than 26 million drove. While 1.8 million immigrants living in California were undocumented, the vast majority of immigrants in California were either citizens or had some other legal residency status. California had more immigrants than any other state, and not just from Latin America: The Philippines, China, India, and Vietnam were all next in line, and in that order.

"What you're dealing with in Haven," Tank continued, "is a fucking cakewalk, baby."

I bristled—because a part of me knew that he was right—and also the term *cakewalk* . . . Problematic.

"These vaquetones and chequadors working for the coyotes," Tank was saying. "They use the same equipment we use. Cell phones, night vision scopes, two-way radios. They get rooms near the border and set up telescopes for a better view, using kids to distract agents and shit. Then they get over here, stay in safe houses or no-tell motels, who are in on it, and then they're free to fucking rape grandmas and preschoolers—"

"Like the Americans raping grandmas and preschoolers?" I rolled my eyes. "Whatever. I'm not calling to argue about immigration reform—"

"Do you know how much these coyote fucks are charging people to cross? Almost three grand. On a good day, they're bringing about five hundred people into this country. *Three grand each.* You do the math."

"Thank you for taking a moment, then, to help me out," I said. "I'm just up here, surfing and cakewalking—"

"Do you think I like stopping folks, arresting them and breaking up families?" he asked.

Yes.

"You think I feel any joy finding dead illegal aliens in the fucking desert or in the trunk of a car?"

Yes.

As a matter of fact, he said he loved these things on his Facebook page last year. He even included video of him and other agents storming a strawberry farm outside Ventura. More than 100k "likes."

God bless America.

"I know you don't think so," Tank continued, "but I'm just trying to protect Americans from what happened to my own mother."

Tank's mother, Helen, was murdered in a home-invasion robbery. The police arrested the four bad guys. One of them was an undocumented person from Ecuador. The other three were homegrown white boys from Lancaster, California. So where was Tank's vim and vigor for *those* three assholes?

But I wouldn't call him out on this. I already had five years ago.

"Hey, I get it," he said now. "The rich guys rely on cheap labor. These people just wanna work. The white guys create the demand. Anyway . . ."

He exhaled. "I called to give you a heads-up. Got a print hit on your John Doe, and once I'm back in the office, I'll send it over. If there's a jacket on this guy, I'll send it too." He paused, then said, "Sometimes this job calls for brass balls, Rush. Guess that's why you're now working in some soft town by the beach." He laughed. "Guess that's why you're calling me."

My skin flushed, and my phone creaked in my hand from holding it so tight. "I'm calling you now because you were grateful that I saved your life with a box of jumbo tampons, and you told me to reach out whenever I needed something."

Silence, and then: "I'll send the file later tonight. See ya, Rush."

The line went dead.

I sat there for a moment, the phone still pressed to my ear. My chest felt heavy, my pulse raggedy. How many hours had my life shortened talking to ICE Tank?

Didn't matter. He had the answer that I needed.

18.

During the drive to Sableport, I stopped at an ATM and withdrew $500 in mixed bills. Back in the truck, I grabbed an old *Fun Guide to Haven* from the back seat and slipped $300 between the pages describing the pier.

My phone vibrated with an incoming call—Brady. "Hey."

"That family murder up in Creekwood," he said.

"Yeah?"

"Bad romance. The shooter was the ex-boyfriend of the dead seventeen-year-old. The baby she carried wasn't his, and he was pissed off about it. So he went to the house with some guns, and that was that."

"So . . . unrelated to Emiliano Rivas's murder?"

"Fucking awful, but totally unrelated." He paused, then said, "So, do you wanna—"

"Thanks for the update." My pulse kicked hard in my chest. "Gotta hop off. I'll check in later."

"Oh. Okay—"

I hit END CALL.

Café Sable looked like every Pacific Ocean–side café on the coast. Distressed dark wood walls, matching wood tables and chairs shaded by big red umbrellas. At this time of day, tourists with their sand-covered kids took up most of the outside seating. That was fine—I hadn't come here for the "world-famous fish and chips." I came here for *her*, the redhead wearing the yellow shirt and standing at the hostess desk. Her plastic nametag said CAITLIN, and she matched the picture I'd found on Honor Butler's phone. The same young woman who'd been at brunch with Honor and Liam.

She smiled at me, poor thing, and welcomed me to Café Sable. "Just one today?"

"Just one," I said, "but I'm here to talk to you."

Confusion made her brows crinkle.

"About Honor Butler," I said.

Her bow-shaped lips went "Oh," and she blushed all the way down to her dermis. Then she turned to a coworker wiping down menus. "Can you watch the desk for five minutes?"

Five minutes. *So optimistic, Caitlin.*

Neither of us spoke as we strolled on the pathway away from the beach.

"Are you a cop?" she asked.

"Not anymore," I said. "I'm a private investigator, and I'm looking into all that happened with Honor."

"She *wanted* to do it," Caitlin said. "Anything to make Liam happy." Then she told me everything Honor had already told me.

"Who is Big Baby?" I asked.

"He was the driver."

"He got a real name?"

"Satan? Lucifer?"

"And Orville Klein?"

"A client. He really liked Honor. He was into rough stuff—she said she could handle it."

"And Big Poppa D?"

Caitlin frowned. "He's our nail tech—he's, like, really good with acrylics." She stopped in her step. "Hey, am I gonna get arrested or something? I didn't force Honor to do anything." Her eyes were hard and tear filled. "If anyone should get in trouble, it should be Liam. I was smart enough to break up with him last year. He tried it with me, but I'm not trying to be anybody's pretty prossie."

Pretty prossie. Honor had mentioned that term.

I said, "Explain to me, then, how you and Mackenzie—"

"Ohmigod." Caitlin turned away from me, and soon, her shoulders shuddered as she hid her face in her hands. Neither of us had tissues, and she dried her tears on the tail of her shirt.

She pushed out several breaths and blinked out at the ocean. "I miss her so much," she whispered. "Can't believe that she's . . . she's . . ." She looked over her shoulder at me. "Did Liam get arrested for that yet? I haven't heard from him."

My heart boomed. "Liam? Arrested? For what? Pimping?"

She dabbed at her still-leaking eyes. "No. Drugs. He was Mackie's connect."

Had Liam—not London—given Mackenzie Sutton the drugs that had killed her?

Seven minutes later, I parked at the Office of the Medical Examiner.

India was showering—she'd just completed the autopsy of a man found floating in an estuary. She wouldn't be able to smell a rose if she stood in the middle of Descanso Garden in the middle of summer.

I sat in India's guest chair and flipped through the notes I'd jotted down in my pad, updating questions with much-needed answers.

India swooshed in wearing clean blue scrubs and smelling like shea butter and, unfortunately, the dead guy from the estuary.

"I know, I know. Give me a minute." She grabbed the phone from her desk and called Toshi, her loc girl, to schedule a last-minute shampoo and trim. After she ended the call, she loudly exhaled and said, "Excuse my piquant aroma."

I grinned. "Has Anthony had the privilege of smelling you after you've autopsied a floater?"

She laughed. "Babe, I can't show him everything at once. Gotta save a little mystery for later, after he puts a ring on it."

My eyebrows lifted. "So y'all are moving in that direction?"

She shimmied her shoulders. "Possibly . . ." She logged on to the computer, clicked and clicked around until she found what she was looking for. "The DNA from the toothbrush that Kwon brought in matches with Emiliano Rivas." She pushed back from the desk.

"Tell me something that I *don't* know," I said, twirling the pen around my fingers.

"The fiber that we found in Emiliano's ligature mark is made of polypropylene. Could've come from packaging, transportation, upholstery, clothing . . . It's flexible. It's heat resistant."

I scribbled notes as she talked. "Has forensics figured out what those fibers came from?"

"Not yet." India squinted at me. "I'm confused."

"About . . . ?"

"About you still asking questions. You did your part—Emiliano Rivas is in one of those drawers back there, found."

My cheeks burned. "I know he's been found. I'm just trying to clean up a few loose—"

"Trying to find out who killed him isn't a loose string. If I know Ivan, I know that he sure as hell ain't paying you to work this case anymore."

I cocked an eyebrow. "I like cleanliness."

"You like *control*," India countered, "and your new job doesn't give you that."

I lifted my chin to counter her counter but sank in my seat. "I can't leave it behind yet."

Chippy's was located in a strip mall alongside a used bookstore and a dialysis center. Nothing like watching bespectacled old ladies loading their old Buicks with bags of books next to a pickup on big wheels and antennae flapping with American flags parked beside an ambulance loading out a patient needing their blood cleaned with an artificial kidney.

The woman behind Chippy's counter looked like Reba McEntire. She narrowed her eyes at me. "What can I do for you, Officer?"

I cocked my head. "Not a cop anymore."

"You still walk like one," Gun Shop Reba said.

"Ah. Let's pretend, then."

"Fine. I'm busy."

I chuckled and looked around the now-empty store. "That's pretty good. I'm Sonny Rush."

"And I'm Bev, owner of this fine establishment. Any information I share will cost ya."

"Good, cuz I can pay." I found the picture of the black glitter and pink rose gun on my phone. "How many of these have you sold in the last year?"

She slid on her reading glasses and stared at the picture. "Only one, and as you can see, it's pretty ugly."

"Yeah, I see it bright and clear. Can you tell me who bought it?"

"Five hundred."

"Three."

She shifted away from me and logged on to the countertop computer. "Here you go." She swiveled the computer screen in my direction.

"And here *you* go." I slid over the cash-thick fun guide to Haven. I didn't bother reading the screen—just took a picture of the record with my phone. "Thanks so much, Bev."

As I left Chippy's, my phone vibrated with a text message from Tank.

Here's your guy!

But then the circle of reception turned and turned and turned.

Only one more bar. I needed just one—
I bumped into a body built like a brick wall.
That body's voice said, "Watch it, pretty lady."
Embarrassed, I looked up and said, "Oh!"
Brady Kwon smiled down at me. "What are you doing here?"

19.

Silent, we walked side by side, not speaking, until:

"Why didn't you mention that you were driving up?"

I flashed a frown. "I have to tell you where I'm going now?"

"No," Brady said, "well—"

"I kissed you one time, and now, all of a sudden—"

"It's not that," he said.

"What is it, then?"

Brady asked that I wait for him while he talked to Bev about the ugly black-and-pink gun. Armed with a badge, he didn't need a bribe and came out of the store with the same information that had cost me a *Fun Guide to Haven* and $300.

Brady returned to me and smiled. "If you'd only waited."

I rolled my eyes and followed him across the street. The Sableport-Haven Division of Mendocino County Sheriff's Office was a tan building that could've doubled as a public library. Behind the grating, the windows were dulled from salt and sand, and any light that survived to brighten the space was dulled. Inside, the desks and chairs looked *Barney Miller*—old—and not one wall had been left bare.

Brady led me down the short, carpeted hallway to his office. He closed the door, then said, "I thought we were working together on some things—"

"We are—"

"And you're telling me everything?"

"I'm telling you *enough*," I said, heat prickling my neck. "Am I gonna tell you how many times I'm gonna stir the batter after I add eggs? No, but I *will* tell you when I'm about to slide it into the oven."

He stared at me, then sat down behind his desk. "You're right. I'm sorry. I'm trippin'."

Which was why I didn't date cops. I'd barely broken the rule by kissing this one, and now, a usually on-the-level, perfectly rational man was pouting because I didn't tell him that I was working my cases.

I settled into the guest chair and said, "What's going on?"

Brady tapped his desktop computer awake and turned the monitor in my direction. "Remember when Araceli said Emiliano left to get propane and never came back home?" He pressed play on a video.

"7-Eleven?" I asked.

"Yeah," Brady said, "the one on Coral Ave, a little over a quarter mile from the Rivas house."

In the video, Emiliano Rivas was lugging the empty propane tank to the store's locker and waiting as the clerk unlocked the cage. After he'd exchanged one empty can for a full one, Emiliano carried the propane tank to his truck parked near the locker. He stopped to talk to someone off-screen.

"Who is he talking to?" I asked.

The clip ended.

Brady said, "Don't know."

"No views of the other side of the parking lot?" I asked.

Brady said, "Nope."

"Play it again, please?"

Propane tank in. Propane tank out. Talking to an off-screen stranger.

"Okay," I said. "He's smiling, which means he may have known this person."

Brady said, "Not threatened."

"Not necessarily," I said. "Could've been someone offering to help him or making a joke about seeing him struggling or . . ." I tapped my finger against my lip. "Is there a traffic cam on this street?"

"Nope."

"Any other businesses?"

"Not with working cameras."

I tapped my lip one last time. "So the gun."

"She tell you the owner?" Brady asked.

"Yep."

"Bev is a hard nut to crack," Brady said. "You threaten her or something?"

"Charm," I said, grinning. "And three hundred dollars."

"Sonny."

"I'm not a cop," I said. "I can offer cash incentives for playing the game. And that's all this is, right? Cops versus robbers? And speaking of ugly guns, who the hell is Jaylayne Merkley?"

Brady logged in to the DMV database and typed in the name that had been linked to the glitter-rose Glock. He tilted his head at the picture on the screen. "Whoever she is lives down in Haven, on Azure Way."

She was a middle-aged white lady with lidded blue eyes, a round cheerful face, and big brown hair. She looked like she enjoyed chardonnay in tumblers and black-glitter guns with pink roses on the grip. She had another name on record.

"Merkley is her maiden name," Brady said. "She used to be Jaylayne . . . *Kruger*."

Our eyes met and my mouth formed into an O.

"As in the *sister* of Dave Kruger?" I asked. "The foreman at Lumière?"

"As in the ex-*wife* . . ." Brady tabbed over to the first window on his computer that had listed Jaylayne Merkley as the gun's owner. He scrolled down . . . down . . . and stopped. "She reported the gun stolen a month ago."

"Do you think Dave stole it," I asked, "scratched off the serial number, used it while kidnapping Emiliano, and the gun dropped out of his pocket when he dumped him in the woods?"

Brady grunted, gave a half-assed shrug. "Whoever dropped the gun was an amateur."

"Who drops a gun and leaves the damned thing?" I asked.

"Someone in a hurry."

"Someone too scared to go back for it. And why did they bring it in the first place? The guy was strangled to death, not shot."

"And strangulation is pretty personal," Brady added.

"Maybe," I said, "Emiliano and Jaylayne were having an affair and Dave caught them and lost it, grabbed whatever-that-was made of polypropylene fiber, wrapped it around Emiliano's neck, and choked him."

Brady grunted. "Maybe."

"Any prints found on the gun?" I asked.

"Nope, clean," he said, rubbing the bridge of his nose. "And you like Dave Kruger for this because . . . ?"

"Because of the dead day laborer who fell from the scaffolding at Kruger's former worksite."

"But Dave didn't push that guy, did he?"

I opened my mouth, closed it, then said, "No." I huffed out a breath. "You're right—it's a stretch."

"But it's not impossible," he said, twirling his pen around his fingers. "I'm just having a hard time finding the 'why.'"

"Will you talk to Jaylayne?" I asked.

Brady nodded, then started moving files around on his desk. "The missing men at Lumière's construction site—the ones Araceli Rivas mentioned."

"Yes? What about them?" I sat up straighter, a dog waiting for a treat.

He found two sheets of paper. "Yeriel Barada and Jared Lebron, cousins from Puerto Rico. Both men are alive, working as welders. They moved down to Temecula to work on another spa project. They didn't give notice—just ditched one day and never looked back."

"So they weren't like Emiliano, then."

"Nope."

I flipped my notebook pages back to my talk with Caitlin at Café Sable.

"Sonny," Brady said.

"Um-hmm?"

"Why are you still doing this?"

I paused in my page flipping and looked up at him.

He was staring at me, his eyes filled with wonder and something else . . .

"Am I making you sad?" I asked, my head cocked.

He nodded.

"Why?"

"You were freed from this burden—"

"I don't see any of this as a burden—"

"Bullshit."

I sent my now-nervous gaze back to the notepad. "So I found one of Honor's so-called friends, Caitlin Hodges. She works at Café Sable as a hostess. I asked her about some of the names I found in Honor's phone and money apps. Are you interested, or do you wanna waste time pitying me?"

"It's not pity. I'll run the names you give me and let you know what I find."

"You can't run them now?" I asked.

"You wanna supervise me?" he asked, eyebrow cocked.

I laughed. "I thought you knew me by now. Of *course* I wanna supervise you. Duh."

He didn't smile. "I'll run them later. I got other shit to do right now." He paused and added, "I may not be you, but I *do* know how to investigate—"

I held up my hands. "I just want—"

"A one-hundred-percent clearance," he finished. "But you don't have to see any of this to the end. That's my job—"

"I was hired—"

"Honor's paying you?"

"No."

"Did you do as Araceli Rivas asked? Find her husband?"

"Yes."

"Then you have a one-hundred-percent clearance."

I blinked at him. My throat tightened, trapping the response I wanted to give. Because he was right. Me wanting and needing to fix things the way *I* wanted and needed them fixed? Yes, it was a burden—and I didn't know how to put it down or let someone else take it from me.

I cleared my throat and said, "You may find it troubling, and useful, to look for this Liam asshole while you're figuring out how Mackenzie Sutton died."

"Why?" He leaned far away from his desk, far away from me. He was now done with the "Sonny" part of his day.

"According to Caitlin," I said, "Liam was Mackenzie's drug connect."

Brady said, "Word?"

"Yeah."

He made a note on his notepad.

My phone buzzed with a notification.

Upload completed.

I tapped the picture that ICE Tank had sent me—and gasped at the image on my phone. "Ohmigod."

Brady said, "What?"

"I got a hit on the fingerprint confirming Emiliano Rivas—"

"I won't even ask how you—"

I showed him the picture that ICE Tank had emailed.

Brady frowned. "Okay. Yeah. So? That's Emiliano."

I shook my head. "Look again."

Brady squinted. "I don't get it. That's Araceli's husband and . . ." He looked at the picture long enough to see the rest. *"Who . . . ?"*

The picture of Emiliano Rivas showed the man's same hard brown eyes, that small scar in his left eyebrow, and the tatted neck. But the name associated with this man?

Kelvin Alamo Quintano.

Born in Jalisco, Mexico, in 1998, not 2000. He was twenty-five years old, not twenty-three. His first arrest: June 2020 for burglary. His last arrest: December 2021 for assault. He was who he was . . . until he became Emiliano Rivas.

Brady sat back in his chair, then stared at me.

For a moment, I said nothing as I stared back at him. Then: "Why did he change his name? He hadn't broken any laws since 2021?" But I already knew the answer to my own question even as Brady said—

"He was probably scared that his record would get him deported quicker."

"Do you think Araceli knows?" I asked.

Brady shook his head. "The woman makes snowmen out of old books." He pushed out a breath, then said, "And now I'm asking you to stop digging on this. You go around asking questions about Kelvin Quintano to the wrong people and you could either put yourself or this case in peril."

"Peril?" I asked, eyes bugged. "You're talking to me like I'm some blonde who runs a cat grooming business and found a chopped-off head in her shampoo bowl. I'm a fucking—"

"*Brunette* private detective who, yes, found out a shit ton of information," Brady admitted. "But now I'm asking that you let go and trust me to do my job. Can you do that?"

"Run Liam's name," I asked. "Right now."

"No," he said, shaking his head.

"Fine. I will." I pulled my laptop from my bag.

"C'mon, Sonny." He sighed and reached over his desk for my laptop.

"Stop." I slapped his hand and typed Liam Dyer into PeopleFinder. Up came a record and a picture of a douchey blond with classic Abercrombie & Fitch vibes combined with Justin Bieber without the talent. He lived on Spindrift Avenue. "Is that street in a nice neighborhood?"

Brady nodded, his eyes glued to my laptop.

I typed in the address: The house stood high on the bluffs of Sableport. Five regular-size homes could fit into this monument to Italian marble and glass. The owner—and Liam's father—was Nigel Dyer, software chip–tech magnate worth a billion dollars. I clicked to open Liam's past history with the law.

"Arrested for drug possession, driving under the influence, assault—oh look, you were the arresting officer when he got picked up for attempted arson. Looks like Liam never went to court for any of these things. Charges dropped. Every. Single. Time." I gazed at Brady. "You fed the beast too."

He blushed but said nothing.

I turned my attention back to the record. "Oh, look! Here are a few articles related to him. Great headlines. Sableport Man Arrested for Illegal Firearm Possession. Ooh, you're quoted in Boy Hospitalized After Being Struck by Sedan. 'I do not believe drugs or alcohol were factors in this accident.' That's what you said. And yet you want *me* to trust *you*?" I cocked my head and stared at him, managing to not burn him with the fire in my gaze. "Are you fucking *kidding* me, Brady?"

He shook his head, squeezed the bridge of his nose. "There's nothing I can say to . . . to . . ."

"You *should* be embarrassed," I said, closing my laptop. "You all look the other way because boys will be boys, and now he's pimping girls up and down the coast—"

"We haven't proven that yet—"

"*We?* You're not *interested* in proving shit because he's a rich kid with a rich daddy. Why else would he be allowed to terrorize young women up here and down in Haven?"

Brady held out his arms. "Because life isn't fair? C'mon, Sonny. What do you want me to say? Stop pretending that Los Angeles prosecutes and arrests fairly—"

"They don't, but I didn't look the other way—"

"Autumn Suarez isn't dead because *you* looked the other way?"

My head snapped back as though he'd punched me.

"That came out wrong," he said, his eyes wide.

I glared at him now, fully and without mercy.

"Sonny, I didn't mean . . . I meant . . ."

"What's going on, fellas?" Will McCann asked out in the lobby.

Hearing his partner's approach made Brady tab out of the window for Emiliano-Kelvin.

I closed my laptop and shoved it back in my bag.

Will McCann opened the door to the office. "We have a visitor," he said. Grinning at me, he sauntered to his desk wearing a gray suit and cranberry-printed tie. "The illustrious, yet disgraced Sonny Rush. What trouble have you brought us, dear lady?" The office now smelled like his lemons-sage-pepper-scented cologne.

I blinked at him. "I was just in the neighborhood."

Brady said, "Anything else, Ms. Rush?"

"Nope." I stood from his guest chair.

"Good." Brady also stood. "I'll be reaching out to your contact in Immigration—"

"For what?" McCann asked.

My heart plunged to my socks—if Brady talked directly to Tank, I was about to be iced out of ICE and out of my own investigation. An investigation he hadn't really cared about until I started turning over dead soil to find new life. There was nothing I could say about it, not with McCann right there, not with my badge in a desk down in Los Angeles.

"Anything else?" Brady asked, hands on his hips.

"No," I said, coolly. "We're done here." I paused, then added, "With everything."

20.

And that included him pretending that he liked and respected me. No—I was a means to his ends, and he was taking advantage of my need to close cases.

I hopped in the Bronco, ready to drive back down to Haven.

Finding the truth and righting wrongs was my destiny. And Brady Kwon was asking me to stuff all that, all of me, into a closet and do . . . *what*? Follow around law-abiding yet cheating husbands for the rest of my career?

I rolled the windows down to air out the haze in my head. The ocean, blue and endless, stretched out to my right, and for a moment, I imagined walking out to the sea and letting the ocean's power pull me under. But that's when I saw her reflection in my side mirror.

Araceli Rivas driving a sleek silver Lexus.

With that cherry Kool-Aid hair and the oversize sunglasses perched on her nose, yeah, I could tell that this was Emiliano-Kelvin's widow. The light turned green, and she followed me through the intersection, then changed lanes.

When the hell did she get a Lexus?

She switched lanes and raced past me.

I followed her, letting two cars separate us.

Maybe I should've gone home. Maybe I should've let her disappear into Sableport and written her off as just another woman with a complicated past. But yeah, that wasn't me, especially after learning that her husband had lied about his name—and probably his entire past. Araceli Rivas could drive wherever the hell she wanted and in whatever car she wanted. But I didn't become a detective to mind my own business, did I?

We rolled past downtown Sableport, past all the restaurants and wineries. The silver Lexus turned onto a side road that wound up the cliffs and toward a vantage point overlooking the Pacific.

Araceli parked the Lexus on the side of the road.

I parked a little ways back and killed the engine. I lifted my phone and tapped record.

Araceli left the car wearing an orange-and-yellow sundress and walked toward the edge of the bluff, hands clenched to her chest.

The door to a black Dodge Charger opened—Emiliano-Kelvin had also driven a black Charger—and a man climbed out. He was short and wore a Phillies baseball jersey. I couldn't see his eye color, but he looked like the mechanic from Liberty Tires & Brakes, where Araceli worked.

Araceli's face lit up seeing him.

He wiped the tears from her cheeks.

She dropped her head before he lifted her chin.

They hugged.

His hands dropped down to her ass.

This was not a church hug, no, ma'am. Not with his hands squeezing her rump like a loaf of bread.

Araceli wrapped her arms around his neck and buried her face in his shoulder. Then she tipped her head back and kissed him. That kiss deepened, and they clung to each other like no one else in the world existed.

Holy shit.

I muttered "What the hell?" not caring that I was recording this.

How long was long enough for mourning?

Araceli had officially been a widow for two days now, and now, here she was . . .

But then again, what had been her relationship with Emiliano before he drove to 7-Eleven for propane? A happy marriage. Yeah, everyone is happily married when faced with the worst. Just like everyone lit up a room or gave sweaters off their backs once they were found dead. There were no unhappy marriages or assholes in cemeteries.

Araceli and this Matais guy had something going on. Fine. But did that "something" lead to Emiliano's death?

The kiss ended, and Araceli stepped back. She brushed her hair behind her ear and said something that I couldn't hear. Phillies walked her to the Lexus and then returned to the Dodge.

I didn't follow either car.

Was this new love? Renewed love? Dangerous love? Did this man know Emiliano Rivas? Did Matais the mechanic *kill* Emiliano Rivas?

I found Araceli's Instagram page and saw that eight thousand people followed her. I wouldn't go through each profile to find the dude she'd just kissed—I had already tapped on ten and was ready to tap out.

In her latest post, she held a blue urn and wiped away a tear as the caption stated that funeral services would only be family, but anyone could give to the GoFundMe.

No—Araceli Rivas's love life was no longer any of my business, but . . .

As I drove back to Haven, I needed background noise, and little did I know: The soundtrack of *Hamilton* was not the perfect pick. Too much similarity in the musical's main character not being satisfied and Araceli Rivas retreating to the arms of her mystery man. That kiss replayed in my head, a bad movie I couldn't turn off.

After hitting replay on "Satisfied" eight times, I finally pulled into my driveway.

Giovanni and Elliott were standing in the space between my place and theirs. Both men were frowning, their arms crossed.

"Uh-oh. Who dropped the baby on her head?" I cracked, grinning at the unhappy couple.

The two men exchanged glances.

Giovanni rolled his eyes.

Elliott forced himself to smile and flicked his wrist. "It's nothing."

Giovanni huffed a breath. "How can it be 'nothing' after you've made it into a 'thing'?"

I blinked at him. "What happened?"

Giovanni opened his mouth to respond.

Elliott said "*Nothing*" louder this time.

Giovanni glared at the peat stuck beneath his shoes, then said, "I'm gonna check on . . ." He stomped up the steps to his porch and ducked inside their house.

With his arms still crossed, and his jaw set into a clamp, Elliott paced and glared at the front door to his house.

"What did Haven do to you today?" I asked, eyebrow cocked.

"According to him?" Elliott said. "Everything."

"And he's mad because you're determined to make Haven heaven."

Elliott stopped pacing and glared at me. "I gave up everything to make Haven heaven."

"But is Haven more important than . . . ?" I gestured to the couple's home.

"Why can't he try harder?" Elliott asked.

"Because Haven hurts," I said, wincing. "This place with its cutesy shops and its cute little pier? It's a fucking lie, with poison and daggers. The few Black and brown people here are the canaries in this coal mine, and our bodies are literally being left in these woods warning y'all about the poison and the daggers, but you can't look at anything except the glass beach and the dog statue made of seashells."

Elliott started pacing again. "San Jose was a hellhole, Sonny, and Gio *now* has this romantic view of that fucking pit. I remember it, though. There were thirty-two murders in San Jose in the last year—"

"And I've been in Haven for less than a month," I said, "and in that time, at least four people have been killed a mile apart. People that you knew personally, not as stories on the news."

He rolled his head on his neck. "I didn't know the man found in the forest—"

"Fucking A, Elliott," I snapped. "That's not my point."

Giovanni returned to the porch. "He knows what you mean. He's just being willfully obtuse."

Elliott snorted, and said, "And you're being a—"

"A what?" Giovanni asked, stomping back down the porch's step.

"Guys," I said, both arms out. "Let's take a breath."

"You want your happily ever after?" Giovanni asked him. "Go for it."

"'But I won't be there,'" Elliott said. He turned to me. "That's what he *didn't* say." This time, *he* spun on his heel and marched past his husband up the stairs and into the house.

Giovanni snorted and shook his head. "This place . . ." He let his gaze soar over the redwoods. "This place may be the end of us."

I found Mom sitting on the couch, in her blue-and-orange dashiki-style housedress, a near-empty glass of wine on the coffee table, her index finger tap-tap-tapping at her phone. Smiling, she didn't even look up as I walked in.

"Texting Quincy again?" I asked, already knowing the answer.

She glanced my way. "He sent this adorable video of his dog. I swear, Sonny, it's the smartest dog I've ever seen. You should look—"

"I'm good," I said. "Dinner ready? I'm starving."

"Long day?" she asked, standing from the couch and shuffling to the kitchen.

"Ridiculous and long."

"Let me sauté the green beans really quick," she said. "I know you like 'em crisp." She grabbed the bag of fresh veggies from the fridge along with a clove of garlic.

"How was work?" I asked.

Mom shrugged. "Good, but . . ."

"But?"

"Drama." Her eyes flicked over to me before settling back on the green beans. "An order got screwed up. Cakes were put in the oven, but someone forgot to turn the damn thing on. The drama part was . . . the cakes were for a retirement party tonight. The boys were not happy."

And they still weren't, not with that argument I'd witnessed moments ago.

"Mom," I said, my belly twisting, "were you supposed to . . . ?"

"Turn on the oven?" She shook her head. "Rule is: Only Gio or Elliott handle the ovens. That way, they can only blame each other."

I let out the breath I'd been holding.

Was the cold oven the "thing" they were arguing about?

As Mom finished cooking, I grabbed my phone and texted Giovanni.

So what was the "nothing" that El didn't want me to know?

Ellipses bubbled on the screen. Then:

Val put a paper bag too close to a heat lamp

Bag caught fire

A customer was the only one who noticed flames

The back of my neck tingled, and my hands shook as I texted back:

I'm so sorry

Please tell me the damages

I will make it right

TBH

Auntie Val has been messing up a lot

El is scared to tell you

We know it's been so hard for U

But I think

Auntie V needs help

I love you Sonny and I'm only telling U this

cuz you need to know

For her sake

For your sake 2

Numb, I joined my mother at the table for a dinner of fried chicken, mac 'n' cheese, and those freshly sautéed green beans. I'd barely taken my first bite when her phone buzzed. She glanced at it, and before I could speak, she was typing again.

"You know dinner's a no-phones zone," I said, half joking.

Mom didn't look up. "It's Quincy."

"Oh, okay, then." I rolled my eyes. "So . . ." I took a bite of a perfectly fried breast and chewed for a moment before saying: "Why is Mr. Quincy so interested in you now?"

Mom blinked at me, then her brows dropped into an angry V. "What does that mean?"

I chewed my chicken, silent, not tasting the five hundred seasonings she'd used for the perfect crust.

"We were both married and had children to raise," Mom spat. "Now our kids are grown and our spouses are dead. How is that strange to you?" Her phone buzzed again, and that frown melted as she grabbed the device. She laughed as she typed.

"Do you want me to just leave you two alone?" I asked.

Her gaze snapped to me. "What is it this time?"

"It's kind of hard to have a conversation when you're glued to your phone." I paused, then added, "You two have a lot to text about."

Mom set the phone down a little too hard, the smile gone from her face now. "Because he knows me, and he knows how I think. Like we're twins. He's a wonderful man."

"Then why didn't you get married back then?"

Mom shrugged. "Destiny. Fate. Maybe we weren't supposed to be together back then. Maybe we needed to work on ourselves before—"

"Are you kidding me?" I asked.

"He makes me perfectly happy—"

"Because he knows you're looking for this perfect love," I said, my mouth now tasting sour. "No man is perfect."

"No shit," Mom said.

"Quincy isn't as great as you think, so stop comparing him to the asshole you ended up marrying." I sat back in my chair. Pain thudded between my eyebrows, and I rubbed my temples to relieve it.

"You don't want me to be happy," she said.

"That's not what I said."

"No," she continued, her voice rising. "It's fine for your father to have his fun, but the minute I try to enjoy myself, it's a problem."

I blinked at her, confused. "What are you talking about? Dad—"

"Is always working," she said. "That's what you were gonna say, right?" She snorted. "You think he's working right now? Please. His

shift's *been* done. He's with one of his girlfriends, Alyson. Yes, *plural.* But you don't seem to care about that."

My fork clattered to the plate. "What the hell are you talking about?"

She scowled at me. "Don't act like you don't know. He's your father, but he's also one of the boys. And *you're* one of the boys. You back the blue, too, no matter what."

My chest tightened. *"What?"*

"I'm not stupid, Alyson," she said, her voice softer. "Let's stop pretending that I am. You don't have to protect me anymore." Mom's fingers futzed with the edge of her napkin. "I'm just sad that you didn't even try to warn me, lay a few clues down for me to pick up and discover on my own . . ."

I stared at my plate of chicken and green beans. "What are you saying?"

"He betrayed me over and over again," Mom said, eyeing me. "And there you were, singing the praises of Pope Alvin Rush the Beneficent."

I shook my head. "I've never canonized him—"

"Bullshit, Alyson. Your whole career has been one station of the cross after the other."

"Wow," I said. "So now I'm an Al fanatic."

She cocked an eyebrow before pushing away from the table, the chair scraping loudly against the floor. "I'm done. You clean up." She tottered down the hall to her bedroom and shut the door behind her.

My eyes blurred with tears. All those years, all those nights, Dad had come home late or not at all. I'd believed every excuse he gave, every lame story about casework or statements or . . .

Girlfriends?

Who?

Tami over in Jails? Busty and blond and quick to laugh at bad jokes?

Melanie down in Vice? She'd bring me rum cakes on her trips back home to Nassau.

My father had been a charming man. He didn't like thieves, especially, and the one time I shoplifted a pack of Bubble Yum, he marched me back to the supermarket and forced me to return it.

Mom had obviously known the truth about his extracurricular activities. She'd known and stayed and kept up the appearance of "Happily Married and Faithful." I *didn't* know that had all been a facade—but was that because I didn't *want* to?

Some light purified. Some light destroyed. Some light did both.

Feeling like shit, I put away the food and washed the dishes. Then I tromped to my own room and sat on the edge of my bed, my body shaking. After taking several deep breaths, I pushed the big moving box I'd taken from Mom's closet out into the open. Inside, I found large manila envelopes stuffed with documents my parents had collected over decades of our lives together.

I dug through the mass and found an unopened envelope from Lenderful. I tore open the flap to find a standard letter addressed to Mom.

"As a past loyal customer . . ."

The letter went on to introduce a new program that offered "flexible capital options."

Past loyal customer . . . Annual percentage rate—37% . . .

What the fuck? When? Why . . . ? *What?*

I dipped back into the box and pulled out tax returns, pay stubs, bank statements, any document that had numbers. My dad's salary from the LAPD had been more than decent. He'd paid for our house in lower Ladera Heights. Private school for me—from preschool to high school to college. Family vacations. The new cars and vans for the bakery. So then why were they past loyal customers of Lenderful?

I studied a bank statement, an ATM receipt, and canceled checks from 2000 . . .

My father's salary in 2000 was $150,000, with $50,000 of that from overtime. Mom's two bakeries made a combined net profit of $60,000. But between private school tuition, vacations to Disney World, mortgage and two cars, not including random expenses like clothes, groceries, or Christmas . . .

The math wasn't mathing.

I went back to the box of shitty finances and found a promissory note from Lenderful Financial for a loan of $50,000.

But this loan was taken out in 2015, the year my father retired.

None of this made sense.

My parents worked hard—they *rarely* talked about how tight things were.

But now, staring at these numbers . . .

I leaned back against the pillows, my mind racing.

I wanted to see the truth. But all light was not the same. Some light showed clarity while other light blinded. Right now, the light was powerful, bright and deadly. The truth sometimes was.

We were all great pretenders.

21.

Morning sunshine streamed through my bedroom window and cut across the papers I'd left scattered on the floor last night. My eyes burned from not sleeping and my mind swirling with questions about my father's affairs and my family's finances.

What new distractions would find me today?

How much more light could I stand?

How many wonderfully delicious chicken dinners in the world had been ruined by fights about money and adultery?

That's what I thought about as I watched my breakfast plate of chicken, macaroni, and green beans rotate in the microwave. Last night, I'd lost my appetite after arguing with Mom, and the only good thing to come out of that was leftovers.

Mom shuffled into the kitchen, not ready to make eye contact with me. "What's your day today?" She grabbed a mug from the drying tray.

I took my plate to the dining room table. "Maybe make progress on Cooper's dog. She's still with the family who backed over Gio's car. After I check that box, I don't know." I poked my cheesy noodles with my fork. "So many adventures to choose from." I smiled at her and pretended to be unbothered.

"You're not working too much, are you?" she asked, pouring a cup of coffee.

"Nope," I said. "You know me: just being thorough."

"But what does that mean now?" she asked. "In this world as a PI?"

Relieved that she remembered I was no longer a cop, I shrugged and chewed, not ready yet to talk existentialism at eight in the morning while wearing boxer shorts and a Notorious B.I.G. graphic tee.

Mom sipped from her cup, then said, "I was talking to Quincy last night, and he was saying that finishing a case as a cop means something completely different as a PI."

I cocked my head. "Was he a cop or a PI?"

"No, Alyson, but that doesn't mean—"

"Mom," I said, holding up my hand. "No disrespect, but I don't need career counseling from someone who has no idea what it means to be me. Oh—Ivan invited us to lunch today over at his house. Wanna join?"

"Nope. Fuck Ivan." She opened the fridge door. "Anyway: I'll be home late tonight—we need to make cinnamon rolls."

My phone vibrated: a text from Brady.

Hey!

I hope you and I are okay

We weren't okay. I bit into my chicken wing—nothing was gonna block today's culinary blessing—

I know who BIG BABY and Orville Klein are

Not even the promise of information.

But you'll have to call me to find out

I turned my phone over.

Fuck Brady and his overt manipulation. Did he think that I would forgive him after he'd insulted me because he had something I wanted? Did he think that I would reminisce about kissing him by the ocean and forget his disrespect?

Autumn Suarez isn't dead because you looked the other way?

I wouldn't forgive nor would I forget. But I would play nice to get what I needed—and I needed light. Right now, though, this plate of soul food took priority over any other needs.

Today was a suede cowboy boots kind of day. I grabbed my red pair of booties and teamed them with wide-legged jeans, a white shirt, and a tan blazer. "Gettin' shit done"—that was today's look.

After pouring a cup of coffee, I returned to my bedroom and plopped onto the mattress, opened my laptop, and scanned the *Haven Voice* website for any updates on London's murder case or dead Emiliano Rivas-Kelvin Quintano being discovered in the woods.

> Featured Pet: Doug the Pug
>
> Where to Celebrate Labor Day
>
> Heat Advisory Issued

There was a letter from Tanner Orr, the editor-in-chief and water carrier for the paper's owner, Boomer Levy, a.k.a. Cooper and London Sutton.

> It is with great sadness that I am resigning as editor in chief of *The Haven Voice*. I am filled with gratitude for the opportunity to lead this group for nearly three years. Today, though, I am disillusioned by the direction the publisher wishes to take this highly esteemed journal. So much has occurred since my first day—some good, some bad. Reporting both kinds of news seems natural. However—

My phone vibrated again.

Another text from Brady.

U there?

Hello???

Please forgive me

I tapped random letters on the keyboard just to fake a response, just so that he'd see those ellipses bubbling on his phone, just so that he'd hold his breath until I responded . . . And then I deleted the gobbledygook and turned the phone over on the comforter.

Fucker.

An email reply had come from Kianna at the California Highway Patrol.

Here's the info on the license plate of the car that rammed into you.

The Honda Odyssey was registered to Lincoln McDermott, and he lived at 713 Serenity Street in Sableport. The picture I found in PeopleFinder showed the same blond, generic-looking man who'd absconded with Figgy in a minivan driven by his wife . . . *Jennifer.*

Lincoln and Jennifer McDermott were both accountants. Their daughter, Noa, was six years old. Jennifer had a bench warrant for traffic tickets. Lincoln shared custody of his other kids with his ex-wife.

Jennifer's bench warrant—if needed, I'd work it to my advantage.

And the ex-wife: her daughter, Lalah, was the same age as Noa. I'd use that math, too, if forced.

I'd make the McDermotts hand over Figgy, and then I would take their insurance information as well as an apology for destroying Giovanni's now-totaled Sentra.

I drained the rest of my coffee and slipped my laptop into my bag. I swiped over to Brady's last "Please forgive me" text message and tapped my response:

Okay

Almost immediately:

OK WHAT??

I tapped nonsense into the text window for that ellipses effect, then deleted it all again.

Since the McDermotts had already shown me that they were fucked up in the head—from taking possession of a stolen dog to hitting my car and leaving the scene—I decided that I'd protect myself from their unpredictable behavior.

I pulled on my shoulder holster, filled by my Glock. Then I texted Araceli.

Hey there

A few things have come up and I wanna chat with you

Available today?

Hi Miss Rush!

Thank U 4 thinking about me

Home all day

Working on E's memorial

Mackenzie Sutton's autopsy was also scheduled for today. India wasn't working on it, but she'd still know things. I resisted texting her. Look at me, growing up.

Mom and I didn't talk much as I drove her to the bakery.

After starting that small kitchen fire, she wouldn't have long before Giovanni and Elliott fired her from Sweetlife. Giovanni had promised to let me know when it was time for her to put away her apron. Maybe that time was now.

I wanted to ask about the loan from Lenderful, but my head hurt. A Rush family hangover from last night's spilled secrets.

"I hope you're not worrying about me," Mom said. "About my . . ." She motioned at her head. "I bought some stuff from the store two days ago that has ginseng, ginkgo biloba, and ashy-ashy-something in it. I've just been neglecting to take . . ." She sighed, not even believing her own bullshit enough to complete the delusion.

I overheard her say the same thing last night as she talked to someone on the phone:

"People act like forgetting a few things is like having cancer," she'd complained. She paused for a long moment, then said, "Because nothing is wrong. Why would I . . . ? I'm fine, and I don't wanna talk about it anymore."

The McDermotts lived on Serenity Street at the end of a quiet cul-de-sac in a picture-perfect house. White picket fence, a well-manicured lawn, and an American flag hanging proudly by the front door. It was the kind of place where you'd expect to find a golden retriever bounding through the yard, tail wagging. This morning, that dog was a goldendoodle, Figgy, with the fig-colored birthmark on her rump. She was rolling in the grass with a guy wearing soccer pants and black-and-white sneakers.

Parked a few houses down, I watched them from the front seat of my Bronco.

Lincoln tossed an orange tennis ball and Figgy chased it, her tongue lolling. Lincoln laughed and took the ball from Figgy's mouth. Lincoln threw his arms around Figgy's neck and smothered her in kisses.

Yeah, I was about to break a whole bunch of hearts to heal one. But right was right—Figgy didn't belong here. And that's why I climbed out of the car and made my way toward the house.

Lincoln spotted me. Immediately, he stiffened and narrowed his eyes.

"Good morning," I said, stopping just outside the gate. "Remember me?"

"Can I help you?" he asked politely.

"I'm Alyson Rush, private investigator. We need to talk about the dog."

He glanced toward Figgy, who was still bounding around with the ball in her mouth. "What about her?"

I reached into my bag and pulled out a folder, flipping it open to reveal photos of Figgy, vet records, and a copy of the adoption paperwork. "She's not yours."

His jaws tightened. "Look, lady—"

"Stop before you start," I said, cutting him off. "We both know Figgy belongs to someone else. I've got all the proof right here, in case you wanna play dumb."

For a moment, Lincoln McDermott didn't speak. His eyes darted between the papers in my hand and the dog. Then he let out a sigh, rubbing a hand over his face. "We bought him, fair and square."

I laughed. "Fair and . . . ? What the fuck kind of answer is *that*?"

His shoulders sagged like the weight of it all was finally hitting him. "My wife found Lucy's listing on one of those dog rehoming sites. Lucy—"

"Her name is *Figgy*—"

The dog barked and trotted over to the fence, panting and smiling after hearing her government name.

"She was for sale," Lincoln said, blushing. "The seller said they were moving and couldn't keep her. We paid five thousand dollars."

I gaped at him. "You paid *five grand* for a stolen dog?"

"We didn't know she was stolen!" he shot back. "How were we supposed to know? The seller seemed legit. They had paperwork, photos, everything. I'll show you . . ." He rushed into the house.

While we waited, I stooped and let Figgy sniff me.

The dog nuzzled my hand.

Lincoln returned to the yard, hunting through the expandable file folder until plucking out a document. "Look. Here." He thrust a pink flyer at me.

GOLDENDOODLE PUPPY FOR SALE
2 YR OLD FAMELE
5000
CURRANT ON SHOTS & VAXINE
POTTY/CRATE TRAINED
SHIPPING ALSO AVAILABLE

Text D.B. Cooper at 555-5398

The flyer had been composed with eighty different fonts and random-ass spacing.

The seller: D.B. Cooper.

I chuckled. "You know who D.B. Cooper is?"

Lincoln's eyebrows scrunched.

"The mystery man who hijacked the plane back in the seventies? FBI still doesn't know who or where he is?" I dialed the number listed there and put my phone on speaker.

"The number you have called is no longer available . . ."

"That doesn't prove that Figgy was stolen," Lincoln said, his chin lifted as the light in his eyes dimmed.

I raised my eyebrow. "You know all this is fake—and Figgy ain't two years old."

He shook his head, his hands still clutching his file of truth. "Look, we just wanted to buy our daughter a dog. She'd been asking for one for years, and we finally had the money. And Figgy's been perfect. Noa loves her."

He swallowed, and his Adam's apple bobbed. "She needed a dog. We'd gone through so much—I'd put her and Jen through hell . . ."

I nodded. "I believe you—"

"I want to give Noa everything—"

"And you can—but not this dog. You're not a dumb man—you knew this was a janky buy, but you bought her anyway, hoping that no one would come looking for her. Right?"

He dropped his head, but he wouldn't agree.

I didn't need him to.

"And I get that," I said, "but she belongs to someone else, someone who's also gone through so much."

His face twisted with frustration. "What am I supposed to do? Just tell my kid that the dog she loves isn't hers anymore? Do you know what that will do to her?"

I nodded, my stomach burning. "Yeah, I do, and I hate that for you, but she's not your dog. Lincoln, look . . . You don't want this turning into a legal mess. Figgy's owner?" I said. "Very rich. Very angry. He would destroy you and salt the earth. I haven't given him your name—please don't make me give him your name. Not with Jen's bench warrants. Not with your divorce from Sarah. Don't force my hand." I set my hands on my hips, which pulled apart my blazer.

His blue eyes widened, seeing my shoulder holster.

"You're now swimming in the big kids' pool," I said, "and you will drown, and I will still get the dog."

He stared at me for a long time, his jaw working as he weighed his options. Finally, he let out a heavy breath. "What do you want me to do?"

"I'll give you until tomorrow," I said. "Prepare Noa for saying goodbye. Then I'm coming back for the dog. If Figgy's not here, I'm going straight to the police and to the real owner."

22.

The drive over the hills that separated inland Haven from Oceanside Haven warmed the truck's interior. Multicolored mid-century houses, many with rotting wood planks and topped with crappy roofs, lined the blocks. Big shade trees and covered porches provided protection from the heavy sun that no one saw much over on the other side of the hills. Araceli's house stood out with its down-home rocking chairs, flowered wreaths, and fairy lights.

This morning, the green Honda Civic wasn't parked in the driveway. Neither was the silver Lexus or black Dodge Charger. But the front door opened, and the lady of the house, wearing paint-spattered denim overalls and a red tank top, smiled at me from the porch as I tromped up the walkway.

"I couldn't tell if you were still home," I said.

"I let family borrow our cars," she said, flicking her hand. "I think I'm gonna let my nephew just take over the note for Emiliano's car—I never liked driving it."

I looked back over to the empty driveway. "The Charger, right?"

She nodded. "Too loud. Too big. I'll keep my little hooptie." She laughed. "Hondas will run until the zombie apocalypse. Come on in—"

"No need—this won't take long."

"Okey dokey." She sat in one rocking chair, and I sat in the other.

"So," I said, "we confirm the identity of the deceased in different ways. Through DNA. Through dental records. Through fingerprints."

She nodded. "You did that already with the toothbrush."

"Yes, but one other result came up through his fingerprints."

Araceli stared at me, and then her eyes widened. "Oh. *Oh.*" She sighed. "His prints came back as Kelvin, right?"

"You know?"

"I didn't think of that until you just brought it up. I don't know him as Kelvin, and so . . ." She shrugged. "I didn't find out about his name until I saw his passport on our honeymoon."

I frowned. "You probably should've mentioned that to me."

"What difference would it have made?" she asked. "He was already dead. It wasn't like he was living a different life. Lee's dead, period. Doesn't matter."

"Well," I said, "what name gets put on the death certificate matters *a lot*."

Araceli chuckled. "You're talking like we got life insurance policies, retirement, and 401(k)s. The government didn't know Emiliano Rivas lived. They barely care if he died. You only care cuz I paid you to. Anyway . . ."

She tugged at one of her overalls straps. "I had no idea how expensive death is. I chose cremation thinking it was gonna be cheap." She snorted. "It's like ten thousand dollars. I don't have ten k."

I remember the sticker shock of the casket and the place to lay my father. Even with help from the police union, Mom and I were *still* looking at almost twenty grand.

"I launched a GoFundMe," Araceli said. "That's how I came up with the money to pay you and how I'm gonna pay for his funeral and stuff. I hate asking people for money, but . . ." She bit her lower lip. "I'm now in a new club, and I can't afford the membership fee, ha. But I can't be paralyzed by it. Nothing gets done if you don't get it done."

She should put that on a plank of wood and sell it in Celi's Secrets: *Nothing gets done if you don't get it done.*

She clutched her heart. "When does it stop hurting?"

My eyebrows crumpled some—Emiliano *just* died and she's already asking for closure?

She caught my facial shift. "Was that wrong to ask? I just thought . . . I mean . . . He's been gone for months, and I thought it wouldn't hurt like this because I'd prepared myself for the worst."

"But now that you know that he's passed . . ."

"It's like the last few months of preparing myself were for nothing."

"There's no timetable on when the pain isn't as *sharp*," I said. "I think the pain always stays sharp—we just deal with it differently."

Araceli tugged at her fingers and then futzed with the wedding band on her left ring finger. "It made sense to me that he changed his name—he needed to be another person to ICE, to the cartels. It was what he wanted—it wasn't up to me to tell him what he wanted to be called. I loved him. Period. And I knew him as Emiliano, and Emiliano was kind and funny and made great carne asada and carnitas, and now . . ."

Araceli looked at me with tear-filled eyes. "People here gotta do what they need to survive."

"I understand—"

"Do you, though?" Her gaze slid from my $200 pair of red suede boots up to my designer jeans. "You may be struggling in a way that I don't see, but I don't think I'm wrong when I say you've never had to hide or lie just to make it through the week. You haven't left your whole family behind just to work a crappy job that didn't pay you what you're worth because you don't speak the language—"

"No, I'm not an immigrant," I said, tamping down my anger, "and being Black in America may look easy to you, but it's not. And I've left my home in LA to come live here, and I've shed blood for a country that doesn't see me as worthy, and to be frank, I'm not sitting on your lovely porch on this gorgeous Wednesday afternoon, willing to participate in the 2023 Oppression and Struggle Olympic Games."

She dropped her head and whispered, "I understand. Sorry."

"It's all good." I stood, tromped back down the porch steps, and turned back to look at the young widow. "I saw you the other day in Sableport. You were with a guy. You looked . . . *close*."

"Matais. My ex." She blushed and patted her cheeks. "You probably saw me kiss him, which was weird—weird cuz he's my ex and we work together at the tire shop. We dated, like, three years ago, before I met Emiliano. I hadn't kissed any man since Lee and me started dating. I wasn't even *interested* in another man. Emiliano Rivas was it for me. And even after kissing Matais again . . . he isn't my Lee . . ." She gazed at her wedding band. "I don't ever see me taking this off."

My mother still wore her wedding rings, and my father had died five years ago.

"I want to move forward," Araceli said, leaving the rocking chair and standing at the lip of the top porch stair. "But that feels like . . . like I'm betraying him. Even when he was still missing and I was hoping that he'd slip into bed beside me one night, I still went to work, and I went to a baby shower and a wedding in my friend's backyard. I still kept living and . . .

"I . . . I messed up—I've been alone all this time, and I've been terrified, and my ex . . . he helped look for Emiliano and did chores around the house and . . . he's not scared of anybody and protected me. And seeing that someone killed Emiliano, I'm glad he's been around and . . . I know he took advantage of me because I've been so vulnerable, but . . ."

Araceli stared out into her neighborhood. "I've come to my senses. Matais was an ex for a good reason." She offered me a sad smile. "Some people make assumptions about me, but they only see a slice of my life. You saw me with Matais, and if you didn't know, you would've assumed the other twenty-three hours weren't filled with writing my dead husband's obituary and eulogy and wondering about the holidays now that he's gone . . . That slice of life you saw me live? That was me taking a breath after living with a ghost in my haunted house."

Her neck turned pink. "How do you stop feeling like shit for still living?"

Ivan's house was tucked away on Sea Cove Lane, a quiet street near the beach, modest but comfortable. Nicer than his Mar Vista home he'd had back in Los Angeles. Not Cooper's architectural masterpiece—no infinity pool spilling into the Pacific. But he had a hot tub and a small putting green.

Good for him.

Uncle Ivan, wearing track pants and a hoodie, opened the door before I could knock. "Before you ask, yes, I *do* know Jesus."

I snorted. "Ha."

He smiled his big, crooked smile, then pulled me into his godfather hug. "Look at you, all dressed up." He stepped aside to let me in, then tossed a look back at my Bronco.

I gave him a quick headshake. *She's not coming.*

His smile died. *Oh.*

"I'm starving," I said, grinning again.

"Well, follow me."

His home smelled like garlic, rosemary, and grilled meat. A mix of cozy and polished, the house had hardwood floors, rugs, and walls painted in muted ocean tones. Lived in, not staged.

My chest tightened, and my eyes burned with fresh tears. Even though Auntie Belle wasn't here, she was. I still smelled her white sage and her Dior perfume. Any moment now, I expected to see her bustling into the room with her arms reaching for me.

"Let me give you a tour," Ivan said, gesturing for me to follow him.

We walked through the living room with furniture that was mismatched but looked comfortable. In the kitchen, copper pots hung above the breakfast bar. The dining room had a beach view. He led me down a short hallway. Guest bedroom over there. Den with a big-ass TV and a bigger armchair over there. Then the en-suite bedroom. A row of framed photos on the dresser. Auntie Belle smiled back at me from many of them. Her arm draped around his shoulders as they sat in front of a Christmas tree or the beach. She was laughing in one picture, her head tilted toward his as he played a ukulele. They looked happy. In love.

Ivan also stared at his wife from the threshold. "Belle loved taking pictures," he whispered. "Every trip, every holiday, she brought that damn camera out. Drove me fucking nuts sometimes, but I'm glad now, because I have proof that she came into my life. She's still here, even if it's just pictures."

I nodded, swallowing the lump in my throat. "I miss her."

"Yeah," he said. "Wish I'd been better for her."

Uncle Ivan had grilled T-bone steaks and roasted vegetables. He added a crusty loaf of bread and soft Irish butter. We sat at the small dining room table, and he opened a bottle of Pontet-Canet, a delicious red blend that tasted crisp and alive with blackberries and black cherries. This wine and the soft roar of crashing waves made me envious. One day . . .

"Weird," Ivan said now. "I never felt in control down in LA. Always felt like I was living in someone else's house, know what I mean? Up here? Haven feels . . . *mine*. Like I finally control my day to day. 'Control my fate' sounds arrogant, so I won't say that—don't want the gods trying to prove a point, ha ha."

I said "Ha," then sipped more wine and rolled it around my mouth. So absolutely perfect.

"I don't miss Los Angeles," he continued. "I was a mess down there. High blood pressure. High cholesterol. Angry all the time. The quiet here makes me feel healthy. The ocean isn't crowded with tourists—"

"It will be, if Coop and the Chamber of Commerce win the fight."

"Ugh. Yeah." He shook his head. "That spa is gonna change our life. I don't know if that's a good or bad thing—I like the quiet, but I like having clients too."

"More people means more problems," I said, "and problems keep the lights on."

"Right." He stabbed a broccoli spear on his plate. "I was hoping to see Val."

I grunted. "Well, not only is she mad at you, but she's also pissed at me. So, worst possible timing for having lunch with two of her least favorite people."

"How's her . . . ?" He pointed at his head.

"Getting worse. I'd hoped that her memory issues had only flared because of the stress of the move. But . . ." I shook my head and told him about the small kitchen fire at Sweetlife.

"Shit," he said. "That ain't good."

I ate a sliver of steak but didn't taste it—numb mouth.

"There's a nice place," Ivan said, "but it's up in Sableport."

"Sunset Park," I said, nodding. "Not cheap. Six grand a month."

"Shit."

"Coop said he'd help pay."

Ivan cut at his steak. "Maybe you should consider accepting his offer. It's the least he can do after selling you a bill of goods to get you up here. Not saying that he owes you, but . . ."

"He owes me," I said, smiling.

"You thought I was being an asshole when I mentioned this before," he said, "but if you wanted to run an office out of Sableport, you could. Get Val settled up there and . . ." He shrugged. "I'm not telling you what to do. Just saying that you have more flexibility than what you think."

"Yep. Speaking of Cooper . . ." I speared a piece of zucchini with my fork. "I stopped by his place yesterday."

Ivan cocked an eyebrow. "You two friendly again?"

"No, it's just . . ." I chewed the zucchini. "I'm worried about him, and I'm also curious. I'm taking Figgy back home tomorrow—I met with the guy who bought her.

"On another note, the Emiliano Rivas–Lumière connection . . . I read an article in the *Chronicle* about how the spa project is over budget and how there have been accidents. Nothing specific, though, about Emiliano Rivas, who is actually named Kelvin Quintano. The mystery deepens."

Ivan said "Bah" and flicked his hand. "There's always chaos at construction sites."

"Workers dying—"

"Other than Rivas, who didn't die at work, who else died?"

"We don't know that Rivas didn't die at or *because* of work," I clarified. "Dave Kruger or whoever could've dumped him in the woods as a cover-up."

Ivan made the face, conceding my point. "Say you're right. But Rivas—" He held up one finger. "—is one guy. About four hundred and fifty people get killed each year in accidents up and down the state. I'll give you Rivas, and that's still no evidence of a trend. Kwon and McCann will hopefully figure out whodunit and we'll see for sure."

I circled back to my visit with Araceli Rivas and that an ex-boyfriend had come back into the young widow's life. "She was fine with Emiliano's lie about his name," I said.

"We're all fine with lies," Ivan said, "until we're not. Even you."

"I'm not fine with lies. It's just . . ." I pushed out a breath. "How can you trust anything else about the person if their basic identity . . . ?"

"You knew everything about Cooper," Ivan said, "and he *still* managed to pull one over on you. As far as cheaters go, you *also* slept with another woman's husband—"

"That's different," I interrupted. "They were getting a divorce."

"*Getting*. She was still Mrs. Sutton, and you were still seeing him."

My cheeks burned.

He pointed his fork at me. "Don't get righteous. Don't lose sight of the real. That's all I'm saying." He scrunched his eyebrows. "I was gonna ask why you were still chasing that ball on Rivas . . . I get it. As for Lumière . . . construction's a dangerous business."

"True, but . . ."

"But what?" he asked, his mouth full.

"Cooper said that you were in charge of the background checks for the principals," I said, keeping my voice even. "Including Dave Kruger."

Ivan laughed. "Of course Cooper said that. Your boy always passes that buck, especially when it comes to looking good to you."

"Is it true, though?" I pressed. "You gave Dave Kruger a thumbs-up?"

Ivan crossed his arms, his gaze steady. "I did my due diligence, Sonny. Checked records, called references, did everything by the book—or as close to the book as you can get in this business. Being a PI? Sometimes it's dirty work. Sometimes you're gonna get splashed with shit. If you can't personally handle that, they're hiring security guards at the mall up in Sableport."

"Ouch." I slumped some in my seat. "I'm not accusing you of anything, sir. I'm just trying to figure shit out. I've been here since the beginning of August, and you have to admit that a lot has happened since my arrival, you know? And I know that I'm not perfect—"

"You're not." He wiped his mouth with a napkin. "And neither am I. Far from. I've done things I'm not proud of, but I'm just an old cop trying to make a dollar outta fifteen cents before I fuckin' kick the bucket."

I nodded, then stared at my steak.

"What's going on?" he asked, slicing another piece. "You got something on your mind."

"Mom told me . . ." I cleared my throat and sat up in my chair. "She told me that Dad cheated on her. All those nights he was working late, all those excuses. I believed him. Every single lie he told me, I believed him."

Ivan's face softened, but he didn't respond.

"I know," I said, nodding. "Cops cheat all the time."

With other cops. With dispatchers. With EMTs and nurses.

I'd never indulged in the candy shop—with free candy or with candy that belonged to someone else. But then again, Cooper had belonged to someone else, even though he had papers proving that he was extricating himself from that person.

"My father," I said. "He was supposed to be different from the other guys. I thought he loved her—"

"He *did* love her," Ivan said. "None of those other women meant anything to Al, and Valerie knew that. She stayed married to him because she knew his heart was hers. I know it's hard to hear, but that's just how it was back then. I mean . . ." He paused and watched me pop a wedge of beef into my mouth, then said, "I cheated on Belle."

I stopped chewing my food and glared at him.

"She eventually found out," he said. "I threw myself at her feet and begged for forgiveness. She forgave me, and I promised her never again."

"And?" I asked, mouth full.

"And I cheated again. And then again."

I dropped my fork and pushed away my plate.

He watched me closely. "Belle had my heart *and* my wallet. Same for your mom. It didn't—"

"No," I said. "It *did* mean something, and if I have to explain that to you, a grown-ass man, why sleeping around on your wife was bad—"

"I know that, Alyson."

"Would you have been cool if Belle had fucked around on you?" I asked. "And now that I know all this, I hope she did."

His face flushed. "Not funny."

"No, it's *not* funny. But I hope she found *immense* pleasure and company with someone who made her feel valued. I hope she didn't spend her entire life waiting for you to act right and to stop lying to her. Same goes for my mother. I hope she fucked the Muffin Man and the guy who came in once a month to check her stoves' pilot lights."

His darkening face quivered with quiet rage, and he breathed through his nose, in, out, in . . . before sitting back in his chair. He rubbed his mouth for a moment, then cleared his throat.

If I hadn't been his best friend's daughter, Ivan would've vaporized me by now.

This version just kept breathing and rubbing his face until his face returned to its true shade of pink. Then: "Maybe Val shouldn't have sprung it on you like that last night, but you kinda forced her hand by lionizing Al."

I squinted at him. "You weren't there. How do you know that I lionized Al?"

He now pushed away his plate. "I don't have to 'be' there. I know you, and I know how much you loved and admired your dad."

I shifted my glare from Ivan down to the steak and veggies on my plate.

"You're acting brand new," Ivan said, smirking at me. "Like some doe-eyed idealist. And next I'm gonna have to explain to you that Leonard Cohen wasn't singing about God in 'Hallelujah'!"

I rolled my eyes. "Be for real right now."

He laughed. "I know you think people should act right. But here you are, just as fucked up as the rest of us, pretending that perfect people exist while you're singing a cold and broken hallelujah with London Sutton's husband."

I guzzled the rest of my wine.

"Val's still talking to what's-his-face?" Ivan asked, filling my glass.

I said, "Yeah."

"Guess I should be happy for her. But that guy?" Ivan grunted and shook his head. "Hard seeing her with someone who's not Al, you know?"

I shot him a look. "That's rich."

He picked up his fork again and pointed it at me. "She's not innocent either."

"What does that mean?"

He said nothing and glared at me over his wineglass.

I nodded and said "Whatever," but my stomach rolled.

Not innocent?

Did she sleep with the Muffin Man?

23.

The T-bone steak sat in my gut like a stone. Not that it was a bad cut, but the talk of adultery could make even the best Wagyu taste like round steak from the laziest cow.

I left Ivan's for the Bronco. My phone made me shift my attention to the text message from Brady.

You busy?

I looked out the windshield and to the sandy beach where kids were tossing a Frisbee.

The phone vibrated again.

Big news

How should I play this?

My stomach twisted around that meat, and I took deep breaths of salty air.

On my way to the office

See you soon

Brady Kwon was waiting at the front door of Poole Investigations as I swung the Bronco into the parking spot next to his black Yukon. He looked great in his blue suit, but I never had issues with his looks.

He smiled at me and said, "You look beautiful."

Nor had I ever had issues with the way I curled my hair or filled out a pair of jeans.

I said "Thank you" and shoved my key into the locked front door.

Cool air pulled us over the threshold, and the bell above the door announced our arrival. I turned on the lights and scooped up the mail from the basket beneath the mail slot.

"Since you started working here," Brady said, "I see your influences."

I made a face. "How?"

He followed me down the hall to my office. "The basket to catch the mail, for one. And it doesn't smell like 'boy' anymore."

"I bought some of those plug-in air fresheners." We passed Ivan's empty office and headed into mine.

Brady plopped into my guest chair.

I slipped off my blazer and pulled my binder and laptop from my bag. "So what's the big news?" I reached into my minifridge and pulled out two bottles of water.

He cocked his head. "You're armed today."

"I had to see a man about a dog." I offered him one of the water bottles.

Brady grinned as he cracked open the bottle. "And that required a gun?"

I leaned back into my chair. "Last time I confronted him and his wife about said dog, she tried to run me over in her minivan. I learned my lesson, and I went prepared." I took a long pull of cold water.

"You *know* that you can call the police—*me*—if you need assistance."

"You *know* that I'm a licensed private investigator with a permit to carry."

He shrugged. "Makes you even more dangerously sexy."

I tossed him the leanest of grins.

"The poisoned cupcakes," Brady said.

"Oh, so you've been *busy* busy," I said, allowing myself to smile just a little more.

"I'm thinking about how you plan to reward me," he said, his head cocked.

"A reward I will most likely rescind as a result of our last conversation and you revealing what you really think of me—"

"Sonny," he said, shaking his head, his cheeks red.

I held up my hand. "The poisoned cupcakes. The guy on the video buying them was Carlos Vega, known associate of Keely Butler."

He nodded. "Correct—"

"Go arrest him—"

"Will you wait a moment and let me talk?" He paused, then said, "So I dug into Honor's phone records and the names you gave me."

"Liam Dyer, Orville Klein, Big Baby."

"'Big Baby' is . . . Carlos Vega."

My mouth popped open, and I blinked at him.

"The driver, the one who drove Honor and other girls up and down the state? The one who purchased those cupcakes that killed that poor raccoon? That's Carlos Vega."

That means . . . the man who'd stood with my mom at the pier that night. The man with Keely on the night I'd snuck into her house . . .

Carlos Vega.

"Ohmigod," I finally managed to whisper. "Vega and Liam Dyer: How are they connected?" I grabbed my pen and legal pad from the corner of the desk. My thoughts were racing too quickly through my head, and my pen was moving too slow to capture everything Brady had just said.

"Vega and Dyer played soccer together back in high school," Brady said. "Then Vega got hired as a driver with Dyer-Tech, Liam's father's company. They have factories down in Mexico."

My eyes widened. "So Vega moves product—"

"And women and—"

"Drugs," I said. "Liam was Mackenzie's connect."

"Also?" Brady cocked his head. "Vega isn't Hispanic or any kind of ethnicity. His mom remarried and the stepfather basically adopted him, and Carlos unofficially changed his name from Campbell to Vega. Charles Campbell—that's his government name."

I bumped my fist against my lip. "Is he affiliated?"

"As in a gang?" He nodded. "With the SSS."

"Who the fuck are they?" I asked, writing down that letter three times.

"Sand Sea Skinheads. They're growing weed and hate up in these redwoods."

"And now they're trafficking?"

Brady shook his head. "Not according to one of my informants. Too much of a hassle—bitches are a bitch, was his quote."

"So Charles being Big Baby—"

"Is extracurricular activity," Brady said, taking a few sips of water from his bottle. "That's him and Liam going out on their own. But that's not the big news."

I dropped my pen and peered at him. "What's the big news?"

He smiled and said, "Jaylayne Merkley."

"Dave Kruger's ex-wife."

"Correct, and registered owner of the pink-rose Glock found beneath Emiliano Rivas."

"What about her?"

"She's dead."

"What?"

"Yep."

"When? How?"

"Last week. Heart attack." He shrugged. "But of course I wasn't satisfied with that. How would the gun come into Emiliano's possession? Did they know each other? Had he done work at her house?"

"And?"

"Still working on it. Since she wasn't killed, there's no box of evidence that holds her phone or—"

"Wait." I sat up in my chair. "Where's Emiliano's phone? He had to have one even if it wasn't with his body."

Brady stared at me, then wrote a note. "There was no phone found in the forest."

"I mean . . . it's probably dead by now, but . . ." I shrugged. "Maybe those last calls he made were to Jaylayne Merkley who needed someone to change a light bulb or something, and she didn't want her ex-husband to do it."

"Maybe." Brady flipped to the next page of his notepad. "We're still waiting for DNA results from beneath Emiliano's fingernails."

I had updates, too, and I told Brady about my quick stop at Araceli's earlier today. "The GoFundMe, the kiss that I saw . . ." I shook my head. "I guess she's just trying to make it. I don't know."

Because really, what do I know about how to live? After lunch with Ivan, it's clear that I don't know a damned thing.

"Is that it?" Brady asked.

"That's all I have."

Brady blinked at me and grinned.

I scrunched my eyebrows. "What?"

"You haven't complimented me."

"On?"

He waggled his filled notebook.

I said, "Good job, Brady."

"That's it?"

I squinted at him. "Did I miss you solving the cases of either Emiliano Rivas or Honor Butler? I mean . . . you're doing what you're supposed to be doing. Being nosy. Asking questions. Chasing phantoms. There's nothing *extraordinary* in what—"

"Really?"

I held out a hand. "Why do you care so much about not only what I think but also to the degree that I think it?"

He tapped his pen against his pad.

"Be the best cop for *you*," I said. "Fuck trying to impress me—"

"I'm not trying to impress you—"

"Fine. Don't try to prove to me that you're a good cop, then. I'll never think you're as good as or better than me. There is no finish line here, Kwon. Don't even have a finish line—I will *never* reach that point where I can no longer ascend, where I no longer care what people think about me. So just . . . *stop*, okay? You're a good cop. Smart. Committed. And I think you're very handsome. Go with God, dude."

He rolled his eyes and sipped from his water bottle.

"Oh," I said. "What about Orville Klein? Who is he?"

The lightest veil dropped over Brady's face as he considered the notes he'd written. "Looks like he's just a guy. Lives in Napa with his wife, Cookie."

I waited for more, then: "That's it?"

"That's it."

His first lie of the day to me.

Who was Orville Klein, and why was Brady protecting him from me?

PART III

The Girl Who Survived the Hornet's Nest

24.

But what about my own family's mysteries? What were the most important people in my life hiding?

Back at home, I ducked into my bedroom and changed clothes, putting the Glock back in her case. After starting a spreadsheet on my laptop, I sorted through everything that I'd found in boxes, tubs, and old envelopes across the bedroom floor: receipts, invoices, vacation itineraries, calendars, checkbook registers, and check stubs. I also pulled Dad's old case files—reports, warrant requests, and transcripts.

A shiny new refrigerator purchased from Sears three days after Dad wrapped a big kidnapping case. A week-long vacation to Maui following the raid of an underground brothel. My first car, a used Honda Prelude, bought not long after a seizure of property tied to a money laundering investigation connected to pimps.

Every time my family had come into something big—something we wouldn't have otherwise been able to afford—an investigation or a bust had preceded it.

My daughter mind said, *But cops got bonuses and worked hella overtime. We saved up for things like every family.* I flipped through the old search warrant requests and evidence logs that had been noted with Dad's badge number and quick right-slanted signature at the bottom of reports or listed as part of the seizure team. There were pictures of bundled cash neatly piled and tied with rubber bands, stacked across tables. In some pictures, my father stood over those towers of money. I stared the longest at these photos.

Did he ever pocket any of these bricks and bring them home? Tell himself that it was harmless, that no one would miss a bundle or two? If the other cops on his team were in on it, who would say that there'd been twelve bundles and not the seven they'd inventoried?

My stomach twisted.

Alabama, Alaska, Arkansas . . .

This was my father. He'd taught me how to ride a bike. How to tie a double Windsor knot. He'd drilled into me the importance of always telling the truth. And now, here I was, sifting through his life . . .

A stranger to me.

And my mother . . . how much did she know? How much had she accepted or questioned?

This evening, she looked smaller wearing her dashiki-printed housedress. We ate leftover fried chicken and macaroni for dinner. She wasn't in the mood to talk, and I wasn't in the mood to pretend. So, we watched *Halloween Baking Championship* on TV in silence until:

"I took a lunch break today," she said, sipping from her glass of wine. Then she cleared her throat. "Went over to Deegan's, and . . . umm . . . I got lost for a moment trying to get back to the bakery."

I glanced over at her but didn't speak.

"And yesterday, I set a paper bag too close to a heat lamp. Started a little fire." Her eyes glistened with tears as she shrugged. "The boys have been really patient with me, and I've tried to play it off, but I've *tasted* my mistakes. The cakes taste like salt and not sugar. The cinnamon rolls don't rise because I forget to add yeast. And getting lost today . . ." She shook her head, then closed her eyes.

"Mom," I whispered, "we can—"

"I'm not ready yet—"

"To?"

"Talk about what's happening to me. To talk about . . . *care*. I want to go to Taos with Quincy to see the hot air balloons."

But I couldn't let her do that alone—I needed to go too. That required money, and any extra money I earned needed to go toward a memory care facility, even if it wasn't Sunset Park up in Sableport, even if it was an at-home nurse.

Money. That's why we were here—and we didn't have enough of it because . . .

Kansas, Kentucky, Louisiana . . .

"Mom," I said, tugging at the string on my long-sleeve T-shirt. "Dad . . ."

She didn't look away from the television screen. "What about him?"

I opened my mouth, then closed it again. "I know about the loans from Lenderful."

She grunted and sipped wine.

"Why? What did Dad do? Why is there no pension? Tell me the truth, please."

Her eyes flicked from the TV down to her glass.

"We might as well discuss this now," I said.

Before you forget.

Mom stayed quiet for a long moment.

I muted the television's volume.

"Your father was a good man," she said. "But he wasn't perfect. Sometimes, he'd come home with something he'd . . . *found* during searches and seizures. Stuff that wasn't worth logging into evidence, I guess."

No such thing as something "not worth" logging, but now was not the time to argue the point. Instead, I asked, "What kind of stuff?"

"Electronics, jewelry, those kinds of things." She shrugged. "He said those things were gonna get auctioned off anyway, so why not? I didn't ask questions. I didn't want to know."

My chest tightened. "Did he ever take money?"

Mom's head snapped in my direction, and she glared at me. "Al wasn't a *thief*, Sonny. He hated the idea of dirty money."

I held her gaze. "Mom, did he ever take—"

"Once," she said, looking away, "but it wasn't his idea. I don't know how much or how they did it exactly—"

"They?"

"—but your dad . . . he regretted it. Lost sleep over it. Said it was a mistake, and that he'd never do anything like that again."

"What did they do?" I asked, leaning forward.

She shook her head. "I don't know. And I didn't want to know. Whatever it was, they didn't get caught, but it ate at him. After that, he never took anything ever again. Not a CD player, not an earring."

I sat back on the couch as tears slipped down my cheeks. "You say this like it's . . ." I shrugged, shook my head. "He was a *cop*. *I'm* a cop . . . Well, I was when he was alive. And you were *okay* with this *and* the affairs, and whose house did I grow up in?"

"You know how I came up," Mom said. "There I was, my brother and his crew running the projects, using dirty money to put me through culinary school. I met and married a good guy. A cop, of all people, and he went from being an honest man to a man who'd take something that wasn't his. But only for good reasons—"

"Good reasons?" I screeched.

"That money helped take care of you, take care of us—"

"Says every criminal that I've ever arrested."

"But we're not them."

"No," I said, "we're worse because *we're* the ones putting people in jail for taking care of themselves and their families by robbing banks or stealing cars or—"

"Totally different circumstances. Your father and Ivan—"

"Ivan?"

"—and the squad only took from the thugs and convicts."

I rolled my eyes. "Oh, okay. Then that's fine."

What the complete *fuck*?

"I'm tired of talking about this. Go wake him up." Mom waved her hand toward the hallway. "It's time for dinner."

My breath caught in my throat. "Excuse—*huh?*"

"Your father," she said, then glugged from her wineglass. "He's taking a nap. Go wake him up." She turned her attention back to the TV. "Turn up the volume—I can't hear."

My hands clenched into fists before I aimed the remote control at the television.

Down in my lap, my phone chimed, and Cooper's face brightened its screen.

Thinking about you

A flush crept over my face as I stared at Cooper's text message. With a shaky finger, I texted back:

I've been thinking about you too

I chewed on my bottom lip and watched the screen.

No ellipses.

He wasn't responding. Maybe he was staring at his phone screen too.

Minutes, then hours, passed without a response from Cooper.

At midnight, I turned off my phone completely—I wasn't going to sleep with one ear and one eye tied to my phone. He wouldn't control me like that.

Morning came, and my phone had burst apart from missed texts and emails—none of them, though, from Cooper.

A flare of worry soured my stomach. Had something bad happened? Had he done something rash? Had he done the worst thing?

I texted him.

Are you alive?

This time, ellipses bubbled on the screen.

Yes

I exhaled, then chose to look out the window at the fog instead of my phone. I had enough to think about, shit that had kept me from sleeping. Like . . .

My father.

How had he stopped himself? *Had* he stopped himself, or had someone in his crew snitched?

No one liked a whistleblower until history books and newspapers proved that we should. If I'd known that my father and Ivan had been stealing, would I have turned them in?

I sat with this for a moment, my gaze trained on that fog—but my pondering had already answered the question.

Had my pink iPod been purchased by my parents or stolen from a drug dealer's house in Palms? Had my mountain bike been brand new or slightly used by a girl whose parents had been jailed for selling crack? My diamond earrings—I'd picked them out at Kay Jewelers on my sixteenth birthday. Had the money that bought them been legit, or had it come from those bundles of cash "liberated" by my father, Ivan, and their crew?

We all knew truth, but my parents had stumbled over it, showed it to me, demanded it from me before they'd stolen from someone or slept with the 9-1-1 dispatcher.

I sighed, then muttered, "Enough." Switching gears, I left bed to grab the file folder I kept for Emiliano Rivas's investigation. Ivan said that only one worker had died at Lumière's construction site. Two, if he generously included Emiliano's death. What could have been the circumstances behind his murder?

Maybe Emiliano had threatened to expose Dave Kruger . . . or even Cooper. Maybe Emiliano had been a whistleblower.

I logged on to Etsy and typed "Araceli Rivas." Celi's Secrets sold everything from mushroom art to seashell bracelets and snowmen made from recycled books. The customers loved her wood wall pockets stuffed with preserved lavender and wood-bowl candles scented with honey and pieces of dried oranges and lemons.

Five stars. **The most beautiful candles I've ever purchased!**

Five stars. **My sister loved this gift!**

I scrolled through her shop and stopped at a picture of a colorful summer wreath made of silk flowers.

An average rating of 3.9 stars, which made it one of the lowest-rated products in Celi's Secrets.

I scrolled through the reviews and stopped at a five-star review written by Jaylayne M.

Was this "Jaylayne Merkley," Dave Kruger's ex-wife?

> **You know I love LOVE LOVE your stuff, A! Everybody, Araceli is the best. She even dropped off my order in person and threw in this wreath!**

A supercustomer, Jaylayne M. had also purchased wall art of the state of California made from seashells and pebbles, a candle ring made with clustered white flowers, and pink crystal suncatchers. Five stars for every piece.

The other customers, though, continued to lower their ratings.

Three stars. **The item arrived and it wasn't made of pink crystals. They were PURPLE! Broke my heart because my decor is PINK.**

Two stars. **I wanted the wreath in the picture. I am very disappointed with the wreath that I got. Too many daisies. Barely any roses. If you can't give me the wreath in the picture, then it's false advertising!! I WANT THE WREATH IN THE PICTURE OR MY MONEY BACK!!!!!**

One star. **These candles smelled like farts.**

But Jaylayne M. had given five stars to each of these products and many customers found her reviews helpful.

I, too, found this helpful—there was the connection I'd been searching for between Emiliano and Jaylayne . . . that is, if the "M." stood for "Merkley."

The most common reasons people were murdered: sex and money. Having met through Araceli and Celi's Secrets, maybe Emiliano and Jaylayne had been having an affair, and maybe Dave Kruger found out. Maybe Dave Kruger and Jaylayne had divorced because of her relationship with Emiliano. Maybe Emiliano had stolen from Dave, or maybe Dave had stolen from Emiliano. Maybe . . .

I needed to take an early-morning walk.

The forest outside my cottage swallowed me up, and I felt like the only person in the world. I tapped the Glock nestled in my hip holster and took in a deep breath, pushing it through clenched teeth before marching toward Emiliano's death site. I hiked past trees that soared to the sky and rotted stumps that now sprouted ferns and mushrooms. Sunlight twinkled between the gaps of branches. The only colors here were shades of browns and greens.

It was easy to find the tree that Emiliano had been propped against. Three unlit candles and a rosary now memorialized the spot. Whoever left these items . . . how had they reached this tree? Where was the road that—

Twigs snapped somewhere behind me.

I looked over my shoulder.

No one there.

"Hello?" I tried to ignore the prickling against my neck.

No one answered.

A good thing.

A bad thing.

I marched west, passing a dry gully and a massive fallen redwood. The path I walked was well trod. The killer had probably taken this—

More branches and twigs cracked behind me.

I looked back over my shoulder with my fists clenched, knees bent. Ready to fight. Ready to shoot. "Who's there?" I shouted.

But no one came out from behind the standing or fallen trees. My ghost was here, though. I smelled his cologne: patchouli, moss, and pepper. I heard him trying not to breathe but failing.

"I know you're here," I said. "Be a man about it and show your face." My eyes skipped from the log covered with mushrooms to the copse of young redwoods. "I can stand here all day. Are you prepared to?"

Leaves crunched . . . Branches snapped . . .

I stood still until those sounds faded . . . faded . . . until that lingering scent of peppery cologne dissipated . . . until . . .

Silence.

The scent of redwoods and fungi wafted, free of other perfumes.

I walked until I reached a two-lane road.

Nothing special—except there were no streetlights to light up the darkness. Someone could've easily pulled over to the side of the road and unloaded the body. Had they carried Emiliano to that place at the tree, or had they pulled him? Pulling would've made a lot of noise—leaves crunching, twigs snapping. Same with using a cart or a wheelbarrow. Too much noise.

According to the autopsy report, Emiliano had been five-five, one hundred fifty pounds.

Who'd be strong enough to throw him around their neck or carry him in their arms?

25.

Life wasn't a straight line, even in a city by the sea. If anything, the ocean was eroding all of Haven's straight lines or erasing them altogether. As I drove to the office, I determined that my life here in Haven had proven to me that I needed new muscles. It had taken me thirty-four years to learn how to move through Los Angeles with confidence—and I'd still stumbled. What made me think Haven required less than a month?

From my desk, I heard the bell above the front door of Poole Investigations jangle, the sound sharp and startling in the stillness.

Instinctively, I reached for my Glock. "May I help you?" I called out, my voice hard.

"Miss Rush?" Araceli Rivas called out.

We met at my office doorway.

Her eyes goggled as she caught me standing with a gun on my hip. She gasped—"Oh!"—and took a step back.

I beckoned her to join me. "Come in. Have a seat."

She wore a damp, loose cardigan over jeans, high-top sneakers, and hair swept into a ponytail dampened by the ocean air. By the looks of her red eyes and gunky mascara, she'd been crying. She sat in my guest chair and crossed her arms.

Instead of sitting behind my desk, I sat next to her in the other guest chair. "What's wrong?"

She crossed her arms even tighter over her chest. She tried to glare at me, but her quivering chin betrayed those hard raccoon eyes. "Ever since they found Emiliano, my life's been turned upside down."

I stayed quiet, giving her the space she needed to say what she needed to say.

"I didn't want this," she continued. "All I wanted was to find him. That's it. I didn't want . . . whatever you're doing right now."

Her words startled me like a splash of cold water. "And what is it that I'm doing?"

"Investigating his death."

I shook my head. "His case is with the sheriff's department."

"People say you're poking around."

I shrugged. "I mean . . ."

"So you *are*!"

I grimaced. "You sound like you're sad that he's been found."

"No, it's not that," she said, shaking her head. "I'm heartbroken that he's gone."

For the first time interacting with each other, I felt Araceli's lie—it was oily and slick, and the smell turned my stomach.

"Everyone is blaming me for his death," she said. "His brother says if it wasn't for me, he'd still be alive in Jalisco. America killed him."

Just like Haven had killed Xander Monroe.

"I'm scared they're gonna do something to me," Araceli said, a teardrop plopping on the back of her hand. She shook her head. "I should've just . . ."

"Let him stay lost?"

"No—I should've just told him no when he asked me out," she said. "I should've just moved to Mexico with him." Another giant teardrop plopped on the back of her hand. She pushed out a breath and snapped a tissue from the box on my desk. "I'm getting out of here."

"Out of . . . ?"

"Haven. I'm not gonna sit around and wait for his people to kill me. I just wanted you to know since you've been so nice to me."

I narrowed my eyes. "Where are you going?"

She shrugged. "I'm gonna pack up what I can and just . . ." She stood from the chair, and together, we shuffled back to the lobby.

With each step I took, I moved slower and slower, drained of energy. As the widow exited Poole Investigations, I listened to the dying jingle of the bell above the door. Then, I stepped to the window and peeked past the vertical blinds.

Araceli hustled down the sidewalk and climbed into the silver Lexus, the same car she'd been driving in Sableport. This time, though, she didn't slip behind the steering wheel.

Because the driver was already there: Matais, her ex-boyfriend.

My stomach dropped as I lifted my phone and snapped pictures. The Lexus backed out of its space, and I took pictures of the front license plate. Once the Japanese sedan reached the end of the block and made a right turn out of my life, I hurried back to my office and texted Kianna, my friend at California Highway Patrol.

You working today?

I bit my bottom lip as I waited for her response.

Am I ever NOT working?

I sent her the Lexus's license plate number and the car's make and model. Then I stared at the screen, blocking thoughts and holding my breath as though Kianna needed all the oxygen in the world to run a simple plate check.

Ellipses.

Then:

Registered to . . .

Ellipses . . . then . . .

Jaylayne Merkley, 7 Azure Way, Haven

Dave Kruger's ex-wife.

I texted Kianna my thanks and sent her a DoorDash gift card. Then I added that note to my file on Emiliano Rivas.

Why did Matais and Araceli have Jaylayne's Lexus? Because maybe Araceli or Matais had bought it from her or from Dave. Jaylayne had just died last week, so maybe the registration hadn't been changed yet? Maybe Jaylayne had never remarried, and Dave was next in line. Maybe Dave had simply *given* the Lexus to Araceli, another person who'd lost their spouse.

But the Lexus was the second item in this case that used to belong to Jaylayne Merkley. The first: that black-and-pink gun found beneath Emiliano Rivas.

Maybe . . . maybe Dave Kruger had discovered that Jaylayne had given both car and gun to her lover, Emiliano, and in a jealous fit, Dave killed the man. Or maybe Emiliano had stolen both the car and gun, and Dave Kruger had killed him for *that*.

And then there was Matais. Araceli had stopped dating him only after she'd met Emiliano. Maybe that had pissed Matais off. Humiliated him. How much? Enough to kill?

What cologne did *Matais* wear? Did it smell like patchouli, moss, and pepper? Was he the man who'd followed me around the forest this morning?

I leaned back in my chair and closed my aching eyes—they felt crunchy and were as sharp as bear traps. The dull thud around my sockets eased the longer I kept my eyes closed. Soon, my breathing slowed and . . .

. . .

. . .

Alarmed, I sat up in my chair.

I'd fallen asleep—only ten minutes had passed, though.

I tapped my laptop keyboard until it popped on. I typed CHARLES CAMPBELL into PeopleFinder.

There were six hits: one in Haven, one in Sableport, one in Mendocino Coast, and three around Fort Hood.

I scrolled the results until I found the man who'd purchased and poisoned the cupcakes from Sweetlife.

His last known address was on Hollister Road.

Sounded familiar.

I tapped in that address: the gray Victorian with dingy pink eaves.

Current resident . . . Keely Rochelle Butler.

My eyes bugged. "No," I whispered, shaking my head. "No, no, no."

Honor had been scared of Big Baby a.k.a. Charles Campbell a.k.a. Carlos Vega because he lived in her house.

"Shit. *No.*" I pressed the heels of my hands against my eyes.

Brady and I had sent Honor back home—and to one of her captors.

I grabbed my phone and called Brady.

No answer.

I texted him.

We need to talk ASAP

I'm serious as FUCK

Call me

PLEASE

Keely and Carlos Vega lived together. As lovers or as roommates? Didn't matter. He'd been Honor's driver, taking her from customer to customer, beating her so much that she'd been too scared to run . . . until she had.

And now . . .

Brady needed to get her out of there.

I gathered everything I had on Honor's case—the notes, the photos, the names—and I marched to the copy machine and made duplicates of every document. Then I bound those copies with a clip and slipped it into a big manila envelope. I wrote FOR BRADY KWON - FROM A. RUSH on its face with a big black marker.

My chest tightened as I loaded my files and this envelope into my bag. I wanted to help Honor, but this investigation was bigger than me. It needed more resources than anything we had available at Poole Investigations.

The desk sergeant at the Sableport-Haven Division of the Mendocino County Sheriff's Office was a round, pink man who wore round, gold glasses. He smiled at me like we knew each other from way back.

"Is Brady in?" I asked him.

"Nope," he said, "but McCann's here."

I pointed in the direction of the office. "May I?"

He nodded and smiled.

A moment later, I knocked on the doorframe of that office shared by Brady and McCann.

McCann looked away from his computer and grinned. "PI Rush! What's happening? Come in!"

Why so happy?

"What can I help you with?" Will McCann asked. He wore another big-boy suit, this one gray pinstripe, and a red tie.

I took a guest chair, placing my phone and bag on the empty chair beside me. I held up the manila folder. "Wanted to get an update and to drop this off for Brady. We're working on something together."

McCann rolled his eyes but then tossed in a good-natured smile. "We haven't found the person who left the poisoned cupcakes on your porch. We'll let you know when we do."

"What about the person who assaulted me?" I asked, playing along.

McCann smiled at me as though he knew something but couldn't say.

"Switching gears . . ." I dropped the manila folder on Brady's desk. "Any new information on Emiliano Rivas? Tox screens? Gunshot residue from that black-and-pink gun? Surveillance video from his last day alive?"

McCann shook his head. "None of that involves you now."

"The bad guy dropped him in the woods near my house—"

"And that's all he did."

"True. Anyway . . ." I stood and offered him a tight smile. "Please let your partner know that I stopped by."

"Yep." He turned back to his computer before I reached the door.

The kind desk sergeant was on the phone, but I waved at him and tromped back to the parking lot, the weight on my chest lighter, feeling better about sharing the burden. I reached for my phone—

No phone.

I'd left it on the seat back in Brady's office.

Shit.

I headed back to the building.

I smiled at the round sergeant who was still on the phone and headed down the hallway, to Brady's and Will's office. I heard the *zzzzht* and growl of a paper shredder. My heart leaped in my chest.

Behind me, the round desk sergeant said, "Was there something you needed?"

I startled, turning to him and forcing my smile. "No—I just forgot my phone," I said, loud enough for Will McCann to hear. Then I knocked on the doorframe again before standing in the threshold.

Will McCann stood at his desk, his eyes on the phone in his hand.

"Hey," I said. "Sorry to bother you."

Over by the window, the paper shredder's teeth still held a document that had almost been completely eaten. The manila envelope still sat on Brady's desk . . . but the binder clip sat on Will McCann's desk blotter.

"What now?" He looked up from his phone, pretending to be distracted by me.

I pointed to the guest chair. "Left my phone." I grabbed it from the cushion and waggled the device for him to see. Then I left the office and headed down the hallway. Right as I reached the desk sergeant's desk again, I heard the *zzzzht* of the paper shredder.

My stomach dropped, and every nerve in my body screamed.

The neat stacks of clipped evidence on Honor Butler's situation had disappeared into the machine's maw, reduced to thin strips in seconds. First, Brady's weird reaction to "Orville Klein," and now his partner had shredded documents related to Honor's trafficking.

Why?

Back in the truck, I opened my laptop and logged on to PeopleFinder.

Who was Orville Klein?

According to Brady, he was just a guy who lived in Napa with his wife, Cookie.

I tapped in ORVILLE KLEIN and added NAPA since Brady had let that detail slip.

The photo on the screen looked like the man who'd held Honor Butler on his lap on that boat. He'd been born in 1952—there'd been a more than fifty-year age difference between him and his so-called date. He lived on Brittany Circle with Arlene a.k.a. Cookie.

Just a guy.

I clicked a link to his social media.

Facebook quickly gave up the goods.

Orville Klein was a rabbi at Congregation Beth Shalom.

There he was, in one post, on the green with some golfing buddies.

There he was, a delegate at the California Republican convention.

There he was, at a bar mitzvah, surrounded by family who'd been tagged in this photo. His wife Cookie, maybe two sons, Adam and Bill, along with their wives, and grandchildren, Seth, Noah, Amy, and . . .

My eyebrows lifted, and I whispered, "Shit."

Will McCann wearing one of his grandpa suits and a yarmulke.

Orville Klein wasn't "just some guy." He was Will McCann's poppa.

26.

Numb.

I couldn't feel my lips, feet, or hands.

Will McCann had just pretended that he hadn't shredded documents relating to possible sex trafficking in this part of California. He hadn't shredded them because he hadn't seen value in my contributions. He hadn't shredded them because he'd wanted to lead his own investigation. He'd shredded evidence because his grandfather had been one of the predators listed in those files.

That's why Brady had played down Orville Klein's identity—because he knew too.

Cold sweat revived my numb skin. A sense of relief washed over me. I'd made copies of the original documents instead of handing everything over to Brady Kwon. Now that I knew McCann and Brady were compromised . . .

There was no one I could turn to in helping Honor Butler. Because how deep did this corruption go? Had it poisoned all of Sableport and Haven?

Before leaving Sableport, I drove by the McDermott house over on Serenity Street.

No cars were parked in the driveway. No one played with Figgy in the front yard.

I knocked on the door and rang the doorbell.

No one answered.

I rang the doorbell again, but this time smiled for the security camera and said, "Hi, Lincoln. You know why I'm here. I warned you, right? I'm gonna run a few errands and return later this evening. Let's just get this done, okay?" I dropped my smile. "Okay."

Then I growled as I stepped off the porch. *Don't force my hand, dude.*

The air conditioner was roaring inside the offices of Poole Investigations, and the sudden cold rattled my bones. Outside, the temperature had already dropped to the low sixties, and fog had once again rolled past the shores of the Pacific Ocean.

I wasn't sure if my shivering came from the chill in the air or from what I'd seen at the sheriff's substation up in Sableport. McCann shredding evidence . . . He was trying to gut Honor's case before it could officially launch. I dropped into my chair, exhausted by all the bullshit and shenanigans. With my eyeballs thudding in my head, I knew that I was edging up to a breakdown. I needed to be done with all of this. I wanted resolution.

But there was no such thing as total resolution—as a cop, I knew this to be true.

Lincoln McDermott—he was keeping me from checking off something so close to resolution, and I hated him for it.

The bell over the front door jangled. Startled, I hopped out of my chair and hustled to the lobby.

A white man who looked to be about fifty years old, and wearing a perfectly tailored suit, stood at the reception desk. He'd been plucked out of a TV legal drama, all crisp lines and polished shoes. He smiled at me with perfect American teeth and said, "You're Alyson Rush." His voice was a honeyed baritone. "I'm Stan Cain, London Sutton's defense attorney."

Stanley Cain gave me his business card, but I already had his number. I'd dated guys like Cain. Looked good in their suits. More interesting than prosecutors. Better with their tongues. Cunning linguists.

Like the men I'd dated, this one was doing his job. He was about to threaten me. He'd be a lousy lawyer if he didn't.

With my stomach sinking, I gestured to the waiting area. He took a chair near the Skittles machine, and I sat across from him. I didn't offer him coffee, water, or candy—I didn't want him to feel welcomed here . . . not until he needed Poole Investigations for future work.

Over the span of two minutes, Stanley Cain and I lobbed opinions about the fog, about Los Angeles, about fire season.

"So let me tell you why I'm here," Cain said, finally straightening in his chair. "I'll be calling you to the stand during Mrs. Sutton's trial."

My throat went dry, but I managed to say, "Why's that?"

He gave a little shrug. "Because you're a key witness in this case. You know and I know that London's actions weren't entirely her own. You know and I know that this normally levelheaded woman was driven to despair—some might even say temporary insanity."

I frowned, already bracing for the twist I saw coming like a meteor in a dark sky. "What does her temporary insanity have to do with me or with her murdering Xander Monroe?"

"Oh, come on," he said, leaning forward. "Don't play innocent. I know all about your affair with Cooper."

Heat rose to my cheeks. "Mmm."

He waited for me to say more.

I wouldn't give him anything else, not even a rebuke of "It wasn't an affair."

"Before you say that it's not any of my business," Cain said, smiling, "please know that it's entirely my business. Because it's wholly relevant to my client's state of mind. You waltz into Haven, disrupting lives, continuing your affair with a married man. That affair left London devastated and unstable. It pushed her over the edge."

Still no response from me.

"You didn't know Xander Monroe when he was alive, did you?" Cain asked.

"No, I didn't."

Cain shook his head. "He had nude pictures of girls from Oakland."

I shrugged.

"He slept with almost all of them."

"High school girls?"

"Yes, high school girls."

"Cheerleaders?"

"A few, yes."

I gasped. "Wait a minute. Are you telling me that . . . ?" I sat up in my chair and gaped at him. "That a handsome, gifted football player had sex with . . . *high school girls*, probably a few of them . . ." I gasped again. "And that some of them were even . . . *cheerleaders*? What the *fuck* is happening with today's youth?" I smirked and sat back in my chair.

"He pursued my client—"

"One of the high school girls is your client?"

"I'm referring to London Sutton—"

"The forty-year-old woman with a medical degree?"

Stanley Cain lifted his index finger. "He threatened her. Followed her on that trail. She had a right to self-defense."

I blinked at him, burning with anger, but letting it simmer. He wouldn't get me with the depiction of Xander as an oversexed Black male predator committed to taking—no, *stealing*—London Sutton's precious white womanhood. And self-defense? Really? Why did she hide him in the bushes, then? Why didn't she call the cops? Why didn't anyone hear her scream? Where were her bruises? And who carried around syringes filled with liquid nicotine when there were guns, knives, Tasers, pepper sprays, and California mountain lions right there as defense tools?

And what about the weeks before Xander allegedly attacked London Sutton? The texts? The secret meetings? The need for expensive condoms?

Cain had yet to mention that a grown-ass woman—a doctor, no less—was sleeping with a seventeen-year-old boy. There was no consent in this relationship. He. Was. Still. A. Minor.

"Tell me: Why did her despair about Cooper lead her to commit statutory rape?" I asked. "Why didn't she fall into the burly arms of a man of even twenty-one?"

Stanley Cain's neck flushed. He didn't respond.

Because there *was* no response.

London Sutton couldn't claim that Xander had lied to her about his age—she had been his pediatric psychiatrist who knew he'd been depressed about his football injury, who knew he'd just moved up to Haven for his last year of high school, which had also contributed to his depression.

Sure, every road in this town was winding, and sure, maybe all the light was blinding, but London Sutton's claim that she was just an innocent was absurdly and clearly straightforward in its bullshittiness.

Though anger bubbled in my gut, I kept my poker face cool. "Whatever problems London's had, they're on *her*, not me."

"Maybe," Cain said smoothly, "but the jury only needs to see you as part of the chaos that sent her spiraling."

I crossed my legs and said "Mmm" again.

His smile, cold, calculated now, sent a shiver down my spine. "Ms. Rush, I will use everything about you to paint a picture of someone who brought chaos to this town. That will include your history with the LAPD."

My skin tightened. "What about my history?"

Now it was Cain's turn to cross his legs. "You were fired, weren't you? And then sued in civil court for wrongful death? You lost that case. And your boyfriend—my client's husband—is helping you pay that settlement."

I narrowed my eyes at Stan Cain and said "Mmm" again. I wanted to scream and tear off my clothing and run naked through the streets of downtown Haven.

"You aren't innocent in this," he said. "And when I present to the jury about your affair and the money and you flaunting your relationship—"

"Flaunting."

"—the jury will see the real you. The woman who drove London to insanity."

His words landed like blows. Exhaustion settled on my shoulders, and I felt the fight already draining out of me. I couldn't deny my relationship or the money or my past with the LAPD. Flaunted, though? Not at all.

"Why are you telling me this?" I asked, my voice barely above a whisper.

Cain tilted his head. "Because I want you to know what's coming. You've already made enemies here, Ms. Rush. I'm just the one who'll make sure you regret coming to Haven and destroying more lives."

I exhaled, then stood from the chair.

"Nothing to say?" he asked, also standing.

"Nope." I motioned to the candy machines. "Would you like some Skittles or Whoppers? They're fresh."

He chuckled, then walked to the front door. He looked back at me with confused confidence.

I blinked at him, poker faced.

The door opened. The bell rang. Stan Cain left the office, and quiet found its way back to Poole Investigations.

Alone again, I let out a strangled "Fuck" and returned to my office, tears hot in my eyes.

I needed a lawyer.

One more expense.

My phone vibrated from my pocket.

An email notification.

> FWD: Valerie Elizabeth Rush's 10/25 Taos, NM trip: Your reservation is confirmed.

27.

Oh, Haven . . .

This town and me . . .

Together, we were a sad love song, the worst dirge ever. Never enemies to lovers. Right now, forced proximity. Not that I ever held romance in my heart—I was a cop, badge or not—but I wanted to give people a happily ever after. I wanted to slay all dragons and ride into the sunset . . . but not this way. In Haven, there were dragons, werewolves, and zombies, and I had one rusty blade with a broken handle in my busted hand.

So far from romance. Very much an American tragedy.

I just needed to make it to the end.

Making the victim into the villain . . . Defense attorneys played this awful trick all the time. This time, though . . . *insidious*. Stanley Cain planned to lean into race, the threat of Black manhood and their wild, voracious sexuality destroying white womanhood . . . and then blaming the Black whore—*me*—for the white woman's continued diminishment.

Xander's parents weren't dumb. I'm sure their attorney knew the angles that Cain would play. But I wanted to tell them since I'd heard that strategy fresh and in person.

But Lori Monroe wasn't answering my call.

I left a voicemail, including as many details as I could so she wouldn't have to call me back—she had a lot on her plate. Burying her son was the most important task right now.

I also wanted to let Cooper know that Stanley Cain and London were taking the tried-and-true bigot path to freedom—but I didn't know the best way to do that. Our text messages would probably be subpoenaed to serve as foundation for her temporary insanity claim. Worse: Stanley Cain probably had his own investigator clocking everything that Cooper did with me.

We both needed to watch our backs.

Although the clock said it was only five thirty, the world felt like it was close to midnight. Mom had made smothered chicken and onions for dinner, and she tried to keep me company as I ate, but she kept falling asleep as *Real Housewives of Beverly Hills* played on the living room television and filled the silence.

I told Mom that I'd clean the kitchen, and she tottered off to bed—neither of us had the heart or energy to discuss her Taos trip.

After completing my chores, I retreated to my bedroom closet and found the lush Hermès dust bag. I'd taken out my red Birkin three times: for a gala for the mayor of Los Angeles, on vacation with Cooper to Palm Springs, and for a sorority brunch in Beverly Hills. That qualified on a resell site as lightly used. Cooper had loved me enough to use his reward—one couldn't just *buy* an ultra-expensive Birkin, and neither of us knew what he'd done to score it—but now I needed it to no longer carry my wallet but to hire an attorney who'd defend me. Just like that, a Birkin bag had become a means to an end. Its prestige and status had become a life-saving buoy.

Yeah, another American tragedy.

I took a shower and tried not to think of anything else except scrubbing and which lotion to use afterward to moisturize my skin. In bed, I glanced one last time at my phone.

I closed my eyes and hoped that I wouldn't dream—I wanted sleep all to myself, not even sharing it with the subconscious me.

If only I'd arrested Royalty Miller, Autumn Suarez would be alive right now. Then I'd be a detective sergeant down in Los Angeles, enjoying Korean BBQ after working a case for forty-eight hours without a break. If I hadn't gone to that art exhibit in Santa Monica and not looked across the hall to see Cooper staring at me . . . if I hadn't fallen in love with him . . . Haven would've remained that place way up there where Uncle Ivan lived.

But my fucking heart . . . feeling compassion for the young mother shoplifting bologna and diapers. Softening for the handsome developer who enjoyed a good burger and my kisses and . . . and . . .

. . .

. . .

The soft chimes of my ringing phone pulled me out of sleep. I squinted against the darkness and grabbed the device from my nightstand.

Ivan.

I said, "Hey—"

"Get to the office," he said. *"Now."* Then, he hung up.

The screen still shone bright in my hand. It was just eight minutes after four thirty in the morning. The haze of sleep melted into a cold knot in my stomach. What bad thing had happened? And then I remembered: I wasn't a homicide detective. I didn't have to go anywhere.

I called Ivan back, but he wouldn't pick up nor did he let it roll to voicemail. The phone just rang . . . rang . . . rang . . .

Ugh.

I pulled on a thick hoodie and sweats, a leather jacket, and a black LA Dodgers baseball cap. I grabbed my gun from her case and checked the magazine. Fifteen rounds. I prayed that I'd have fifteen rounds when I came back home. I left a sticky note on the microwave for Mom:

Emergency @ office. Be back soon.

Hopefully I'd be home before she awakened.

The fog outside was thicker than I'd ever seen it, curling around the cottage like a ghostly shroud. Driving that mile into town was a slow crawl—the Bronco's headlights barely pierced through the white soup. I held my breath most of the way.

I turned onto Seaview Way and spotted Ivan, a shadow made by the closest streetlight. He stood in the middle of the road in front of the office and aimed a brightly shining flashlight at a body at his feet.

No. *No, no, no.*

My heart bucked in my chest, but the Bronco bucked more as I slammed her into park. I threw open the door and shouted, "Who is that?" The cold air slapped me, but I didn't slow down.

Ivan's face was as pale as the fog. He wore a gray USC sweatshirt and jeans. No blood. He shook his head and gestured to the body on the asphalt.

Dave Kruger.

"What happened?" My wild gaze swept over Ivan.

"I got an alert that someone was fucking with the door," he said, rubbing his face. "So, I came over and found him . . ."

I stepped closer to the man sprawled unnaturally against the asphalt.

Dave Kruger's face was slack, his eyes wide open and glassy. His black T-shirt was ripped and glistened with something wet. A dark pool of liquid spread beneath him and seeped into the cracks of the asphalt.

"I called it in before I called you," Ivan said, his voice low.

I squinted closer at the dead man's chest. "Is that . . ." A piece of paper was stuck to his chest, so bloody, it almost looked black. A scrawled message had been written in thick black marker.

LET IT BE OR YOU'RE NEXT

"Who would do this?" I asked.

Ivan shook his head. "Don't know."

"Who is the 'you' in 'you're next'? You? Me? All of Haven?"

Ivan shook his head again. "Don't know."

I shivered as the fog pressed in around us, muffling the world and amping up the silence. Standing there . . . it was like Ivan and I were the only two people left alive in Haven.

Until I heard the sirens.

Pods of lookie-loos had gathered behind the yellow tape now strung across Seaview Way. Many held up phones to record the early-morning drama.

My gaze roamed the growing crowd.

Was the murderer here?

Or was the murderer working the scene?

Brady saw Ivan and me standing on the civilian side of the tape—and he pretended that I was just another face in the crowd.

McCann—I didn't see that fucker. Was he still at the office shredding documents?

I wanted to tell Ivan about Will McCann, but then I'd have to tell him that I was working with Brady Kwon on Honor's case . . . and also explain to him why I called Brady on the night Honor showed up on my porch and not him.

Ugh.

Dave Kruger wasn't dead yet, but he was lingering in its immediate presence. The waxy pallor and the distant eyes . . . Just a matter of time. But he had something to say to me—at least that's what the paramedic told me after finding me standing behind the yellow tape.

Ivan and I exchanged looks.

"Record it," Ivan whispered as I ducked beneath the tape.

"Yep." I'd forgotten about my transcription software but now found the app and tapped record as I followed the paramedic to the ambulance. I climbed into the back of the rig and settled on the bench beside Dave Kruger's stretcher.

The paramedic pulled the door shut. The driver up front put the wagon into drive and hit the siren. Guess I was going to the hospital too.

Dave Kruger wore an oxygen mask. His heart rate was slowing and blood pressure dropping. In addition to the smell of diesel and iodine, I whiffed the scent of patchouli and moss. The same loud cologne I'd smelled in the forest yesterday. Had Dave Kruger been the one following me?

I leaned over and said, "Dave, it's Sonny Rush. Looks like you pissed somebody off real good."

He tried to smile. "Huh . . . huh . . . heart."

"Your heart is the least of it," I said, my eyes skipping around his bloody T-shirt.

"Juh . . . Jay . . . Jay . . ." he said, then his lips moved but no sound came.

"Jay?" I asked. "Jaylayne? Your ex-wife?"

His eyes brightened. "Chu . . . chu . . . check."

My eyebrows scrunched. "I don't understand—"

"Huh . . . heart. Check." His hand wagged in the restraints and his pulse sped up.

I took his hand.

His pulse slowed. "Stop it . . . Her."

"Stop what, Dave? Her? Who?" I placed my second hand atop his and watched his pulse quicken. But then the long beep sounded, and the paramedic sighed.

5:55 a.m.

Dave Kruger was dead before we reached the emergency room bay at Sableport Presbyterian Hospital.

Brady Kwon had taken over an empty doctor's office and now sat back in the chair. After working a crime scene so early in the morning, he looked like shit—dark circles under his eyes, whiskers along his jaw, rumpled jacket. He hadn't returned my messages, and by the hard line of his dried lips, he wanted to keep not talking to me. But alas, Brady's victim had offered his last words to the woman Brady now . . .

Loathed?

Hated?

What the hell was Brady's problem with me?

He wouldn't answer that question when I asked. Instead, he said, "Can we just . . . ?" He rubbed the bridge of his nose.

"Fine," I said.

"What did Dave say to you?" he asked.

I squinted at him, then played my conversation with Dave Kruger.

Brady asked me to play the recording two more times.

I did and sent him both the audio and text files.

"Anything else?" I asked.

He said "Nope" and stood from the chair.

"What's your problem?" I asked again.

He chuckled and glared at the ceiling. "I don't have a problem."

His response was supposed to be "What makes you say that?" and I was prepared to offer him my list of grievances. But he didn't.

Frustrated, I pushed my hair off my forehead.

He made a dramatic sweep of his arm to look at his watch. "Anything else? I gotta get back to Haven."

"Would it trouble you to give me a ride back?" I asked.

He turned to leave the office. "Come on."

I followed him through the crowded hallways filled with injured people on stretchers. Out in the waiting room, loved ones paced as other patients waited their turns for treatment.

Brady approached a female patrol officer with a hard-gelled hair bun. Her nameplate said Reyna Bell. "Hey, Rey," he said. "This is Sonny Rush. Sonny, this is Deputy Bell. Rey, would you mind driving Miss Rush back to Haven?"

My eyebrows lifted.

“Sure thing,” the patrol officer said.

Brady flicked a smile at her, nodded at me, then stalked past the double doors to the parking lot. Out there, dawn had broken across this part of California. According to my phone, it was now almost eight o’clock.

28.

The sky had lightened beyond the fog's white veil. Neither Deputy Bell nor I spoke during the ten-minute drive, not until I asked that she drop me at Poole Investigations, the street still being held captive by a few sheriff's deputies and crime scene technicians.

There were no news vans ready to shoot live in downtown Haven. Would anyone outside this place ever learn—or care—that Dave Kruger, the foreman of Lumière Spa and Resort, had been killed?

Ivan was leaning against the front door of the Victorian and scowling at his watch. For homicide investigations down in Los Angeles, we'd keep the street blocked off for most of the day. Here in Haven, tourists had to be spared the horrors of lingering bad things like murder and loss—these cops and CSIs wouldn't be here long, not with brunch starting soon.

Deputy Bell tossed a wave to the deputies working the scene, pulled alongside the curb, and put her sedan in park. "So this is the famous Poole Investigations."

I cocked an eyebrow. "Famous?"

She chuckled. "Almost every cop I know wants to work for Ivan. I know that he's got a waiting list."

I shrugged. "Guess Ivan wants to keep it small."

She said, "Sure. 'Small' is one or two people. Five is . . . *not.*" She chuckled again. The radio *blurp*ed, and the dispatcher called her name. She reached for the handheld.

Five?

I muttered "Thanks for the ride" and hopped out of the patrol car just as Brady Kwon pulled into a spot behind her. I glared at him as I marched to join Ivan at the office door.

Since we had precious CCTV that would be useful, Brady Kwon let Ivan and me enter the building, even though the scene was still being processed. He followed us down the hallway to Ivan's office.

Ivan played the footage that had first alerted him to someone futzing with the door.

Dave Kruger, his face hidden by a balaclava and baseball cap, had parked his Subaru in my usual spot. He had hurried over to the front door and wiggled the doorknob.

"Why did he think someone was here?" Brady asked.

"I keep a light on upstairs," Ivan said.

A car approaching off-screen lit up the side of Dave's truck with its headlamps.

Dave had turned and started to back up, threatened by whoever was approaching. He'd held up his hands as he talked and walked and—

"Wait," I said. "Stop. Go back."

Ivan pressed the rewind button.

"There," I said.

Dave had been talking and . . .

"That," I said. "He's talking to two people. One person's taller than the other."

Ivan tapped rewind and played the recording again, and yeah, Dave had started talking to one person, and then his head tilted up to address the second person. That second person's hands shot out.

Dave had blocked his face and grimaced.

"Pepper spray?" Ivan asked.

I said, "Yep."

The shorter person, also wearing a cap, burst into view, big knife out. Stab in the chest, stab in the arm, slash to Dave's neck. Dave had stumbled back and out of view. The second killer's profile followed him until Dave came back into view, now standing in the middle of Seaview Way. That's where he'd collapsed.

The knife guy bent over, stabbing Dave again and again. He placed the note on Dave's chest before stepping away.

Then both perps hustled in the direction they'd come.

The light in the side panel of the car had dimmed . . . dimmed . . .

Dave lay there, still.

Ten minutes passed and the side of Dave's Subaru lit up again. Ivan lumbered into view. He'd stopped in his step, and then he'd hurried over. He stayed down for two minutes until he stood and started pacing with his phone to his ear . . . He kept pacing until he'd been lit up by approaching headlamps. And then there I was, gaping at the body on the ground.

Brady asked Ivan to email him the recording. Then the investigator hustled out of the office and down the hallway.

Ivan and I stayed seated and listened to the bell jangle over the door. My godfather didn't speak, just stared out the window, his face lined with exhaustion. Then he loudly exhaled, then rolled his chair over to the credenza. He pulled out the bottle of bourbon and two short glasses.

He didn't ask if I wanted any. He just poured, pushing the second glass toward me before sighing loud and long and sinking deeper into his chair.

I held up the glass—the amber liquid glinted in the dim light. "Starting early, are we?"

Ivan's chuckle was more air than sound. "We've earned it."

I cradled the glass of bourbon but didn't drink yet. My hands were still trembling.

Ivan took a long sip before setting it down with a soft thump. "Want more bad news?"

"No."

"Araceli never paid her fee," he said, his voice flat.

I blinked. "You're kidding."

He rubbed a hand over his face. "She said that, technically, we didn't find Emiliano." He paused, then said, "No more promises of a digital cash payment. Cashier's check or cash deposits only, and *then* you start the case. Fuck this 'It's not going through' and 'What do you mean, it didn't transfer' bullshit."

My ire sparked, and that's when I took my first sip. The alcohol, though, wasn't as hot as my anger.

Ivan stared at his glass like it held answers to this morning's madness.

The silence stretched.

Ivan's shoulders were shaking. He leaned forward, resting his elbows on the desk, and buried his face in his hands. "I don't know if I can keep doing this," he said, his voice muffled. "Getting too old for this shit."

He slowly lowered his hands. When he looked at me, his eyes were shiny, and the lines of his face were deeper than his regret.

I pulled up the picture I'd taken of the note left on Dave's chest.

LET IT BE OR YOU'RE NEXT

Ivan refilled his glass with more bourbon.

"Dave Kruger was following me in the woods yesterday," I said.

That made Ivan pause. "*What?* Why?"

"Don't know. I didn't see him—just . . . smelled him." Then I told him about my walk in the woods.

"Because you'd asked him about his dead worker?" Ivan said.

I shrugged. "I guess. Maybe he was trying to intimidate another worker on the job and they caught him and—"

"Killed him?" For a moment, Ivan looked skeptical, but then he cocked his head. "Maybe." He reached into his desk and grabbed a small manila envelope. He pushed it across the desk. "You've got mail. Someone slipped this into the mail slot."

I tore open the envelope and dumped the contents on the desktop.

A regular house key on a plastic dumbbell fob. Two pieces of folded paper. The first sheet: a death certificate for Jaylayne Merkley with a sticky note on it. The second sheet: a printout of after-clinic visit notes for Jaylayne Merkley.

"What the hell?" I muttered.

Ivan read aloud the sticky note on the death certificate. "I may have hated her with all my heart, but she didn't deserve this. I will stop by tomorrow. D.K."

D.K.

"Dave Kruger?" Ivan said. "Why the hell would he send—"

"Her heart," I said, remembering my time with the dying man in the ambulance. "He said to check her heart."

Jaylayne Merkley's after-clinic visit was dated August 1, weeks before her death noted as August 13 on her death certificate. Dr. Jones-Smith said that Jaylayne had been a healthy woman. Good heart. Good weight. Good cholesterol. Sure, she had high blood pressure, but nothing to be worried about. He gave her some water pills and sent her on her way.

Thirteen days later . . . heart attack.

Both Ivan and I said, "Hmm."

"What could've brought on a sudden cardiac arrest?" I asked.

We drank as we thought about that. Then:

"I knew a cop," Ivan said. "Oscar Lynch. Picture of health. We were called to a scene. Accident. Lotta cars. Lotta bodies. Lynch sees a little girl, and her leg is trapped in the door of an old Buick. She's bleeding out. Only one Jaws of Life at the scene, and they were being used to pry open the door of another car. Lynch couldn't let this girl die—he's got one at home that looks just like her.

"So he rushes over, and I'm following him. The damn door isn't opening. But that doesn't stop Lynch. He uses his bare fucking hands and the will of fucking Satan and the great United States of America to pry open this fucking door . . . His veins are pressing up his face and his neck, and he's lookin' like the fuckin' Rock, and . . ."

Ivan's eyes glazed as he remembered. "And he gets the door open. The girl—she's pulled out of the car, rushed over to an ambulance, and . . ." Ivan sighed.

I sipped my bourbon, waiting for more. "And then . . . ?"

"Oscar Lynch drops dead right there. Heart attack."

I said, "The exertion?"

Ivan nodded. "His heart just said, 'Fuck it.'"

I said, "Hmm."

Too much.

"Is that what Dave thought?" I wondered aloud. "That Jaylayne's heart had done too much of something and gave out?"

"Maybe that's why he gave you . . ." Ivan pointed at the house key on the dumbbell fob.

"Maybe."

"Check it before you give it away," Ivan said. "Once MCSO takes over, you'll be locked out." He sipped bourbon, then said, behind the glass, "But I guess you know that already."

I stared at him.

"I warned you about Kwon," he said. "You didn't listen."

I grunted and sipped my bourbon.

"This is all my fault," he said. "You coming here. I shouldn't have—"

"Cooper was here," I said, "which meant that I was coming to Haven even if you didn't ask me to work for you."

"You're about to break apart sitting there," he said. "Being a stubborn ass and bourbon are the only things keepin' you together."

I waggled my head. "I just . . . I need a breath." I gulped more bourbon and closed my eyes as my limbs warmed, as the muscles around my neck loosened . . . but not all the way. I didn't know who I'd be with soft shoulders.

And I needed them hard—didn't know what bullshit I was about to face. And anyway, my set of armor was hard earned and hard to come by.

After finishing our morning libations, Ivan and I left the office for the cold outside.

No CSIs. No sheriff's deputies. No cameras.

Ivan sighed. "If you can, go get some sleep."

I snorted and rolled my eyes. "Okay."

"Maybe you'll eventually get some deep sleep in with Val away."

"Away?"

Ivan stretched. "For the hot air balloon festival. She'll enjoy her time away, and you can sleep with both eyes closed."

"Yeah."

But . . .

I hadn't told Ivan about the hot air balloon festival.

Maybe, after she'd confessed about our family finances, Mom had called Ivan to let him know that our family shame was no longer a big secret. Maybe, in that same conversation, she told him that she was now long-distance-dating an old friend who'd invited her to Taos to see hot air balloons.

The thought of Ivan and my mother talking again made me smile. That I'd been shut out of that, though . . . But then, I'd been shut out of almost everything in my life. I'd become an outsider, and this reconciliation between my mother and godfather was just one more thing.

Morning sun pushed past the fog to light up the cottage like a waystation. Brady's Yukon was parked in the gravel driveway. Seeing him standing there in his rumpled MCSO polo and chinos made my head explode. My mouth tasted sour from the bourbon lingering on my tongue. I hopped out of the car, almost forgetting to turn it off first. "Is my mother okay?"

He cocked his head. "Huh?"

I tried to run past him and up the porch.

Brady caught my elbow. "She left with Giovanni and Elliott."

I yanked away from him.

"Sorry," he said. "Didn't mean to scare you."

"What do you want, then?"

He motioned to the cottage. "Not gonna invite me in?"

I lifted my eyebrows. "I don't bring strangers into my home."

"Honor Butler—"

"—was a stranger and also a minor in danger."

He said "Ah," then nodded. "You okay?"

I waved a dismissive hand. "Doesn't matter." I folded my arms and leaned against the porch banister. "Why are you here?"

"I wanted to check in," he said. "After this morning and, you know, everything else."

"Anything you can share about Dave Kruger?" I asked.

Brady shoved his hands into his pants pockets. "C'mon, Sonny. The investigation just started."

"Sure," I said, squinting at him.

"What's that look for?" he asked, grinning.

"You're standing here like we're . . ."

"Like we're what?"

"Like we're okay again."

"We aren't?" he asked.

I gaped at him. "Wow. That's some skillful being willfully obtuse."

He laughed. "What? Fine. You want me to say Kruger's death is related to Emiliano's? That Honor is Dave Kruger's secret daughter?"

"Don't mock me." Because there *was* a thread connecting all of this—I just couldn't see it. I swallowed to get rid of that sour taste of defeat—it was worse than morning bourbon.

"Have you talked to Tank?" I asked.

Brady said, "Yeah. Great guy."

I snorted. "Great guy? Are we talking about the same immigration officer who'd be just as comfortable on a front lawn burning a cross as he is roughing up young brown women holding newborns to their bosoms?"

Brady winced. "When you put it like that . . ."

I paused and waited for more. "So what did you discuss?"

A veil dropped over his eyes. "Can't say. It's an active investigation."

I lifted an eyebrow. "I'm aware—and I helped *a lot*, which is why you have that scary man in your phone directory now."

Brady said "Sure," but then he didn't say anything else.

"With these new rules you now have, is there anything you can tell?"

He rolled his eyes. "I don't have new rules—I can't just . . ." He pushed out a breath and said, "Liam Dyer."

"What about him?"

"He left Haven two days ago. He's now in Portugal for study abroad."

I nodded. "Last time I checked, Portugal extradited Americans."

"*Rich* Americans?" Brady asked. "Cuz that's what Liam is."

"Are you saying he's gonna get away with running a sex trafficking operation—"

"Allegedly—"

"I'm not a lawyer," I blurted. "I can say what he is—"

"And you're not a cop either—"

"Which means I can *really* say what he is." I held Brady's gaze—a quality of character that I used to see there no longer twinkled. It had tricked me into trusting him, trusting whatever he told me.

"Why didn't you tell me that you received the tox results on Mackenzie Sutton?" I asked him, unblinking.

"Your old boyfriend didn't need to know that until we were ready to tell him."

I cocked my head. "Oh. So, you think I rush back to tell Cooper everything I find out? Is that why you're freezing me out? Because you think I'm back together with my ex? You were the one who wanted to go there with me, remember? I wanted us to remain professional, but you told me that you were a big boy, that you could handle it. Either you lied or you believed your own hype."

He backed away from me. "I didn't come here to fight with you—"

"What *did* you come here for, then?" I asked. "Cuz it's not to share information or move anything forward on any of these investigations."

He held out his arms. "I fucked up. Yes, I believed that I could compartmentalize. Wrong. I can't. I want to take you to dinner. Getaways up and down the coast. But not with you the way you are. What you are."

I narrowed my eyes. "This isn't about me—"

"The hell it isn't."

"No." I kept squinting at him, at the vein ticking along his jaw, at his clenched fists, the way he covered his eyes with a shaky hand. "What happened, Brady?"

He looked away, his neck flushed all the way to his ears. "How did you do it?" he asked.

"How did I do *what*?"

"Move to a new town and start over?"

"You make it sound like I succeeded—"

"You have."

"Do you *see* me?" I asked, a manic grin on my lips. "Do you see my reality?"

He shrugged. "But you're moving ahead no matter what the LAPD thinks about you. Despite what they did to you."

I clomped up the porch steps. "Guess we have different definitions of 'success,' then." I paused, then said, "Honor Butler."

He shook his head. "I'm handing that over to the FBI. We don't have the capacity to handle something that big."

"Handing it over," I said. "So you got the envelope I left you—"

"On my desk? Yep."

"And you reviewed everything?" I asked.

"I did."

"The phone records?" I asked.

"Yep."

I hadn't included phone records because I didn't *have* phone records. "And the transcripts of the voicemails?"

He nodded. "And I'm meeting with an agent down in the Bay to discuss it all."

"Great." Except that I hadn't included transcripts either. What I *had* included had been shredded by Will McCann.

Brady had just lied to me. I no longer had to doubt him—I knew for sure not to trust him.

Silence fell between Brady and me, and he smiled and gazed at me beneath his brows. “You know, we could use a real meal. How about dinner tonight? This time a place with cloth napkins.”

I blinked at him.

His smile warmed and widened. “Just dinner. We haven’t talked in a moment.” When I still didn’t respond, he said, “Think about it. Totally selfish—I need you to save me from my newest murder book.”

I said, “Mmm.”

He said, “Call you later?”

I said “Yep” and trudged into the cottage, my body weary, my mind gooey. I undressed and climbed into the shower to wash off the sick and the dead, refusing to think about Brady’s visit and the real reason he stopped by my—

I cocked my head.

What’s that?

I peeked past the soapy shower door to see my phone buzzing from the sink. I rinsed away the soap, turned off the water, and grabbed my phone.

No, this message hadn’t been left by Brady. Nor was it a text. The video loaded slowly, then the first frame played.

My heart plummeted.

Mom stood at the end of the pier, her face pale, her body rigid. The camera reversed to show someone wearing dark glasses and a balaclava to hide their features.

“Leave Haven,” the person said, “or you’ll never see her again.” Then the video ended.

My hands trembled as I gripped the phone. A cold sweat broke across my skin as I tapped Ivan’s number.

He answered on the first ring. “What’s—”

“Go to the bakery *right now.*”

29.

Mom wouldn't answer my call, and I kept being sent to voicemail. There wasn't an AirTag in the shoes she wore, and mSpy wasn't refreshing. No one answered the phone at Sweetlife.

My drive over to the bakery was a blur.

Pennsylvania, Rhode Island, South Carolina, South Dakota . . .

I zipped around the corner and spotted Ivan's truck already parked near the shop. I burst into the bakery to see Mom sitting in a booth with my godfather who still wore the gray USC sweatshirt he'd been wearing the last time I saw him.

"Mom!" I said, nearly shouting.

"Sonny? What's wrong?" she asked, bright in her blue Sweetlife T-shirt.

Relief and anger rolled through my chest. She was fine—unharmed, oblivious. She scooted out of the booth and said, "You two are scaring me."

I pulled her into a tight hug. "I just . . . I got . . . freaked out."

Ivan peered at me. "You don't just freak out."

I said, "Let's talk in the office."

Mom led Ivan and me behind the counter, into the workroom and into the sun-filled office of Sweetlife. Giovanni and Elliott were designing a cake on a large touch-screen monitor. Their eyes widened seeing the three of us invade their space.

Giovanni sensed trouble first. "What happened?"

I told them that I'd been taking a shower when the message came. Then I played the video for them. Elliott gasped. Giovanni squeezed my hand.

Mom wandered to the window and peered out to the ocean, her cheeks quivering with rage and sadness. "I'm too young for this," she whispered, then closed her eyes. "Not now, Lord. Please. Not now."

Ivan, his fists clenched, spoke first. "We'll find whoever's behind this, Val. They won't get away with it."

Oh, but they'd already won.

I didn't care anymore. Not about Araceli reneging on her bill. Not about dead Dave Kruger and dead Jaylayne Merkley. Not about any of these strangers I'd met in my time in Haven, because that's who they were: strangers. I hadn't taken a vow before God and the mayor of this city to protect and serve this slowly dwindling population madly intent on killing each other.

Fuck Haven. Ain't gotta tell me twice.

Ivan drove Mom back to the cottage, their reunion now forced by necessity.

I pulled up to Cooper's house. After parking, I sat there for a moment, gripping the steering wheel. I didn't want to be here. I didn't want to ask for help. But right now, I had few choices. After finally working up the nerve, I left the Bronco and trudged up the walkway to his front door. My legs felt lead-heavy, and the pit in my stomach deepened with each step I took.

The door opened before I could knock. Cooper stood there, head cocked, confusion and concern a mix on his face.

Before he could speak, I blurted, "I need your help."

"What's going on?" He stepped aside to let me in.

But I remained standing at the threshold. "I'm not sure that's . . ." I shook my head.

He squinted at me for a moment. "I'm not gonna stop living just because Cain is trying to catch me doing something."

My eyebrows shot high on my forehead.

He beckoned me to follow him.

"Sonny, sweetheart," Auntie Emilie LaPlanche called from the kitchen.

Uncle Frank LaPlanche sat out on the deck, reading the newspaper and drinking coffee. The older woman wore an Emory University sweatshirt and looked like she'd come straight from the hair salon to Haven—her short silver hair had been edged within an inch of its life. And now she pulled me into a tight hug and said, "I was hoping to see you."

Uncle Frank waved at me from the deck.

Auntie Lee asked me about my mother, about my health, about my relocation.

I told her the truth and sighed. "Wish I had a better update than that."

She cupped my cheek. "Tiens bon."

I gave her a sad smile. "I won't give up—I promise."

Cooper said, "Gotta steal her, Auntie."

She squeezed my shoulder. "It'll all work out."

A moment later, I stood in Cooper's office, a space dedicated to glass, more glass, and an expansive view of the Pacific Ocean. "Coop," I said, "I didn't come to—"

He aimed a remote control at the large monitor on the wall. "Behold." The screen filled with the renderings of the sunroom at Lumière. Creamy ceramic flooring with deep-blue tiling in the small pool. Large windows lined the wall and ceiling.

My eyes filled with tears. "You're still building it?"

He looked back at me. "Of course I am." He then clicked to advance the slideshow.

Potted plants and glass tables and light-colored chairs.

My shoulders eased just looking at this oasis.

"I never lied to you about my heart or my love for you—" He looked back at me again, and this time he saw the tears and fear in my eyes. He came over to me and cupped my elbows with his hands.

I swiped my wet cheek against my shoulder. "I shouldn't have come to Haven. But I did because I fucked up so bad—"

"But you didn't," he said. "Showing mercy wasn't fucking up, babe. You have to forgive yourself—" He hugged me.

I wanted to finally exhale and relax against him, but I couldn't—too much work to do. "I need to stay at the condo in Sableport," I said, "and . . . I need to place Mom in Sunset Park." I showed him the video of the threat made against Mom and me, then said, "I just . . . I need to get away for a bit. And I need her somewhere safe."

He nodded, then padded over to his desk. "You know you can stay there as long as you need. And we'll look at Sunset Park tomorrow." He found the keys and tossed them to me.

"I can't just let you give me this," I said, shaking my head. "What do you want, Coop?"

He thought for a moment, took a deep breath, and said, "I want you to forgive me."

Not even twenty-four hours had passed, and I had fifteen bids for the Birkin; the top price—$15,000—had been offered by a woman down in Pacific Palisades.

Back at the cottage, I thanked Ivan for looking after Mom and told him that we'd be staying at India's for a moment. He gave me a hug and then climbed into his Toyota Tundra.

I found Mom standing in the living room. Her eyes lit up, but then she remembered—and remembering made her smile wobble.

"I'll be ready in ten," I said, my voice steady. "We're staying in Sableport."

"With Indy?" she asked.

"No. At a friend's condo."

"Which friend?"

"Doesn't matter," I said. "Be ready to go in ten minutes. Just pack a bag."

"First." Mom sat her phone on the breakfast counter between us. On the phone's screen: the mSpy app. After a long pause, she placed something else beside the phone.

An AirTag.

"What are these things?" she asked.

I swallowed. "Trackers."

Her lips pursed, and her jaw clenched.

"Just spit it out," I said, already beat up by the day. Might as well stay clenched in my protective ball and take the hits.

"You just wanna lock me up in some fancy jail," she accused. "You don't want me to have friends because you don't have any—"

Ouch.

Mom glared at me. "It's like you're a possessive boyfriend."

"Because I don't want you hit by a logging truck or kidnapped, raped, murdered, falling off cliffs, or eaten by bears?" I asked.

Her lips turned into a hard line. "I can handle myself."

I scoffed.

"I'm going to Taos with Quincy," she said.

"How you getting to the airport?"

"I'll take an Uber."

"Using whose phone?"

"I can put it on my phone."

"Using whose credit card?"

She didn't have credit cards anymore. Tears shone in her eyes. "I'm going—"

"Give me his number."

"Why?"

"I want to talk to him."

"Why?"

"Because I'm a possessive boyfriend," I snarled. "I'm not putting you on a fucking airplane to the desert to be with some man I haven't seen in five years. Don't act like I'm being unreasonable here."

She watched me for a moment, and her jaw unclenched. She swiped on her phone and recited his phone number.

The line rang . . . rang . . . rang . . . An automated lady told me to leave a message.

I did leave a message—and even sounded like I was thrilled to talk with him soon. I ended the call, and the smile I'd pulled on fell back off. "He needs to call me."

Mom nodded. "He will."

I looked at her, chin up. "You may not want to admit it, but I know the truth. I've been the one answering the phone and being told to come pick you up from the grocery store or police station because you'd wandered off again. I've been tracking you, and I've still managed to lose you. I'm standing right here, in front of you, and wondering if the next thing you're gonna say will be 'Go wake your father up.'"

Horror crossed her face, and she started to shake her head.

"You talk about him in the present tense, Mom." Tears, hot and fat, burned in my eyes.

She glared at the AirTag and shook her head. "How many times?"

"Isn't once enough?" When she didn't answer, I swiped my wet cheeks. "In the last three days? Maybe five times."

She mouthed, "Five?"

I just wanted to climb in bed and pull the sheets over my head, drink until I drowned, skip tomorrow, and wake up next year. Happiness couldn't exist in this town, in this neighborhood, in this cottage. That is, if happiness—genuine forms of it—still existed in this world.

Mom exhaled and pushed the AirTag into her hand. She took off her shoe and placed the device back in the tongue. "He makes me feel like . . . Val again."

"I'm sure he does."

"I can't wait to see him again." She pulled me into a hug and kissed my cheek.

"I know," I said. "He needs to call me."

"He will."

She really thought that I'd just . . . *let her go*.

Mom left me with one last kiss before turning to the fridge. "Are we eating here or in Sableport?"

"Sableport." I backed out of the kitchen and headed toward my bedroom, feeling like shit.

Was this my own biological fate? Would I inherit my dad's liver or my mother's mind? Or would I suffer with both, that is, if the gods wanted to be even crueler than what they'd been? And if this was my future . . .

Why the hell was I wasting it chasing other people's demons?

Before leaving Haven for Sableport, I stopped at FedEx and shipped the bag to the woman in Pacific Palisades. Then I collected my digital payment.

By two o'clock, my mother and I were in the Bronco, on the road, heading north. Mom sat quietly in the passenger seat as we zoomed past stretches of rugged coastline and rolling hills bathed in sunlight.

"You're too quiet," she said, breaking the silence.

"Just thinking," I said.

"About?"

I sighed, my chest aching with the weight of everything I couldn't say. "About whether I can keep doing this."

Mom turned to me with clear and sharp eyes. "You're stronger than you think."

I let out a bitter laugh. "Am I? Because right now, I'm barely holding it together."

"You think no other woman in the world hasn't felt that way?" she shot back. "Raising you and running a bakery, basically a single parent with your father's schedule. You think I didn't have moments when I wanted to give up?"

I glanced over at her.

"Don't you dare give up, Alyson," she said, her tone softening. "Not when you're doing the right thing. No matter how much it costs."

"And what if it costs too much?" I whispered.

"Then . . ." She reached over and placed a hand on mine.

Then . . . *what*?

I pointed at Sunset Park Senior Living. "That's the place."

Eyes big, Mom gasped. "Oh my. That's gorgeous."

I pulled into Sunset Park's driveway and slowly rolled past the large, rolling green lawn. A group of seniors were in the park slowly moving, practicing tai chi. Others tossed bocce balls while a few walked dogs.

"Looks expensive," Mom said. "We'd be able to afford this?"

No.

"We'll figure it out," I said.

Her eyes glimmered. "The rooms must be really nice."

At $6,000 a month, they better be Liberace suites.

She turned to me and smiled. "And you wouldn't be far away?"

"Nope." I pointed up ahead on the road. "You can almost see the condos from here."

She nodded. "Okay. But only if we can afford it."

I patted her knee. "I'll figure it out." I already knew that I'd do anything to keep her safe.

The last time I drove through these gates, Cooper had tried to convince me to move here. I'd balked. So much had changed since then.

India stood at the door to unit 7A. After hugging Mom and me, she opened the trunk of her car to show us bags of groceries. *I may not have lots of friends, Mother, but this one . . .* She was silver and gold.

I unlocked the door to unit 7A and led Mom and India inside. The condo was sleek and clean with big windows overlooking the ocean. But as I stood there in the quiet, watching the waves crash against the rocks below, I couldn't shake the feeling that no matter how far I ran, shadows—Haven's, Los Angeles'—would find me.

Hey are we doing this?

Dinner I mean

I turned over on the outside deck chair and ignored Brady's latest message just like I'd ignored I'll be done at around 5 and Surf or turf or both and I'll find a spot that has all the neon lights working. He didn't get to do that—lie and ice me out before we'd even slept together. Lying and icing were reserved for lovers only.

I'd responded to Cooper's texts because he'd been my lover, and also, I was now living rent-free in his condominium. So when he texted EVERYTHING OKAY? I'd responded with a simple YES THANKS.

Ivan texted too.

You good?

Yes

Tell India that I owe her

OK

Let me know when you're ready to head back

Didn't know when that would be. If that would *ever* be. I mean . . . sure, I needed to go back for our personal belongings, but beyond that . . .

The sound of a text message being tapped pulled me from my thoughts.

I looked back to see Mom inside, leaning against the breakfast bar with the iPhone in her hand, that one finger tap-tap-tapping at the screen. She was texting Quincy . . . who hadn't returned my phone call. She came to stand out on the deck and took pictures of the ocean. The world briefly lit from the flash. She grinned as she texted the picture. "It's beautiful out here," she said, slipping back into the living room to send Quincy the shot.

I groaned and rolled out of the chair. Back in the living room, I watched her texting for a moment before saying, "Why hasn't he called me back?"

She paused, and her smile dimmed some as she joined India in the kitchen. "Oh, that's right. Let me tell him . . ." Her fingers tap-tapped at the screen, then whoosh. "I just reminded him." Her phone chimed just as she grabbed a wooden spoon. She read the text, grinned wildly, and said, "He's driving right now but said you can call him at any time."

I retreated back to the patio under Mom's watchful gaze. I turned on the firepit and plopped into my cushioned chaise longue. After taking several deep breaths, I called Quincy's phone number.

The line rang two times before: "Hello?" The man sounded like he was driving through a canyon on Saturn.

"Is this Quincy Johns?" I asked, voice raised.

"Alyson—" Two beeps and the call dropped.

I tried calling again. This time, I said "Hello—" before the signal dropped.

A moment later, Mom stood at the patio door with her phone. "He's driving through some dead spots. He'll call—"

My phone rang.

"Alyson," the man said, "this is Quincy Johns. Sorry about that."

"Hi." I blinked, shocked that I was actually hearing his voice. "Hi . . . Thanks for calling."

"I know it's been a while since we've seen each other," Quincy Johns said, "and my condolences again." He sounded strong, and with his voice that deep, as big as a sequoia, a rare size for the air force.

"Mom says you're living in Ojai now," I said. "It's a different town now."

He chuckled. "More Range Rovers, less healing arts, right?"

His laugh took me back to the past, at our house after Dad's funeral. He and Mom had stood in the garden—she'd been crying, but he'd placed a hand on her shoulder. Mom and Quincy had stayed out there, and a few of their friends had joined them, and he'd made her laugh. He'd kissed her cheek as he said goodbye. She'd clenched his forearm, her eyes closed . . . I saw that as grief, sadness, the fear of being alone. Not . . . *sex.*

Quincy Johns and I talked a few minutes more, and I ended the call.

Back in the living room, Mom said, "Well?"

I shrugged—every man was a yellow light when it came to my loved ones, and with Mom's diminishing mind, that light would never change.

For dinner, Mom and India made shrimp risotto and an asparagus salad. We drank pinot grigio and ate tiny Bundt lemon cakes for dinner. We talked about India's quick trip to Marin and the kids' fall school year. We laughed as though nothing ridiculous and dangerous swirled at the borders separating Sableport and Haven.

I washed the dishes as India packed up leftovers. "Wish I could stay over tonight," she said, "but Brooke and Sam have a beach cleanup tomorrow that I'm supposed to be leading."

"You're a good momma," I said, whipping the towel at her. "You're gonna screw 'em up regular-style."

She smiled and said, "I needed to hear that. Sometimes, I worry . . . and feel guilty . . . and feel totally inadequate."

"Come on," I said, grimacing.

"Picking them up late at after-school care," she said. "Not making the cookies from scratch. Not showing up for the Halloween parades—"

"You're trying," I said, "and the kids know that you are. I'm telling you: They know who the real villain is."

She laughed and crossed her fingers.

Mom said, "Alyson?" She was standing at the dining room table and holding a small manuscript box. "I need to give you something."

I whispered to India, "Speaking of screwing kids up . . ." I tossed the dish towel on the counter and turned to my mother. "What's that?"

She placed the manuscript box on the breakfast bar. "You should read what's in here."

I looked back at India, who'd cocked a worried eyebrow.

"Why are you giving me this now?" I asked Mom.

"You . . . I . . ." Mom took a deep breath, then touched her neck. "You deserve to know before I forget." She stared down at the box, her face and will starting to crumple but her spine remaining straight, like she would accept the fallout no matter what.

I held my breath and stared at the blue cardboard box.

She tapped the top of it and stepped back.

Box in hand, I returned to the deck. Out there, the salty breeze whipped around me. The crash of waves against the shore had softened as the sun started its slip below the horizon, leaving the sky streaked with ambers and lavenders.

30.

At sixty-eight years old, my parents were supposed to be that couple in those Ensure and diabetes medication ads. They were supposed to be enjoying river cruises on the Rhine and Danube, wearing white to Smokey Robinson concerts at the Hollywood Bowl. Grandkids and soccer games and Christmas programs—I'd failed to give them a tutu-wearing grandkid dancing and twirling on stage to "Flight of the Bumblebee."

Mom and India sat in the living room, both pretending to be deep into *Real Housewives of Beverly Hills*—but I felt their eyes on my back.

Down at the beach, no one walked or jogged on the sand. No one slipped into the ocean for one last dip before bedtime. The world looked abandoned.

I slowly exhaled and opened the blue manuscript box. With trembling fingers, I flipped through the documents: bank statements, court documents, legal correspondence . . . The chaos of my parents' life. I paused on a page that mentioned the house in lower Ladera Heights, the house that I'd grown up in and had believed to have been lost to a fucked-up reverse mortgage.

But the document that I was now reading wasn't about that reverse mortgage.

It was a cover letter from Dad's police union attorney.

. . . This was the best I could do, Al.

Then I read each page after that, slowly and with great intention, until my eyes had glazed over with stunned, unfallen tears.

What the . . . ?

Our house hadn't been lost because of a predatory loan. No, our house had been seized as part of a restitution agreement tied to my father's . . . *plea bargain*. He'd been caught stealing from crime scenes but hadn't been sent to jail. This deal had kept him out, but at the cost of everything else—the house, the bakery, Mom's sense of security.

The *fuck*?

Where the hell had *I* been during this time?

I looked at the dates of these documents.

College . . . police academy . . . distracted . . . dating hot assistant DAs . . .

My mind buzzed with angry half-remembered words, and I gripped the edges of the chair to keep myself grounded. The most recent stories Mom had fed me, combined with the ones I'd believed my entire life—more lies. The house *hadn't* been stolen from us by some faceless bank.

Dread burrowed deep into my core as I reached for an email from Captain Joseph Wagner of the LAPD.

> Al-
>
> You really think I'm just going to look the other way? I saw you do it. I heard Poole bragging about it. FUCK YOU and him. If it were up to me, you'd never taste freedom again. You think you've gotten away with it by retiring early but you still got a daughter in blue, dumb-ass. Think about that on the jet ski you bought using money from the trap house off Centinela.

Revenge.

I read this email three more times, and each time was a slap in the face.

Captain Wagner had led the investigation that ended my career. A tall, broad man with an air of authority that bordered on arrogance, he and my father had joined the LAPD around the same time. They'd been friends, and I thought that friendship would help me in the Autumn Suarez investigation. Not at all, and I'd never understood why Captain Wagner had come down on me so hard, why he'd taken such satisfaction in destroying me.

But now I knew.

My dismissal from the LAPD hadn't been about Autumn Suarez—freeing her murderer or making the wrong call. My ending had been *personal*, a calculated act of vengeance designed to humiliate me, yes, but to humiliate my father most of all.

I'd been a pawn.

On weak legs, I stumbled into the house and through the living room. I burst into the bathroom and dropped in front of the toilet and vomited. My body twisted as my stomach launched everything I'd eaten all week into a watery grave. Behind me, Mom rushed to wet a face towel as India held back my hair. All of it didn't matter as I retched and winced and retched some more.

A cold towel cooled the back of my neck.

The toilet flushed.

I vomited some more, and my body twisted into a paper clip.

Wet towel.

Flush.

And then I gagged on air—there was nothing left.

Tears spilled down my cheeks, and I slapped away my mother's hands—she wanted to comfort me, but I didn't want anything from her. She knew. All of this. Everything. *She knew.* I buried my face in my hands, and my shoulders shook with my silent sobs.

Everything that I'd worked for, everything I'd believed in . . . all of it had been a lie. I'd thought I was making a difference, pursuing justice, standing on my own two feet. But every step I'd taken had been tangled up in the web of my father's pathology. A pawn in a game I didn't even know was being played.

I sat in the bathroom, and eventually, my tears stopped, leaving me hollow, numb.

India whispered, "Wanna talk?"

I shook my head, not sure I had the strength to keep going. I stood and whispered, "Take a shower." Someone—*me?*—turned on the shower spigots, and the bathroom filled with steam.

This fight felt too big, the lies too deep. I'd never be able to put the pieces of my life together. I didn't even have a reference point to look at—my origins were fractured and still shifting.

Did I even *want* to fix it?

I didn't want this kind of light, not anymore. I didn't want any more truth. No more illumination. No, I wanted to close my eyes and enjoy the glare that blinded. No, no fixing.

I closed my eyes and did nothing as I stood beneath the hot water.

I was paying for the sins of my parents. No matter what I did—professionally, romantically—this life was never gonna be simple for me. My story was never gonna be straightforward or end well. I was never meant to have a happily ever after.

And Mom knew all of this and did nothing, ensuring my fate. And I, stubbornly, clung to the belief that if I tried harder, things would shake out in my favor, not knowing that the dice had been cast the moment my father thought about stealing evidence.

All this time, I'd thought the threat was all external. No—the most harm had come from the ones who'd patted my back and hugged me: Ivan and my own father.

Sadness washed over me and then filled me up again. Sobs broke from my chest like those waves breaking against the shore. I couldn't breathe, my weeping was that deep and all consuming. In between the mania, there were gaps of clarity, my mind assuring me that it wasn't that bad, that everything would be okay. But then another wave would hit and wash away that beautiful sandcastle of lies that the optimist in me had just constructed.

The baddies won.

India was sitting on the bed in the room I'd chosen as mine. She winced seeing my swollen red eyes and swollen nose. She patted the spot beside her and said, "Your reaction is totally valid."

Wearing pajamas and wet hair, I plopped on the bed and tried to speak—but the word-making part of my mind was now waterlogged. And that made me start crying again.

India held out a box of tissues.

I plucked a sheet, and whispered, "I don't even know what to say. 'What the fuck' works, but even that . . ." I dabbed the tissue against my damp cheeks. "And now here I am, staying in my ex's condo. The jury's gonna love this."

"You are not the reason London did what she did," India said, wagging her finger at me. "How many women have their marriages end but don't go and date minors that they then kill? She wanted what she wanted and got caught, and you're easy to blame. The jury will see through that excuse just like they'll see through Xander being some aggressive, oversexed thug who attacked her. Not one piece of forensic or medical evidence supports that."

She brushed a lock of my wet hair off my forehead. "Want me to make an appointment for you?"

"My hair's that much of a hot mess?"

India winced. "You're looking like a drowned turkey."

I laughed at that one. "Yes, please."

"Silk press?"

"Absolutely."

"You okay?" she asked.

I shrugged. "I'm not gonna walk into the ocean, if that's what you're worried about."

She placed her forehead against mine. "It's gonna be okay."

I whispered, "Whatever that means, right?"

She sighed. "Right."

India and I walked back down to the stairs and hugged at the front door. I cried some more, and she held on to me as I settled down again.

"You good?" she asked.

I gave her a thumbs-up and a stronger smile.

India squeezed my shoulder. "I'm glad Coop let you stay here."

"We're visiting Sunset Park tomorrow to check them out."

Her eyebrows lifted. "Uhh . . ."

"More financial assistance."

Her eyebrows climbed higher.

I shrugged. "Call it guilt and reparations. Right now, I'm in no position to say no."

I didn't want to talk to my mother. I knew that I wouldn't be able to look at her without a scowl. Maybe Quincy Johns could come up and take her on a drive through wine country. Give me time to exorcise the hate now brewing in my gut for her and my father. Now that she'd told me the truth, she was free to sip wine and nibble cheese and enjoy shit as I carried forth my nervous breakdown.

PART IV

The Girl Who Fell Through Fire

31.

A week ago, I'd flirted with a hot winetender. My muscles had ached from pedaling that wine-bike trolley, and I'd started looking into the death of Emiliano Rivas.

I'd done a lot of living in seven days.

But now it was Monday morning, and it was time to start living again. Staying at the condo was restorative. Staring out at the ocean and those waves crashing onto the shore . . . Smelling that salty air and the smoke of the firepit . . . If I quit Ivan's firm, what would I do for a living? Yes, Sableport was bigger than Haven, but still not as big as Los Angeles. This town wasn't cheap.

I could return to LA and fight to clear my name, win a few hundred thousand for wrongful termination . . . Even if I won, though, it would take years to receive a single dollar from the city. What would I do until then? And if Cooper paid Mom's bill to live at Sunset Park, would I want to be that far away from her? From India? From . . . *him*?

Ten minutes to eight, Mom and I sat in my Bronco, driving to Sunset Park Senior Living. The golden light of a new day cut across the windshield, and the hum of the tires against the road lulled me into silence. Mom, wearing nice jeans and a lilac cotton shirt, sat in the passenger seat with her hands folded tightly in her lap.

Cooper couldn't make it up to Sableport to tour with Mom and me. That was fine—we weren't family, and my mother wasn't his mother-in-law. Even after I'd tried to absolve him of this particular bout of guilt, he'd insisted on paying for Mom to stay a couple of days to see if she liked it.

Once I pulled into Sunset Park's parking lot, Mom and I finally looked at each other.

Mom said, "It's very pretty."

I nodded and said, "It is." Then I climbed out of the truck and slammed the door.

An older blond woman who resembled Jane Fonda but with Joan Collins's teased updo met us in the lobby. She wore perfume that smelled like almonds, vanilla, and baby powder. The ring on her finger could fund my life. Her name was Calliope. "But you can call me Cali," she said in a faded Southern accent.

Mom gave me a small, weary smile before following Miss Calliope down the hallway.

A pang of guilt flickered in my chest, but I pushed it away. I had a right to be angry at her.

Miss Calliope led my mother and me around the grounds of Sunset Park. Mom liked the duck pond and nearly burst with excitement visiting the professional kitchen. She gasped at the fourth-floor atrium and praised God for the view. If she chose to stay, her room looked out at that duck pond, and if she wanted, she could volunteer in the kitchen.

"Are we allowed to have weekend guests?" Mom asked.

"A maximum of three days," Calliope said.

Always thinking about Quincy Johns now.

"You will thrive here," Miss Calliope said to Mom. To me: "The safety of our residents is our number-one priority."

Price definitely wasn't.

As we stood alone back at that duck pond, Mom reached for my hand—I let her take it but refused to look at her. "Are you ever gonna forgive us?"

I snorted. "You held all this information from me for how many years? You dump all of it in my lap last week, and now you want me to get over it forty-eight hours later? *Really?*"

"I want to be here, mentally, when you do, that's all."

I pulled my hand from hers. "Again . . . you had *years* to tell me all of this. But now there's a clock. *Your* clock. And it's still all about you. Fuck my life and all the shit I've had to face without even knowing why I was facing it and—you know what?" I turned to her and held my arms out to the side. "Do you want me to just say the words so you'll feel better? Fine. I'll say them. *I forgive you.* That better?"

Her eyes shone with tears.

So did mine. Because she *still* hadn't apologized to me. Just *Here you go, here's the truth. Now you know.*

Years and months and days—I'd never get them back. By my third year on the force, my reputation had already been stained and trashed by unseen forces. What were my parents thinking? As much as they'd want to say "We were thinking about you," I'd call bullshit. But Mom hadn't said that—*we were thinking about you*—because she knew it was bullshit.

"So back in the day, did you and Quincy . . . ?" I kept my eyes on that duck pond, my nostrils flaring.

"No, we did not have an affair," Mom said. "Is that what you're about to ask me?"

I didn't respond, keeping my jaw clenched.

She gazed at me, then said, "After your father's third so-called 'slip,' I thought about it."

"But?"

"Quincy was transferred, and there was no one else I wanted to . . ."

Opportunity, not fidelity, had kept Quincy and Mom apart—and now, knowing all that I did about Dad's affairs . . . I couldn't blame her for trying.

"I don't know what I was thinking, Alyson," Mom said as we walked toward the lobby. "I shouldn't have let your father expose you—or even *me*—like that." She chuckled. "Me losing my memory . . . a fitting punishment."

And living out that sentence in a room with a view of the Pacific Ocean and a duck pond, paid for—not by the man she'd married, but by the man I couldn't.

If that was some kind of bullshit fate . . .

"Don't worry about that," Cooper said once I climbed back into the truck. "I have the money." He exhaled into the phone's speaker. "I want to do this for her. For you."

I thanked him and headed to my next appointment: hair.

After a vigorous wash, Santoy slathered deep conditioner into my hair and sat me under the hair dryer for twenty minutes.

If my father had his home taken away as punishment, what had been Ivan's? He didn't go to jail—at least not that I knew of. But then again: What did I know about the people who'd helped raise me?

When I returned to Haven—*to quit?*—I'd ask Ivan. Fuck manners and consideration. I was tired of the lies. No more. I wanted all the light—to see the obstacles, to cleanse my soul, to chase away the phantoms. *Done.*

I left the salon with trimmed ends and healthy locks. Something about a silk press that gave me cocaine-bear energy. Wearing these jeans and these Doc Martens and this cashmere sweater, I was standing on business today. The bitch was back—and with new hair and a clean Glock. Mess with me if you dared: I'd go off not because I was manic but because I was clear eyed. The ancestors stood at my side.

I stopped at the office of the *Haven Voice*, the town newspaper without an editor in chief or the backbone to print the entire truth about this fucked-up town. Not much activity happening for a newspaper—most of the desks were empty, and Tanner Orr's office was dark. I smelled brewed coffee, so someone still worked here.

Faith, the redhead who didn't like me, had survived. She actually smiled as I entered the building. "How can I help you today?" she asked.

I cocked an eyebrow. Had she been body-snatched since my last visit? "You know I'm working the Suttons' missing goldendoodle case."

She made sad eyes. "Yes. Poor Figgy. Poor Cooper. He's had so much tragedy."

I said, "He has, but I have a lead." I told her about the ad that had been placed on the paper's website. "Could I have the sales slips and all that?"

When she said "Sure, let me get it," I nearly puked across the desk.

Why the change in energy?

Faith tapped at her keyboard, and a moment later, the printer spit out three sheets of paper. Faith snatched them from the tray, stapled them, and handed them to me. She smiled and said, "Hope this helps." She widened her smile. "Please tell Cooper that we're thinking about him."

I squinted at her and said, "Sure."

That's right—Cooper was a single man again. Ladies would soon be lining his walkway with casseroles, bottles of wine, and lacy lingerie.

By the time I got to the office, the sun sat in the middle of the sky and its light slanted through the windows in long, golden streaks. Ivan wasn't here. Good. I wanted to tell him my next steps—but I needed to first solidify that plan.

Figgy: I would get the goldendoodle back today. My nervous breakdown had benefited Lincoln and his family. But that version of Sonny was now dead . . . or at least passed out in her bed.

LAPD: I needed to hire an attorney . . .

"Maybe the police union will pay for it," India said over the phone. She'd called to make sure I hadn't throttled my mother during the tour.

"Even then," I said, sipping a cup of K-Cup coffee, "do I want the world to know what my father did? Like . . . I was already horrified when I thought that I'd done nothing wrong—"

"And you've still done nothing wrong."

"But my parents, my godfather . . . they're . . . *Ugh.*" My cheeks were blazing. "And then to go up against Captain Wagner—"

"You have proof."

"I know."

"So maybe the city will settle," she said. "Maybe you can get Maxine Waters to be a big mouth on your behalf. Round up Kamala and Michelle. Beyoncé. RuPaul."

I laughed. "That's a helluva coalition of powerful queens." I took a gulp of coffee. "And don't forget: *You.* You my ace girl."

"Always and forever," India said. "Let's burn Wagner's thin-blue-line ass up and take your pension and badge back."

After ending my call with India, I grabbed my binder and found the sales papers for the DOG FOR SALE listing in the *Haven Voice.* Lincoln McDermott had shown me that janky ad with the MacDraw and QuarkXPress vibes. The billing address . . . a post office box. But the name on the credit card: Charles Campbell.

A.k.a. Carlos Vega.

Keely Butler was involved—I knew that, even though I didn't see her name on any piece of paper. She hated the Suttons, and stealing their dog was the perfect way to get back at them.

But Carlos Vega a.k.a. Charles Campbell was a problem. This dognapping was just one slice of banana on this banana split—and he was a dangerous man. It wouldn't be smart to confront him alone about Figgy or Honor or his assault against me.

Out in the lobby, the bell above the front door rang.

"Hello?" a man shouted.

My hand quickly brushed against the Glock on my hip before I slipped down the hallway.

Lincoln McDermott stood in the waiting room along with a tall goldendoodle with a fig-colored spot on her left rump.

Figgy!

I gasped seeing them both.

Figgy had only met me once, but her tail swung like crazy as though we were favorite cousins.

"You brought her," I said.

Lincoln's eyes peeked at the gun. "You were very kind to give us a few more days with her." He offered me the pink leather Versace leash. "She's a good girl."

I accepted the leash and kneeled before the dog. "Your daddy's gonna be so happy."

Figgy nuzzled my cheek.

"Noa, Jen, and I are visiting a no-kill shelter after school today," Lincoln said. "We'll pick out a dog there instead of going through a private buyer." He sighed. "It's been heartbreaking."

"I know," I said, nodding. "Thank you for doing the right thing."

Lincoln's face crumpled. "We're gonna miss her." Then he shuffled out of Poole Investigations empty handed, closing the door softly behind him.

I sat down on the carpet, and Figgy sat beside me. She licked my hands as her body vibrated with excitement. For the first time in forever, I smiled a smile that reached my soul. The world was still a mess, and my list of problems hadn't gotten any shorter. But at least I had Figgy back. And for now, that was enough.

32.

I grabbed the sales slip order and ad that Charles Campbell had purchased to sell a stolen dog and tucked it into Honor Butler's case file—he was the overlapping wedge in this Venn diagram. Selling dogs. Selling sex, including the seventeen-year-old daughter of his "known associate," Keely Butler. Xander Monroe's funeral was in Oakland on Thursday. A perfect day to stop by the FBI field office.

As Figgy and I walked out to my truck, I stared at the spot where Dave Kruger had lain dying. A single candle sat on the curb, the only testimony that a life had been lost here. Around that slice of now-washed blacktop, the world moved on. People stood in line for dinner at Deegan's. Kids licked ice cream cones as big as their heads. And I was about to return this happy, tall dog to her owner. Me lingering here—the only person lingering here—and then moving on felt like the job of a professional mourner.

I opened the door to the Bronco and Figgy hopped up into the back seat. I placed an arm around Figgy's neck and held up my phone. "Smile for the camera, Figgy!"

The dog's breath warmed my cheek as I took our selfie.

Click.

A perfect pose of a dog and her detective.

I attached the picture to a text message.

Hey Coop!

Look who I ran into!

Almost immediately:

NO FUCKING WAY!

Figgy?!

Are you sure???

I took a picture of the pink Versace leash and the fig-colored birthmark on her rump.

Positive!

I'm man enough to admit that I'm crying right now

I scratched Figgy behind her ear. "Your poppa's happy."

Not at home though ☺

on the other side of Haven

Call me when you're home

We'll be at the condo

I smiled at Figgy. "You're now an official PI assistant, Miss Figgy. We got lots of shit to do today before we tell Haven to 'suck it.'"

She wagged her tail and sniffed around the cabin before settling down on the seat, one paw atop the other, like she now owned 51 percent of this truck. A very demure, a very decent dog.

I gave her a quick scratch behind the ears before shutting the door and hopping behind the steering wheel. "I know Mackenzie didn't," I said to the dog's reflection in the rearview mirror, "and I'm not even gonna say the other one's name, but did Coop ever play you some Lauryn Hill?"

Figgy panted, "Yes."

"Good." I hit the stereo button and "Intro" came on. I snapped my fingers and smiled at the doggie in my rearview mirror. "Let's get it, Miss Figgy." I pulled onto Seaview Way, heading east to reach Highway 1.

At the traffic light, the Range Rover ahead of me turned left. Matte black, black rims, gorgeous. The driver: Araceli Rivas. Her cherry Kool-Aid hair was swept to one side, and her sunglasses pushed up on her head.

"What's going on, Araceli?" I asked. "Miss 'I'm Not Paying My Bill.'" I turned left, too, since Sableport was that way. I eased into the lane behind her.

Araceli and I had started our adventure together with her driving a beat-up Honda, and in just a week, she'd leveled up. As I drove to a beachside condo in Sableport, I guess I had leveled up too.

But I didn't have a dead husband to bury.

The goldendoodle barked once, yawned, and placed her head on her paws. "Enjoy your nap, Miss Figgy."

I kept a safe distance behind Araceli Rivas as we both headed north to Sableport.

We eventually turned off Highway 1 and onto Main Street, home of Sableport's high-end, open-air mall. Shoppers came here for their Gucci, their Louis, their Prada and Escada. Sushi, iced matcha lattes, and acai bowls in between all of their shopping. Araceli found a parking spot in front of a Nordstrom entrance. I rolled past her and found a spot across from Adidas—I could watch her there without drawing attention.

Figgy, awake now, sat up in the seat, then climbed onto the center console, ready to be a doggy PI.

Araceli stepped out of the SUV.

Figgy barked, "Girl."

My jaw nearly hit the steering wheel. "What the . . . ?"

The young widow wore Christian Louboutin heeled boots—the signature red soles glowed in the sunlight—and a Louis Vuitton bag hung casually from her arm. She wore a body suit and a long camo jacket. Her lips were the color of her hair.

"Figgy," I said, "who dis woman?" She was not the grieving widow I'd met last week. The woman who couldn't pay Ivan my fee. The same one who'd launched a GoFundMe to fund her husband's cremation. Paint-spattered overalls. Goofy sweaters. Craft-kid kitsch. No, ma'am.

This glamazon strutted into the Gucci store like she knew where the Gucci family kept their good silverware. Where the fuck was she getting the money for all this?

I did the math. Those shoes: almost $1,500. That bag: almost $3,000. Even a used Range Rover cost $60,000. And the matte job on top of that?

I grabbed my phone and texted Brady Kwon.

I'm still not talking to you

But I'm seeing something strange right now re A. Rivas

Call me ASAP

I stared at the screen.

No ellipses. No response.

Was he busy working? In a meeting? Away from his phone? Was this "Really, I can't talk right now" instead of simply ignoring me?

Ugh.

As I waited, I took pictures and video of everything I was witnessing.

Twenty minutes later, Araceli emerged from the store carrying a shopping bag with the iconic Gucci logo. She slipped her sunglasses over her eyes, tromped back to the Range Rover, and tossed the bag into the SUV's back seat.

My grip tightened around my phone as I recorded. I was done following her around town, but my questions wouldn't change: Where had this money come from? Who was bankrolling her new life? And what the hell was she doing in Sableport, dressed like a contestant on *Love Island*?

Still no response from Brady Kwon.

I took the last shots and video, including the Range Rover's license plate.

Figgy yawned and whined.

"Yep," I said, "we're leaving right now." I reached back and scratched her ear. "Looks like we've got a little more digging to do, Miss-Miss."

Araceli was spending all this money . . . and she hadn't paid my fee. Oh, hell no.

Yeah, something was wrong here . . . and I wasn't letting this case go without pulling it, kicking and screaming, into the light.

The space. The ocean. The quiet. I could get used to life in Sableport. With Mom safe just a mile and a half away in an equally beautiful spot . . . Yeah. Maybe I'd even adopt a dog. A tall, leggy one like Miss Figgy.

I settled in the condo's living room with my laptop. Figgy curled up on the blanket at my feet that I'd spread out for her. As she snored, I visited Araceli's Etsy store again. A top-rated seller, Mrs. Rivas enjoyed more than a thousand reviews, including those left by dead Dave Kruger's dead ex-wife, Jaylayne Merkley.

On the sale page for the hanging crystal stones, I sorted the reviews to Most Recent, and—

Uh-oh.

One one-star review after the next, with customers posting pictures of cracked crystals, broken strings, displays made with one type of stone and not the variety as described.

The same thing that had happened with her multicolored wreaths.

Broken, bent, shoddy.

Celi's Secrets hadn't enjoyed a solid run of four- and five-star reviews since the beginning of the year. What had happened for this shift in quality and care to manifest? Marital problems between her and Emiliano? Illness? Whatever it was had decimated her reputation—she hadn't fulfilled orders since late April.

Emiliano disappeared on May 13, the day before Mother's Day.

Etsy disputes weren't unusual, but something about these complaints bothered me.

A woman named Theresa had ordered a custom jewelry box:

> She promised me a refund but that never happened. Then, I found out she'd done the same thing to a dozen other people. She was using fake tracking numbers. I reported her.

Kenya from the Bronx left a one-star review for a multicolored glass suncatcher.

> If I could, I would give this ZERO STARS. I first received a broken one. She then promised to send another one but with more glass. But I never received it!!
> DO NOT USE THIS STORE!!
> UPDATE: I reported this seller to the US Postal Service!! They'd already had an investigation open!!
> UPDATE#2: DO NOT USE THIS STORE!! She isn't supposed to even have a store anymore! Mail FRAUD!!

Update: OMG SHE OPENED ANOTHER STORE!! SHE'S NOT SUPPOSED TO AND ETSY HASN'T CAUGHT HER YET! I'VE REPORTED HER. DO NOT BUY FROM HER! YOU'VE BEEN WARNED!!!

My stomach sank. "C'mon, Araceli."

I opened a new tab and found Araceli's GoFundMe page.

The $10,000 goal had been met and exceeded by $2,000.

She wasn't buying new Gucci, Louis Vuitton, and Louboutin shoes with only $10,000, though.

I swiped over to the widow's Instagram page.

No updated posts or reels since she'd shown the world the urn she'd chosen for Emiliano's ashes. Death was taking a social media holiday.

Why did I still care, though? Why was I giving this woman any of my wobbly bandwidth?

But now that I could see clearly, I wasn't ready to look away. There was too much of a glow around this still-bouncing red ball.

Figgy rolled over onto her side, staying close enough to keep my foot against her fur.

I'd only met one of Araceli's Instagram connections—Jessica over at Liberty Tires—and now I clicked on Jessica's profile. Pictures of tailgating, tequila shots, and freshly manicured nails. Jessica was into lowriders and French bulldogs.

There was a group shot at a brewery. At the end of the bar . . .

Matais, Araceli's ex. He'd been tagged, so I clicked into his profile and . . .

There he was, the sunset behind him, posed in front of a black Range Rover. The woman draped across him: Araceli Rivas wearing a pink camisole dress.

Another shot. This time, Matais was visiting Rosarita Beach down in Baja, California. He was writing in the sand with one hand while holding a longneck bottle of Corona in the other. His partner in these shots: shit-faced Araceli Rivas.

Both posts were dated August 2.

After clicking on the picture of Araceli posed nude with hundred-dollar bills covering her lady bits, I clicked out of Instagram.

She wasn't paying my bill. She'd balked at the price on the day she first visited last Sunday. But here she was, on social media, buck naked beneath a blanket of Benjamins.

I found Emiliano Rivas's autopsy report and scanned it again. Polypropylene fibers had been found in the ligatures around the dead man's neck and wrists.

"Okay," I whispered, typing POLYPROPYLENE FIBER into a search engine. "But what is it used for?"

I clicked on the first result.

> ". . . found commonly . . . netting for basketball hoops and soccer goals."

Figgy was slowing my trek to Brady Kwon's office. Everyone—from citizens and civil service workers to deputies wearing khakis and badges—stopped to greet the dog. Loving the attention, Figgy's tail wagged so much, I feared she'd break it. She caused so much commotion, that the badged and khakied man that I came for actually left his office to see what the fuss was about. Seeing that I was tethered to the fuss, Brady's excitement withered.

After petting the dog, he said, "This must be Figgy, the dog who started it all."

I said, "Verily."

"You come to see me?" he asked.

I nodded. "Can we talk in your office? But only if McCann's not there."

His brows furrowed. "He's gone for the day."

A moment later, Brady was closing his office door. He reached in his desk drawer and pulled out a dog biscuit for Figgy.

She immediately took the treat and settled at my feet to start crunching on it.

"What's up?" Brady asked, sitting back in his chair.

"A lot," I said, "and I've left messages for you that you still haven't returned."

He held up his hands. "Busy. You know how it is. You have me now, though."

And so I told him about the ad in the *Haven Voice* being connected to Figgy's theft and to Carlos Vega a.k.a. Charles Campbell. I told him that I'd seen Vega and Keely Butler unloading pet supplies at their house just almost two weeks before.

Brady scribbled into his leather binder. "Okay. Anything else?"

"Araceli Rivas," I said.

"What about her?"

I told him about her Etsy store, the negative reviews, the mail fraud, and the investigation launched by the US Postal Service.

"Don't fuck with the post office," he said, writing and smiling.

I narrowed my eyes. "Sounds like none of this is blowing your mind."

He shrugged. "It did when I first learned about it."

"You knew?"

He nodded.

"And you didn't tell me?"

"Why would I?" he asked. "This isn't your case. You were supposed to find Emiliano—"

"He's been found."

"The end." He blinked at me. "Who Araceli is and how she fucked over her customers has nothing to do with your investigation."

I snorted. "The hell it doesn't."

"How? She paid you to find him. He's across the street, waiting for the crematorium to pick him up. End of story."

I shook my head. "No, not end of story. And since you brought it up, she didn't pay me."

"So because she didn't pay you, you're doing *more* work for her?"

"I'm not doing work for her—"

"Who's your client, then?" Brady asked.

"My *client*?"

"Because you're now a private investigator, Alyson. You're not working this case for the people of Mendocino County. You're not working this case for Araceli Rivas. So who *are* you working for?"

I blinked at him. "Hmm."

Brady squinted at me. "You no longer trust her because she skipped out on paying your fee. You're going in on this girl—"

"Going in?" I said. "Are you fucking high right now?"

He looked up to the heavens. "The great Sonny Rush—"

"Stop it—"

"—being petty and trying to make a young widow into a villain—"

"Brady—"

"Because, why?" He tilted his head and peered at me. "Unbelievable."

I nodded. "You're right. It *is* unbelievable—but not for what you're thinking."

We were done here. Even though he'd already lied to me about Orville Klein, I'd still hoped that lie was a one-off, that, ultimately, he was a good cop. A good guy. I was sitting here now because I'd been willing to trust him again. Because I needed to trust *someone*. But Brady checked his watch. "I gotta head."

I shrugged. "You probably should."

He paused, staring at me, wanting to ask what I meant by that. With my arms crossed and my mouth a hard line across my face, he knew what I meant. Still, he said, "We really didn't get to talk about us."

I chuckled. "Yeah, we did."

"Ah. Okay." He knocked on the desktop and stood from his chair.

That was my cue.

Figgy jumped up before I could—she sensed the tension, too.

I wandered over to the doorway but looked back at Brady one last time and said, "Good luck."

"With what?"

My gaze skipped from the desks to the shredder before finally settling on the man I'd come to see. "Everything and nothing."

Since Figgy liked her, I played Lauryn Hill on the drive back to Haven. The goldendoodle hung her head out the window, tongue wagging, as I drove down Highway 1, mentally cataloging all the evidence I planned to take to my meeting with the FBI on Thursday morning before Xander's funeral.

The late-afternoon sky was streaked deep orange and indigo as I pulled up to the cottage—I needed more clothes, including my funeral suit and shoes. Figgy's body vibrated with excitement. Her tongue hanging out, she gave me a happy bark.

I loved this dog.

Before I climbed out of the car, though, I made one call.

Honor Butler's line rang and rang. She'd come to me, not her mother, in the middle of the night. She'd asked for my help, and even though her situation needed the resources of an entire government body and not one woman at a small agency, I still cared.

Finally, the line clicked. "Hello?" Honor sounded stronger than the last time we spoke.

I smiled so that she could hear it in my voice. "Hey, it's Sonny Rush."

"Oh. Hey."

Stony silence.

My grip tightened around my phone. "I'm just checking in on you. And . . ." I cleared my throat, my neck flushing with embarrassment. "Last time we talked, you hadn't heard about Mackenzie dying. Are you okay?"

"Yeah."

I paused and waited for more. "I know she was like your big sister—"

"I'm good. No worries. Just getting ready for school," she said. "You know, the usual."

My eyebrows furrowed. "You can't talk."

She chuckled. "Not really. No cross-country this year."

In the background, I heard a muffled voice. Honor, muffled now, said, "Mom, relax. It's just an admissions counselor at Sableport Community College."

"I haven't forgotten you," I said, my heartbeat notching up. "But I'm bringing in law enforcement—"

"No, not really."

"Not Sableport, not Haven, not even Mendocino County, okay?"

"That's awesome. Okay, thanks for calling—"

"Are you safe for now?" I asked, tears burning in my eyes.

"Totally. Okay. Bye." She ended the call before I could say anything else.

33.

Elliott and Giovanni had left our mail on the foyer table—bills, including a lending statement from Lenderful.

I placed a bowl of water and a few chunks of cheddar cheese on the kitchen floor. "We won't be long," I told the dog. "I know you're hungry."

Figgy hoovered the cheese, took a few laps of water, then roamed from room to room, exploring and sniffing. She found me in my bedroom, grabbing Honor's canvas shopping bag that held many things, including a dead phone, a dead digital camera, instant camera photos, pieces of mail, a gas station map of Mendocino County, and a FasTrak sensor.

I grabbed one of my suitcases from the closet and threw in more clothes. I grabbed my black pantsuit and a pair of black loafers. No heels since I'd be helping to carry Xander's casket to its final resting place.

Figgy barked from over at the window.

"I'm hurrying," I said.

I called Mom to check in on her stay at Sunset Park.

"We're playing *Family Feud*," she said, laughing.

"Oh, wow. That sounds incredible. So I'm guessing you're liking it?"

She laughed. "I'm loving it. Tell Coop that I forgive him for fucking you over." She laughed, and the joy came deep down in her toes.

My phone vibrated: a text message from Lori Monroe.

Please arrive at CHURCH by 10 AM on Thursday morning

The service is set to begin at 11 AM

Thank you again for doing this for our family

After confirming with Lori, I texted one of my favorite FBI agents at the LA office.

Cherise Foreman responded immediately:

How do you like it up there?

My husband and I are thinking of transferring to SF/OAK

I told her that Haven was a vibe, that I hadn't rested since I'd been here, and that I needed her to connect me with an agent in Oakland for Thursday morning, *early* early.

Ellipses. Then:

OK!

Livinia Holland handles sex crimes

Busy but she could see you at 8

Perfect—I could meet with Livinia and give her everything that I had before driving to the church for Xander Monroe's funeral. I thanked Cherise and promised to pay her back.

You still with the hot developer?

Complicated

Pay me back with a stay at Four Seasons or Ritz-Carlton

Done

Figgy plopped down at the foot of my bed. She closed her eyes and almost immediately started to snore.

I watched her body rise and fall, and calm settled over me. Just hearing the simple rhythm of her breathing eased something raw in my chest. My thoughts, usually racing and jagged, softened, and yeah, I needed my own Figgy. Someone who'd remind me that not everything in this world was broken.

Honor's canvas shopping bag tumbled over to the floor and most of the items shoved inside of it fell out—including a matchbook from Luc(k)y's, the dive bar in Sableport. I hadn't noticed these matches before . . . nor had I noticed the handwritten phone number inside the cover.

Curious, I created a new phone number using the generator app just to call this mystery number.

The line rang . . . rang . . . rang . . . rang . . . No voicemail picked up.

I turned on Honor's phone and searched the call log for this number ending in -3243.

Call made on August 5, 2023.

I tapped the information button—no picture had been linked to the number. I scrolled to the first of three messages sent by the person at the end of -3243.

I get it

this shit is scary

but no risk no reward

If you ever need an out find Sonny Rush

She's now living at that cottage where you were busted

last time

That's how I'll know

Whoever this was . . . they'd been the one to send Honor in my direction—and I'd only arrived in Haven just days before.

I tried calling that number in the matchbook again.

The line rang . . . rang . . .

"Yeah?"

I froze and held my breath.

He said "Hello?" and sighed before ending the call.

I couldn't feel my lips, but my ears were burning.

I knew that voice:

Brady Kwon.

My phone buzzed in my hand.

An alert from the security system.

I swiped across the phone screen to the app's camera and—

Figgy's sharp growl startled me.

I stopped moving and noticed the goldendoodle standing by the window, her ears perked and her body rigid. Her growl stayed low and steady, her dark eyes locked on something outside.

Adrenaline surged through my blood as the security app on my phone chimed again.

Figgy's warning wasn't bullshit—someone was out there.

I moved to the window, my heart hammering as I peered out.

Trees. Bushes.

I looked at my phone again. In real time, the video showed a figure creeping along the north side of the cottage, gun down to his side.

Figgy barked and growled.

Shit!

Someone was on the front porch. The intruder's face hid beneath a black balaclava. He gripped the doorknob with a gloved hand.

My heart leaped in my chest, and I turned as the front-door sensor chimed. The floorboards in the entryway creaked.

He was inside!

I crept out of the room, closing the door and locking Figgy inside. Tiptoeing down the hallway, I pulled the Glock from my hip holster.

Footsteps.

I was shocked that I could hear any sound—my heartbeat was thunder and cannon fire.

Gun cocked, I pressed my body against the wall.

The intruder stepped closer . . . closer . . .

The floorboards creaked.

He crept closer . . . closer . . . smelling like weed and sweat.

Closer . . . closer . . .

He stepped past me, moving to my closed bedroom door. He reached for the doorknob.

I lifted my gun and said, "Hey."

He swiveled to face me, his eyes wide. By the time he remembered that he also had a gun, I'd already kicked him in the crotch. He didn't go down hard, but he did go down and drop the gun.

I kicked his gun away.

He grabbed for my foot but missed.

I kicked his hand and slammed my Glock against his nose.

He shrieked and grabbed his face.

In the bedroom, Figgy barked and scratched against the door.

With his hand covering his nose, he turned over and made it up to one wobbly knee.

I slammed the Glock against his head.

He toppled over again.

I grabbed the intruder's gun and pushed the barrel of mine against the top of his head.

He lifted his hands.

I pulled off the balaclava.

Carlos Vega a.k.a. Charles Campbell, and his blood was now fucking up the nice runner I'd bought on sale at Bed Bath & Beyond. He laughed, something men with guns to their heads should never do.

"You find this funny?" I asked, shouting over the din of the barking dog and my thundering pulse.

"Who the fuck are you gonna call, Superdick?" he muttered. "They've been watching you since you got here."

"Who is 'they,' asshole?" I demanded.

He snickered.

I pressed the gun's barrel harder against his skull. "Who is 'they'?"

"You're not gonna pull the trigger," he said. "You aren't dirty like that, and I'm not a threat. You can't claim self-defense. So make the call."

This man wasn't scared.

I stepped back but kept the gun trained on him.

He sat against the wall, using it to brace himself as he stood up.

"Why'd you come here?" I asked.

"Why the fuck you think?" He used the tail of his T-shirt to stop the flow of blood from his nose.

"Who wants me dead?"

"Who doesn't?" he asked. "You've fucked everything up. You won't leave. You won't quit. You gotta go."

I squinted at him.

He flicked blood off his fingers and it splatted against the wall and ceiling. He cursed and said, "Bitch broke my nose." He glared at me. "Make the fucking call. They'll send somebody out. Take a report and then . . . *what*?" He nodded at his gun now in my hand. "Keep it. Everybody's a badass with a gun. Got any questions, ask ya boy. He don't want you here either."

My boy?

Who . . . ?

Carlos Vega started back down the hall.

"Hey, Vega?" I nestled his gun in my waistband and my Glock in its holster.

Aggravated, he sighed and turned back to face me. "What—"

I grabbed his wrist, turned it clockwise until his palm faced the ceiling and those splats of his blood.

He dropped to his knee and yelped in pain.

"Since you're here." I twisted some more.

His cries sharpened.

"This is for the cupcakes," I said, gritting my teeth, "and for jumping me that night . . ." I twisted harder.

His face was now the color of strawberries. The veins pushed hard against his skin. His cries were almost louder than my heartbeat.

One more twist would do it. Break it nice and easy.

"Stop, please!" he managed.

"You leave me the fuck alone and I won't dislocate your shoulder." A little more twisting.

"Okay, okay, okay!"

"You really think I believe you?" A little more . . .

"I swear!"

I didn't believe him.

Pop!

He screamed the scream of three hundred men. He grabbed his arm and let his forehead rest against the hardwood floor. He finally caught his breath.

With angry tears in my eyes, I stood over him. "Get the fuck outta my house."

Carlos Vega a.k.a. Charles Campbell made it to his feet again and staggered down the hall and back out the front door. His face was as red as a stop sign and streaked with tears, blood, and snot.

I followed him down the walkway and all the way up to the main road. He climbed into the front seat of a pickup truck. With the tap of his brake lights and the turn of a key, the engine rumbled and zigzagged down the thin road.

Loaded down with two guns now, I plodded back down the gravel driveway, my mind slowing and racing at the same time.

They.

My boy.

Brady Kwon?

34.

After photographing the hallway and taking swabs of Carlos Vega's blood, I grabbed bleach cleaner and rubber gloves, and I scrubbed that man right out of my cottage. The floor, the walls, and even the ceiling—I wiped all of it down, knowing that luminol would still light up this now-hidden blood like the Milky Way if I needed to prove that Vega had invaded my home.

As I scrubbed and cleaned, my mind wandered.

They.

Ya boy.

Carlos Vega said that he wouldn't return—and he may have been telling the truth. But he'd send someone else in his place.

I showered, then changed into the softest leggings and the softest T-shirt I owned. After I finished packing for my trip to Oakland, I grabbed another suitcase and packed more of Mom's things. Finally, I fetched Figgy and headed to the truck, peering out into the darkness—anyone could be hiding out in those trees.

The goldendoodle knew that she was home. Her tail wagged like a metronome set on high as I parked in front of her *real* house. Once I opened the Bronco's door, she almost knocked me over and bounded up the walkway like she'd been on the longest walk ever. She scratched at the closed door, and by the time I joined her, she and Cooper were already entangled.

Cooper, on his knees, closed his eyes as the dog licked at his face. He made a sound that landed between a laugh and a sob as he buried his face in Figgy's fur.

Joyful light danced in his eyes as he looked from my face to Figgy's—but then he saw and that light dimmed. "What happened?"

"Life." Near tears, I smiled at him and took a few steps back.

"Where are you going?" he asked, craning away from Figgy's sloppy kisses.

"Back to the condo."

"Will you talk to me?" His face darkened and even Figgy, feeling his shift in energy, stopped her celebration. "What happened?"

"I'm not pulling you into this," I said, shaking my head. "I'm good. Don't worry—"

"Come inside," he said, stepping aside. "Not a request."

I sighed, rubbed my forehead . . . then marched past him into the house.

The inside of Cooper's home no longer smelled of cigarettes and the holy trinity. There were no pots of simmering goodness on the stovetop. No blaring volume on the television.

"Your family's gone?" I asked.

"Yep." He unclipped Figgy from her leash and the dog did a few zoomies up and down the hallway. Cooper, wearing basketball shorts and a T-shirt, padded over to the bar cart in the living room and grabbed the bottle of bourbon and two glasses. He pointed to a stool at the breakfast bar and said, "Sit."

I sat.

He poured that beautiful amber-colored liquor into both glasses and handed me one. He held up his and said, "To kicking the world's ass . . . and whoever you just beat up."

I sipped as my gut swelled with fire. "How did you know I got in a fight?"

He sipped, keeping his gaze trained on me. "Two guns, but only one's properly holstered."

"Ah. Yeah." I pulled Vega's gun from the small of my back and set it on the counter. Then I took another sip of bourbon. "Believe it or not, I got my hair done this morning."

He snorted. "Kicking some guy's ass sweated out your press? You always hated that."

"Twenty-four flawless hours, that's all I ask."

"Why didn't you call the police?" he asked.

"Because something weird and fucked up and dangerous is happening with some of these Haven-Sableport deputies. The guy who got his ass kicked tonight has connections there."

Cooper's movements slowed and he searched my eyes. "You're shitting me, right? Brady Kwon is crooked—"

"I didn't say Brady Kwon."

"But you would've called him tonight if he was a straight shooter. I know you two are . . ."

I cocked an eyebrow. "Are what?"

He blushed. "Together."

I tilted my head. "Bad intelligence."

"You're not?"

"Not even in casework—and I ended the investigating part earlier today."

"Ah." A small smile formed at the edges of his lips. "Sorry to hear that."

I smirked. "Are you?"

"About the investigation—yeah. The part about you two being a couple, absolutely not. You can't see it right now, but I'm dancing like Snoopy at Christmastime."

I snorted, then finished drinking the booze in my glass.

"Why did you go back to the cottage?" Cooper asked, over at the fridge again.

"Needed more clothes," I said. "Needed my suit—Xander's funeral is Thursday."

Cooper pulled out a pack of salami and placed it on the counter. "I want to go, but . . ."

"No, not smart."

He opened the salami packet. "He was a good kid."

"Yeah. The Monroes are good people."

Figgy kept darting around the house, pausing to sniff at everything, reacquainting herself, and looking for the rest of her family.

"I loved having my aunt and uncle here," he said, "but it was time for them to go. They were buying up all of Haven's dairy foods, and I was about to stroke out from eating too much butter and salt."

I told him that Mom loved Sunset Park.

He casually mentioned that he may have already paid her lease for the year.

I said nothing, just stared at him while rubbing my left temple.

"There's a catch, though," he said.

"There's always a catch."

"Be Lumière's chief of security, just like we planned."

My stomach rolled. "We planned a lot of things."

"None of it is off the table," he said. "But let's take it one by one. This, first."

I sipped my bourbon and enjoyed the warmth still building in my chest. "This town . . ."

"Six-figure salary. Benefits. Housing. The best tech. Wine." He paused. "I'll even build you a house."

A new start on the other side of Haven.

"Nothing's changed." He plucked a salami slice from the packet and ate it. "Think about it. Take the week, but I need to put someone in that slot. And I want it to be you."

What about Ivan and Poole Investigations?

I had been planning to quit and leave Haven altogether, a clean break. But now . . . Quitting but living on the wine side? I'd be betraying my uncle.

"I need another favor," I said. "A comped room at either Four Seasons or the Ritz. Not for me—for a friend helping me out on something."

"Give her Anastasia's phone number," Cooper said, "and she'll make the reservation."

"Thank you."

"Mm-hmm." Cooper's shoulders were shaking. At first, I thought he was laughing, but then he buried his face in the crook of his elbow.

A teardrop plopped onto the front of his shirt.

I hesitated for only a second before moving closer to him and wrapping my arms around him. He clung to me like I was his lifeline, and for a moment, maybe I was. Two broken people holding each other together in life's wreckage.

Then, he pulled back, wiping his face. "Sorry," he whispered, heading over to the kitchen sink. "I didn't mean to fall apart on you."

"It's okay," I said.

He washed his face and hands. Cleaned up, he ran a hand through his hair, then tightened his jaw.

We sat back at the breakfast bar, silent, trying to catch our breath. An impossible task.

Cooper exhaled, stood up again, then said, "Anything else happening around Haven that I've missed?"

"Dave Kruger's dead," I said.

Cooper grabbed a bag of tortilla chips from the pantry and a jar of salsa from the fridge. "I heard. That guy was an asshole, but he didn't deserve to . . . Well . . . I'll just shut up."

"You're not shocked he's dead?" I asked, frowning.

Cooper set the chips and salsa between us. "I mean . . . he was a genius at running sites, but he wasn't the nicest person. He rallied people to do the job, but then he pissed them off."

"Why'd you hire him, then?"

"He'd helped put up some of my favorite spots. He was a gifted builder, and that's what I needed. Someone fearless. Someone with vision." He dunked a chip into the salsa, then crunched it. "We fought about the budget at least twice a week, and I threatened to can his ass every other month."

I grabbed a chip from the bag. "I read about the budget. What the hell, Coop?"

Cooper chuckled. "Dave absolutely hated the mobile clinic and the lawyer wagon. But I wanted people—not just the guys who worked there but their families and, really, anyone in the community—to have access to doctors and lawyers. Dave was constantly triggered about that."

I frowned. "Because it was free?"

"No, because with every injury, we had to report to the state. And the time workers took getting stitched up meant that they weren't working."

I nodded. "Oh, yeah. And with a lawyer there—"

"They knew their rights." Cooper shrugged. "I know: It's not cheap, but I . . ."

"Am a bleeding heart."

He smirked. "As much as a crass capitalist can be a bleeding heart. And the health clinic isn't costing too much—I'm partnering with UCSF for that and Stanford Law for the lawyers on wheels." He shrugged again. "I sleep better at night, which means it's still all about me." He grabbed the chips, salsa, and salami. "Let's change spaces."

I grabbed the bottle of bourbon and followed him down the hall and to a study with overstuffed couches and glass walls that looked out to the Pacific.

"Don't you feel exposed?" I said, not sitting down yet, aware that too many pairs of eyes were searching for me on the other side of this glass.

"You can see out," he said, placing the food on a coffee table. "But no one can see in. It's magic. Sit." He plopped into a cushion.

I stared at him, at those muscular calves and hard jawline, his tousled dark hair and strong hands. "I really shouldn't. I . . ."

He didn't speak. Just sat there, eyes on the lights of Haven, sipping his bourbon.

I loved this man, and I knew where this was headed. I wanted to go in that direction, to live in that world, but . . .

I knew what would splash cold water on this smoldering fire.

"Who do you think killed Dave, then?" I asked, choosing now to sit.

Cooper clinked the ice cubes around his glass. "The husband of the woman he was sleeping with. 'It's always the husband.' Isn't that what you always say?"

"Cuz most times it is," I said.

This time, though, maybe not. The words of the note left on Kruger's chest were not those of an angry spouse.

Who could've written it?

Carlos Vega—but what did he have to do with Dave Kruger?

Brady Kwon and Will McCann were "investigating" Emiliano Rivas's death. Had they received kickbacks or something from Dave and he had threatened to out them, but they killed him instead, leaving that note to confuse everybody and pull people's gazes from them to some random phantom? The video *had* shown Kruger being attacked by two people.

"Aren't you gonna ask if I killed Dave Kruger?" Cooper asked now, his eyebrow cocked.

"How long will it take to replace him with another experienced foreman with a vision?"

He groaned and squeezed the bridge of his nose. "At least three weeks."

"You're gonna lose how much a day on this slowdown?"

"Thousands upon thousands of dollars."

"A crass capitalist and developer on a schedule and already over budget?" I snorted. "You didn't kill Dave Kruger."

He laughed, then rubbed his bleary eyes. "Fuck, no."

Sitting here and drinking good booze with Cooper . . . This was how it was supposed to be. This was the flag at the top of Everest. Just six months ago, it never occurred to me that I wouldn't even reach this peak. But I'd failed in both love and career.

Made me want to take the bottle of the brown liquor, go find a closet to hide in as I drank and cried.

Cooper ran his hand through his hair and then clamped that hand over his mouth. It was his tell—he wanted to say something, but fear kept him from saying it aloud. But then he exhaled and leaned forward, his elbows on his knees. "I asked you to forgive me, Alyson, but I know that I don't deserve it."

I didn't respond.

He ran that hand across his mouth again. He stared out at Haven's light again, his jaw clenching and unclenching. "I'm waiting to reach the bottom of my hatred for London so that I can move on. But . . . I haven't reached the bottom of the well yet."

I cocked my head. "You'll deny yourself a good life until then?"

He gave a one-shouldered shrug.

"You'll miss out on some good shit."

He smirked. "Listen to you, the lady of the never-ending descent."

"Ha. Yeah." I tapped the rim of my glass. "Have you thought any more about Mackenzie's memorial?"

He shook his head. "Later—that's all I know. Something small. Probably just a few family members. We both decided on cremation."

"We"—him and London.

"I'm so sorry about Mackenzie," I said. "Addiction is already fucking hard, but it's just extra dangerous now. The amount of people dying from fentanyl being laced in regular shit . . ."

Cooper's mouth set into a hard line. "I want to find that bastard and squeeze his fucking neck. I know I'm not supposed to say this aloud, but if I see Liam Dyer again, I'm gonna fucking kill that guy. I'll hang for it, I don't care."

"I hear he's in Portugal."

Cooper nodded. "His father is hiding him. Mackie isn't the only person who got bad shit from him."

"No?"

"Nope. He gave a few laced joints to the niece of some cartel fucker a few months ago. She's dead. They finally figured out Dyer was her supplier. He's already dead—he just ain't realized it yet. I hated him the first day Mackie brought him to the house."

"You *do* know that he was the one pimping out Honor Butler."

Cooper made a face. "Not Keely?"

And now I made a face. "The guy who drove Honor to her so-called 'dates.' He's living in the house with Keely and Honor."

"He's living there *now*?" Cooper asked, gaping at me. "I reported him, like, a year ago. Hell, even London filed a complaint."

"But?"

He shrugged. "No one did anything. And then, this last time, when Honor left for good . . . Who knows, babe? I'm in no place to talk about anyone else's daughter when mine is . . . She's . . . Yeah." He tossed back the rest of his bourbon.

I touched the back of his head.

He turned to me, his eyes searching mine.

I placed my hand on his cheek.

He covered my hand with his.

"I hate saying this, but . . ." I paused, then took a deep breath. "No one compares to you, Cooper Sutton."

He smiled. "No one compares to you, Alyson Rush."

I sighed and placed my head on his shoulder. We sat in the silence, with Figgy curled at our feet, hidden from the world, trying to figure out how to live . . . and how to love.

There were no sunbeams to warm my face and pull me from sleep. I blinked—glass walls, overstuffed couches, the gray ocean. A hard shoulder . . .

Cooper.

I'd fallen asleep in his arms. His hand was draped across my hip as we lay twisted around each other on the couch in the sunroom. I stared at him as morning broke across Haven. His eyes cracked open, and he whispered "Hey," then "Ouch." We both shifted and he pulled me close.

I whispered, "Good morning," and gave him a hint of a smile.

He peered out to the gray waves and the gray sky. "Gonna be a Sonny day."

I chuckled. "Your favorite kind."

We stared at each other for a moment, and then we kissed. Just the brush of his lips against mine made me shiver, like we'd never kissed before. But this simple kiss was the promise of a new start. It was the most precious kiss ever.

"Bacon and eggs?" he asked, nuzzling my nose.

"Sounds good."

"I'll need to take Figgy out first."

The goldendoodle lifted her head, hearing her name. She'd slept in her bed in the corner, the first night in her home in weeks.

Cooper's aunt had told me days ago, "Tracasse-toi pas." *Don't worry.*

I was starting to believe her. Yeah. It would all work out.

But the glow that I'd enjoyed after waking up to Cooper was dimming. My worries always came to find me in these alone times.

Nothing had changed.

I'd tried love and had a career that I'd enjoyed—and I'd failed spectacularly in both. Who's to say I'd succeed this time? At least being a lonely private investigator guaranteed some kind of stability. Did I want to forsake that for the unknown with Cooper and a new job ensuring the safety of a staff and countless guests?

Yeah, I wanted to be chief of security at Lumière. I wanted to investigate the crime that would happen at a rich-people's spa. I wanted that salary and those benefits, semiregular hours, and a smaller queendom than Los Angeles. And yeah, I wanted Cooper.

How would I tell Ivan that, not only was I quitting Poole Investigations, but that I was also going over the hill to work with my . . . whatever Cooper was about to be?

Ivan probably knew by now that I knew about his and Dad's schemes. That I knew my dismissal wasn't about Autumn Suarez's death but about a score needing to be settled because of what he and Dad had gotten away with. The job at Lumière would be the break from the mess made by two of the most important men in my life.

Yeah, Cooper was the developer of Lumière, but security would be mine to create from the ground up. Hiring my own staff. Creating codes of conduct. And all the wine I could drink. I'd be a fool to let that pass.

After taking care of Figgy, Cooper poured fresh hot coffee into my cup. An MSNBC news program played on the countertop television—it felt like old times . . . Almost. He slid the creamer carton and sugar bowl in front of me and turned back to the bacon frying on the griddle.

My hands shook as I fixed my coffee—everywhere I looked, I was reminded of the women he'd loved, the women who'd lived here. The snapshot of Mackenzie standing in front of the Eiffel Tower. London pretending to glug from a large bottle of wine. On the fridge door, souvenirs from their trips around the world: sea turtles and Santa Claus on the Alps.

Cooper turned to see what I was gaping at. He said, "Oh. Sorry about—" He plucked the photo from the magnet. "I thought I'd taken out all the—"

"It's okay," I said. "That's your kid and wife—"

"Ex-wife." He held my gaze. "I wouldn't have asked you to stay overnight if the divorce hadn't gone through."

I sat up straighter on the stool. "When?"

"A few days after you dumped me—I was getting a divorce for *me*, not for you. If you and I had reconciled, then, great. If not, I was free to exist without her. And I knew I needed to do some healing and self-reflection before I told you and . . ."

Sounded familiar.

After eating bacon and eggs, I gathered my guns and bag.

"What protection do you have other than . . . ?" He chuckled and pointed at the Glock and Beretta.

"A strong heart and a clear mind," I said, slipping my gun into the hip holster.

He took my now-free hand as we walked to the front door.

"Hopefully, I can go about my Tuesday morning without being accosted or inconvenienced."

He snorted. "Would you even know a Tuesday morning free of bullshit?"

"There was that one Tuesday, November 4, 2008." I paused, then added, "Seriously. I'll watch my back—I've been trained to do that, remember?"

At the front door, we hugged, tight and long.

"We'll figure this out?" I asked, my eyes closed.

"Yeah." Then he nuzzled my ear before stepping back to open the door. He smiled and whispered, "I never stopped loving you."

"That was your first mistake." I kissed the tip of his nose and whispered, "And I never stopped loving you."

35.

Unlike Cooper, I didn't believe that Dave Kruger had been killed because he'd been sleeping with another man's wife. Not with that note left on the dead man's bloody chest.

LET IT BE OR YOU'RE NEXT

As I drove toward Jaylayne Merkley's house on 7 Azure Way, I hoped that something there would tell me what the dead man couldn't.

Located three blocks over from Cooper, Jaylayne's Victorian had tall windows and a wraparound porch with flaking white paint and a decent view of Haven's rocky coastline. A black Hummer was parked in the driveway, covered with sheets of dust that would require two trips through the car wash. No newspapers were piled on the porch. No mail was shoved in the slot. Jaylayne had been dead since August 13. Had Dave been the one maintaining the property?

I pulled on a pair of latex gloves, palmed the house key that Dave Kruger had left me, and stood on the porch.

Let there be light.

No one had lived in the house, and so it smelled . . . *alone*. No vibrant snaps of soap. No warm smells of a burning fireplace or fresh-brewed coffee. Framed photographs hung between commendations and ribbons of a muscular, deeply tanned white woman with Farrah Fawcett hair. Most pictures showed her wearing a tiny yellow bikini and striking a pose to show off a million muscles rippling across her body.

Looked like Jaylayne Merkley had been a bodybuilder but only after she'd stopped competing as a weightlifter. On every flat surface and every bare wall, there were medals for figure bodybuilding, ribbons from the NPC, IFBB, and WBFF, trophies from winning at VIRUS, IWF, and on and on.

But then, as the wall of medals turned to pictures, I saw that she'd replaced weights and coconut oil for sensible pumps and a Dress Barn suit to become a life insurance agent with State Farm. There she was, shaking hands with a fat cat in front of a rambling ranch. There she was, wearing that famous State Farm red polo at an open house on the coast.

The faint crunch of gravel outside snapped me out of my scrutiny. The roar of a lawn mower and a shadow walking back and forth along the front yard told me who had come. To confirm, I peeked past the living room blinds.

A man wearing a long-sleeved cotton shirt, khakis, and a sunhat wore earplugs. He was pushing a lawn mower between Jaylayne's front lawn and the house next door. He wasn't following me—just doing his job.

I exhaled and forced my breathing to slow, continuing my walk-through.

I reached a home office and stood at Jaylayne's desk. There, I flipped through an expandable folder filled with clipped documents, including copies of life insurance policies. I recognized the names of two people in the bundle: Araceli and Emiliano Rivas.

Hmm.

Another connection between Jaylayne and the Rivases. The couple had insured each other for $350,000 each. Emiliano was the beneficiary in the event of Araceli's death, and Araceli in the event of Emiliano's. She won that race. Had she collected yet? By the way she'd been shopping in Sableport? Probably.

I searched the desk drawers and couches, hoping to find a cell phone.

No luck.

But I knew the truth like I knew my name: Beneath the Kool-Aid hair and the goofy crafts, Araceli Rivas, grieving widow and the creator of snowmen made of recycled books, was a fraudster . . . and a black widow. Where was her ex-boyfriend, Matais? Probably getting ready to die—that is, if he wasn't dead yet.

I returned to that folder of life insurance policies.

Jaylayne Merkley had a life insurance policy on Dave Kruger for a million dollars. But she'd died of a heart attack on August 13 . . .

The day after Emiliano Rivas had been found dead in the forest.

Hmm.

What if . . . ?

"No," I said aloud.

Well?

What if . . . Jaylayne Merkley had carried Emiliano Rivas to his death spot in the forest? She may have been thinking "No big deal, 150 pounds" because she'd been a weightlifter. But that had been how many years ago? Maybe Emiliano's weight had stressed her heart, and that hike from the main road to the spot in the forest had been too much.

Shit.

I flipped through the Rivas life insurance policy and found the last of two pages—but it was not policy related. No, this area map had been printed out August 13. Someone had used a yellow highlighter to outline a space with trees located east of Highway 1.

The last page was another printed-out map, this time of East Haven. Printed out on May 9, 2023.

Directions to 32250 78th Street

I tapped that address into my phone's map app:

7-Eleven.

Emiliano Rivas was last seen on May 13 at the 7-Eleven on Seventy-Eighth Street. He'd gone to refill the propane tank for a family barbecue. In the convenience store's CCTV, he'd been seen chatting with someone off screen. He'd been found dead, months later, in the forest with a black-and-pink gun beneath him.

Jaylayne's gun. Jaylayne who had a map of where he'd be. Who'd sold a life insurance policy to Araceli Rivas. Jaylayne, who'd had a heart attack a day later.

I returned to the hallway and glimpsed a staircase—not leading up a level, but down into the darkness.

A finished basement.

I hit the light switch at the top of the landing.

A closed door.

I crept down the stairs and stood in front of this closed door. My breathing quickened—there was something on the other side of this door—the crackly sensation of fear and discovery pricked my skin.

I turned the doorknob and . . .

The stink of decay and waste—spoiled meat, shit, rancid vomit—wafted from the dark space.

Not good. I shuddered as that stink bloomed, as my pulse thundered in my ear and the natural instinct to run, hide, and cry rolled over me. But that horror never completely rolled away—it always lived at my edges, adding to my existing lacework of trauma. With trembling hands, I tapped record on my phone, and said, "This is the basement of 7 Azure Way." I sounded shaky. That didn't stop me, though. I stepped across the threshold like it had been sprinkled with nitroglycerin.

Another light switch.

On.

Dark wood ceiling beams. A wet bar. A floor plant. Three pairs of shoes lined the wall to my left. The largest pair: women's Skechers, white, size ten, the soles thick with dirt.

Crumpled in the corner to my right . . .

White netting now stained brown. Polypropylene fiber? Soccer goal netting?

And . . . a stained athletic sock, ADIDAS across the foot.

The smell was strongest here—tan carpet, but this spot in the corner was darker than the rest. The baseboard and lower half of the wall had been stained with . . .

What am I looking at?

Round brown smears. The back of a head?

Emiliano Rivas . . . he had been kept here.

What is . . . ?

I held my breath and bent toward the piece of paper caught between the baseboard and carpet.

An Uno card. Draw Four. Half of it burned.

Hands shaking, I kept the camera recording as I backed away from that reeking corner.

Back on the first level, I took deep breaths of cleaner air and closed my eyes to slow my pulse. Calmer, I opened my eyes and . . .

In the middle of the hallway: the touch-screen security panel.

I tapped the camera icon and selected ACTIVITY.

The last video captured had been of me, an hour ago, walking up the porch.

I swiped up the activity list and stopped at video clips recorded on August 12.

A figure wearing a hoodie, dark sunglasses, and dark sweats had approached the porch and rang the bell.

The door had opened, and the visitor standing on the porch asked, "You ready?" The hood slid back just enough for me to see a wisp of hair the color of cherry Kool-Aid.

I spread out Emiliano Rivas's autopsy and forensic reports across the Bronco's dashboard and chose a science-heavy document that I hadn't paid much attention to.

Bugs.

The *Papilio cresphontes*, though, was no ordinary bug. While its larva looked like broken brown twigs, the adult butterfly, the eastern giant swallowtail, boasted a beautiful black body with yellow flair. This butterfly populated warmer parts of the country, especially locations near citrus orchards.

Haven was not a warmer part of the country—and there were no citrus orchards here. So, how did a butterfly like this manage to lay eggs in Emiliano Rivas's wounds? Where had she come from?

I called my California Highway Patrol friend, Kianna, and asked her to run the license plate number of the black Range Rover that Araceli had been driving the last time I followed her to Sableport.

Kianna popped her chewing gum as she tapped the computer keyboard. "Registered to Paul Martinez."

PeopleFinder told me that Paul Martinez lived in Sableport and ran a pest control company, Pest-B-Gone. He wasn't married. Had been in the army before receiving an honorable discharge. Pest-B-Gone had two offices, including an office on Main Street in Haven. I entered that address and clicked on Street View . . .

Two doors down from Liberty Tires & Brakes.

Did Araceli and Paul meet the old-fashioned way? Face-to-face, live in person, at the tire shop?

My phone vibrated: a text from Dr. Nicole Pugh, my therapist.

See you on Friday

Hope you're doing the work

Well . . . I *was* doing the work. Maybe not the work *she'd* assigned.

I reviewed the notes I'd made throughout my investigation of Emiliano Rivas. Araceli and I had first met on Sunday morning, August 12. I'd still been recovering from my wine-bike booze cruise, and she'd wanted Ivan and me to find her missing husband. Later that night, an anonymous caller had found Emiliano Rivas in the forest.

Who'd made that anonymous call?

The next day, I had taken the case.

On that Tuesday, August 14, Brady and I had visited Araceli at her home and gave her the official death notification: The man in the forest had been Emiliano Rivas. I'd used my fancy transcription app to record that meeting.

I found that entry on my phone, tapped play, and read the transcript.

ARACELI: I thought I was ready to hear the news. Especially after I heard they'd found someone in the forest . . . Was that him?

I had nodded.

ARACELI: How?

ME: We're still figuring that out.

ARACELI: Can you tell me . . . ? Was it natural? Like . . . heart attack or . . . ? His only brother died last year. He had some undiagnosed . . .

We talked a few times later. But then, on Friday, she'd come to see me and tell me that she was leaving Haven. I found that interview with her and tapped play:

ARACELI: They're saying that he's not there.

ME: *They* meaning . . . ?

ARACELI: His mother, his brothers—

That.

His brothers.

She'd told me that Emiliano had only one brother who'd died from heart disease.

A lie?

Did it matter?

When it came to murder, *everything* mattered—and Araceli Rivas had 350,000 reasons to kill someone. She couldn't get paid if Emiliano Rivas stayed lost.

Yeah, Jaylayne Merkley, champion weightlifter, could've easily carried Emiliano Rivas, who'd been tied up in her basement since May. He'd probably been emaciated enough that she felt confident in lifting him. She'd carried the gun with her to the woods—why, if he was already dead?—and as she dropped Emiliano against the tree, that gun had fallen to the dark forest floor. Winded from the trek, she hadn't noticed that she'd dropped the gun—or she had, but it was too late, and she'd been too scared to return for it. Something had kept her from returning to retrieve that gun. *Or someone had kept her*... Because then she or Araceli had made that anonymous call.

Emiliano Rivas was never lost.

By the time I parked down the block from Araceli Rivas's house, the sun had slipped behind the hills. The drive had taken forever to reach the other side of Haven—construction flatbeds hauling wooden beams to the spa site had hogged the two-lane highway.

An older man with a square jaw and a soldier's haircut and wearing flawless Air Jordans was sitting in one of Araceli's porch chairs. He matched the PeopleFinder image of Paul Martinez. The matte black Range Rover was parked in the driveway.

"Hi," I said, strolling up the walkway. "Araceli here?"

From the corner of my eye, I saw the living room curtains move back some.

"Nope." He tossed me a look, then went back to texting on his phone.

"Know when she's returning?"

"Nope."

Paul Martinez, CEO of Pest-B-Gone, didn't fit in with the cutesy signs and pumpkin-spice vibe. With that haircut and sharp jaw, he looked like he killed things.

My gaze skipped around the front yard and to the side of the house. On my last visit, I'd spotted bags of fertilizer, folded patio chairs, and two soccer goalposts . . . without a net. *White polypropylene fiber* . . . Araceli had told Brady about Emiliano coaching kids' soccer.

I stared at that netless soccer goal and said to Paul Martinez: "Could you ask Araceli to call Sonny Rush as soon as possible?"

He said, "Yep."

"You Paul Martinez?"

He startled and looked up from his phone. "Yeah. How do you know my name?"

I gave a one-shouldered shrug. "I'm not the one you need to worry about, Paul." I nodded toward the house. "Araceli," I said, louder, to the living room window, "you need to call me."

Then a large black-and-yellow butterfly—the eastern giant swallowtail—fluttered around my head and landed on my left shoulder.

36.

I dared to smile as I slid behind the Bronco's steering wheel. I now knew the truth about Emiliano Rivas's death—the wife did it for money. And she'd do it again for money—to Paul Martinez next time, if no one stopped her—

My phone buzzed, and I glanced at the screen.

AIRTAG ALERT: Val's location no longer available.

Shit.

"No, no, no." I refreshed the app.

The little dot that marked Mom's location at Sunset Park in Sableport was missing and its signal lost.

I called Mom's phone, and the line rang . . . rang . . . rang . . . My chest tightened the longer my call went unanswered, the more I stared at my mother's picture in the screen. But then, on the fifth ring, the line opened and I heard background noise. I shouted, "Mom—"

"This isn't your mom," the man said.

"Who is this?"

He laughed.

Then my phone beeped three times and . . .

Silence.

Back on my screen, the AirTag blinked to life again and my mother's icon was moving toward Highway 1, away from Sunset

Park Senior Living and north toward Downtown Sableport. I swiped over to the mSpy app to confirm . . . but the app—which also meant her cell phone—was now headed *south* toward Haven.

My mother had either split to become two people, or the man I'd just talked to had either stolen her shoes or her phone.

Nausea swept over me, and bile burned up my throat.

Which do I follow?

Someone could've easily stolen her phone.

Follow the AirTag in her shoes.

A headache pushed against the back of my eyes. I'd left Haven and had placed my mother in a safe environment.

But they *still* came for her.

And Carlos Vega—how did he know that I'd be at the cottage that day, at that time?

Being watched.

"Then watch me get her back," I growled, throwing the Bronco into buck.

The roads blurred as I sped from the other side of Haven to the ocean side of Haven. The dying light and roving mist had turned the world into a hazy mess of shadows, and I gripped the steering wheel so tight that my knuckles hurt. My breath came in short, panicked gasps of states, presidents, and books of the Bible, failed attempts to ground myself.

Alaska, Alabama, Genesis, Leviticus, Obama, Roosevelt . . .

My eyes ping-ponged from the road to my phone screen and that icon of Mom wandering the streets of Sableport. Over on mSpy, the phone was closing in on the cottage. Who the hell was headed there—and what were they trying to find?

The image of my mother's face haunted me, especially that cocky smile of hers dimming along with her memory. Her already-sharp words had turned sharper because she'd become angrier—at me, at Dad, at her failing mind. The thought of her wandering Highway 1—hell, a mall, even—confused and vulnerable, made me lightheaded, and . . . and . . .

Jefferson, Proverbs, Myanmar, Fiji . . .

"Where are you, Mom?" I muttered, scanning the roadsides even though her AirTag placed her miles away. But I couldn't put my trust in technology—because technology was also telling me that she was headed to the cottage. And maybe she was.

Ivan.

I called my godfather, but the call immediately rolled into voicemail. Frustrated, I slammed my hand against the steering wheel before leaving a message. "Damn it, Ivan. Where the hell are you? Mom's in trouble."

My phone buzzed: Cooper's face flashed on the screen.

I'd only said his name when he said, "What's wrong?"

"Mom," I choked out. Then, I told him about the AirTag and about the predator answering Mom's phone.

"Want me to go to the cottage?" he asked without hesitation.

"Yes, please," I said, relieved.

"I'm heading out now. Call me if you hear anything."

He'd also lost his mother—she'd wandered away too . . .

The phone rang again, but this time India's face filled the screen.

"Sonny," she shouted, "I just found your mom!"

"What?" I asked, my heart pounding.

"I found her on the side of Highway 1."

"Where is she now?"

"I'm driving her to the hospital," India said.

I called Cooper and told him that Mom had been found.

"I'll meet you at the hospital," he said.

Ten minutes later, my tires skidded as I jammed into a parking space at Sableport Presbyterian Hospital. I'd come here just days ago with Dave Kruger, and now I found my mother in an emergency room triage bay with India standing at her bedside.

I choked out, "Mom." My voice and soul were breaking.

Mom's head lolled in my direction. Her face was bruised, her lip cut. "There you are," she whispered. "I'm okay. I got away."

I took her hand and kissed it. "I'm so sorry."

"For what?" she asked, chuckling. "You didn't jump me."

India took my free hand and said, "She has a few bruised ribs, a fractured thumb, and some abrasions. She's tough."

"Damn right," Mom said, settling back into the pillows. "I got in a few licks too."

I lifted her hand—blood had dried beneath her fingernails. The DNA of her attacker lived in that blood.

India noticed me noticing. "Swabbed."

"What happened?" I asked, pushing back tears.

Mom patted the puffy circles beneath her swollen eyes. "He said he was gonna spend the weekend with me."

"Who?" I asked, trying not to shout.

"Quincy," Mom said. "He texted me this morning."

"You didn't tell me—"

"I'm not a child," she snapped. "He was gonna pick me up, and we were gonna have a picnic at the park near the lighthouse."

"Okay . . ." I said, my skin hot. "But . . . ?"

"But he had his son text me," Mom said. "His phone died or something, and he was at Best Buy. Anyway, he had his son pick me up."

"His son," I said.

"Quincy can't drive long distances like that anymore," Mom explained, "so his son—"

"Drives with him," I said.

"So a real nice car pulls up," Mom said, "and . . ."

"And . . . what?" I asked.

"And . . . uhh . . ." Her eyebrows crumpled, and she shook her head. "And I . . . and . . . he took me . . . He took me . . ." She shook her head again, but now her eyes darted from me to India to the IV in her hand.

Shitshitshit.

"Corkscrew," she said. "For the wine. For the picnic. I stabbed him with the corkscrew, Sonny. I . . . I think I hurt him bad."

"You stabbed *who* with the corkscrew?" I asked, my voice tight. "Quincy?"

Confused, Mom's face crumpled, and she whispered, "I . . . I . . . No."

Was this trauma or dementia blocking her ability to remember?

Relief and frustration warred inside of me. My mother was alive, and she'd fought back and won—but the answers I needed were locked somewhere in the mists in her mind.

I scowled at the baby-faced deputy now taking Mom's statement.

Would he do something about this, or would he put her report in the shredder?

Will McCann was dirty. So was Brady.

So, hell no, I didn't trust this Deputy O'Connell—he worked out of the Sableport station, and too much bad shit was now happening in this town. Just like the town south of its border.

The emergency room physician returned to Mom's bedside for another examination.

India and I returned to the waiting room and met Elliott, Giovanni, and Cooper. Giovanni's shirt front was covered in white powder, presumably from baking pastries.

"What happened?" the men shouted.

I opened my mouth to speak but nothing came out.

As India caught them up, my hands started to shake—the events of the day were slamming into me. Before I could stop them, tears were spilling down my cheeks. I covered my face to catch the sobs racking my body.

Cooper held me tight in his arms. He whispered "It's okay" and "I got you" until I'd calmed some.

Giovanni offered me tissues and a handful of Skittles.

"But Miss Val is okay?" Elliott asked again.

"Yeah," I said, pushing smashed candy from my back teeth. "And she stabbed his ass with a corkscrew, whoever he is."

Brady Kwon rushed into the waiting room. Eyes wide, breathing heavy, he said, "Hey, Sonny—"

Cooper blocked him from approaching me. Both men stood the same height. Both had hard jaws and curled fists.

"What the fuck do you want?" Cooper demanded.

"Is Mrs. Rush okay?" Brady asked. Then he looked past Cooper to me. "Sonny—"

Cooper moved again to block his view.

"Dude, what's your fucking problem?" Brady challenged.

"Dirty fucking cops, *bro*," Cooper spat. "Want me to name a few? You know 'em all."

Something in Brady's eyes shifted, and he whispered something that only Cooper could hear. Cooper's ears flushed red. He glared at Brady for a moment, but then he set his hands on his hips and stepped aside.

Brady nodded at him and walked toward me. "Can we talk?" he asked.

I didn't say a word as I followed him to a private phone cubby. Then: "You and McCann—"

"He's no longer with MCSO," Brady blurted.

"Where is he?"

Brady shrugged and shook his head. "In the wind."

"You next?" I asked, eyebrow cocked.

"Here's the truth," he said. "I've been part of an internal investigation—"

"Oh, really?" I asked, smirking, arms folded.

"Really," he said. "Because *yes*, there *is* corruption in Sableport and Haven, and *yes*, a bunch of cops, including McCann, are involved. Drugs, trafficking, extortion . . . You started to figure it out, and I needed to push you away and pretend like I was a part of it."

I rolled my eyes. "Uh-huh."

He gripped my elbows. "I'm telling you the truth. Will's grandfather is one of the men in Honor's pictures—"

"I know, and Will—"

"Shredded the evidence you provided," Brady said, nodding. "I knew this because he told me—"

"Because you were a part of it—"

"Yes. And no. I'm in on the investigation. It runs deep, Sonny." He let go of my arms and took a deep breath. "And someone you love is also involved."

My pulse snapped to his. *"What?"*

"Yeah."

"Who?" I closed my eyes, waiting to hear—

"Ivan."

I squinted at him. *"Ivan?"*

"Yeah."

"How?" I asked. "As a good guy or . . . ?"

Brady frowned. "Sonny, he's not a good guy."

I blinked and my eyes felt dry and crunchy. "But . . . but . . ."

"He hires problem cops," Brady said. "I don't know how deep he's involved, but he reports to Will McCann. He's on the books for the Dyers. I don't even know where to begin."

Money, once again.

All of me had gone numb—I couldn't feel my face, my legs, or my feet, but somehow, I was moving. "I'll ask him myself."

"What does that mean?" Brady asked, frowning.

"Don't know." I rubbed my temples and stared at the pay phone on the wall. "I need to think about my mother first."

And handle Quincy Johns.

I called that number, and the line only rang twice before:

"Hello, Alyson!" Quincy Johns sounded happy.

I put the phone on speaker so that Brady could hear. "Hi, Mr. Johns. Are you in Sableport yet?"

He laughed. "No—I thought I told Val that I couldn't make it. I'm still stuck in Ojai."

"Your phone," I said.

"Just needed an update." He sighed. "This 'getting old' business is bullshit."

"Did your son drive up here?" I asked.

He paused, then said, "My son? Honey, he's in Houston, in the delivery room with my new grandbaby." He sighed again. "Oh no. Is Val's memory flickering again?"

Tears burned in my eyes. "Afraid so." I paused, then said, "I'm about to request something strange, and I hope you'll . . ." I squeezed the bridge of my nose, then said, "Could you send me a pin of your location right now?"

"A what of my what?"

I walked Mr. Quincy through the process and my phone dinged.

Yep, he was still in Ojai, a nine-hour, five-hundred-mile drive away.

Mom had been attacked—but not by Quincy Johns. And a quick Facebook check confirmed that Dejanae Johns had been born in Houston around the same time I arrived at Sableport Presbyterian Hospital.

Thinking about it now, the man who'd answered my mother's phone when I last called . . .

Sounded like Will McCann.

37.

Since I refused to trust another sheriff's deputy in Sableport, Cooper hired private security to guard Mom's hospital room. Brady had balked at the two booted and suited former San Francisco Police Department cops built like Iron Giants, but he knew I had receipts of his coworkers fucking up and fucking me and my family over.

But then, the unexpected happened:

Brady and Cooper turned their dueling swords away from each other to aim them at me.

"You can't do this, Sonny," Cooper said, shaking his head, pacing the empty hospital conference room Brady had commandeered.

"The hell I can't," I said.

"What if he's not alone?" Cooper asked. "What if you bring someone with you, and they're just waiting and watching? He's not gonna show up without an extra pair of eyes and you shouldn't either."

I grinned. "You wanna be my extra pair of eyes?"

Cooper shrugged. "Or one of the security guys in an unmarked car."

"Like in an Acura or something that won't call attention?" I asked.

He said, "Uhh . . . they don't drive Acuras."

I snorted. "Then no."

"This is far too dangerous," Brady said. "Let me—"

"You?" I said, grimacing. "I've been a cop longer than you, in a city three million times larger than yours. What makes you think that you're better equipped than me to confront this asshole?"

Brady said, "Well, because . . . because . . ."

"Because of your *dick*," I said. "Am I right?" When he didn't respond, I rolled my eyes. "You both can track me, if that calms you down some." I took Cooper's phone and added my number to his Find My. I also downloaded the transcription app I had on my phone onto his phone—he'd be able to read my conversation with Ivan in real time.

Brady held his hand out to be added to Find My.

I cocked my eyebrow at his gesture. "I don't trust you yet." I nodded toward Cooper. "Feel free, though, to ask *him* where I am."

Brady said, "Fine."

"Who's part of McCann's clique?" I asked, checking my Glock again. "Carlos Vega? Liam Dyer? All of them and more?"

"And more," Brady said. "But we'll catch them."

I forced a tight smile and said, "Sure you will."

Call me faithless, but no, he wouldn't. And I wouldn't either.

This town was lost in a fog that I no longer wanted to penetrate. Let the monsters lurk—just leave me and mine the hell alone.

And if anyone was going to find out who'd hurt one of mine, it would be me.

My phone rang. "It's Ivan." I answered and said, "I was just about to call you again."

Ivan said, "What's up?"

"We need to talk in person," I said. "I need to tell you something, and not on the phone."

My godfather paused before saying, "Okay. See you at the office?"

"No," I said. "I'll let you know once I get there."

"Everything okay?"

I'd left him a frantic voicemail. *Mom's in trouble.* And now, for him to ask . . . ?

I chuckled. "Everything is shit." My throat tightened with fresh tears. "See you soon."

He didn't even ask about Mom.

I stared at the red dot on my phone of my mother's phone moving around Haven. Whoever had Mom's phone had gone to the bakery and then to Poole Investigations. Looking for me?

The cool night air hit me as I left the safety of the hospital. I tugged my jacket tighter around me, wanting to return to the condo and collapse in the deck's lounge chair from exhaustion. Not just yet—at least for the collapsing part. I peeked at the phone again—whoever had Mom's phone was now circling the cottage.

Would the thief come to Sableport Presbyterian next?

I wouldn't be there, and guards now stood at Mom's door.

The phantom couldn't touch her.

I hopped in the Bronco and watched the fog roll in from the Pacific and onto land.

Would a jury convict me of first-degree murder for killing the person who'd hurt and tricked my mother?

Was Brady being truthful about being the snitch—and if he was, how did I feel about that?

I swiped into the mSpy app on my phone—the person who had Mom's iPhone was less than four miles away from the lighthouse.

Brady and Cooper trailed behind me in India's olive-green Fiat.

The road unwound before me, and the lighthouse materialized out of the fog. Stark, white, rising nearly one hundred and twenty feet on the jagged peninsula. No sound except for that crash of waves against the cliff and the soft howl of wind off the Pacific.

The phantom with Mom's phone was a mile away.

I found a bench that looked out to the sea and tapped a message to Ivan:

Just got here

Sitting on a bench

And then I sent him my location. Seconds later, my phone vibrated with Ivan's response.

Be there in 20 minutes

Just wrapping up my meeting with Lyric Sydney

Case is yours if you want it

Cheater Lyric Sydney would have to bust her cheating bigamist husband, Kameron Trevino, without me.

The roar of the ocean did nothing to calm the storm raging in my mind. Neither did the car now pulling into the lighthouse's parking lot. From the sound of the engine to the crunching of the tires . . . sounded like a truck.

Or those footsteps . . . Rhythmic. Heavy. A man.

I tapped record on my transcription app and set the Glock on my thigh.

"Strange place to meet," he said, walking up behind me.

I closed my eyes, then opened them again. I turned to face him. "I thought you wouldn't be here for another twenty minutes?"

Ivan shrugged. "Magic." He wore a gray sweatshirt—and blood had seeped through the bandage at his wrist.

I glanced at the mSpy tracker on my phone—the big red dot that represented Mom's device was standing beside me. I held the map out so that my godfather could see what I saw.

"We don't have to bullshit anymore," I said, holstering my gun. "I'll ask again: *Why?*"

"Why, what?" He shoved his hands into his pockets.

"Trick Mom into thinking Quincy was coming up here? And then to attack her?"

His eyes bugged again. "I didn't attack—"

"She remembered and told me that it was you." A lie. "And I'm looking at your wound right now."

He held my gaze, refusing to peer down at his injury. No more light in those eyes. They were as hard and black as a shark's. "She was fucking around on Al with him—"

"He was cheating on her," I shouted. "With more than one woman."

Ivan sniffed.

"Revenge twenty years later?" I asked.

"As long as it takes," he said.

"You're so fucking dirty," I said, gaping at him. "She trusted you. That's why she got in the car with you." I pushed back the sob creeping up my throat. "If she didn't have that corkscrew, what were you gonna do to her?"

He paused, then gave a one-shouldered shrug. He knew—he just didn't want to tell me. "You need to leave Haven. You should've never come up here."

"You invited me—"

"No, I didn't," he snapped. "You came up here to be with London's husband—"

"London's *husband*?" I cocked my head. "Sounds like you've chosen a side in this battle. May I ask why?"

He shrugged. "The highest bidder wins."

"She hired you to work the case, didn't she?"

He chuckled. "She wanted the best."

"And I guess I was occupied."

He laughed.

"And I *am* the best," I said, "but I haven't believed that for a year now. I thought I was the worst cop in the world because I'd been fired, but then I learned about you and Dad and Captain Wagner. You three? The worst of the worst—and I was caught in the middle of your bullshit."

Ivan wandered to the edge of the bluff, his silhouette stark against the silver mist. My stomach churned watching him there, my heart mixed with fear and sadness. His face was hard and unreadable. His jacket billowed in the wind. The bandage wrapped around his wrist peeked out from beneath its cuff.

I stood from the bench, and salty wind whipped around me. From here, I could see the ocean crashing against the jagged rocks below and the silver fog rolling in from the horizon.

Ivan's lips curled into a faint smile, but it didn't reach his eyes. "We've been busy since you got here."

"Busy searching for the truth," I said. "The dog, the football player, the dead, the girls . . ."

"What can I say? I'm a busy man. Gotta keep working—America doesn't take care of its old people, ya know?"

I gawked at him. "Seriously?"

He shrugged, his expression calm. "I told you, Sonny. Haven's a small town. Everybody wears more than one hat."

"How is it that you kept your life together?" I asked. "You got your house near the beach. A PI firm, and some money in the bank. You did the same shit as my father, *with* my father, and yet . . ."

I gasped, then narrowed my eyes. "*You. You* snitched on him. *You* were the whistleblower."

Ivan blinked at me. "We were wrong to do what we did."

My jaw dropped—speechless.

"Survival of the fittest," he said. "And Val . . . He did all that for her, and for her to sneak around with *that* fucker. Nuh-uh. Not on my watch."

A teardrop rolled down my cheek. "You're a piece of shit."

He shrugged. "Yeah, and so was Al. And so is Valerie."

"Killing her—"

He flicked his hand. "I wasn't gonna kill her. I needed to get you outta Haven—"

"And I left!"

"Sableport, Haven, Fort Bragg, it's all mine," he snapped.

"*Yours?* What the hell, Ivan?"

He stared out to the ocean.

"Are you working for McCann?" I asked.

"Working *for*?" He snorted. "That son of a bitch works for *me*."

"Carlos Vega," I said. "He tried to kill me—is that because you told him to?"

This time, Ivan met my gaze and held it.

Yes.

"And Dave Kruger?" I asked.

"Was a problem," Ivan said. "He chose his side—he didn't care about money anymore. He liked the idea of Lumière more. Clean money, he called it. No more kickbacks from the inspectors, from OSHA. He wanted to go straight."

"Who did it?"

"Carlos and Will. But they fucked up—they weren't supposed to *kill* him. Idiots."

"Ivan—"

The flash of the gun in his hand shut my mouth. He held it steady.

"Why . . . ?" I swallowed the lump in my throat, aware that I needed to have this on record. "Why are you pointing a gun at me?"

Worse, his eyes were colder than the steel. "I'm not going to jail, Sonny," he said, calm. "You think I've done terrible things? You're right, I have. Shit you can't even imagine. And everything you now know? You'll take to the grave."

"They all know you're here, and . . ." I held up my phone again. "All of this is being transcribed in real time. Technology is a bitch and a wonder."

My phone buzzed with a text from Brady.

I read it and smiled at Ivan. "Was McCann parked in a white Honda down the road?"

Ivan's eyebrows furrowed. "Yeah. Why?"

My phone buzzed again with another text. "And is Charles Campbell . . . ?" I looked back at the parking lot and spotted the black pickup truck. "Parked right there?"

Ivan gazed at the lot.

"Will's been arrested," I said, "and Campbell will be arrested in about three minutes."

The man standing before me—my play uncle, my godfather, mentor, and boss . . . I hated him. There was nothing good about this lying, cheating, stealing, murdering . . .

The silence stretched between us, broken only by the crashing waves.

Ivan took several steps back, his heels hanging over the edge of the bluff. "I'm not going to jail," he said. "Not for you. Not for anyone. I'd rather—" He took another step back.

I shouted, "No!"

And then, he was gone.

I rushed over to the bluff's edge. The wind tore at my hair as I peered down at the waves exploding around the slick, jagged rocks below.

No sign of Ivan.

Just that churning water. Just that rolling mist.

I stood at the bluffs, waiting.

Minutes felt like hours as a dive team combed the waters beneath the bluffs. Bright lights lit up the night, and the squawks of radios competed with the ocean's noise. All that light above nor the bright search lights below couldn't push through the murk to find anything except rocks and foam.

Brady, grim faced, approached me and said, "Nothing."

I kept staring out at the Pacific.

"We'll figure it out, Sonny," Brady said. "And this goes beyond Ivan—I told you that. He had help. Partners. Connections."

Ivan was gone, his body being battered somewhere in the surf, but his web of corruption still entangled Haven. That web wouldn't trap me here, though. No, this slice of heaven had nearly sliced my neck.

Fuck this place.

38.

Thursday, August 23, 2023

Before India and I leave the condo for the Bay, Cooper brews fresh coffee, fries bacon in the broiler, and makes scrambled eggs with onions and bell peppers. His silence is heavy—he's still dealing with so much—and now, learning that Ivan had been working as London's private investigator . . .

I promised to bring him foil-covered plates of food from the funeral repast, including every lemon-flavored dessert on the buffet table.

As he cooks, I listen to the transcribed audio of my last conversation with Ivan. He sounded so cocky as he admitted to all the evil he had done. He didn't think he'd be caught—not until he realized he was being recorded. Once he realized that Brady was listening in real time . . .

What choice did he have but to risk it and jump? A dirty ex-cop like him sometimes thrived in prison. Did he want to take that chance, though? A savvy judge could've shuttled him off to a place where he was just another asshole cop, hated and targeted by gen pop.

Even though Brady and his superiors vowed to be on the right side of justice, I don't trust anyone in Haven—I included the transcription of my confrontation with Ivan in the files I'm handing off to FBI Special Agent Livinia Holland at our meeting this morning.

I ride shotgun as India pulls onto Highway 128 South. She taps my thigh. "You good?"

"Yep," I say.

"What time is your meeting with the FBI?" India asks.

"Eight thirty." I peek at the back seat and the expandable file that contains information on Honor Butler's case as well as Ivan's racketeering operation. I've also included information on Araceli Rivas and the role she played in the murder of Emiliano Rivas.

My phone vibrates.

A selfie from Cooper: at the beach with Figgy. The Monroes had extended an invitation to him, and he'd come close to joining India and me on the drive down to Oakland but decided against it.

"Don't wanna be a distraction," he said. The ex-husband of their child's murderer attending that kid's funeral: That was a lot. Instead, Cooper made a large donation to the scholarship fund Lori and Devon had established in Xander's name—money that would support high school graduates interested in physics, comics, and sports. Xander loved all three things.

I put away my phone. For the first time, I'm zooming down Highway 128 and witnessing its beauty. Those redwood trees and rock formations, glimpses of the Pacific Ocean, the way the sunlight slants across the asphalt.

India drives this highway with one hand on the wheel, totally at ease. She doesn't clench as a logging truck rumbles toward us.

Sometimes, you need to let someone else take the wheel as you learn how to drive.

I'm staying put, but not in Haven by the Sea. Hell no. I'll stay in Sableport, at that lovely condo close to Mom at Sunset Park. As chief of security for Lumière, I'll have to drive past the seaside part of Haven to reach the other side, but I refuse to live there. I need to tie up loose ends at Poole Investigations since the ocean turned over Ivan's body. Those files in the file room, that loft, that building—my circus, my monkeys.

My godfather had been the godfather of Haven. Did he know Honor Butler had been caught up in Haven's trafficking ring? Was that why he'd never committed to finding her—because he knew exactly where she was?

Not all light brings clarity, but a lot of light shines down on all that is real, all that's important to me.

Mom. India. Cooper. Those in need. Those without voices. Clean air. Good wine. Sweet potato cupcakes. Figuring out how to live. And living the best life that I can. Starting now.

And in October, I have a date with my mother—we're soaring over Taos, New Mexico, in a hot air balloon. Yeah, we have some memories to make.

Acknowledgments

Readers, I can never thank you enough for picking up another RHH story. I think of you every time a random idea pops in my head. Every morning at zero dark thirty, my mind turns over the same questions: *Will they like this? Will they laugh? Will they gasp? Will they trust me again?* Thank you for trusting me again.

Thank you, Jill Marsal, for continuing to be the best agent in the world. To my editors Jessica Tribble Wells and Clarence Haynes: Thank you for helping me see past the mist to the shore.

To my friends: Thank you for the love, for the hot tea, for the plot twists, for making me leave my house and desk sometimes. Thank you, new friends Jason Blitman and Amanda Blitman, for introducing me to more of the Palm Springs reading community and to the Georgian as a wonderful writing retreat. I did a lot of good writing at that lovely blue palace across from the Pacific.

To Mom, Terry, Gretchen, and Jason: Your love and support sustain me. Hugs and hugs and hugs.

And thank you, David and Maya, for all the adventures, for all the good meals, for being okay with being still sometimes and finding joy in the quiet.

About the Author

Photo © 2023 Andre Ellis

Rachel Howzell Hall is the *New York Times* bestselling author of *Fog and Fury*, *The Cruel Dawn*, *The Last One*, *What Never Happened*, *We Lie Here*, *These Toxic Things*, *And Now She's Gone*, *They All Fall Down*, and, with James Patterson, *The Good Sister*, which was included in Patterson's collection *The Family Lawyer*. A two-time *Los Angeles Times* Book Prize finalist as well as an Anthony, International Thriller Writers, and Lefty Award nominee, Rachel is also the author of *Land of Shadows*, *Skies of Ash*, *Trail of Echoes*, and *City of Saviors* in the Detective Elouise Norton series. A past member of the board of directors for Mystery Writers of America, she has been a featured writer on NPR's acclaimed *Crime in the City* series and the National Endowment for the Arts weekly podcast. Rachel lives in Los Angeles with her husband and daughter. For more information, visit www.rachelhowzell.com.